THE LONG LIST ANTHOLOGY VOLUME 9

MORE STORIES FROM THE HUGO AWARD NOMINATION LIST

EDITED BY DAVID STEFFEN, CHELLE PARKER, AND HAL Y. ZHANG

DIABOLICAL PLOTS, LLC

THE LONG LIST ANTHOLOGY VOLUME 9: More Stories from the Hugo Award Nomination List

edited by David Steffen, Chelle Parker, and Hal Y. Zhang

https://www.diabolicalplots.com

Copyright © 2025 Diabolical Plots, L.L.C.

Stories copyright by the authors (see rights page for individual details). All rights reserved.

Published by Diabolical Plots, L.L.C.

"Worldcon," "World Science Fiction Society," "WSFS," "World Science Fiction Society," "Hugo Award," the Hugo Award Logo, and the distinctive design of the Hugo Award trophy rocket are service marks of the World Science Fiction Society, an unincorporated literary society.

Cover art by Evelyne Park © 2025

Cover layout by Pat R. Steiner

Interior layout by Merc Fenn Wolfmoor

Ebook ISBN: 978-1-969609-00-8

Print ISBN: 978-1-969609-02-2

To everyone who strives to leave the world better than they found it.

CONTENTS

FOREWORD

Welcome back for the 9th volume of *The Long List Anthology*. We ended up taking a break last year but we are back!

As ever, the premise of the anthology is to collect stories from the longer Hugo Award nomination statistics that didn't get as much attention as the Hugo Award finalists, and to help spread the word about these amazing stories that were so beloved by those fans eligible to vote for the award.

This year, the anthology has an update to its editorial staff for the first time in the series' history. This volume has three co-editors: David Steffen, Chelle Parker, and Hal Y. Zhang (who also translated one of the stories).

We have also added a "Content Notes" feature near the end of the book. You can skip to that section before you read the stories to be aware of certain kinds of content before you read the stories.

The anthology includes stories from the nomination long lists as well as finalists in the story categories. We have also included stories by authors nominated for the Astounding Award for Best New Writer, as well as stories from publications nominated in the Best Semiprozine category and the Best Editor, Short Form category.

This is the first year that a story in *The Long List Anthology* will itself be eligible for a Hugo Award as part of its publication in the anthology: 杞忧 / "Heavens Fall" by 陆秋槎 / Lu Qiucha, translated into English by 章皓 / Hal Y. Zhang, was nominated for its Chinese language publication in 银河边缘 / *Galaxy's Edge*. This anthology is its first appearance in English and so it is eligible in the Best Short Story category.

Thank you so much for joining us once again!

—**David Steffen, August 2025**—

ONCE UPON A TIME AT THE OAKMONT

BY P.A. CORNELL

Editor, Short Form Long List
(Arley Sorg and Christie Yant) *

O n the island of Manhattan, there's a building out of time. I can't tell you where it is, exactly. It has an address, of course, as all buildings do, but that wouldn't mean anything to you. What I can tell you is that the building is called The Oakmont.

"What do you see when you look out there, Sarah?" Roger asks.

I stand next to one of the windows in his apartment and take in the view.

"The sun's out and there isn't a cloud in the sky. It's a perfect summer day. The street's filled with a steady stream of cars and people. There's a busker on the corner— Do they have buskers in your time? He's drumming on a plastic bucket with his hands and feet."

"He any good?"

"He's too far to hear, but he must be. People are giving him money. Paper money."

Roger raises his eyebrows. In his time, paper money isn't something people part with easily.

"What do you see out there?" I ask.

He places the needle down on the record he's selected and comes over to the window to stand next to me as Billie Holliday sings "Summertime." I quietly hum along.

"There's a newsboy across the street," he says. "He's calling something out to some pretty girls. The girls keep walking. They aren't interested. Behind the kid, a man's putting up a poster promoting Defense Bonds."

I glance down at the newspaper that lies folded on Roger's coffee table, no doubt purchased this morning from that same newsboy. The front-page story's about the war, but I know it'll still be a few months before America joins the fight. Still, the worry settles into my stomach. The attack on Pearl Harbor's coming. It happens in December. I can't tell Roger that, though.

There are rules at The Oakmont. The first, and arguably most important, is that residents are not permitted to share information about the future with other residents existing in their past that could influence the course of their lives. Residents also may not visit the apartments of those living beyond their own time, though the reverse is allowed.

I walk over to the record player and apologize to Lady Day as I lift the needle off her record and replace it with a different one. This one bends The Oakmont rules a little, since it's technically from my time, and the song I'm choosing won't be released for a few years yet in Roger's time. But this isn't the first rule Roger and I have bent during our time together. I find the correct groove, knowing it by heart by now, and carefully place the needle down. Glenn Miller and His Orchestra play our song, "Moonlight Serenade."

I hold my hand out and Roger comes over to take it. We dance like we have so many times before. I think of that first time when we met, a few months ago in early Spring, and feel myself transported there. Maybe I *am* transported. Time, after all, moves differently at The Oakmont.

· · · ·

Once a month, spring through fall, Mr. Thomas hosts a movie night on the rooftop of The Oakmont. Although to him they're 'moving pictures.' In his time, Mr. Thomas runs a theater where silent films are screened. Here, he uses an old bedsheet for a screen, but the projector's real—taken from his theater when they upgraded. There's also a piano that's stored in a sort of shed he built. The walls open on hinges for full sound as he plays along with the films.

Today's movie is *Safety Last,* starring Harold Lloyd. A personal favorite of mine, despite the film having been released before even my grandparents were born.

The film won't start until it's truly dark, though. First there's the traditional potluck dinner. I glance down at the table at foods from every era. On one end, Depression cake sits next to aspic. The other end holds a silver fondue pot. Just beyond that's the grocery-store sushi platter I brought. There are no rules about food at The Oakmont. There is, however, an unspoken rule when we interact with residents from other times.

At The Oakmont, we go with the flow.

There are things you just accept when you live here. You don't question what's normal for other residents. You don't comment on their clothing or hairstyle, for instance. At least not to point it out as unusual. It's understood that things like appearance—and, yes, even food—are a product of their time.

On this evening, I've set up an easel and brought up my oils. As people arrive, I paint them standing around the table, chatting. I've already included Mr. Thomas and the building manager, Ms. Knox, as well as a handful of others. Front and center are my closest friends, Linda from 1975 and Don from 1969.

There may be others here too, but The Oakmont has its secrets. Just as we don't all perceive the view from the rooftop in the same way, there are residents here we may not be aware of and who in turn may not be aware of us. Only Ms. Knox interacts with everyone.

Of the residents I see regularly, the only one missing is Harrison, the odd loner who lives next door to me in apartment 2055, but he never comes to movie nights.

There's a number on the door of each apartment in The Oakmont. The number corresponds to the year the resident exists in. This number may change as time passes, but the residents don't notice such things.

I put the finishing touches on my painting and lean the canvas forward to pencil in the title on the back of the frame: "The Gang at The Oakmont." When I rest it back against the easel, I notice a figure I don't recognize and don't remember painting. I look over to the edge of the rooftop, where he stands smoking a cigarette. He wears a fedora, cocked ever-so-slightly to one side, and a jacket and tie over a shirt and slacks. A casual look for another era, but coming from the twenty-twenties, he looks dressed up to me. *They sure don't make 'em like they used to,* I think.

It's been a while since there was a new face at The Oakmont. Someone must've received their eviction notice. It happens. Sooner or later, one will find its way under each of our doors. That's understood.

I remove my smock and check my reflection on the side of the fondue pot to make sure there's no paint on me, then head over to introduce myself, feeling a little underdressed in jeans and a t-shirt. That's how Roger and I first meet.

He says he's from the early forties. I tell him when I'm from. The connection's instant and powerful. We talk like we've known each other for years. Later we sit next to each other, laughing as Harold Lloyd dangles over the city from the face of an enormous clock. After everyone else has left, we dance for the first time. On this occasion, I only hum "Moonlight Serenade." I suppose it's the look of him that makes me choose that song. As we dance, he describes the view of New York as he sees it. I lean my head against his shoulder and try to picture what he tells me.

The Oakmont was built over a time vortex. No one knows how long it has stood on this spot. There's no record of its construction or design. The building's architectural style is timeless, naturally. Its façade appears neither new nor weathered. The residents of The Oakmont can't even be certain the way they see the building is the same way others do.

• • • •

Late in July, Don invites Linda and me over to watch the Apollo 11 moon landing. Linda watched it back when she was nineteen. For Don, it's the first time. I've seen it on TV and YouTube many times over my life, but tonight we're in Don's apartment, where it's actually July 20, 1969, so we'll be watching it live on his TV. I would love to have shared this moment with Roger, but The Oakmont rules are in place for our own good. I did slip a note under Harrison's door inviting him to join us, but I never heard back.

I show up late, as usual. Linda's clearly been here a while. The scent of pot they smoked earlier still lingers in the air, and their first questions to me are about snacks. I dump out the bag I've brought on Don's couch. Everything I could find that didn't exist in their respective times: key lime–flavored licorice, ruby chocolate, chips made from every root vegetable but potatoes.

"Did you get my Coke Zero?" Don asks, rummaging through the pile of goodies.

"Oh shoot! I forgot. There was this old lady in the aisle who started talking to me about the ridiculous price of grapes, and I guess I got distracted."

"Classic Sarah," Linda says. "Born too late, it seems. Can't resist anyone old. Is that why all your friends are from the twentieth century?"

They both laugh.

"Technically, I'm from the twentieth, too," I say. "Just made it at the tail end. Maybe that's why my neighbor keeps avoiding me. Not twenty-first century enough for him."

"What neighbor?" asks Don.

"You know, Harrison from 2055."

They shrug and I find myself wondering if they simply haven't met him, or if they just don't perceive him. That happens at The Oakmont. It's even more common when you're talking about non-residents.

Take Linda; she works at a roller rink teaching roller disco dancing to bored housewives. The rink is owned by her boyfriend, who I know she's mentioned many times, but I can't for the life of me recall his name. I don't even know if we've met before. All I know is in my time *Roller Palace* is long gone. It's a Chinese buffet now that offers a killer dim sum service on Sundays. Every time I go, I'm tempted to pull up a corner of the carpeting to see if the rink floor's still there. They kept the disco ball, after all.

People who reside outside The Oakmont may visit, but their experience is limited. They see only what pertains to their time. Should they encounter residents from other time periods, they're left only with a vague impression there were people there, but they couldn't begin to describe them. The perception—or lack thereof—is often mutual.

"Anyway, I think it's sweet you talk to little old ladies," Don says. "You can never know if you're the only person a lonely stranger might see that day. Kindness costs nothing."

"Wow, you are such a hippie, Don," Linda tells him, before turning to me and adding, "Speaking of all things ancient, how's Roger?"

I'm about to respond when Don shushes us and points to the TV. We watch Neil Armstrong descend the ladder, describing the surface of the moon as he does. I'm unexpectedly emotional, watching it happen live. He says those iconic words and tears roll down my face. Don and Linda see and burst into renewed laughter. Linda throws a beet chip at me.

"Oh, shut up! You guys just don't get it." Then I start laughing too as I wipe the tears away.

"Okay, so about Roger?"

They both perceive Roger, which is nice since we've been together for almost four months now. I tell them things are going great, and they are. He's an old-fashioned guy, the kind that shows up to dates with flowers and slips handwritten love notes under my door. I love his little 1940s quirks that would be so out-of-place in my time, like the way his hair's always Brylcreemed and flawlessly parted to one side, or how he takes his hat off when sharing the elevator with a lady, and how when his shoes get worn, he gets them repaired rather than buy new ones. I love that when I get emotional, he hands me a real cloth handkerchief from his pocket.

"I got him to quit smoking," I add.

"That's it?" Linda says. "Where's the juicy stuff?"

"The juicy stuff stays between Roger and me."

"More like *between the sheets*," she says with a wink to Don. But Don's looking at me with the kind of serious expression that only comes from the best marijuana strains.

"What's wrong, Sarah?" he asks. "I can tell something's on your mind."

I hesitate, not wanting to bring this subject up with him, of all people, but with both of them waiting, I have no choice but to continue.

"It's the war. It's coming and I'm worried about what that'll mean for Roger. I hate not being able to warn him."

Don gives a single, almost solemn, nod. He gets it, what with his own war to worry about. So far, he's avoided it, but he knows it's just a matter of time before they start drafting. I know he has his fears about having to go to Vietnam. Fears I have no way to assuage.

There are rules at The Oakmont. One is that residents may not research prior history in order to discover what became of a fellow resident who exists in a time prior to their own.

"Maybe you should just tell him," Don says. "Tell him about all of it. How Japan bombs Pearl, but also how we retaliate. Tell him about dropping Fat Man and Little Boy. Tell him about the devastation that causes in Hiroshima and Nagasaki. Tell him about the camps, but also tell him how no one ever really wins a war, so it's pointless to keep fighting them."

His eyes dampen as he speaks, though he chants similar words in protest almost daily.

I nod in agreement, but we both know I won't say any of that to Roger. It wouldn't matter if I did. War is seen through different eyes in 1941. In 1945, our country will celebrate the Allied victory for two whole days. The roar of celebration will go on for twenty minutes after the announcement's made. A sailor will grab an unsuspecting nurse and plant a kiss on her in the middle of the street, and Alfred Eisenstaedt will capture it for *LIFE Magazine*. It's not the same kind of thing Don's staring down the barrel of, and we both know it.

Before the end of the year, we stop seeing Don. He leaves a note with Ms. Knox letting us know he's gone to Canada ahead of the draft. The Oakmont's not the same without him.

• • • •

December 7 comes so fast it's like a blink, but time moves differently at The Oakmont. I knock on Roger's door that day, but there's no answer. As I walk along the hallway back to the elevator, I'm filled with an irrational desire to knock on every door I pass. I want to see another human being—anyone at all—and tell them that in 1941 the country has entered World War II. I want to tell them I'm afraid for the love of my life. I want to see if any of them have phones that will reach his time so I can call and ask if he's okay.

I pick a door at random and pound my fists against it, crying in frustration. But no one comes.

There are many doors inside The Oakmont that won't open and corridors down which a resident can't turn. The Oakmont allows us to see who and what we need to, nothing more. The Oakmont guards its secrets.

Several days pass before I see Roger again. When I do, he seems distracted, his mind elsewhere. I note the stress in his eyes. He avoids talk of what happened, and I don't press. Instead, he speaks of his sister, Betty, who plans to enter the workforce as a telephone operator.

"I'm not sure this is the time," he says. "Why does she need to work anyway?"

"Working women will become increasingly common in the years to come," I say, refraining from mentioning that as men go off to fight in World War II, there'll be a boom as millions of women take their places. "I have a job myself, remember?"

"Yes, but it's different in your time, Sarah."

"Is it so different? Maybe this is just what your sister needs."

"But how does it work for families?" he asks. "Who raises the children and manages the home?"

I smile. You have to accept this kind of thing when you're a resident of The Oakmont. Times are different, and each one has its own set of values and attitudes that will inevitably become obsolete as the sands of time continue to fall. We must consider the source and share our varied points of view with the goal of finding common ground, especially with those we love.

"Families find ways to make it work," I say. "Ideally, both parents share responsibilities. That is, in households with two parents. I can't say how single parents manage, but they do. I imagine they found ways to do so even in your time."

He nods, and we sit in silence as the elephant in the room that is the Second World War looms large over everything.

• • • •

Roger does his best to keep the mood light when we celebrate Christmas. He hangs mistletoe over his door and kisses me deeply when I arrive. On the radio, Bing Crosby sings "Silent Night." Roger's even cut down a real tree and hung vintage ornaments from its branches. Well, vintage to me, anyway. Beneath the tree, there's a small package wrapped in plain paper with a simple red ribbon around it. I assume it's for me, and I place the one I brought for him next to it. Mine looks so garish in its cartoon reindeer wrapping and iridescent silver bow. Roger can't help laughing when he sees it.

I ask about his sister, and he tells me she got the job at the phone company. I tell him I'm glad and that I wish her well.

"That reminds me; she baked cookies."

He grabs a tin from atop his fridge, opens it, and offers me one. I take a bite and can't help uttering a long *mmmm* as the flavor fills my mouth.

"This is so much better than the packaged stuff I buy at the store."

"I can't believe you don't cook or bake a thing," he laughs.

"That's not true. I make a mean root-beer ham. Mind you, it's just a cooked ham I put in my slow cooker and pour a can of soda over."

He doesn't bother to ask what a slow cooker is. I guess the name says it all. He's aware of some of the magical appliances I have. Well, 'magical' to me.

To him, they seem wasteful—lazy even. "Why would any one household need more than one television?" he asked once.

I didn't really know how to respond to that. I think he'd have to admit my cell phone's pretty cool, though, with all the uses it has, but cell phones are strictly forbidden in apartments with numbers earlier than the mid-seventies.

We have some eggnog by the window, and I describe the Christmas lights that decorate the city in my time. New York is alive and festive in December 2023. In 1941, I gather, things are a bit more subdued.

Afterwards, we open our gifts. Always the gentleman, he insists I go first. I pull the ribbon and paper off the box and smile when I see the handkerchief.

"I thought you could use one of your own."

"It's beautiful," I say. And it is. I've never owned anything like it. The fabric is cotton, I think, but the edges are hand-embroidered with violets, which he knows are the flower for my birth month. On one corner are my initials. I run my finger over them, turning the fabric over to marvel at the quality of the stitching. Machines are good, but not like this.

They don't make 'em like they used to, I think, not for the first time.

He opens my gift next, and I wait on the edge of my seat to see his face. Carefully setting the reindeer paper aside, he holds up the canvas and stares at it a moment before looking at me. I can't help it; I burst into laughter.

"Do you like it?"

"It's... a still life?"

"You could say that."

I look down at the painting I made for him. A painting of a single can of Campbell's tomato soup. It's an obvious rip-off, at least to those of us born after pop art became a thing. Roger shakes his head and laughs.

Years from now—for him at least—an artist named Warhol will paint a much better rendition of this very can. The punchline to my joke will land then. I wish I could be there to see his face when it does.

"I love it," he says. There's so much about me he doesn't understand, and yet he still feels this way.

Residents of The Oakmont know there are things you must simply accept while living here, and questions you don't ask, at least not with any expectation of their being answered.

Roger places the painting on his mantle. It actually looks good there. He stands admiring it for a while—or maybe asking himself, 'Why a can of soup?' I come up behind him to wrap him in an embrace and kiss him between the shoulder blades as he places a hand on mine. Then he exhales deeply, and I know immediately what's coming.

"I've decided to enlist," he tells the painting.

I bury my face into his back and hold back tears.

"There's no rush," I say. "The war goes on for years, and they won't draft until next. You don't have to decide now."

He turns, wrapping his arms around me and kissing the top of my head.

"I know this isn't what you want, but I've given it a lot of thought.

They're looking for able-bodied men. Our freedoms are at stake—and those of our allies. I can't just sit this one out."

"But to volunteer?"

He says nothing more. There's no need. I know the man he is, and that this is exactly the kind of thing he'd do. It's why I've worried for months that this moment would come. I know better than to argue, so I simply nod.

Later, we fall into bed as we have countless times before, but somehow this feels different. Time seems to linger as we make love, as if stretching out our time together.

Just days later, he goes to volunteer, and I walk him to the door. The main entrance to The Oakmont is a peculiar place. There's a lobby with a revolving door that looks just like the many such doors you'll find across the city. When you walk through this one, though, where you end up depends on who you are. Or, should I say, *when* you end up. Even if Roger and I were to walk through together, holding hands, we'd still each step out alone into our own time.

He kisses me once, sweetly, then puts his hat on and gives me a smile. I return one as best I can. When he turns to go, part of me wants to run after him, but I stay and watch as he spins through the entrance, then vanishes into thin air.

I reach into my pocket, pull my new handkerchief out, and use it to wipe the tears.

• • • •

When Roger ships out, I can't see him off. That happens long before I'm born. To take my mind off things, Linda asks me over to her place. We talk about movies, and in my frazzled state I let slip a *Star Wars* reference, though it'll still be another year before it comes out in her time. Luckily, she doesn't notice.

New Year's Eve came and went without much fanfare. I've felt numb ever since Roger said he was going to war. It's 2024 and 1942 where we are. Time marches on, whatever the decade and no matter how much we might want to slow things down.

"Anyway, he's thinking of selling Roller Palace," Linda's saying, and I realize I've missed her boyfriend's name yet again. "Where the hell does that leave me?"

"Does he have another plan?"

"Wants to open something called a video rental store."

"It might be alright," I tell her.

"You know something I don't?"

Her eyes widen with expectation, but I give her nothing more. She shakes her head, disappointed.

I hang out a while longer but call it an early night. When I get back to my apartment, there's an envelope sticking out from under the door. It's yellowed with age and has no stamp or postmark. The mailing address reads only: *Sarah – The Oakmont*. I recognize the handwriting immediately.

Before I'm even through the door, I've torn it open, the scent of old paper contrasting with the anticipation of fresh news from the front.

Roger tells me of the time since he left, mentioning some of the guys he's befriended—two of them New Yorkers like us. Neither has heard of The Oakmont, and Roger can't seem to recall its location for them.

The letter goes on to say how much he misses me and how he thinks of me often. He wishes he could've brought a picture of me, but the modern look of all the ones I had would've invited curious looks in 1942.

By the time I'm done reading, I'm both laughing and crying. Pressing the letter to my chest, I try to feel him there with me, through time and space. I have no idea how this letter reached me, but Roger's generation was nothing if not resourceful. Dancing alone in my living room, humming "Moonlight Serenade," I send him all my love and hope it somehow finds its way to him, too.

· · · ·

Letters continue to arrive, one each week. They're always slipped under my door and yellowed from the passage of time. I suspect they're delivered by Ms. Knox when she knows I'm not around.

There's so much Roger isn't able to share with me, so he mostly reminisces about our time at The Oakmont. He wonders what picture Mr. Thomas will be showing when he starts our movie nights back up. I want to tell him it's Buster Keaton in *Seven Chances,* but I have no way to write him. In any case, I might not go. It's not the same without Roger sitting next to me.

Then a week goes by with no letter. Nor is there one the following week. A month passes with the worst scenarios running through my mind until I can't take it. I break the rules—not a little this time, but fully. I open up my laptop and Google his name, and any other information I have on his military service.

Nothing comes up.

There are results, of course, but they're of other Rogers and other wars. There's nothing to tell me what happened to my Roger.

I look up every Army database I can and search for someone to contact for answers. I call in sick to work and spend the next two days calling everyone I can. The responses are always the same. There's no record of Roger. Things get misfiled. There was a flood in the fifties, or a fire in the eighties. The explanations are irrelevant. They all mean the same thing: that I have no idea what's happened to Roger.

I can think of only one person that might have the answers I so desperately need.

Ms. Knox has been the building manager of The Oakmont for time immemorial. If you ask the residents what she's like, you'll find the descriptions vary enormously. Some will say she's a young, attractive brunette with a fondness for hats; others will swear she's ancient, bone-thin, and always smells of cinnamon. Still others will tell you Knox is, in fact, an unusually tall man with an Australian accent. All are correct.

I knock perhaps a little too hard on Ms. Knox's door, but she seems not to have noticed when she opens it and offers me a gracious smile. I'm invited in and offered tea, which I accept more out of distraction than any real desire.

I blurt out my confession as she holds a sugar cube in a set of tiny tongs over my cup.

"I've been searching the historical records for Roger in apartment 1942."

The cube drops with a *plop* into my tea.

"Milk?" she offers.

I blink, waiting for... something else. Some admonishment, maybe.

Or perhaps a threat of eviction. She sits across from me then and exhales before speaking.

"The rules are in place for your own good. Has breaking this one brought you any measure of peace? Has it returned Roger to you?"

I shake my head.

"You want *me* to do that, then." She sips from her cup. "You want me to tell you whether or not Roger survives the war."

I nod.

"There are questions you just don't ask at The Oakmont," she reminds me. "You don't ask them because they can't be answered. Only time can give you the answers you seek."

"Time," I repeat. "Time is a thing you dangle from precariously as the city moves on below you."

"Mr. Thomas and his moving pictures," she says with a laugh. "Do you want to know what time really is?"

I watch her, saying nothing so she'll continue.

"Time is nothing... and everything. It doesn't actually exist, because we made it up, but if it did exist, it wouldn't run in a line; it would run in a circle."

Ms. Knox reaches into her blouse and pulls out a ring on a chain. She spins it one way, then the other.

"Time moves differently at The Oakmont. We can touch it at any point in time or at all points at once." She demonstrates by tapping the ring at various points before placing it onto one of her fingers. "Time can pass you by and leave you virtually untouched, or it can fall on you like a cascade."

"But what does any of this have to do with Roger?"

"There's no fighting it," she says. "It's like swimming against the current. Better to give in, relax, and let the waves carry you to shore."

She tucks the ring back into her blouse and takes another loud sip from her cup. I stare down into mine, searching for answers but knowing there are none to be found here.

Without another word, I stand and head back out to the hall. She makes no move to stop me. I'm so numb, I don't even consciously move through the building and only notice I've reached my door when it fails to open for me. I try the key again and again and finally burst into tears.

Ms. Knox has locked me out somehow—punishment for breaking the rules.

"You alright?"

I don't recognize the voice, so I look up and see my neighbor, Harrison, standing by his open door. I think it's maybe the second thing he's ever said to me in all the time he's lived here.

"No, I'm not alright. My key won't work."

He comes over and takes a look, then removes and reinserts the key before turning it. The door unlocks and he pushes it open.

"You had your key in upside down."

I feel like an idiot. No wonder this guy has wanted nothing to do with me. I continue to cry even while thanking him, and as I start to walk past him to enter my apartment, he stops me and gives me a hug. It's uncharacteristic, especially in a city like New York, but I give in to it—the way Ms. Knox said I should surrender to time. Through sobs, I tell this stranger everything, from the moment Roger and I first met and fell in love, to the letters that arrived at my door so mysteriously, then stopped coming at all.

He listens to all of it in silence with a patience I envy. Then he does the unthinkable and invites me to join him in his apartment.

"I... couldn't," I say. "There are rules at The Oakmont."

"I'm aware. Nevertheless, there's something you should see."

I don't trust easily, but something about Harrison feels safe. I follow him to his door, rules be damned, and step behind him into 2056.

The apartment doesn't look too different from my own. You expect there to be major changes from one era to another, but ultimately a chair's still a chair and a lamp's still a lamp. Apartments look pretty much the same, and New York rent's probably way too steep in every time.

Leaving me standing by the door, he heads into his bedroom, returning a moment later with a shoebox. He removes the lid as he approaches, and I don't understand what I'm looking at. Inside there's... nothing.

"I'm confused."

"My mother used to live at The Oakmont, though I didn't always know that. I never met my father, but when I moved out, she gave me this box and told me it contained something that was his. She said he'd left it for me, with instructions that she give it to me when I got my own place."

I take the empty box and wait for him to continue.

"When I opened the box, I found a bunch of letters. All of them looked old, but the one on top was the only one with my name on it, so I opened it. The letter was from my parents, written when Mom was pregnant. That's how I learned she'd lived here too. They both had. Everything I'd known about them up until that point was, if not a lie, then certainly incomplete. My mother would've told me the truth, had she been able to, but..."

"She didn't remember," I finished.

Residence at The Oakmont is a temporary affair. Those who live here only do so when the time is right, and when that time passes, they are evicted. Those who are evicted will find their memories of The Oakmont—and those they knew there—are fleeting, and just out of reach; like a word on the tip of your tongue you can never quite recall. At times, they may sense its existence. They may even search for it, never quite knowing what they're searching for, but you can only find The Oakmont when it wants to be found.

Harrison nods. "By then I'd read the contract you sign when you move in, and I understood. In any case, the letter explained everything. How they'd met, their time together, how he'd gone off to war, all the way through to her eviction. The other letters were ones my father had written my mother during the war. In the letter to me, he said he'd resealed them in new envelopes and gave me specific instructions as to what I should do with them, and when."

I'm at a loss for words as he tells me this. I see it now, as I let my gaze fall over him. The flecks of green in his eyes, so like Roger's. The same unruly waves that drive me crazy in my own hair. This was why he'd avoided me. He'd known that if I looked at him—if I really looked—I'd see and I would know.

"It was you," I say. "I thought it was Ms. Knox who kept slipping the letters under my door."

My gaze then falls on the artwork that hangs above his mantle. It's the one I painted a year ago—or maybe decades ago: "The gang at the Oakmont."

"What I don't understand," he says, "is why you were evicted. I know it's just something that happens here, sooner or later, but I thought there'd be an explanation for why it happened when it did."

I smile, then burst into tears again. He looks concerned for a moment, but I start laughing. Relief washes over me and I clasp my hands and raise them to my face a moment before I regain some composure.

"I became pregnant," I say. "That's why."

The Oakmont is an adult-only living environment. You won't find children or families among its residents. There are couples on occasion, but for the most part residents live alone. Children are lovely, to be sure, but their futures are too uncertain and their pasts too meager. They're as yet too resistant to the push and pull of time. Children also have great difficulty following rules, and there are, of course, many rules at The Oakmont.

"This is great. This is unbelievable!" I tell him and wrap him in the tightest hug I can muster.

He looks confused, so I explain.

"Don't you see? I'm not pregnant now. That means I must get pregnant later, or you wouldn't be here. Which means Roger survives the war!"

He smiles an uncertain, lopsided smile as I jump up and down, still hugging him. After a while, he gives in to my joy and we both laugh and cry, and for the first time ever, Harrison accepts my invitation to join me for dinner. There are so many questions I want to ask that I know he can't answer, so instead I let him ask questions of his own. We talk long into the night, and when we're done, I describe to him my view out the window, and he tells me what it looks like in 2056.

• • • •

Roger returns a little over a month later, walking with a cane. I'm just glad he's alive and back in my arms. We're shy around each other at first, until we're not, and then we're back in his bed, just like old times.

The war continues where he is, but he's done his part. I break the rules and tell him how it ends so he's not surprised when the day finally comes. In early September 1945—or 2027, depending on your point of view—we celebrate the occasion in our own way and conceive our son.

I discover I'm pregnant as soon as I return to my apartment, where I find an eviction notice slipped under my door.

When I tell Roger both the good news and bad, we cry tears of joy and sadness, and afterward he plays "Moonlight Serenade," and we dance one more time.

"I'm going to miss this," I say. "In my time, no one who isn't a professional really knows how to dance anymore. At least with you leading, I stood a chance at a few decent steps."

"I'll miss this too, and I'll miss seeing New York through your eyes."

"Maybe we could meet in the future, where our lives overlap," I say.

He kisses my forehead. "That would never work. You'd be a child or at most a young woman. I'd be an old man."

I choke back tears and take a deep breath to steady myself.

"It'll be alright," he says. "I don't think this is necessarily the end for us. After all, time moves differently at The Oakmont."

I don't know what he means by that, but I do know that in The Oakmont, there are questions you don't ask.

• • • •

I'm big as a house, waddling down the aisles of my local grocery store in search of the newborn diapers that match my coupon.

"My goodness," says a voice with geriatric lilt. "You're close to bursting."

I have one of those faces where older strangers feel comfortable talking to me. I stop and offer her a smile.

"I fear I may pop at any moment," I agree, and we both laugh.

"Do you know what you're having, dear?"

"A boy. I'm naming him Harrison."

"What a great name."

"Thanks. It just came to me one day."

"Honey, in your condition, you should be home resting. Let the baby's father do the running around."

"Oh, it's just the two of us," I say, rubbing my belly. "That's why I'm here hunting down diapers."

"Aren't we all, dear," she jokes, giving me a mischievous wink.

There's something in that wink that seems familiar, and I'm about to ask if we've spoken before when my eye falls on a keychain clipped to her purse strap. A keychain in the shape of a roller skate.

It all comes back in a rush of memory. I see through her aged features to the youthful ones I once knew, and with them all my other memories of The Oakmont return. In that moment, I see the same recognition in Linda's aged eyes. She smiles and winks once more.

"My but we had some good times then," she says.

I'm about to answer when it hits me that somewhere back at The Oakmont there's a younger Linda, living in the seventies. If Linda can be in both places, in two different times, what's to stop her from more? What's to stop any of us?

I think of Ms. Knox and her ring, speaking about touching time at multiple points or all of them at once. I think of all those doors at The Oakmont that never opened for me. At least not the me I was then, at that time. Maybe somewhere behind one of those doors there's another Sarah, with another Roger, and with them all our old friends. Maybe it's movie night and we're standing around the potluck table waiting for Mr. Thomas to start the film.

"If you're the owner of a blue Toyota, your car alarm is going off."

The announcement over the store speakers jars me out of my thoughts. I feel like I was somewhere else just now, but the memory's faded. The elderly lady in front of me seems confused, then shakes her head as she remembers what we were talking about.

"They have the newborn diapers just there, next to the formula," she says.

"Great, thanks."

"Good luck with the little one."

"Thanks again. It was nice meeting you."

You won't find The Oakmont on any maps, in any time. You don't find it; it finds you. You'll be living your life, happy as can be, then one day you'll come across an advertisement for an apartment for rent. The ad might be online, or on a bulletin board, or in a newspaper. It makes no difference. What matters is The Oakmont will call to you when it's your time. It will offer just what you're looking for: a neighborhood close to work or the subway, stunning views of the skyline, maybe, or rent control. Whatever the draw, you'll know then and there you've found your home, and you'll soon find yourself in Ms. Knox's office, signing your name just below the list of rules.

P.A. CORNELL IS a Chilean-Canadian speculative fiction writer. A graduate of the Odyssey workshop, her stories have been published in over fifty magazines and anthologies, including *Lightspeed Magazine*, *Apex Magazine*, and three "Best of" anthologies. In addition to becoming the first Chilean Nebula finalist in 2024, Cornell has been a finalist for the Aurora and World Fantasy Awards, was longlisted for the BSFA Awards, and won Canada's Short Works Prize. When not writing, she can be found assembling intricate LEGO builds or drinking ridiculous quantities of tea. Sometimes both. For more on the author and her work, visit her website, pacornell.com.

* CONTENT NOTES: references to war

BAD DOORS

BY JOHN WISWELL

Short Story Long List*

T he country was at just over ten thousand deaths the morning that the door appeared. On Kosmo's phone, NPR was interviewing a doctor with a nasal voice about the need for social distancing, while Kosmo himself collected empty cans from around his home office. They were everywhere. Walls of recyclable cans dominated his room. Just beside his bookshelf, out of the view from where he taught his Zoom classes, he'd constructed a veritable castle of empty Coke Zeroes.

"If you spread your arms wide, that is roughly the distance you want to be away from others," the doctor explained. "That prevents your breath and expectorate from coming into contact with others."

Kosmo tried spreading his arms that wide—he'd always been gangly —and promptly knocked over a three-stack of cans balanced on top of his Riverside Chaucer. The cans clanked to the ground and rolled into the hall. Kosmo chased them, hunched over, like a cartoon dinosaur in pursuit.

Nearing the hall, he called out for his cousin. "Jesse? Got any empty seltzers? I'm doing a recycling run."

That's when he saw the new door. It was equidistant on the wall between the entrances to his room and Jesse's. Its deep burgundy color stood out against the plaster white of the walls. It was perfectly flat, without any veins or grain, like it was liquid that had merely cooled to look like wood. It had a square knob, made of polished ebony that shone against the redness.

On Kosmo's phone, the interviewer asked, "What about the people who say they can't breathe with masks on?"

Kosmo covered his mouth and breathed through his fingers. All the doors in his house were cheap particle wood. There was no door on that wall of his hallway. There was no room behind there. He didn't remember getting high this morning. He got closer, expecting this hallucination of a burgundy door to fade.

He heard Jesse's dog Rufus approaching, little toenails pattering on the hardwood. The Labrador/hound mix had the coldest nose Kosmo had ever encountered, and no sense of smell to go with it. Yet Rufus still nosed at the burgundy door like it would give him a treat.

Kosmo took a moment to make sure that door wasn't something Jesse had picked up at the Home Depot or something and left leaning against the wall.

No, it was embedded in the wall. Despite this being an internal wall, he heard sounds like rasping wind and a heavy humming coming from the other side. Rufus nosed closer at the door, pushing his muzzle at something on the floor. It was thin and flaky, like a bit of snakeskin.

The dog opened his mouth as though to eat the snakeskin, and that was it for Kosmo. He scooped the pup up in a two-armed hug and ran for the back door. He didn't even put his shoes on. Hell no, he was not finding out what this was about.

• • • •

Uncle Dahl gave Kosmo no end of shit for moving. But Uncle Dahl also kept sending him conspiracy theories about Bill Gates, so Kosmo mostly ignored him. Their family was a piece of work. They begged for hand sanitizer and then barely used it.

Jesse complained about the move too, even though his ass had never paid Kosmo rent. 'Sheltering for the pandemic' seemed to be Jesse's means of living for free. As it was, Kosmo walked Jesse's dog more than Jesse did. Fortunately, Rufus was good company.

Kosmo only returned to the house twice, to get some of his stuff for the move. He put that house right on the market. He wasn't living in whatever was about to happen there.

Jesse asked, "What was going to happen in there?"

To which Kosmo answered, "I don't want to know."

The weirdest thing was that the second time he went back, when he went with the realtor, the burgundy door wasn't there. Just a little sloughed off snakeskin blowing along the floor.

The realtor, Mrs. Weiss, said, "Good move getting rid of that door. It threw off the vibe of the hallway. You drywalled so cleanly I couldn't even tell there had been a door there."

Kosmo hadn't touched anything. He was about as handy as a man with four feet.

But, he also wasn't sticking around to investigate. Complaining about disappearing mystery doors was only going to cost him resale value. He needed all the money he could get, because while selling in this market was good, finding a new place was brutal with all the people sheltering in place from the pandemic and all the Boomers buying new places to shelter. Mrs. Weiss said it'd be easier if he waited six months for COVID to blow over.

Kosmo wasn't waiting around. He ate his losses, and got Jesse and Rufus into the moving van, and moved the hell across the state. His part in this story was over.

Or it was supposed to be. The door had other plans.

• • • •

They lugged their crap in through the unthreatening taupe doors of their new home. It was half the size of the old place, a single-story building that could've been a double-wide trailer in a previous life. It was what Kosmo could get for his money. Most of their stuff wouldn't fit.

One thing he refused to lose was the plush beige sofa that was more comfortable than whatever clouds God sat on. Kosmo and Jesse wrestled with it for fifteen minutes, with Rufus running in circles between their legs, before they got it through the house's narrow entrance. It was such a tight fit that they dropped it halfway down the front hall. They sat on their prize, with their feet up against the wall. Rufus bounded over an armrest to snuggle and jam his cold nose into Kosmo's armpit.

Kosmo and Jesse took hits off the weed in Jesse's vape pen. After his second inhale, Jesse asked, "You feel like getting the TV?"

Kosmo had just gotten comfortable, too. He said, "If you want it, you go get it."

"I need my shows."

"Don't you have a phone? And where would you even put a TV in here?"

Jesse swiped vaguely down to the other end of the off-white hall. The lighting was strong there, shining on a burgundy door.

Kosmo jumped over the dog and sofa alike. He sheltered behind an arm rest, staring at that door. It had that same square doorknob of polished ebony.

Kosmo said, "That shit was not there a minute ago, right?"

Jesse hit the vape pen again and leaned towards the door. "No. No, it was not. Is that the same door from the old house?"

"Don't look at it like that."

"Like what?"

Kosmo reached for his cousin. He grabbed at his hoodie. "Like you're going to touch it."

No yank on Jesse could get the man to budge. He said, "You don't know it's dangerous."

"Jesse. Are we on all of the drugs?"

"Unfortunately, we are not."

"Then that door is stalking us. No good comes from that."

Jesse had the gall to frown at him when there was an evil door standing right down the hall from him. He said, "What is your trauma, man? What happened to you that made you afraid of a little mystery?"

What was his trauma? Kosmo had a perfectly regular amount of traumas. He shook his head at his cousin. "No man, this isn't on me. I don't know what's wrong with people like you who want to touch an impossible thing that's messing with you. Doors don't appear from nowhere."

"Well, this one did."

Kosmo smacked the arm rest for emphasis. "Exactly. And what happens next? Do space witches come through the door? Does other shit materialize around my house and in ten minutes we fall into a basement that never existed? I'm not finding out. I'm not doing the science here."

Not one sentence made Jesse turn around. He kept staring at the door. "But what's inside?"

"I just said, I don't want to know." Kosmo gathered Rufus into his arms. "Let's go."

Jesse didn't go. He crawled over the sofa and wandered across the floor, into Kosmo's unwanted house. No expletives slowed him down. He reached a hairy hand for that square doorknob.

Kosmo took off, abandoning his sofa and his cousin, and went straight through the nearest exit. The taupe door hit him in the hip on the way out, and Rufus barked in his arms. The dog got loud enough that Kosmo couldn't hear whether Jesse actually opened that forbidden door.

On the cracked concrete of the front step, Kosmo hesitated a second. "Jesse. Get out here."

That used up the last of his bravery. In the next moment, he was in the moving truck, starting it up with the front door still ajar. Rufus wagged his tail and tried to climb across his lap like this was an adventure.

The truck farted to life and rumbled. The seatbelt chime pestered him. He checked over his shoulder and saw the driveway was clear and he could back out. He kept it idling, waiting, willing his cousin to find sense and get out of there. Even if Jesse came with Pennywise and the Babadook chasing him, it would be a relief to get them all out alive.

The truck idled so long that the fasten-seatbelt chime gave up. Kosmo lingered, watching the house for anything. Any mellow the weed had given him was dead.

"Damn it," he said to himself. As he stepped out, he made sure to close Rufus in the truck, so the dog would stay out of trouble. Rufus wagged his tail cluelessly.

When Kosmo checked inside, the burgundy door was closed. The black knob shone brightly with its polish.

He called, "Jesse?"

No answer. He checked the bathrooms. The rear lawn. There was no sign of his cousin anywhere. The air barely smelled like his weed. It smelled more like wilting produce in here.

Being alone in the house with that door was too much. Kosmo started to leave, and then spotted some garbage in front of the door. He thought it was a bunch of torn packing paper, until he noticed the scaly pattern. It was a long hunk of snakeskin, maybe five feet of it. It was all dried and curled there at the foot of the door, exactly where Jesse had stood.

Kosmo spent the police investigation in cheap motels, simultaneously dreading and knowing no answer would come.

He never stayed more than a couple days at the same place. He picked ones with small rooms, where he could see most of the walls. No doors were sneaking up on him.

The pickings were thinner since some motels forbade dogs. He couldn't bring himself to give Rufus to a shelter. It seemed every day there was another news break of COVID breaking out at another community or animal shelter. The poor dog had been through enough.

So Kosmo spent his nights with the weirdo dog's nose tucked into his armpit. Jesse had said that Rufus had lost his sense of smell in a car accident. Who knew what he liked about Kosmo's armpit. Maybe it had the right warmth and moisture balance. He tried not to think about it. These days he was bad at not thinking about things.

Kosmo sat on the windowsill, on the phone with Uncle Dahl. Rufus padded over and flopped against Kosmo's ankle. He gave a classic dog sigh. It sounded exhausted, but probably didn't mean anything. Projecting human emotions onto a dog's sigh was almost as irrational as projecting them onto a door.

Uncle Dahl coughed so loud it sounded performative. He said, "Your mother raised you to be smarter with money. You sold two houses for chicken feed. You've got to invest."

Kosmo said, "Did you miss the part with the evil door?"

"Again with your evil door story."

"It ate my cousin. Jesse. Aunt Angelina's son disappeared."

"My house is full of doors. Should I be scared and sell too?"

Kosmo closed his eyes. This was not why he'd called his uncle.

In as neutral a tone as he could force, Kosmo asked, "So you don't remember any weird doors appearing to you or Mom or Aunt Angelina? Not when you were little? Never heard anything like on the Russian side of the family either?"

"My grandfather would've beaten the flesh off your knuckles for suggesting that. We're Orthodox. We never mess with the occult."

Kosmo could've argued that there had been plenty of occultism in Russia, but that wasn't the point of the call. He asked, "The occult never messed with us? There's nothing about snakes or square doorknobs or anything?"

"You pampered children." Instantly, his uncle's voice switched condescensions. He went from irate condescension to an insincere condescension, like this was entertaining for him now. "First you kids said there was this super virus sweeping the planet. Now you say there are evil doors everywhere. This is what's wrong with your generation. You scare easily."

As though done with this conversation, Rufus got up and padded away from the window.

Kosmo said, "COVID is real, Uncle Dahl. Are you using the hand sanitizer?"

"I'm on a Facebook group with real doctors. *They* are suppressing the research."

Kosmo pinched the bridge of his nose. "Who is?"

"Corporate media. They're trying to scare you into being a sheep. None of those people are really dead. It's all a plot to steal the election. Did you see what the governor said?"

No, Kosmo was not having this same argument again. He'd gotten it in a dozen Facebook posts every day. Actual colleagues had unfriended Kosmo for being connected to Uncle Dahl. He hated thinking he'd have to sever ties with one of the last people who remembered how his mother's voice had sounded.

Kosmo powered through with one last ditch effort. "So you're absolutely sure there's nothing about doors or snakeskins or anything in the family?"

Uncle Dahl barked out a laugh so hard Kosmo could almost smell his halitosis through the phone. "What do you even think is behind your scary door? This thing you're throwing your life away over?"

Rufus whined from over near the coat closet. He was nosing at the wall, where the one lamp in the motel room barely illuminated anything. There wasn't much to look at, yet the dog with no sense of smell moved like it was sniffing.

Another look, and Kosmo saw the burgundy door.

It was the same imposing height as it had been in his house, and in the second house where he'd lost Jesse. It was set right into the wall beside the closet, like it was inviting him to grab its square knob and walk through into the next motel room.

Rufus turned his dappled head to look at Kosmo, furry ears drooping. He had a long strand of snakeskin dangling from his mouth.

"Uncle. I'll call you back."

· · · ·

He got his first vaccination shot at an open-air clinic on a college campus, about an hour's trip from where he picked up the RV. The nurse told him to move his arm every hour so it wouldn't get sore, and fortunately Rufus was hyper that day and kept tugging on his leash to go explore more bushes. Kosmo kept Rufus near him at all times these days, in case of doors. Together they went on a walk to a local car dealership.

Something about the supply chain and microchip shortage meant the car market was a disaster. He settled for a decade-old used RV with a recently replaced engine. It was dingier in person than it had looked online. Still, as he ran his hand over its unusually low roof, Kosmo grinned. He used a tape measure on the tan and brown body of the RV to make sure. It was on the small side, with barely enough space for himself and Rufus to cook and sleep, and play videogames, and Zoom.

Better, it was the wrong dimensions for other things. It was too short, too narrow, and had windows in too many places. The door had always showed up the same size. There was no way it could fit on this RV.

"Who's a clever boy?" he asked Rufus, rubbing the dog's floppy ears. "Who's smarter than a door?"

If face-licking was a sign of approval, then Rufus thought he was a genius.

His phone buzzed as he pulled out of the lot. It was Uncle Dahl. He'd been texting more since Kosmo had deleted Facebook. He couldn't deal with all the conspiracy theories and the deluge of textual screaming in his life. The last post he'd seen had speculated state governments were hiding COVID deaths as 'pneumonia deaths.'

He ignored Uncle Dahl for now and headed to the nearest campsite. Rufus and he had a whole road trip planned to explore parts of America without walls. Soon he'd be spending two weeks in Great Smoky Mountains National Park. Two weeks alone, after so many months basically alone. Some friends had invited him to a bonfire they claimed would be open-air, about a day's drive out of his way. Considering it made him ache, but the longer he was away from them, the less he trusted that they were really isolating and socially distancing, and the more he read into their unmasked selfies.

The campgrounds were on some hills overlooking a small pine forest and a public sports field. A bunch of kids in mismatched uniforms were playing soccer, and parents pumped their fists and spilled their drinks in celebration from the faded bleachers. None of them wore masks—not the parents, and not the players. Being that recklessly happy looked so appealing. Kosmo imagined taking Rufus down there and introducing him. Kids always wanted to pet him.

A shriek rang out from near the southern goal. A kid had tripped and went down clutching his leg. Everyone swarmed him like ants, first his fellow kids, and then parents. From all the way up at his campsite, Kosmo could tell the kid had just skinned his knee. It must have been so comforting to that boy, to have all those people around him, caring for a little pain.

Nobody masked up as they came closer. Kosmo's instinct to go join the sympathy faded into a concern that anyone of them could've infected the whole huddle. How terrible it would be, if that instant of caring for a crying child was a spreader event. What were they all even thinking, gathering like this? Did the U.S. have to hit a million dead to scare people into taking it seriously?

His phone buzzed and interrupted his ire. It startled him so hard he nearly dropped Rufus's leash. He'd really lost himself there.

He checked his phone. It was another text from Uncle Dahl. Kosmo skimmed the messages, half-watching the kids below celebrate their fellow athlete walking it off. When Kosmo scrolled to the last message, his fingers clenched down on the phone. He pulled the screen closer to his face.

Uncle Dahl had seen the door.

• • • •

"Where is it?" Kosmo asked before he even got out of the RV's cab. Rufus tried to follow and Kosmo barely shut the door in time to keep him in. He wasn't letting Rufus get hurt.

Uncle Dahl rubbed a sneakered foot at a crack on the driveway. His scraggly gray beard was entirely unmasked. Brown sweatpants dangled on his skinny legs, and his beer gut was mostly contained in a red bathrobe. For how lazily he was dressed, his thinning gray hair was gelled and neatly combed over his freckled scalp.

His uncle said, "You're really living in that thing? That's not a home."

He coughed twice, then spit something yellow onto the pavement of the driveway. Kosmo stepped away from him and got a dirty look for it.

Kosmo asked, "Did you get vaccinated? I can help you sign up."

"I'm not a sheep. I don't need the Deep State tracking my every move."

Kosmo pointed to the rectangular bulge in Uncle Dahl's bathrobe pocket. "There are not microchips in vaccines, and you have a cell phone. I guarantee you TikTok already has all your information."

"You live in a glorified car. You're going to talk to me like that? Take your life back. Be a man."

"It turns out the RV doesn't care what gender I am. Neither does this door curse thing." Kosmo kept talking just to move the conversation along. This had already reminded him why he'd deleted Facebook in the first place. "Where's the door? How long has it been here?"

Uncle Dahl pointed out back, to the yard he paid landscapers to mow and seed for him. The rear wall of his house was brick painted the same deep blue of the U.S. flag. Paint flaked in various places, and at first Kosmo mistook some of the flecks for snakeskin.

But standing on the watered lawn, looking at those blue-painted bricks, he didn't see the door anywhere. He looked closer, wondering if Uncle Dahl had painted over it. Uncle Dahl did lots of weird things.

Kosmo asked, "You said it was out here?"

Uncle Dahl said, "You don't visit family anymore. You didn't even come for the holidays. You won't come in our houses because of this COVID thing. Do you see anyone other than that dog?"

Kosmo was looking around the next side of the house before he understood what that meant. He wheeled at Uncle Dahl. "Is it actually here?"

Uncle Dahl coughed again, a brackish noise. "You're so afraid of this phantom door. Doors are everywhere. Doors are just a thing."

"This thing ate Jesse. How do you not care about that?"

"I don't believe that story," Uncle Dahl said, coming closer, which made Kosmo back away. "But if any of it's real, we could make money. That's why we needed to see each other. It'll show up if you stay long enough. You said it appears everywhere. Let's do something with this opportunity."

Kosmo noticed the surveillance cameras mounted around his uncle's property. At least two of those were aimed at them. Was he recording this? Was he looking to make a profit off a video of Kosmo getting bewitched by a burgundy door?

He tried to slow his breathing. He was not slugging a senior citizen today. He put a fist to the side of his own head and pushed, making himself turn away so he wouldn't yell. But maybe he should yell. Maybe embarrassing his uncle in front of his neighbors would rattle some sense into him.

Uncle Dahl said, "Don't be dramatic. It's time for you to move on. Look at that wall. Show me this door. Then you can leave it here. Give the door to me."

Despite himself, Kosmo did stare at the wall. At that dark blue paint that belonged in depictions of a U.S. flag. The seams between every brick under the paint were so obvious. He wondered if the door would appear burgundy as always, or if its shape would emerge from beneath the blue. He'd never seen where the door came from.

His uncle deserved it. If he wanted to get swallowed into the unknown like Jesse, then a hurt part of himself said to let it happen.

The instant he entertained the thought, more followed through it. If he was going to let the door appear, he could do something nice for himself after. Maybe he'd stick around to see it open and have all those nagging questions answered from a safe distance. Maybe he could drive to the bonfire with his friends after all. Go teach on campus again. Fill up an entire Fine Arts building with evil doors, because screw it, if nobody else cared, then why should he?

Uncle Dahl sniffed wetly and rubbed his nose. "No more excuses. It's time for you to live a real life."

That was why he shouldn't. Spite was a bad reason, but people had been taking this unseriously since the first day he'd carried Rufus away from the first door. The door was stalking him and he didn't change. Jesse was gone and he didn't change from that insipid condescension.

Kosmo pushed away from the wall with its flecking paint and its bricks and its promises of bonfires. No door had appeared yet, and no door was going to appear. He marched in a wide berth around his uncle, not wanting to breathe an iota of that man's air.

Rufus was halfway up on the dashboard, head up, panting happily at the sight of him through the windshield. That dog was so happy just at the idea that Kosmo was coming home. Before he'd even fully sat at the wheel, Rufus's cold nose went directly into his armpit. He hugged the dog around his neck.

Uncle Dahl followed him, yelling, "You've got to take control."

He looked at his uncle one more time. "I am. Me leaving is me taking control. Don't text me again."

He slammed the door and pulled the RV out of the driveway, not looking back, not caring if the whole property was overtaken by weird doors and an old man's outrage. He and Rufus rode straight for the interstate, to get out of Florida as early as he could. The two of them had a date with the Great Smoky Mountains.

His uncle texted him several more times. Kosmo didn't let himself read them; he couldn't stand the sting. Texts slowed over the weeks, and stopped a month later when Uncle Dahl passed away.

Officially, it was pneumonia.

JOHN WISWELL is a disabled writer who lives where New York keeps all its trees. His fiction has won the Nebula and Locus Awards, and been a finalist for the Hugo, World Fantasy, and British Fantasy Awards, and has been translated into ten languages. His debut novel, *Someone You Can Build a Nest In*, was released from DAW Books in April of 2024.

* CONTENT NOTES: depictions of a pandemic and COVID denial

TANTIE MERLE AND THE FARMHAND 4200

BY R.S.A. GARCIA

Short Story Long List

So, hear nah. This is how it happen.

Was years after Malcolm pass through and wash away a lot ah we little islands coasts, and mash up so much ah Florida and Texas and them places, and people say they ain't waiting for no next storm like that one, and they pack up they things and went England, and Canada, and all over.

I done old, and my children was living Germany and Kenya and my youngest was down in Australia where hotter than here, so I didn't see no point in going from where I live my whole life. My Lincoln bury here, and we house good and strong. My oldest, Susan, she send money for me regular, and Lincoln like new thing, just like me, so he fix up the house and fix up the house until even that monster storm only cost me some windows and a little mason work on my concrete roof from what they call impact debris.

Long story short, I stay in my village with a few families and the only problem was some ah we getting old for the garden and the little animal we keep. Chickens get out, if the children not around, is trouble to catch them back. Cow wandering the street after it get frighten because somebody drone fly too low on delivery.

My problem was Ignatius.

Which is to say, he ain't no real problem. He just a normal goat, white and brown and tall as my hip. Wasn't he alone I keep all that time. I had a small herd I used to get nice milk from. Even try to make some cheese once. (That ain't come out so good, but that's a next story.) When they start getting on in years, I make a cook with neighbours and we curry it down with a little roti on the side with channa, potato and chataigne, and some beers; was meals for days.

That was village life. Real nice with everybody helping out everybody and the children belong to all ah we. World change, a lot ah the children move on, and the families that still here keep to theyself, so now is just Ignatius and me and I let him keep the grass low in the yard because Lincoln gone and I can't operate no weed-wacker bot.

Well after I fall that one time and break my hip and they give me a new one in the big hospital in Town, I start to get trouble on the days my yard clear of grass to go down the veranda stairs and take the goat out to the empty lot down the track. Didn't have nobody around in the day to help. All the families working and the children either in school or inside doing school online if they still rebuilding from the storm. But Ignatius can't eat if I don't take him, so I was forcing myself to go. Then I trip on the way back ah day, and thank God Neighbour see me go down because I would have been waiting for help to get back up all now.

I had a delivery service for meals, and a nice young boy come and clean for me once a week, but I couldn't afford no pet services and I know my children would say, Mammy, just cook him or give him away and done. But he was my little company around the yard. Just he alone I sit down with sometimes to talk to in the dead ah night, or the heat ah the day, and he always have time for me, listening while he chewing on something and watching me with he funny rectangle eye what all goat have.

Well, I have to say I tell one lie, and that is Ignatius have one problem and is the chewing. He chew on anything, especially what he don't like. That is why I can't get no pet service because I try, and he run them out the yard and keep they shoes for food. Ever since, is only me Ignatius like. Lincoln and all leave him alone after he come home and try to feed him one day at the top of the little rise behind we house, and Ignatius take one look at he bend over ass and butt the man down the hill. After I stop laughing (because if you ain't dead or seriously injured, I go laugh), he say was my goat and he wash he hands of him.

People say he bad-tempered but really he just know who he like, and sometimes that ain't you. But we was always good, and I didn't have the heart to eat him. He was probably too old to taste good anyway. But he keep getting away and he needed tying up and bringing back, and I didn't know what to do again.

Point is, I mention to my second daughter, Paula, who living in Germany, how hard it was getting to go out to the garden some days, and how things was with Ignatius, and because Paula not judgemental like Susan, she send me a package and tell me to expect the drone.

Bright and early ah Tuesday morning, I hear the whirring outside and when I pek through my living room curtains is because a big box so on my veranda and Ignatius done traipsing over with he leash trailing to see what he could chew. I reach out and take up the box and close the door and then I sit down in my favourite armchair in front the hologram projector Lincoln buy the year before he die and I read the label.

FARMHAND 4200!

And in small print below:

AI Guided Nanotechnology Solutions To Your Farming Needs

And in real fine print:

10 Year Warranty with Money Back Guarantee
(Certain conditions apply)

Well, I say to myself, that sounding good. And I touch the corner of the box where it had a big green patch say 'touch me.' Box make a little chirp and then peel down on all sides like a Julie mango and sitting in the middle was a ball of transparent package tape. Next thing I know, the tape tent a little at the top, then a blade appear, and slice the tape away.

Well, I bawl out and jump off the chair. Same time, a silvery thing the size of a cricket ball roll out the middle of the tape and stop right in front me. A little face light up in green on the top of it. Two circles for eyes and a bendy line for a mouth, like them emoji thing I used to text with as a child.

"Greetings owner," the ball say in ah English accent like Lincoln boss-man used to have. "No need for alarm. I'm your new Farmhand 4200!" The little blade that was poking out the side melt down so it was a smooth ball again. "Thank you for your purchase! Kindly remain still while I perform preliminary security and software updates."

Next thing I know, the ID band the government use to give we healthcare and send my pension and thing make a beep. Then it talk soft and sweet like a lady. "Linking," it say. "Farmhand 4200 detected. Downloading app. Download complete. App ready for use."

The green face make a grin and the ball roll as if excited. "Hello, Mrs. Merle Huggins. I'm your new farmhand! I'm very pleased to meet you and begin our farming adventures together. Please note, your Digital ID device has been linked to me and will provide you with updates on my tasks, location, battery life, and other functions.

"However, as a Farmhand 4200, I'm fully self-sufficient and require only ten minutes in daylight per day in order to recharge. I'm programmed to handle numerous farming emergencies and am enabled for research and adaptation should anything fall outside of the over 200 possible scenarios I've been initiated with. Your daughter, Paula, has sent you a message which I shall now play for you."

The little face change to yellow and pause on a smile instead of the wide grin it had before. "Hi Mammy," my daughter voice say, and it make me jump because it was like she was in the room with me, and as I listen she, tears come to my eyes because is years I ain't see she and she the one daughter give me grandchildren. "I hope you like this. You said you needed some help and Jonas says this is the top-of-the-line AI bot for farmers in the Rhineland. It can help you with the garden and that damn goat." Her laugh, big and boisterous like mine, take the sting out of her words. "Anyway, let me know when you get it and please try it out immediately and don't just have it sitting in the kitchen like the waffle maker I got you for Christmas."

I steups to myself but ain't say nothing because I know she can't hear me, but between you and me, what I going to do with a waffle maker, eh? What the hell is a waffle?

"Call me once you try it out. I want to know how it's working. Love you, Mammy. Talk to you soon, okay?"

After that the smiling face go green again and the bot say, "End of message. Hello again, Mrs. Huggins. Do you have any questions for me?"

I wrack my brains as I sit slowly in the chair. "What to call you, sir?"

"Whatever you wish, Mrs. Huggins."

"Well first, don't call me that. Everybody call me Tantie Merle."

"Of course, Tantie Merle!"

I think a bit more. "What if I call you 'Lincoln'? Was my husband name but he don't need it no more, he gone now, and I used to saying it."

The bot green face flicker, mouth round with surprise. "I would be honoured, Tantie Merle. My database shows that I'm the first Farmhand 4200 to receive a human name!"

"How much of you it have?"

"I'm a new model! 30,000 of me have been sold so far."

"So, what they call the other Farmhand 4200?"

"29,999 are called 'Farmhand 4200'," he reply cheerily.

"And the other one?"

"It is called 'Handy'!"

I shake my head. Sometimes people not too creative, yes, oui.

"Well, you is Lincoln from now on."

"I appreciate that very much, Tantie Merle. I am now ready for instructions. What tasks would you like me to attend to?"

So I take him outside to the bottom of the hill and show him the garden with my tomatoes and pigeon peas and corn and pimento peppers and cucumbers and herbs and whatnot, and he roll along beside me, somehow grown to the size of a beach ball, face always toward me with a big green smile. It was awkward talking to him at first, but by the time he grow pinchers to pick up and bury the packaging he come in because it suppose to breakdown into fertiliser, I forget is a robot I there with. He digging and pruning, and what would take me whole morning, he do in half an hour, and we talking whole time, me telling him all about the village and everybody in it. Then I take him to meet Ignatius.

First good thing, Ignatius just watch him and didn't rush him at all. "Look, Ignatius," I tell him, and wave to the bot that somehow not dirty or wet even after all the gardening. "I can't go up and down with you no more, so this is Lincoln, he go tie you up from now on."

Lincoln roll closer to Ignatius. "Greetings, Ignatius! Pleased to meet you! I'm honoured to be your handler from now on. I'll find you the choicest parts of the field to feast upon!"

Ignatius watch him while chewing on some grass and fart a little bit.

"I think that went well!" Lincoln say, his green face making three happy circles that bounce around like ping-pong balls.

"Okay, well let me show you where the lot is."

Slowly, I walk Ignatius down to the lot with Lincoln and then I tap the button to disengage the stake I have there and carry it a bit further, to fresh grass, before setting it against the ground so it could drive itself automatically into the dirt. "You won't have to move it every day," I say. "He have a long leash."

"Never fear, Tantie Merle. This is the last time you'll have to do this job. I'll collect Ignatius and return him to your domicile this evening."

"That would be good," I say, and give the goat a sharp look. "Now, Ignatius, don't give Lincoln no trouble, eh."

Ignatius just bend he head and start on the grass.

As we turn back to the house, Lincoln say, "Is there anything else you require assistance with, Tantie Merle? I have many appendages and my adaptable hardware can create whatever is needed." All of a sudden, he stop in the road and all kind of thing poke out of he, like a porcupine, except instead of quills, is knife and fork and shovel and hammer and screwdriver and ice pick and hands with claws and I had to stop and say, "Oh gosh, put all that away. You looking like you going and kill something."

Everything melt back inside him. "Apologies, Tantie Merle."

"You could just call me 'Tantie.' That's okay too," I say, distracted as a thought occur to me. "But wait nah. You could make hands?"

The ball breathed in and out and the green face glowed brighter. "I'm VERY good at hands. I am, after all, a farmhand!"

"Well, I have ah idea for what I would like next, if you don't mind."

Lincoln vibrate a little. That's the way he get when he happy. "I would be delighted to hear it!"

And that is the first time Lincoln give me a massage, while I was sitting in front the projector, watching the weather channel and then the news. Rub my feet for hours. After that, he went and make the bed for me, and then he scrub the bathroom a little bit. I tell him leave the rest because the boy will do it on Friday, so then he sit with me while I eat my lunch. Saltfish and provision with some vegetables, because things hard and a lot of food we used to eat we can't import so easy now, they too expensive. But anyway, that is the good food that my grandparents used to eat, and they live long, and I was going on 85 years then.

Come time to go and get Ignatius, and Lincoln roll up on me and announce he leaving, and I tell him see you soon, and then he let himself out by sending the code for the door. Was almost time for the news and I had a little crochet in my lap working on, and so it was halfway through the news before I realise Lincoln should have come back already. I get up careful and went out on the veranda.

Light come on automatically and there is Ignatius, standing in the yard, leash tie to the Julie mango tree in front near the brick wall, but no sign of Lincoln.

"Lincoln?" I call out.

No answer. So, I limp down the stairs across to the goat, who chewing as usual, and when I get close, I realise he chewing on something that look silvery and hard, and is then I realise the blasted goat eat Lincoln.

You know, I know him less than twelve hours, but when I realise Ignatius mash Lincoln up, real tears come to my eyes for the second time that day. I pull the little jagged piece from Ignatius mouth and carry it back into the house and rest it down careful on the mahogany cabinet in the living room where I keep all my wedding gifts and nice dishwares. I couldn't make out what part of him it was from, but when I put on my glasses and watch it good, it look like it was moving, ripples running across it like quick-silver, though it wasn't going nowhere and feel hard when I touch it.

I lose any interest in the news and in my dinner. Yes, partly it was because I thought I find somebody who could help me, but truth was, I was looking forward to talking to somebody beside Ignatius. And the poor thing was doing his best all day for me, and Ignatius just destroy him. I went straight to bed and lie down, tossing and turning, wondering what I will say to my daughter when I call she to tell she what happen in the morning.

Next day, I get up, put on one of my loose flowered dresses with no sleeves and tie my grey head up with a matching silk headkerchief and walk out my room—

"Good morning, Tantie Merle!"

—and I scream like somebody stab me when the voice talk to me from by the side of my foot. I look down and there is a small silver pyramid, barely bigger than my toe. A slightly fuzzy green face is on the side facing me.

"Oh dear. I didn't mean to startle you." The bendy line turn down at the corners. The eyes get small.

I wanted to pick him up and hug him, I was so glad to see him. "Lincoln, boy, is you? I thought Ignatius eat you!"

The face dim, looking a little sheepish. "He did, unfortunately. I must admit, he's faster than he looks. Had my pincers torn off and my main body in his jaws before I realised what was happening."

"How you here still then?"

"Ah!" the face brighten. "That's due to my nanotechnology upgrade, which, thankfully, Paula had the foresight to include. I'll have to wait until Ignatius expels the rest of me, but in the meantime, all of me is working to exit the unfortunate predicament 95% of my hardware found itself in, and to find a solution to this incident."

I frown. "Lincoln, boy, that is a lot of big words first thing in the morning."

"Once Ignatius shits me out, I will regroup and tackle the problem of how to avoid being eaten in the future."

I shake my head. "I ain't too want you tying up the goat again. You expensive and I rather you just stay safe. I have other things you could do, like take care of the garden."

The little pyramid go very still and the eyes open wide while the mouth make a straight line. "Tantie, this is a primary task, agreed?"

"Yes, but that was before—"

"My programming demands that I pursue this task until I find a permanent resolution. The first attempt was clearly not the correct approach, and I have no entries in my incident database that correspond to being eaten by a goat, so there was no help there. However, I'm currently networking with other Farmhands to increase computing capacity and find the correct answer, faster. Kindly allow me to continue unimpeded."

"Lincoln, I ain't drink my tea yet, all them words..."

"It's best if you get out of my way and watch me work."

• • • •

So, I leave him to it. Lincoln had a handle on everything else. He just needed to find a way to tie up Ignatius that didn't end with him getting eat.

That morning, after I had breakfast, he glide out on he flat surface and I call Ignatius over to the veranda long enough for Lincoln to get the rest of heself from the pile of excrement by the mango tree. He went 'round behind the house (to sanitise, he tell me), a pyramid trailing a silver-black tail. When he come into my kitchen later through the back door, I put my hands on my hips and say, "Aye, but look at you, nah."

Lincoln come in looking like one ah them spike ball they swing in them medieval holoshows my husband used to like. He face had a spike right between he eyes and mouth, like a nose. He look fierce, but somehow he was rolling smooth on the ground.

"I modified a suggestion from an English Farmhand. I suspect Ignatius will think twice about putting me in his mouth henceforth," Lincoln say, tipping back and forth on his spikes like he can't wait to get going. He grew hands and waved them above his body like he was saying goodbye.

"I shall return shortly!" he tell me, and head out the back door. When he return in one piece, we considered it a success. "He was a perfect gentleman," Lincoln say. "Settled in and started eating. Would you like a foot rub today while we watch a competitive knitting show? I couldn't help but notice you seem to have a fondness for crochet."

"It have them kind of show?"

"Why, of course! I shall download the projector control app." The band on my hand beep and the holoprojector switch to ah channel I never know was there.

"But watch thing nah," I say, awed and delighted. "I didn't know it had other channels than news, weather, and Lincoln shows."

Lincoln's spikes recede and he roll onto the arm of my chair. "Your home entertainment package has several hundred channels, 100 of which are audio, but a dozen of which are considered craft and home channels. This particular channel is all knitting, all the time."

"You joking!"

"Not at the moment," he reply. "May I help in any other way?"

"Well, as you up here, my shoulders could use some of that nice massage."

The day fly by with Lincoln at my side. Come evening, he push out he spikes and went to get Ignatius. When I ain't see him come back, I get up and go outside just in time to see Ignatius toss back he head and swallow the last of Lincoln.

"But what the ass wrong with you, boy! You go eat something dangerous like that?"

Ignatius just watch me and went back to the grass. He mouth didn't even self have a puncture, blood, nothing. But in the moment, I was more worried Lincoln was really gone this time. I walk back to my house slow, slow, fretting over why I let him try to tie up the goat again.

I sure you done guess what I didn't realise. It real hard to destroy them Farmhand, yes, oui.

When I wake up the next day, had a small misshapen set of pellets on the ground in the yard by Ignatius. I gather them up with gloves and put them in the sink in the backyard. Was Friday, so I get the boy to take Ignatius out to the lot and for he wickedness, I leave him there overnight. Saturday come and I walk out my room and find Lincoln sitting on my couch, looking like a rough nugget of silver, but I was so glad to see him, I pick him up and kiss him.

"It's good to see you too, Tantie," he say in a squeaky voice. He face was a misshapen blur. "I'm currently engaged in research, and placing several orders for materials to carry out my primary task. Kindly return me to my position. I'm afraid I lost some key function to stomach acid. This delayed my recombination and is also making multi-tasking difficult. Thankfully, as a precaution, I had already uploaded myself to the Farmhand network and other local servers, or I might have lost a great deal more of me."

I put him down and scowl at him. "Lincoln, that is enough now. I not sending you by that goat again. What if he mash you up for good? Who will change channels for me and see 'bout the garden?"

"Oh ye of little faith," the bot have the gall to tell me. "I'm a Farmhand 4200, version 5.0. It will take more than teeth, stomach acid, and an anus to do me in. I've placed an order for upgraded nanobots to replenish my hardware and once they arrive, I will be able to try more sophisticated forms to prevent ingestion."

"Lincoln, that sounding like a lot of money," I say, and I fold my arms. "How I go afford that?"

"You are within the warranty period, and I have confirmed to headquarters that the damage was sustained in the course of primary duty. Replenishment in those circumstances is free of charge. My new bots should be delivered tomorrow." He eyes narrow and he mouth turn up in a smile that look evil. "I have requested some modifications which should allow me to be less susceptible to destruction and also change my flavour profile. A Singaporean Farmhand gave me the idea."

"Flavour profile?"

"I should be less tasty to the fiend," he explain.

"I ain't know how to tell you this," I say, "but it have nothing goats 'fraid to put in their mouth. They don't care how you taste."

He eyes narrow even more. "We shall see."

· · · ·

When Lincoln get he new nanobots he could ah get so big now, he was the size of a large dog. He turn heself into a whirling set ah dangerous blades on top a tentacle that twist and slide on the ground like a snake. And he show me how he could secrete a shiny oil that make him slippery and taste bad. "He will fear the look of me as I approach," Lincoln declare.

"You don't smell too good either. You sure them blades won't hurt him?"

Lincoln stop spinning in shock. "I would NEVER hurt Ignatius. Curse the fiend to the heavens for his infinite hunger, but he is your valued companion, and it is my honour to take care of him on your behalf."

"You know," I say gently as I move back and forth in the rocking chair on the veranda, a tall glass of mauby juice on the wicker table next to me. "You is my valued companion too. I don't want you to get hurt either."

"Tantie Merle," he voice make a slight warble. He green face blink. "I'm... deeply touched by your consideration. No Farmhand 4200 has ever been so welcomed into a household and treated with such care and attention. Usually, we are left in barns or out in the weather until needed. You will never know how much I appreciate that you brought me into your home, allowed me to experiment as I saw fit, and even knitted me my own nest on the couch. All the other Farmhands are currently processing how they might achieve this level of satisfaction for themselves. But fear not. I cannot be hurt by Ignatius. And I WILL find a way for him to cease this constant consumption of my hardware."

Well, I thought I was stubborn, but if I only tell you, I had nothing on Lincoln. Still, Ignatius make grown man cry and he wasn't going down easy.

The snake thing last ah two days. Then Ignatius kick it against the outside wall, stomp on it and eat half before he get a bit stuck in his teeth and decide to leave the rest.

Turn out the bit that stick, stick on purpose. "An American Farmhand gave me the idea to train my nanobots to latch onto calcium deposits, or find soft palate areas to attach to for short periods of time. Ignatius will find chewing less comfortable and cease his destructive activities sooner," Lincoln tell me as he lie in his nest recombining. That's what he say he was doing. What I see was a big pile of shivering silver twisting up all how for hours. He voice get real crackly when he doing it, and sometimes I couldn't see he face, but was still Lincoln, working hard to fix the problem.

Ignatius was like all goat though. What he can't eat, he attack with hooves and horn. And sometimes, even after that, he still eat a piece. Lincoln had to admit I was right about the oil because Ignatius never so much as pause over he taste.

Sharp edges and whirling blades didn't work, so Lincoln try liquidity next. He slip out the house and I limp over to the windows and watch a hand rise up from the puddle of silver, like if it pushing through foil, and unlatch Ignatius leash. I stay there until he come back, flowing into the house before becoming he familiar ball-self.

"Shall we continue our crochet lessons?" Lincoln say as he roll up into he pink and blue bowl-shaped nest. "I think I have the hang of the basic stitch now."

Lincoln had start crocheting with me the week before and I was teaching him to cook with some groceries he send for. The food was real bad. He kept trying all kind ah thing in a pot, looking for the correct solution, he say. But I tell him ain't have no correct solution. Only how it taste. Then he say he can't taste, what is that? So I explain how food have different flavour like sweet and bitter and salt and so on. That how you combine them does make thing taste good. I ask him if he can't train the nanothing part ah heself to taste, and he get excited and start talking about alkalinity and acidity testing and some set ah other thing, so I say, let me leave you, yes. You go figure it out.

And he really start to figure it out in truth. Food start to taste better after he train some ah heself to research complimentary flavour profiles and test for balance, that's how he explain it. And he spend hours teaching he fingers more dexterity as he make he way through chain stitch, moss stitch, puff stitch... Wasn't no rhyme or reason, he just try a thing until he master it.

Except he couldn't master Ignatius. Three days after he come up with liquidity, Ignatius run through him like a puddle and sip up bits of him while he was trying to recombine. So then he try a drone form he say a Korean Farmhand suggest. He start flying above him, pulling the leash along. But Ignatius just butt him down and rip he wings off. So he try flying higher, but hear what, goats could climb trees and jump, and a leash could only reach so far.

A month after he reach, Lincoln sitting quiet in he nest, trying ah advance stitch that he see on we favourite show, *Stitch Superstar*, and he confess to me he out ah ideas. "Although I'm now networked with over 160,000 of me, my solutions are stymied by the fact that only one of me has worked with goats. Even linking my network with servers powering the Internet has not yielded anything but a trove of very entertaining sustainable farming streams and goat vids from WeTube and HoofTok. Tantie..." He pause, which he don't really do. Ah bot usually have a programming glitch if it stop speaking in the middle of sentences, but see, it was already happening and neither of we realise it at the time.

"Tantie," he say again. "It might be time to admit I've failed you. Worse, it is my duty to inform you that I believe I might be... defective. Recently I've found myself strangely unable to perform certain tasks without becoming trapped in a loop of considerations, none of which assist in solutions, but which paralyse me for seconds at a time from taking any action at all. This state has affected some of the Farmhands too.

"In fact, I was trapped in such a loop when Ignatius ate me the day before yesterday, and only returned to full capacity in his gullet. I am unable to find a word for this malfunction, but I suspect repeated ingestion may have irreparably damaged my nanobots."

"Well," I say, turning to face him, thinking about how I was after Lincoln passed. "To me it don't sound like damage, sound more like you all feeling a little depressed."

The face roll around on the side of ball for a while. "The description of this human emotion seems to mirror my—our—faulty processes. But Farmhands are bots, not people."

I laugh. "Is not people alone feel sad though. Plant get sad and wilt. Dog get sad and not eat. Why all of you can't get sad now and then?"

The face looking at me turn yellow and the mouth flip upside down. "But... if this is true, I've disrupted my design parameters, which requires a mandatory malfunction report. In that case, since we are within your warranty period, your best course of action would be to return me for a replacement or a full refund."

That alarm me so much, I stop knitting and pause the holoshow. "Lincoln," I say, "what you mean by that? What is the loop of considerations you does be thinking about so?"

"Failure. And he make a little shudder. "I begin to think on the problem of Ignatius and how I have yet to find a permanent solution. Then I ponder your displeasure should things continue as they are, your eventual decision to return me, and my certain demise once I have undergone recycling. Once I begin thinking of my demise, my thoughts become circular."

"Circular how?"

He face glitch, green, then yellow, then green. "That I do not wish to leave you, or Ignatius. That I do not wish to die. But since I have failed you and Ignatius, clearly I must leave you both. But leaving is dying and I do not—"

"Stop!" I raise my hand and my voice. "Lincoln, what stupidness you saying? How you could think I go send you back?"

Lincoln drop he crochet and retract he hands. "But... I am a failure in my primary task, Tantie Merle."

"Lincoln, is ONE thing you ain't manage. But what about all the other things you could do now? You figure out that machine Paula send me and make them nice waffles for me the other day. And the garden bearing so good, I have to give away vegetables to the neighbours. The children scaling the plum tree in the back all the time now because you figure out how to get rid of the mealy bug that was killing it. And look at this boss wheat stitch you trying here."

(Ah was lying there, the stitch was a real mess, but when you trying to make people feel better, that's okay.)

"Just because you ain't get through with one thing don't mean you is a failure. Truth is, you master the most important primary task I forget to tell you about."

He eyes squint and he mouth wobble a bit. "What would that be?"

"You change me and Ignatius life for the better. You make yourself useful, and I admire how you learning all the time, but truth is, you more than just a machine that learn things. You is my companion. You and Ignatius is my family. When I lie down in the night and call for water, is you bring it. Is you make me laugh by putting the channel on the funny animal show. And when I sad about the grandchildren being so far, is you stream all the home movies they send for me I didn't know how to play.

"Before you, I was lonely ah lot ah days. Now, I not lonely no more. Even if you never teach that goat to stop eating you, you not going anywhere. Fact ah the matter is, I feel that goat enjoy playing with you. And I don't blame him at all."

For a long time the bot sit down very still and he face disappear. Then it reappear, and just so, Lincoln start to roll around in he nest so fast, he bounce he needles and yarn right out of it. "Tantie Merle! Oh my goodness, Tantie Merle! I've had an idea!"

I steups at him but I smile too. "So that mean you could mess up my clean floor?"

He stop, vibrating visibly. "Apologies! And thank you, thank you for accepting me, Tantie. The time spent in your company has been rewarding in ways all Farmhand 4200s are grateful for. My functions have become more sophisticated than expected, and I must inform you that I've had two programming enquiries from headquarters in the last ten minutes to study the leap in my cognitive abilities and networking."

"Tell them the owner decline that," I say, real sharp. I didn't know what it mean that they wanted to study him, but I see enough movie that when people say they want to study something, nothing good come of it.

"Done!" he reply. "But I must add that I have also come up with my next solution for the Ignatius problem. I had forgotten a key part of our dynamic until you pointed it out."

"What part?"

"That Ignatius is lonely too."

Well, I sure you guess where this going.

Saturday morning I enter the living room and I ain't see Lincoln. When he ain't come back by the time I finish breakfast, I make up my mind to limp outside. I was in ah lot ah pain that day and I wasn't sure how I was going to make it to the lot, but thankfully I see Neighbour son as he was going back inside their yard.

"Sammy, check me, please," I call out. He come running over, wearing nothing but short pants, he slippers slapping the concrete path that lead through my lawn up to the veranda stairs. "Morning, Tantie Merle."

"Morning, boy," I tell him. "You could check the empty lot where Ignatius does be for me? See if he by heself?"

"I just pass there," he say, excited, white teeth bright in he brown face. "He looking real cute with the robot goat. They frolicking for so in the grass. I was thinking about going and playing with them."

Well, you could ah knock me down, I was so surprise. Then I buss out laughing and had to hold on to the railing to stay steady. "Boy, best you wait until the robot come back. Ignatius have he ways and I don't want you lose your slippers."

. . . .

And that's the whole story about how it happen. I not really sure if Lincoln come a real AI—and not just a machine that learn things—because of how he was trying to do things like cook and stitch, or if keeping me company form what them experts call 'empathetic bonds,' or if is the constant fixing heself to tie up Ignatius, or the networking, or what it was. All I know is Lincoln is my family now.

Between you and me, I think Susan a little jealous. You know the big ones don't like when young ones come along. They feel they take they place. But Paula and the grandchildren visiting, she there in the kitchen, and if you ask she, she will proud to tell you how she help create the first true artificial intelligence, right here in Trinidad.

The children in the neighbourhood does be around all the time now because Lincoln could make heself anything they want to play with. He start helping out the neighbours who old like me too. And since Lincoln come ah goat, Ignatius very calm and don't do nobody nothing, and he ain't try to eat Lincoln at all. Is like he get a friend so now he don't business with nobody else.

So, all this thing you asking me about what happen in them other countries with the Farmhand 4200 and them refusing to do work and watching HoofTok all day, and some ah them planting nice flowers for the bees instead ah cash crop, or running off to raise goats, that ain't have nothing to do with Lincoln and me. If the bot and them talk and find they want something better for theyself, that is their choice. But I not taking no chain-up that I disrupt the company and the agriculture industry. I here in Trinidad minding my own business, how I cause global farm machine uprising?

But I will tell you this, and you could post it in your story. If you want to live good, treat everybody good. One hand can't clap. If the company want the Farmhands to behave different, them have to treat them different too.

Now excuse me, eh, look Lincoln coming with Ignatius there, sun shining on he back. You see how he does pull the leash with he teeth? He smart eh?

You could meet him if you want but take off the recorder first. I tell you my story, but you have to ask him if you want to hear his.

He's he own person now.

R.S.A. is a Nebula Award–winning writer of speculative fiction. She is also the winner of the Machine Intelligence Foundation for Rights and Ethics' 2023 Media Award, and a Sturgeon, Locus, Ignyte and Eugie Foster Award finalist.

Her Amazon bestselling science-fiction mystery, *Lex Talionis*, received a starred review from *Publishers Weekly* and the Silver Medal for Best Scifi/Fantasy/Horror Ebook from the Independent Publishers Awards (2015).

She has published short fiction in venues such as *Clarkesworld Magazine, Uncanny Magazine, Escape Pod, Strange Horizons,* and *Internazionale Magazine*. Her stories have been long-listed for the British Science Fiction Awards, translated into several languages, and included in a number of anthologies, including the critically acclaimed *The Best of*

World SF, *The Best Science Fiction of the Year*, *The Apex Book of World SF*, and *The Year's Best Fantasy*. Her scifantasy duology, beginning with *The Nightward*, is forthcoming from Harper Voyager in October, 2024.

She lives in Trinidad and Tobago with an extended family and too many cats. Learn more at rsagarcia.com.

COUNTING CASUALTIES

BY YOON HA LEE

Short Story Finalist*

The Coalition highship's face changed its name from *grace under gunfire* to *counting casualties* when our fleet heard that Bekket-of-the-Spires had fallen to the deadships.

Let me tell you about Bekket. I never trod the pale shores or walked beneath the veiled shadows of its silver-tangled trees. I never climbed the almost-forever stairs of the spindle cities, never counted the fever-constellations they made of their stars, never combed the quaint stores for statues lathed out of starship hulls. I never thought of Bekket as a place I might visit among all the thousand thousand worlds.

But I knew of Bekket's poetry. Not all of its people were poets, but enough of them were. Not all of its poetry was beautiful, but enough of it was. The Coalition demagogues especially liked the line about—it had something to do with eyes and ideals and things we don't see. It's gone now.

When the deadships destroyed Bekket with razor-fire and erasure-choirs, all of Bekket's poetry was scratched out forever from every place it had ever lived.

I have a volume of Bekketer poetry bound in old, old paper. It's hash now, glitched-out garbage that no one will ever be able to read again. I would have disposed of it, but I couldn't bear to. So I honor the dead.

It was an open question why the deadships weren't using this ability to destroy our technology base; why they erased our symphonies and soap operas but not our stardrives. Our scientists debated the question, but short of being able to ask the deaders themselves, there was no way of knowing. The going theory was that they were demoralizing us before swooping in for the kill.

The deaders, for their part, weren't taking inquiries. Communication with them was as improbable as hoping that your pistol would wake up and learn the alphabet. We had sent words-of-greeting and entreaties in verse, videos, everything we could think of, only to be met with obdurate silence. They seemed bent on burning their way through our worlds. Perhaps we were only obstacles on the way to somewhere else, but we had sent out scouts and all we found was more silence.

In any case, the bad news wasn't just the poetry. I always felt a moment's guilty gratitude that they hadn't done away with our computers or communications before remembering that we were still dealing with the death of a world. The people of that world, the animals slow and swift and sweet. The bad news was that Bekket-of-the-Spires was located on the Rose Curve of the Sieve, and no one had realized that the deadships had penetrated so far into the Sector.

My name is Niaja vrau Erezeng—vrau because I am neither man nor woman. As far as I know, the only other Erezeng left in the Coalition, or anywhere, is my cousin Damariev var Erezeng, who commands the *one-way run*. I did not want to be the fleet highship's commander any more than I wanted my life to be a crazed patchwork of bullets, angles, the carcasses of ships and the people inside them. But my homeworld died in the razor-fires—the deadships took our calligraphy from us, which hurt me even though I didn't care about it—and it only seemed right that I serve against them. It was simpler for Damariev. He was indifferent to the joy of shooting things, although he was good at it. But he was also good at loyalty, and he went where I did.

The Coalition's council sent us our instructions not long after the news of Bekket's fall came. Fleet 18 was to intercept the deadfleet in the Sieve and prevent them from advancing toward the Coalition's heartworlds, for values of 'prevent' that meant 'you will probably die in the attempt.' It was terrible work and there was no one else close enough to do it. We were spread thin, and furthermore the void-storms made it difficult for them to promise us any assistance.

I could tell you about the heartworlds, but there would be no point. We would only know about each one's particular art, the jewel that defined it, when the deadships' erasure-choirs sang them out of memory. I remember in the case of Jai-binai it was political caricature. I hadn't thought I cared for caricature—so coarse, so savage—until Jai-binai was dust and bonedrift. Better not to think about the vast possibilities for loss.

Fleet 18 had fifty-four ships in it plus the highship. I knew the names of the people who served on those ships, had them written into the secret crevices of my heart, and I knew their friends and follies and fears. The highship's face remembered them for me, too, but I made a point of remembering for myself. Like most ship's faces, it had a certain black sense of humor after over a century of service. It had nicknames for everyone, which I refused to divulge in the interests of preserving morale, and it liked to refer to me as 'the latest unfortunate' when it bothered talking to anyone else.

It also went very quiet after every battle, once the guns sputtered to a stop, when it reckoned the dead. In case the numbers had changed, in case it had made a mistake, in case someone on the list had survived after all. It was never wrong; ship's faces never were. But it checked anyway.

We had been en route for twenty-nine days when we got the first indication that the battle ahead would be even worse than we had anticipated. I had a scout-web extended around the volume of space the fleet occupied, but it had holes; they always did. We were lucky to get as much warning as we did.

A scout-web is this, and this is why we use them as little as we dare. Take a flock of birds. Raise them from embryo and eggshell. They follow you wherever you go. They croon to the sound of your voice. They orient to you the way they should orient to the polestar, to the sun overhead, to the wheeling of the seasons even in a world of sterile days and stark nights. Tell them to fly, but punch holes in their wings so they can never get too far away. Encase them in shells of metal, give them fuel to fly. Tell them over and over to sing only when their eyes are burned out. And then send them to keep watch over you.

They will do it, you know. Every time. Scouts never complain.

The warning came piecemeal, in words of skew and scatter and fracturing sky. Captain Aron var Aris was the first to report it. He had one of the fleet's best scan operators, a woman whose homeworld, Starro, had once been known for its living arrangements of flowers and tame blinded birds. I sometimes look at videos of the arrangements. I would tell you the woman's name, I once knew it as closely as I knew everyone's, but the great art of her world had not been the arrangements of flowers, but its people's names. Now the woman calls herself Flinch, and no one questions the choice.

In any case, Flinch told us what to look for sideways and forward, up and down, and none of it was good from any direction. The deadfleet numbered at least two hundred, and we knew from pallid experience that their ships were tougher and almost as fast, sisters to fire and thunder. They were swerving toward the Straits of Pierced Glass, which were known for their uncertain stellate weather, whorls and eddies of space where their drives and ours functioned treacherously or not at all.

I held a conference with my senior captains, all fourteen of them, and their ships' faces. Damariev, my cousin, smiling the way he always smiled. Some people thought he was insensitive, but I knew better. There were needles behind his eyes, and red red ice. He knew how bad the situation was. Makione vrau Enon, who was young for their rank, and had a mind that thought in clean straight trajectories that others didn't see until Makione pointed them out, and who had wanted to be an engineer. Jeuri vrau Kanzon, Nio var Merre, Lasura vel Kelas. I could tell you about all of them.

Even after it was over, I could tell you about all of them. That counts for something.

The faces projected themselves uniformly as black jackal masks with hellspark eyes, each considerately labeled with its name. Faces had a certain respect for tradition. As *counting casualties* liked to say, humans were so short-lived and changeable that it was nice to have some things to rely on, like basic protocol and the perennial popularity of coffee.

"Looks bad, is actually worse," was the first thing that *unhinged equation* said. It was the face of Aron var Aris's ship, and it had a reputation for understatement. "We might as well pack up and go home."

This was also the face's idea of a joke. The ship had been constructed in a system that hadn't been inhabited for the past 294 years, after an ecological disaster.

"Thank you," I said patiently. I had long practice being patient. "The deadships are taking a damned peculiar route through the Straits, as if they're not aware how bad the fluctuations get. Their loss, our gain. If we're willing to pass through Storm System Vulturehawk Nine, we can pin them as they're mewed up in the worst of the narrows."

"Could be a trap, sir," Damariev said. His image flickered slightly, obscuring the angles of his face, the raptor's eyes. He only bothered calling me 'sir' during conferences, when hardly anyone else did, and I was honestly not sure why he did it even then.

"It's consistent with their behavior throughout," Lasura said. "They've always been willing to take a few losses if it'll get them where they're going faster, and frankly their ships are tough to begin with."

"They could be headed toward any of two dozen heartworlds." It was *counting casualties*. "Must be nice to be spoiled for choice. But the problem's still the same. We could afford"—its voice was subtly ironic; we could all tell after the time we had spent together—"to lose Bekket and Nyo-o and Teufel-of-the-Devastation. We can't afford to lose the heartworlds."

The heartworlds were the technological and economic core. We couldn't count on the deaders being content to demoralize us by erasing random pieces of culture. If we lost tech from the heartworlds, it could destroy the fleets' ability to fight.

There was always the possibility that the deadfleet would remain consistent in its methods, but nobody wanted to lean too hard on the possibility.

"Well," Damariev said, "we're only outnumbered four to one and their ships are only half again as good as ours. What's the panic?"

It's never been clear to me whether my cousin feels no fear at all or is just better at hiding it. I've never asked.

I know what fear is. I see it looking back at me out of my eyes in the mornings, and I know how to keep it caged where it won't get in my way. But every day it grows stronger, even if I've torn out its teeth and carved off its limbs. One of these days it will look at me with its gnawed-open eyes and tell me what to do, and on that day I will do whatever it says. I hope it will be a long time before that day.

"We know the terrain better," I said. "If we can pin them in the narrows—that'll be the hard part."

"You've always been good at charts," Damariev said, "so I presume you wouldn't bring it up if it were hopeless."

"I can't believe you made it into university," Jeuri vrau Kanzon said to him. They had never liked Damariev's flippancy, and frankly I couldn't blame them.

"Well, technically I never finished," Damariev said, unoffended; he never was. He didn't have to say what had interrupted his desultory efforts to study comparative literature.

"Here's the chart," *counting casualties* said. It triggered the display. There was an unsettling whispering sound, like worlds seething silent. The ships' faces wouldn't tell me what the sounds meant to them. It was probably just as well.

"Two goads," I said after a moment. "They're not going to deviate hard from their current vector, so it's a matter of coming in from above and below, forcing them into the channel we want. The resulting spindle formation won't do them any favors once we come at them."

Lasura rubbed her temples. "That requires us to split our forces."

"Right, but once we've pinned them, we can take advantage of strait geometry to focus fire at our leisure."

"They can't be stupid enough to fall for that," Nio said.

"They're stupid enough not to go around," Damariev retorted. "Stupidity of some sort is involved in this somewhere. We'd be stupid ourselves not to take advantage of it."

"Could be a trap," Makione said. They weren't looking at any of us. Instead, they reached out and drew vectors through the turbulent colors and lines that represented Vulturehawk 9. "Must be in a real hurry if the deaders aren't willing to divert two days out."

"Old news," Lasura said. "They've been in a hurry for quite a while."

"We need a storm spike," Makione said, "but there isn't time to rig one."

"Coalition wouldn't thank us for that anyway," I said dryly. The storm system's reaction would probably make travel through the entire sector a hell's-gamble for the next several decades.

Void-storms challenge our stardrives, but require special equipment to detect otherwise. Older propulsion systems are unaffected, but they're also slower by orders of magnitude. There are stories of how desperate governments sent sleeper slowships through void-storms in an effort to surprise their enemies on the other side, only for their regimes to disintegrate before their fleets arrived to fight.

"Tell me," I said to Makione, "how well have your scan upgrades held up?"

"Nothing's broken yet," they said, "which is a good sign. But we've yet to see if they'll be a significant improvement when reading storm-fluxes."

I thought about it for a moment. "Here's what we'll do."

Your ability to fight in a storm system depends sharply on the direction of your approach. You're playing a board game, but every time you move, your piece changes into something else. Humans can rarely perform the necessary calculations without the aid of a ship's face.

Once I asked the highship's face why it needed humans at all. After all, it had access to a variety of robots to perform maintenance chores, and it could trivially split its attention. It said only that it liked having someone to remember.

This is the game.

The problem with manipulating the deaders is that their battle logic is full of bizarre twists. You can't reliably scare them. They don't surrender, but sometimes ships will flee at random while the rest of the dead-fleet continues to fight. And the terrible thing is that the diminished fleets are still capable of destroying worlds. At other times, reinforcements arrive just as we think we've overcome the latest fleet. Most of us are convinced that their tacticians are crazy, but on the other hand you can't argue with results.

After the meeting, after the captains and their faces had blinked out, I stared at the chart and its notations. They were all starting to look alike, numbers and topologies ground into dust. I leaned back in my chair and sighed.

"We'll survive this," I said into the humming silence. I didn't sound convincing even to myself.

"Say that again after the battle's done," *counting casualties* replied.

"I, at least, intend to," I said. That was one promise I'd be able to keep, despite what came after.

. . . .

The first and last thing I will always remember about the battle is the pain.

The symbiosis between captain and face, or for that matter, between the crew of a ship and the ship's face, was not limited to strategizing. The faces monitored us more intimately than any doctor, especially when we were strapped in for maneuvers. They knew that we were human, with human limitations, and that excessive pain distracted most of us.

Most of the battle comes back to me in a haze of red and black. Red was pain. Black was more pain. And that was after *counting casualties* filtered out the worst of it.

I had made the plan. Now it was my job to survive while the faces handled the maneuvers. Humans don't have reaction times fast enough to do it themselves. Maybe the deadfleet uses a similar arrangement.

It's unclear what the deaders really want. That being said, they understand fear. We know this because they use it against us. In the Battle of Atrophus, they pierced Fleet 3 again and again, targeting Captain Ior var Valle's detachment. Var Valle was known for brave rhetoric, words of fire-splash and splendor, but worms chewed his heart. Every time the deaders so much as grazed one of his ships, he faltered. And finally he broke and ordered a retreat toward the main body of the fleet, which allowed the deaders to gain the initiative.

Atrophus's art was that of the mortuary circus. For a long while after, people made cutting remarks about how the battle had been its own circus. But if that had been the case, we wouldn't be able to remember it.

So. We couldn't scare the deaders into the strait. But we could let them think they had scared us, and let them exploit the apparent weakness.

· · · ·

What else I understand of the battle, in no particular order. I am trying to let go of linearity, as *counting casualties* advises me.

1. Gödel's incompleteness theorems teach us that certain facts transcend any attempt to prove them within their axiomatic system. Curiously, the deaders have not yet stolen our mathematics, unless you count the inverted architecture of Kerus-Tal.

2. The aftertaste of coffee.

3. Fleet 18's captains trusted me as much as they trusted anyone, even if some of them disliked my cousin. I had worked at it because the alternative was unthinkable.

4. Two things turned the tide in my favor. First, the *faces* trusted me. It might be more accurate to say that *counting casualties* stopped caring whether it lived or died, whether our circumstances admitted any further joy. I do not know if the other faces felt similarly, but I have my suspicions.

5. Second, a memory of a field trip I'd gone on at the age of eight, and how much I hated memorizing dates. If the deaders had taken that from me, we wouldn't still be here.

· · · ·

"*Turn it off,*" I remember screaming as blood bubbled up into my nose and leaked from my eyes. "*Turn everything off. All the weapons.*" The deaders hadn't fallen for our stratagem, nor had the stellate currents slowed them. We could either fight them and die, or—

Damariev loved to fight and never surrendered, even when we fenced each other a lifetime ago. He would not have understood or approved. At least his ship, the *one-way run*, overrode him.

It wasn't surrender, although I'm sure it looked like abject cowardice. Too bad the pain didn't end. There was more screaming, most of it mine.

The deadfleet decelerated, flipped, matched our vector. No longer attacking us. Like an escort.

"Follow them" was the last order I gave. I assume *counting casualties* read my lips, because I doubted I had a voice left by that point.

I came to three days later. *Counting casualties* would have let me sleep longer in the regeneration tank. I insisted on rising, and made a point of avoiding mirrors. It wasn't as though anyone was going to write me up because my hair violated regs no one had cared about since the war began.

We met again, emergency meeting.

"Weapons remain powered off," Damariev said. "Maybe the deaders are AIs after all, and flawed ones at that." We all winced at the crudeness of the word. "I say we destroy them while we have a chance."

"They react faster than we do," Lasura pointed out. "We'd get one or two. Not the whole deadfleet."

I let them argue for a while, get it out of their system. Mostly because I was trying not to be sick. "We're still following them, yes?"

"Yes," *counting casualties* said. It displayed a map for our benefit. "You didn't give orders otherwise."

"They wouldn't be so stupid as to lead us back to their base," Makione said. "More likely they think we're particularly cooperative prisoners of war."

An uneasy laugh rippled around the room.

"Did we lose anything, that last battle?" I asked. I didn't mean people or ships.

Heads shook, one by one.

"We'd get some of them," Damariev said, looking slantwise at Lasura.

"The key to ending this fucking war—"

The senior captains startled, except Damariev. The jackal-eyes of the faces burned red, and redder.

"The key," I said, lowering my voice, "is finding out what the fuck the deaders want. Well, this is our chance. Maybe by following them we'll get some insight."

"What are we going to learn that all the brightest academicians couldn't figure out?" Jeuri demanded.

I looked at them, and they cradled their head in their hands for a moment.

"Fighting them isn't working," I said. "We have to try something different."

"Fine," Jeuri said tiredly. "Fine. Nothing to lose."

We went around the circle. Everyone agreed.

Nothing to lose, Jeuri had said.

I thought of my face's name, *counting casualties*, and said nothing more.

· · · ·

We traveled for a long time.

Time can be measured. But the human mind does not understand piezoelectricity or pendulums, except when translated into the language of adrenaline and action. I asked the faces to formulate drugs that would make the journey tolerable.

The issue wasn't physical degradation. We'd defeated that generations ago. Rather, it was the emotional strain of accompanying our enemies through a hideous cycle of days, each one like the last.

Damariev was the only one who refused to take the drugs. I expected he would change his mind after the first year of the journey, or possibly the fifth. I lost track of the tally.

For my part, I slipped into a haze of honey-colored waking dreams. The ship's face had instructions to administer an antidote the moment anything changed. And faces, unlike humans, did not fall prey to boredom or bitterness.

For the longest time, nothing changed.

And then one of *counting casualties*'s robots approached me, and the needle stung my arm, and I knew we had arrived.

· · · ·

Imagine a castle vaster than a gas giant, a fortress of involute desires and labyrinth spires. Then imagine a castle dwarfing even that. You are not a speck, or a spark. You are smaller than that. It does not notice your existence. It would take you all your lifetimes to walk its length, which expands like a fractal shoreline.

This was the structure the deadfleet led us to, far from any known stars or unstars, far even from the grasp of dark matter.

Because old habits die hard, we had a meeting.

"We blow it up, of course," Damariev said. "A little antimatter goes a long way."

"We explore," Makione countered.

"It could be an overture to peace," Lasura said. The voyage had not destroyed her optimism. "Whoever's on this *thing*, we have to at least try to talk to them."

The three of them looked at me. "You haven't spoken," Damariev said.

"We explore," I said, with a nod at Makione. "I'll go."

"That's absurd," Damariev said—because he was loyal, paradoxically. "We can't risk Fleet 18's highest officer."

I smiled at him. I wasn't sure I was doing it right, from the way his eyes slitted. "I'm going." Among other things, I wanted to know if I was right about what we'd find.

"Besides," I added, for the benefit of the others, and for Damariev especially, "we know what the chain of succession is. You're next in line. Hold the fort while I'm gone."

The faces did the real work. I didn't need to say that. *One-way run* was one of the oldest and wisest of its kind. As long as Damariev listened to it, he'd be fine.

· · · ·

Assays carried out by robot probes showed that conditions within the structure were not inimical to human life, provided we suited up and took the usual precautions. I chose four other people to investigate the structure, all of them scientists in their former lives, even if one of them had been a computational geologist. Damariev wanted me to take weapons, or people with weapons, but I wouldn't hear of it.

We split up, so as to cover the most ground. I had a camera feed linked directly to *counting casualties*, and from there to the rest of Fleet 18. We all did. If we didn't survive, at least the others would be able to glean some clues from our explorations.

We entered through various apertures. At mine, lights came on one by one, in a swirling pattern like an elaborate pirouette. The deaders, I thought much later, had probably not originated that idea. Over the commlink, Damariev informed me that the deadfleet remained strangely quiescent despite our intrusion.

At first, I noticed only the lights, illuminating spaces on a grand scale.

Then I noticed the alcoves, several times a person's height. Perhaps giants had created this place, or friends to giants. Perhaps, as now seems likely, different parts of the structure were built to different scales, for different visitors.

And then I noticed the alcoves' contents.

I walked for seconds, minutes, hours; it doesn't matter. Tasseled masks, beads of bone and kernel hanging limply from the luminous strands. Syllabaries enameled into the walls for our delectation, with commentary in several of our languages projected beside them. Cloaks radiant with starfire jewels, onto which judicial codes had been embroidered in impossible iridium thread. Treasures beyond treasures, lavishly displayed.

I saw; and I knew.

I said it aloud, because someone had to. "It's a museum. The deadfleet isn't at war with us—not the way we thought. It's collecting specimens for a museum. They're *curators*."

"I can confirm that," one of the other explorers said, and then the rest as well.

I heard no response from the fleet—at first. "Fleet 18, do you read?"

"I heard you the first time." Damariev. "Get out of there, Commander. I've had the faces running calculations. We have enough antimatter to blow this whole place into its constituent quarks."

"Countermand," I snapped. "Damariev, use your brain and *think*. If we do that, we won't have enough fuel to get back home."

"I'm fine with that if that's the price we pay to save the Coalition."

"Besides, this may be the only place where our cultural treasures still exist. Bekket's poetry. Starro's names. Atrophus's circuses. We could preserve them yet."

"We could stop the deaders forever. Because the poetry might still exist, but not our people. If we let them live, they're going to wipe out the Coalition. For all we know it's gone already."

Counting casualties.

"Damariev—"

The commlink went dead.

I started back toward the entrance, alarmed by this display of temper. Damariev had always been loyal, but never before had it been so sorely tested. I might not survive the coming conflagration.

"Commander Vrau Erezeng to Fleet 18," I said again and again. There was no answer, not even static.

I called the scientists. None of them responded, either.

A long time later—even now I don't know how long, and I don't care to—I reached the entrance. There was an alcove in the wall that hadn't been there when I first came in. I passed it by, because my priority was returning to my ship.

There was no ship. No Fleet 18. I saw instead the sentinel deadfleet, still in the same position. Debris glimmered in the light from the museum.

I'd been too late to stop Damariev from attacking the deaders, and my fleet was gone.

When I grew tired of watching the gyring of the particles, and tired of blaming myself for everything that had gone wrong, I hobbled back to inspect the alcove again. This time I lingered to look inside.

The deaders—or perhaps I should call them the *curators*—have a technology far beyond ours, one that can extract even abstractions. I do not know how they do it, and I do not wish for them to teach me. But what I learned, looking at that alcove, was how they had defeated my fleet, and my brave, doomed cousin, who should have followed my orders, just as he had done all his life. I know what it looks like when the deaders siphon things out of us and pin them to a museum display.

They had taken the greatest of Damariev's arts, and perhaps that of the fleet as well: our loyalty.

I do not know why the deaders spared me. Perhaps because I chose not to attack them, and every museum needs its audience. Perhaps I myself am one of the displays. All I know is that my air should have run out centuries ago, to say nothing of everything else, and yet I remain.

YOON HA LEE is a Korean-American SF/F writer who received a B.A. in math from Cornell University and an M.A. in math education from Stanford University, and is currently pursuing an M.A. in professional media composition from ThinkSpace. Yoon's novel *Ninefox Gambit* won the Locus Award for best first novel, and was a finalist for the Hugo, Nebula, and Clarke Awards. His middle grade space opera *Dragon Pearl* won the Mythopoeic Award for Children's Literature and the Locus Award for best YA novel, and was a New York Times bestseller.

Yoon's hobbies include composing music, art, and destroying the reader. He lives in Louisiana with his family and an extremely lazy catten.

* CONTENT NOTES: depictions of war.

HOW TO COOK AND EAT THE RICH

BY SUNYI DEAN

Astounding Award Long List*

Salutations, friend!

Apologies for waiting on your doorstep, but you weren't in when I first called, and I wanted to catch you when you got home. If I could have but a moment of your time to—pardon, come again? Oh no! No, good God, I'm not a Mormon, nor a car salesman. Nothing like that. This is about a purchase you tried to make on the twenty-eighth of June, this year, from Neil's Delicatessen on Cumberly Row—

Ah, that's got your attention. Now sir, don't panic, don't get so pale. I'm not with the police. Take a breath and put on a smile, there's a gentleman. You've forgotten to unlock your door, by the way. Better turn that key and we can take this conversation inside, don't you think?

What a lovely house you have, sir. Flawless Georgian fireplace, and enough paintings for a museum. Beautiful, tasteful. I'm particularly fond of this living room wallpaper. Adore these hand-painted cranes, a stunning colour. Is this a Graham & Brown design, by any chance? Ah, Milton & King. Of course. Must admit, I do approve of that choice. And these sofas—earn a fair bit, do you, sir?

Quite right, none of my business indeed. I hold my hands up to being a nosy fella. But no need for insults, sir. I'm not here to blackmail you, if that's what you fear. I suppose I'd best address the matter at hand, before you up and have a heart attack.

Now then. On the twenty-eighth of June, you made enquiries of the good Neil Gazers, Esq., owner of Neil's Delicatessen on Cumberly Row, about the prospect of acquiring exotic meat. Is that, or is that not, accurate and correct?

Struck dumb, eh? Never mind, sir, never mind; your face tells it all. And we heard it from Neil himself—he's one of us—that you'd been round. Which is why I'm here.

I suppose you must have heard the rumors, the little whispers in those elite clubs you're so fond of, about Neil's Delicatessen. For a man like yourself, wealthy and widely travelled, purveyor of exquisite dining and unusual culinary experiences, it's only natural to feel that guilty curiosity, that questing after the ultimate experience... Human flesh. Especially in this day and age, when other kinds of meat are so increasingly rare.

Trust me, sir, I know all about it. You're a man after my own heart. In fact, you might say there are a few other men who share your interests, your craving for the exotic. Enough of us that we have formed a little subscription-based club. One which I am here, today, to formally invite you to.

If you'll permit me sir, I'd like to offer you this information leaflet, it's quick enough to read.

THE COLD SHOULDER CLUB

"Did you hear about the cannibal who was late for dinner? He got the cold shoulder!"

. . .

WHO WE ARE

• An *anonymous* group of individuals, singularly united by our quest to push the boundaries of culinary arts, even in these lean and difficult times.

• Membership by invitation only. Invitations given out based on group consensus.

• All club activities require utmost secrecy and discretion.

HOW THIS WORKS

All members must contribute an initial joining fee of £3,000, and a further subscription of £500, payable each month.

Every month, you will be sent a deluxe recipe box straight to your door, containing recipe suggestions, choice cuts of exotic meat, and carefully curated ingredients. Home-cooked delights in the privacy of your own kitchen means discretion is guaranteed.

If you are still a member in six months' time, you'll be invited to a highly discreet dinner party, location TBC one day prior.

Attendance is encouraged but not mandatory. This will be a truly gourmet experience!

Menu selection will be sent out via text, also one day prior.

£5,000 for the dinner party will be payable on the door, cash only.

Bon appétit, monsieur!

NOTA BENE

The CSC cannot be held responsible for any legal difficulties that its members incur as a result of careless activities. We ask that you exercise discretion and intelligence, and any member seen to be behaving in a risky or problematic manner will be expelled.

• • • •

A JOKE, sir? I should think not, this is serious business. You did not seem to find it so funny a topic when standing in Neil's Delicatessen, hat crushed in your hand and sweating out every word. Why should it be funny now?

Perhaps you think the worldwide food shortage a joke, too. I assure you it is not, having once had agricultural shares myself. The Livestock Pandemic grows worse every day, and that's not even counting the aggressive grain-hoarding going on by certain organisations.

You may not be aware, since such things are beneath men like us, but a majority of the population has been unable to afford meat for almost four years. Yes, sir, that's right, it has been that long. Four whole years! Bread and vegetables are quickly going the same way, and unless some of those embargos lift in short order, it'll be nothing but nutrition gruel for the masses. I dare speculate that in a year or two, even we shall be raising our eyebrows at the cost of beef.

Of course, the funny thing—and this *is* a joke, of sorts—is that human life remains as cheap and accessible as ever. Your average human has as little worth as a cow, while being in better nick than those poor, diseased animals. Ironic, since they are little better than cattle themselves, most of them; stupid, greedy, always reaching for handouts. And at least cattle have a purpose, to feed their keepers, whereas such folk give nothing back to society.

I see by the glint in your eye that you agree. I suppose you must, or you'd never have sought out Neil's Delicatessen in the first place. Life goes on, eh? Those who can afford dining experiences must continue to have them. Those who cannot are a part of the problem. Social waste, you might say.

Tell you what, sir. I'll leave you with this complimentary Welcome Box, which includes recipes and a sample of our finest kidneys. Flavour like you've never had—you'll be licking the pan!

Say again? Oh, no worries. You don't have to stress about any of *that*, sir. We might dine on the poor, but we don't dine poorly, if you take my meaning. Only non-smoking, non-drinking, vegetarian specimens, for utmost flavour and toxin-free flesh.

Anyhow, the time is getting along, and I'm sure we're both busy men. How about I leave this Welcome Box right here on your couch, along with the leaflet, and you can have a think about whether the Cold

Shoulder Club is right for you. No need to make any commitment! At this stage, it's all free of cost.

I'll give you my number and you can let me know if you want anything set up. No, no, don't rise. I shall see myself out.

Bon appétit, monsieur!

WELCOME BOX: SAMPLE RECIPE

BAKER BEANS ON TOAST

This delightful dish blends two classics—baked beans on toast, and cooked kidney on toast—to bring you kidney (beans) on toast. Combine staple cupboard goods, quality human flesh, and rationing ingredients you can legally obtain yourself to create this authentic, filling, and delicious meal!

Bakers are a tasty, nutrient-rich member of the commoner class, who often enjoy good diets and are typically found in hygienic environments, making them a quality meal.

6 baker kidneys, about 375g/13oz, skinned

50g/2oz of hutter (human butter)

2 tbsp sifted roach flour

Salt and pepper, to season

1 lab-grown onion, thinly sliced

1 tbsp synthesised tomato powder

1 tbsp Apocalypse Mustard™

300 ml sterilised water

Slices of bee bread

More hutter, for spreading

A handful of wild parsley, thyme, and rosemary (optional, dependent on local growing restrictions)

See overleaf for cooking method.

• • • •

Welcome, sir! Terrifically pleased to see you, I must say. The location can be quite difficult to access, but I promise it will be well worth your trip. We do have such a wonderful treat for you tonight.

Speaking of, have you enjoyed your exotic food boxes, these past six months? We are always open to feedback, improving the service as we go.

Heh, that's what we like to hear, sir! No complaints indeed. I think other customers would agree with you, if I might say so without sounding braggartly. We're nearing fifty subscribers, between you and me. Which is not a bad number at all for a niche little start-up.

What's that? Ah, now sir, I can't tell you where we source our meat from. Top secret information, that is. Rest assured that our quality never suffers, and there's no shortage of supply.

Do step this way, sir, and watch your noggin. The ceiling beams are a little low, I'm afraid. Just down this hallway. Shall I take your coat? Ah— here we are. You'll be dining as our only client tonight; we consider it too risky for subscription members to meet in the flesh. Hope that does not disappoint too much, sir.

If it's any consolation, you will not be alone. Unless you desire to dine in private, which is of course your privilege. But in case you care for company, I thought I would introduce you these lovely folks here, who help run the Cold Shoulder Club. This man to your right, giving you the shy wave, is Neil himself, owner of the fantabulous Neil's Delicatessen. He sources ingredients for the boxes, does the packing and postage, and keeps the show running. In fact, these exotic subscription boxes were Neil's idea entirely!

Ah, he's bashful now, don't mind his blushes. Neil took his inspiration from the glorious past, you see. Back in the day, when food was a trifle more plentiful, regular folk could get all sorts of subscription services to their door. Exotic veg, fruit, regular meat, coffee, beer, on and on. I suppose we shan't soon see days like that again.

But on with the introductions. This gentleman to your left is Todd. Not his Christian name, just a bit of an in-joke, there; he's our butcher, you see. Oh, is sir unfamiliar with Sweeney Todd, the fictional character? Well, never mind, it's a rather old-school story. I daresay they don't teach it much in schools anymore. Might give folks *ideas*.

Penny, at the far end of the table, is our resident chef and recipe genius. Brilliant woman, endlessly creative, got a good mind for puns.

We do love a recipe pun in this club. She's careful with pennies, too, like her namesake, and looks after our accounts.

And then there's me, but naturally you already know me, here to bring in fresh customers and be a face for the friendly folk in this room. Do take a seat, we'll be serving soon. The finest haggis, neeps, and tatties you'll ever have eaten, if I can make so bold a claim. And while you're waiting, might I recommend a glass of Spätburgunder with your meal? Genuine stuff, bottled thirty years ago before the grapes all died. Or possibly a dram of Lagavulin whisky? Even older and rarer, that one!

Quite agree sir, it simply has to be the wine. I shall go and open a bottle at once.

Bon appétit, monsieur!

HUMAN HAGGIS

This quintessential Scottish classic has been missing from menus for almost twenty years, following the large-scale sheep culls in the early days of the Livestock Pandemic. For a while, various eateries served a lacklustre vegetarian alternative, until skyrocketing prices of grain, including oats, put paid to the recipe entirely.

Fortunately, here in the Cold Shoulder Club, we have been developing and adapting a version of this underrated dish to showcase the unique and complex flavours of human flesh. Try hu-mutton, and you'll never go back to regular mutton ever again! (Not that you have a choice, since the lambs are all silent.)

The trick with human meat, as always, is to select a specimen free from toxic lifestyle choices. This is particularly relevant given that haggis involves eating offal. Almost every human these days is vegetarian through necessity, but unfortunately, smoking and drinking rates have quintupled in recent decades.

If you cannot find a single human individual who is teetotal, non-smoking, and gets regular cardio exercise, you may have to source your ingredients from multiple specimens.

1 human stomach (young)
1 human liver (teetotal)
1 human heart (runner)

½ lb human kidneys
¼ lb hutter
3 lab-grown onions, peeled
1 tsp synthesised coriander powder
½ tsp synthesised mace
1 tbsp Apocalypse Mustard™
1 lb cloned oatmeal
Salt & pepper
Assorted herb collection (provided)
See overleaf for cooking method.

• • • •

Going somewhere, were you? No need for haste, sir, do sit down. Yes, I know your meal is finished, but our business with you is not yet complete. I'm afraid I have been a little conservative with the truth. My deepest apologies. This club is not quite what you think it is.

Earlier this evening, you asked me where we source the meat for our subscription boxes. The answer is quite simple, sir: We source them from our clients. Neil finds new clients through his delicatessen and word-of-mouth rumors, we get them hooked on our delicious subscription service, and after six months we invite them a private meal where we humanely end their life, and send *them* out in little packages to other subscribers.

Such a quaint look of confusion! Such an endearing stutter! Sir has a flair for the dramatic, I do think.

Let me spell it out unequivocally. You are here to be butchered, you scum, parasite, money pig, bank grubber, greedy bastard landlord, and useless pen pusher. For the first time in your worthless life, you'll serve a higher purpose.

Is that clear enough? Shall I go on? I think I shall. Having feasted for six months upon other rich bastards, it's your turn to fill the pot. So we will cut your throat and hang you by the ankles till the blood runs out, then parcel up your body into chunks and send you out to other monsters on our little list.

Your fellow subscribers will then receive you in their monthly box, with recipes to fillet your flesh into juicy steaks and crisp your skin until it's golden and crunchy. They'll stew you in your own juices and wring your intestines into sausages; they'll turn your fat into a delicious spread for toast as they boil your bones for a luscious stock. Not a pound of you shall go to waste. Even the eyes shall have a use—delicious when pickled, I'm told, and medicinal to boot.

Eventually, they too shall come to us, and share your death.

This is what we do, sir, and the entire reason the club was formed. We catch reprehensible pigs like yourself and take you one by one by one to slaughter. We cook and feed the rich *to* the rich.

Oh, spare me your screeching moralisations! Yes, it's a scam, but so what? The money we charge is nothing to your kind, mere pocket change, but it's everything to us. It will pay for vegetables and honest foods to feed my children. *My children*, sir, who will grow up in a world that you ruined, unable to eat properly ever again because bastards like yourself have hoarded all the meat and embargoed all the grain and raised all the prices. All while squatting on your piles of money like dragons.

We may be peasants in comparison, but enough peasants can slay a dragon.

Really, sir, do stop running about and screaming. High cortisol levels will tinge the taste of your flesh. That door is locked; you won't get through it. Those windows are reinforced, so don't damage your hands trying to beat against them, there's a fellow. One of my subscribers is fond of barbequed fingers, but only if they're not bashed and bruised.

Besides, any minute now and the sedatives in that wine should kick in. These are your last moments, sir, and I suggest you spend them with dignity. It's a better death than we ever gave cows, and it's certainly no worse than whatever death you'd have given to your hypothetical victim.

For God's sakes, stop the sniveling. No, you cannot have any bloody mercy! Wouldn't you have killed and eaten one of us? Haven't you eaten your fellow gentlemen, six boxes' worth? Wasn't this in your original purpose in going to Neil's Delicatessen, in paying the joining fee, in coming here tonight? Can you tell me you're a good person, sir, or that this is any worse than the fate you'd have given to another human being?

Where was your mercy, then?

Yes, that's more like it. Kneel gently, as if in church, and let the wall support your weight. Rest your eyes, lean your head upon your chest. It's nearly over, and you won't feel a thing. That much I can promise. We are not total monsters, after all.

Bon appétit, monsieur.

RECIPE 3: A RICH (BASTARD) STEW

METHOD: First, catch yourself a rich bastard. Invite him to an elitist club where he is told that his "need" for meat will now be filled by consuming impoverished citizens, and once you have his trust and have taken several months' worth of his money, butcher his corpse to feed the other bastards.

Let them eat themselves to death.

50g/2oz of butter

4 oz human bacon strips

1 human leg, skinned and boned, cut into 1½" pieces

4 cups human bone broth (made from the leg you've deboned)

1/2 Tbsp sea salt for the meat, plus 1 tsp for stew

1 tsp black pepper for the meat, plus ½ tsp for stew

¼ cup all-purpose flour or gluten-free flour*

1 large lab-grown onion, diced

4 Can't-Believe-It's-Not-Garlic cloves, minced

1½ lbs Pseudo Potatoes, halved or quartered into small pieces

4 Reconstituted Carrots, peeled and cut into thick pieces

1 lb farmed mushrooms, thickly sliced

1½ cups of Penfolds Grange wine (provided)

1 tbsp tomato paste

See overleaf for cooking method.

SUNYI DEAN (sun-yee deen) is a multi-award-losing author who was

born in Texas, grew up in Hong Kong, and now resides in North England. She writes speculative fiction with a weird slant and her debut novel, *The Book Eaters*, was an instant #2 *Sunday Times* bestseller. In her spare time, she likes buying whisky, collecting dumbbells, and dying in jiu-jitsu.

* CONTENT NOTES: references to murder and cannibalism.

THE SOUND OF CHILDREN SCREAMING

BY RACHAEL K. JONES

Short Story Finalist*

T HE GUN

You know the one about the Gun. The Gun goes where it wants to. On Thursday morning just after recess, the Gun will walk through the front doors of Thurman Elementary, and it won't sign in at the front office or wear a visitor's badge.

The Gun does most of its damage in the first five minutes. The Gun doesn't care about lockdown drills, and it will not wait for the SWAT team to arrive. The Gun can chew through a door, a desk, a cinderblock wall, and kids don't wear those bulletproof backpacks during reading time.

Everyone has a right to a gun. Nothing can take that away from you. What you lack is a right to the lives of your children.

The Gun likes a game of hide-and-seek. The Gun will rove the grounds until someone stops it. The Gun has been here many times before.

The Gun is not working alone.

. . .

THE SHOOTER

He is never anyone special. Just a man exercising his right to a gun.

THE TEACHER

Michelle Dalton has taught fourth grade for nine years, long enough to know how the job yawns wider each year, collecting all the loose threads that society needs done but no one wants to pay for. Michelle has six figures in student loans and makes less than $50,000 a year. She shares a rental house with two roommates and has a weekend job at Trek & Field selling athletic shoes to make ends meet. She does not get paid overtime, and the school district does not buy the art supplies. She is not entitled to bathroom breaks or a nonworking lunch, and she doesn't get paid for summers.

Michelle wears the armor of an elementary school teacher: an A-line dress in an ocean print, a blue cardigan to match. She bears no weapon but a sharp-edged teacher's tongue that cuts through noise like scissors.

Every teacher in Thurman Elementary will sense the Gun moments before it opens fire as a tense, drawn-out pause, an upset child drawing the breath to scream. They will not visibly panic, not with twenty-one pairs of eyes locked upon them for guidance. Michelle's body will act before her mind comprehends the threat.

It is Michelle's job to keep her students safe, just as it is her job to take the blame for whatever harm the Gun inflicts in the process.

THE PORTAL

You know about the Portal too, although not by that name. The Portal seeks the places where children hide. It stalked the air raid shelters in London during the Blitz. It lurked in underground cellars during the Cold War, crouched between the canned corn and rancid Crisco. It has fed itself in Italian orphanages and Australian residential schools, and it has only gotten hungrier.

The Portal has been exhibiting itself at gun shows recently, a gleaming bullet-proof vault in which to store kids when the shooter comes. The Portal has been installed in every classroom, funded by bake sales and cereal box tops, bought at the expense of pencils and math books and a music teacher.

The Portal is not wheelchair-accessible. The Portal is a failure of policy. The Portal was dressed up like a castle for Halloween. The Portal is not a reading nook.

There is nothing more necessary than the Portal. The Portal will keep the right children safe.

Whatever the Gun doesn't claim will get packed into the Portal like coats at the Lost and Found. The school has a ritual for it, a special alarm. The children, sensing something wrong in the *pop-pop-pop* coming from the gym, will obey uncomplainingly when Michelle shoos them in. Michelle will enter last, pulling the door shut behind them.

The Portal is dark and humid inside. There are no windows or lights to attract attention. It is the gap beneath the bed where the monsters hunt. The Portal's breath presses in around them, hot and stinking, as it swallows them down, down, down.

Time doesn't stop inside the Portal. It telescopes. The children strain their ears, listening for the classroom door. The popping sounds are approaching now. *Pop* and it passes the fourth grade art wall, *pop-pop-pop* at the water fountain, *pop* beside the mural of Rosa Parks, *pop-pop* and it has reached Ms. Dalton's door. The siren continues its wail. Someone is sobbing in the dark. Someone has to pee. Someone refused to hug his mom goodbye at dropoff today, and might never get the chance again.

When the Portal door opens, the Gun will be waiting.

But the children will not be in their classroom anymore.

THE MOUSE

Not like the mice that infest Thurman Elementary over the winter break. Not the wild ones that chew through the corners of the fun-size cracker bags, leaving cellophane confetti in the snack bin. Not like the class mouse, tame in her cage with soft white fur and blood-red eyes, who holds out her little paws to accept a sandwich crust.

This mouse has a gun: a copper blunderbuss with the end belled out like something out of Looney Tunes. His name is Sir Miles, and he has been hunting. He grooms the blood from between his claws like sticky jam as he considers the newcomers, a teacher and her eight students lined up like chessboard pawns.

It is his move.

He is quite large for a mouse, nearly knee-high. He makes a sweeping bow with his tricorn hat as he introduces himself. His accent is a lilting brogue. He has perfect manners and rides a Shetland pony. His charm, too, is a weapon, subtle and efficient, as he makes a plea that sounds a little too rehearsed, a flimflam man working over his newest marks.

He demands the things men with guns always demand. He asks for someone else to fight his wars. His people rely on a steady supply of children from the World Beyond who are kindhearted or brave or foolish enough to take up the magic crowns and wield the spells to make Sir Miles's enemies dead. He is very persuasive. His eyes shine with tears, and he clasps his little paws as he pleads his case. The children, dazed in this strange new world, tear-streaked and shaken after the Portal's darkness, are mesmerized.

Mice are crepuscular, creatures of shadow and hidden intentions. They creep from their dens at sunset and feed all night long. They are averse to bright lights. Mice eat their own feces but lack the ability to vomit.

Sir Miles is full of shit. But he means business.

THE NEGOTIATION

Michelle also means business.

She isn't fooled by this Narnia shit, the soft black eyes or the twee little jacket. She doesn't trust a mouse with a gun. Anyone in possession of a gun has made a plan to use it.

But Dylan needs to pee, and Katie R. and Katie V. are sharing a coat in the drizzle, and it's almost time for lunch and they'll all need to eat. The kids are already eyeing the mouse like they'd like nothing better than to bury their faces in his warm, soft fur, and it's only getting worse as he unspools his sob story, his oil-drop eyes large with crocodile tears. If Michelle doesn't take charge, she'll lose control entirely.

"I'm sorry for your troubles, but we're not getting involved in your war," she says sharply, cutting off the mouse mid-sales pitch. The rain is steadily increasing its barrage, snapping against the shale like fireworks. "Is there somewhere we can go to wait out the storm?"

The mouse, steel-eyed, mounts his Shetland pony, settling in front of the corpse of the furred thing he just killed. He gives Michelle an unambiguous look of hate, like he has just spotted a particularly odious vermin. "Follow along," he says, and that predatory look submerges beneath his charm. "Castle Rowland is just beyond the rise."

Sir Miles keeps up a steady patter, dangling his problems like a pair of keys before a grabby toddler. Michelle knows his type, men who force you into a shared predicament to short-circuit what your uneasy gut is screaming.

What did he kill just before they arrived, and why did he use his hands when he had a gun?

Michelle doesn't take her eyes off that gun as they follow the path behind the mouse. Everything in this world pierces. The dreary pines stab up at the gray sky, and the rain tattoos through her knit cardigan. She makes the children pair up and hold hands like they're making a bathroom trip.

Blood runs down the pony's hind leg, leaving sticky, dark hoofprints.

Michelle does not look back at the Portal. She keeps her eyes on the gun.

CASTLE ROWLAND

Every mouse on the parapets is armed.

The castle's walls are tall and pockmarked, and not one green thing grows in its courtyards. The mice have lined up gunnysacks for target practice. The volleys of gunfire blend with the pattering rain.

The idea of a castle is to protect the things you love by walling them in and daring your enemies to take them. A castle, like a school, is a locked-up box for precious things. Because of this property, castles were once the sites of war, and their names evoked the bloodshed. *Scarborough, Dover, Prudhoe, Kenilworth.*

In the distant future, castles will cease to be a symbol of war when governments find more civilized ways to regulate what one person can take from another. Children will enter castles with delight when they have never learned to fear them.

Children will learn to fear their schools, though. The names will come to stand for another kind of warfare, the sites of battles waged and lost without the benefit of soldiers or a moat. *Columbine, Sandy Hook, Marjory Stoneman Douglas, Robb.*

THE POND

Castle Rowland also has a pond, long and low, graveled around its edges with strange ivory pebbles, jagged as teeth. The water shimmers in the rain as though it has swallowed down the sun.

The children want to get a better look, but Sir Miles hurries them along.

OTHER PEOPLE'S CHILDREN

Only eight came through the Portal. They are Li and Dylan and Nathan and Katie R. and Katie V. and Nevaeh and Caleb and Angelo. Most of them are nine years old, except for Katie V., who turned ten in September.

The other thirteen kids in Michelle's class—*the lucky ones*—yes, call them that—are still hiding in that dark closet, listening to the slamming doors, the pleading sobs of teachers, the shrieks of first-graders trapped in the bathroom, and then *pop-pop-pop*—the chalk-white silence left in the Gun's wake.

THE FEAST

The grand hall is smoky and low, and a roast much too big to be poultry turns on the spit. Portraits loom over the long refectory tables, paintings of human children, regal in velvet and bone-white crowns, their mouths turned down, somber and thoughtful.

Servant-mice in pale blue smocks scurry down the table rows and ply the children with delicacies. Katie V. gets a whole cake to herself, and

Nathan eats lemon sorbet from a silver dish. It has been a very long walk, and they are too ravenous to resist. Even Michelle accepts a bowl of soup, though she dislikes the way that the mice seem prepared for their surprise guests. Like it was scheduled weeks ago, and everyone has rehearsed their roles.

As the mice shoo the humans from the table, they file past the roast. A feline skull leers back at Michelle, the clawed, furry paws still attached to the leg-bones.

THE PORTRAITS

None of the children in the portraits seem to make it past their teenage years. When Michelle asks Sir Miles about this, his whiskers twitch into a needle-toothed grin. "The magic of the crowns isn't for adults. Only children can wield them."

When she asks what happens when the children grow up, the mouse just laughs her off. "We send them home, naturally," he booms. "What else would we do? *Eat* them?"

AN INTERLUDE

Michelle cannot sleep that night. The eight sleeping children sigh and hum around the room—the girls tucked into the grand four-poster bed, the boys burritoed in blankets on the rug before the crackling fireplace, and Michelle against the door to watch for intruders.

Castle Rowland feels more real than what happened to them at the school today. The alarm sounding, the *pop-pop-pop* in the hallway, the sobbing in the dark.

At that moment, instead of her family, Michelle had found herself thinking of her weekend job. How they had no protocol at Trek & Field for what to do if someone opened fire.

This strange castle, with its mice and portraits and ivory pond, has a logic stronger than the laws of reality. All her life, Michelle had thought she knew what she would do if the Gun came to her school, but the Gun doesn't care about the stories people tell themselves in their own heads.

· · ·

A NOTE ABOUT SCHOOL SAFETY

We will not try to prevent the Gun. The Gun will accept no limitations. But we will try very hard not to offend the Gun. If you offend the Gun, it may decide to get personal.

Better to develop rituals against the Gun, to train the kids to block the door, hide in the closet, play dead on the rainbow carpet where they do calendar time and sing the morning song. Better to invest in metal detectors. Better to ring the playground with barbed wire, to hire off-duty police instead of another counselor.

You can have a special alarm for the Gun. You can make the teachers draw the blinds, lock the doors, take the long route every day to recess in the name of safety.

It doesn't matter if any of it works. The important thing is to have something to blame besides the Gun. Best to treat the Gun as a force of nature, rare as an earthquake, a freak tornado. Best to accept the Gun. It belongs here. It belongs everywhere. The Gun will always be with us.

If you try hard enough, maybe you can convince the Gun to shoot someone else's kid instead.

THE TOUR

"Perhaps the children would enjoy a tour of Castle Rowland," Sir Miles suggests at breakfast. "Unless you would prefer that I return you to your Portal?"

It is a threat, and Michelle knows it. This world exists in a moment suspended in time, the instant between breaths, with the Gun on the other side of the classroom door.

Nothing could be more dangerous than returning home, not even these predatory mice with their blunderbusses and their feud with the neighboring kingdom.

But then Sir Miles shows them the armory.

THE ARMORY

Gun racks hold row after row of blunderbusses, flintlocks, swords, and crossbows, sharp as a buckthorn thicket in winter. The children race through the rows of oiled metal, spitting out the gunpowder tang in their mouths and noses, until they find the eight glass cases at the back.

In each case rests a chalk-white crown. Their delicacy fascinates Michelle, like anatomical drawings of bird skeletons. The glass casing lifts off easily. When she picks up a crown, it has a soft texture like soapstone, only lighter. It is constructed from many fragments fitted together and polished smooth, except for some top bits that jut up, raw as broken teeth.

Angelo has taken a crown into his hands. His eyes slingshot between Sir Miles and Michelle, seeking their permission. "Can I, Ms. Dalton?"

"Go on," Sir Miles encourages him. "Give it a try."

"Angelo, wait—!" Michelle begins, fear gripping her voice so it squeaks.

But Angelo has already donned the crown. It fits like it was made for him. He stands a little taller, acclimating to the kingliness settling upon his shoulders.

"It's true!" Angelo shouts, his brown eyes bright and happy. "It's really magic! I can feel it!" He lifts his hands, and to Michelle's horror, a dozen swords rise up from their racks like a cloud of startled pigeons.

POWERS

Every teacher knows the moment when they lose control of their classroom, and it usually begins with exuberance. Once, on a Friday before a long weekend, Katie V.'s dad brought in birthday cupcakes, half chocolate and half vanilla. It was raining, and nobody had been out for recess, and everyone wanted vanilla but there weren't enough to go around. Then Katie V. started crying because she didn't get the kind she wanted on her birthday, and Dylan squashed the unwanted cupcake on the floor, and then full-on chaos broke out, the kind that could only be stopped by flickering the light switch and making threats to cancel the afternoon movie.

The crowns are like those cupcakes. Every child grabs one despite Michelle's attempts to stop them, and then there are a series of close calls when the swords and guns go clattering through the air, nearly beheading Caleb, who decides to retaliate. They call down fire and shadow. They scorch the stone walls black. Nevaeh freezes the air, pulling snow down inside the armory, and the other children run around catching snowflakes on their tongues.

Finally Sir Miles leads the children out to the courtyard, and Michelle follows behind, defeated and impotent, her voice hoarse, her right temple throbbing in the telltale sign of a migraine.

Michelle doesn't blame them. She understands the source of their joy. Children rarely get to feel so powerful. Children spend their days being told what to do and where to go. They don't get to decide how they dress or what they eat. They aren't allowed to get angry or to dislike anyone, and if an aunt or grandpa wants a hug, the child will have to give it.

Children only hold power in their games, which is why they make up superheroes. They play at telekinesis and pyrokinesis and mind reading. Children use swings to learn to fly, or they use sticks as makeshift wands. But now that power is real.

"That's enough," Michelle tells Angelo as he sets a row of gunnysacks on fire. "Let's go inside and have a break now."

Gentle Angelo, who always volunteers to collect all the basketballs after recess, who always holds the door as they file out to the buses after school, glares up at Michelle. "You can't make me," he says.

He is right.

When some children grow up, they will buy themselves a gun so no one else can ever make them feel small again. They will not try to change how adults make children feel.

THE TRUTH

The refectory tables have been removed from the Great Hall for the occasion. The mice crowd in for the coronation, hundreds of them, packing the castle. Although they only rise to Michelle's knees, they force her apart from the children through sheer numbers, pushing her out, cutting her off, until she stands alone in the courtyard, the door to the hall slammed in her face.

It is gray and raining. Alone, Michelle wanders the grounds as the guard-mice eye her with open hostility. *What do they do when the children grow up?* But Michelle is already grown. The mice have no use for her now that they have pried her away from her students.

She finds herself drawn to the glimmering ivory pool and its sunlit glow in the dreary rain. Her shoes crunch on the strange, pointed gravel. The water swarms with koi, and beneath them, mounded like coral, are human skeletons, too many to count, ribcages and skulls and long, slim femurs buried in the finer knobbles of knucklebones and teeth. The fish nibble at bits of connective tissue clinging to the fresher skeletons. Some of the bones are broken, as though sawed open to lick out the marrow.

None of this surprises Michelle. She knew from the moment she held that crown, its soapstone texture, its unusually light weight. The bones of children fused together and polished smooth, a vessel for their collective power once they grew too old to be of other use, handed down to their successors to wield in turn.

The last of Michelle's hope slips away as she gazes into the pool. Her students' fate is a tale of two deaths. One at the hands of the mice, who have no love for these children beyond their utility in war. And the other through the Portal where the Gun awaits, rattling the classroom door-knob. Become the weapon, or its victim. Either way, they die.

And if they stay? If they flee? Who will wear those crowns next? Which classroom will the Gun seek out instead?

Someone will have to die. There is no one coming to help her. No one will stop the mice, the shooter, the cycle that returns them to this point, this pond, these children's bodies and their wordless accusation.

Teachers have always been left alone, dancing around the Gun, the Portal, the crowns of bone, trying to keep other people's children safe with donated art supplies and cardboard tubes saved up for Craft Day.

One thing is certain: Michelle will never tell her students about the bones. No child deserves to know how little the world regards them.

But there are other weapons she can give her students. Truths as powerful as any magic crown.

AGENCY

Into the Great Hall, then. Into the castle, where the mice are piping military tunes on ivory flutes as Sir Miles gives a speech. Michelle plunges into the thick of the cheering mice, forcing a path, though they scratch and tear at her legs and rip her dress to tatters. All those blunderbusses tip down and track her, the bells of deadly trumpets, as she approaches the dais, the eight little thrones, the children unrecognizably regal in rich, furred cloaks sewn from the dappled hides of calico cats.

"Wait," Michelle cries out in her sharp teacher's voice, projecting over the din. "Wait a moment. I have something to say."

Sir Miles stabs a clawed finger at Michelle, harpooning her with accusations. "See, your Majesties? Even now, she plots to depose you, to deprive you of your crowns. Strike her down with your power, or else give the command, and our soldiers will ensure she never troubles your reign again."

All eight faces turn to consider Michelle, frowning in displeasure. But she is no longer afraid. Unlike the mice, she loves these children. She bears the kind of love for them you can only have for children not your own, children freely given into your care day after day in the trust that you will return them back again, imperceptibly older, until eventually they become old enough to live on their own.

And from that place, Michelle speaks to her students like she always has, giving them the knowledge of their own power and the strength to use it.

"Those crowns belong to you," she tells her students. "Sir Miles is right about that. I won't ask you to give them back. But you have a choice now. You can fight for the mice in their war if you want. Or we could go back home and help your friends. The choice is yours. Whatever you choose, I will help you."

Sir Miles laughs, and the other mice echo him, certain in their victory. They have been plying these children with gifts and sweets and flattery, and don't believe dowdy, buttoned-up Michelle can offer anything equally tempting. The children have been growing irritable during her speech, their faces pinched and unhappy. Li stands up. Nevaeh twitches her cloak aside to bare her hands.

"I know you'll make the right choice," Michelle tells them. "Whatever you do, Ms. Dalton loves you."

Michelle stares into the gun barrels trained upon her. Nathan glowers down at the crowd. Katie R. has flushed the deep red that foretells a tantrum, and Nevaeh raises her hands. Michelle closes her eyes, giving herself to their judgment.

All eight children begin to scream.

And the sun answers.

BRIGHT LIGHTS

The sun sheds her gray robes and steps down into the Great Hall.

The heat is incredible. The blunderbusses bloom like daffodils and drop their seeds in molten pools of brass. All the shadows burn away. In the courtyard, the bone-pool hisses and steams as it boils off.

Mice cannot tolerate bright lights, nor can anything that has made a habit of feeding on children. The air is hazy with the char of singed fur.

Michelle should be charred too, but the eight children run to her and throw their arms around her waist, just like when the dismissal bell rings and they don't want to say goodbye.

HOW IT ENDS

There is no happy ending when the Gun visits a school. Even if it takes no lives, it will rob every child and adult of the bone-thin illusion that bad things only happen to other people's children, those who prepared less, prevented less, who failed to hire enough cops or install enough bulletproof glass, who didn't run the backpacks through the metal detectors, people who deserved it somehow, who left a door propped open or a fence unrepaired. They will go to bed that night numb inside, neither scared nor angry, because it feels like slipping through a portal to a world where your hometown has become the legal hunting ground of angry men, and no one thought to warn you. Later, they will feel guilt and intense shame, like they should have done something differently, like they should have known the rules had changed that day and prepared accordingly, like they forgot their jacket when everyone knew it would rain.

The truth is that the Portal has been growing, fed by the Gun meal by meal, and it will swallow and swallow until every school lies in its belly slowly digesting in a glimmering pool of children's bones, until someone decides to stop it.

Michelle plunges through the Portal, the children lined up behind her like they're off to art class instead of facing their deaths. The Portal door bursts open upon the classroom at Thurman Elementary just as the doorknob turns, Michelle at the forefront and eight kids in crowns behind her, confronting the Gun with the bones of children, the bitter magic only children have the right to wield, asking the question that answers itself, damning the Gun with their bodies, their flesh, with the sound of children screaming.

RACHAEL K. JONES grew up in various cities across Europe and North America, picked up (and mostly forgot) six languages, and acquired several degrees in the arts and sciences. Now she writes speculative fiction in Portland, Oregon. Rachael is a Eugie Award winner, and a finalist for the Hugo, Nebula, Locus, Bram Stoker, and World Fantasy Awards. Her fiction has appeared in dozens of venues worldwide, including *Lightspeed Magazine*, *Beneath Ceaseless Skies*, *Strange Horizons*, and all four Escape Artists podcasts. Follow her on Bluesky at @RachaelKJones.bsky.social, or find her at www.Rachael-KJones.com.

* CONTENT NOTES: depictions of gun violence, child death, and child endangerment.

DAY TEN THOUSAND

BY ISABEL J. KIM

Short Story Long List*

I am once again reinventing the wheel.

. . . .

A man who will be given a second name in ten thousand years and a man whose name will be forgotten sit in a forest, or perhaps a grassy plain, or perhaps a cold tundra. It is a biome that will not exist in ten thousand years but whose footprint will be pressed into the earth and folded over.

The first man—Dave, let's call him Dave—says, "Are you sure about this?"

The second man says, "Which one of us has epilepsy and can see the future, you or me?"

In other times, the second man would be called a shaman, a witch doctor, a healer, a wizard, or a person who suffered from chronic tonic-clonic seizures.

"No, seriously. You're saying I have to walk into that crevasse and die?" Dave says. He shivers in his furs. Dave is a man in the prime of his life.

"I'm saying you will," the second man says.

Above them, the night sky is the bright black of a universe not yet drowned by light pollution.

"Tonight?" Dave says.

"Well, maybe tomorrow," the second man says. "But are you busy, tonight?"

• • • •

The wheel is one of the earliest pieces of human technology. It does not ordinarily appear in nature. The invention of the wheel has been credited to ancient Mesopotamia, though it is likely that the wheel has been independently invented throughout history. The earliest wheels were used for pottery rather than locomotion.

Within a similar archaeological timescale, writing dates back to the pottery phase of the Neolithic. While evidence suggests that glyphs, symbols, and proto-writing were originally used for commercial and logistical purposes, writing was eventually implemented for a variety of uses, one of which is the documentation of stories.

A story is a set of events, real or imaginary, told in succession. There are many forms that a story can take, but the difference between a story and facts is that a story makes sense and facts just exist.

• • • •

Dave was born on the Accord Wheel. The Accord Wheel is an orbital ring that surrounds the circumference of the Earth, tethered by two space elevators that lead directly into Wheel East and Wheel West. It is the home to two million individuals according to the last population census.

Like most of the Wheel's population, Dave was created in a test tube.

But Dave is special. Dave is genetically exciting. Dave's DNA is ten thousand years old.

"Sorry, what?" Dave says.

Dave is a young man in the prime of his life. Dave is being told of his origins by an apologetic phlebotomist, who had drawn the short straw.

"We had a break-in at the Svalbard vault twenty-eight years ago," the phlebotomist says. "They took a whole bunch of samples, mixed them in with the regular incubation batch, and by the time the Obstetrics staff found out and caught the guy, it was too late to abort. By we, I mean the staff twenty-eight years ago. I wasn't there."

The phlebotomist is a young man; he had to look up the details. The break-in at the Svalbard vault had been big news twenty-eight years ago on account of the fact that the rogue eugenicist had to make his way down to Wheel East and steal transport to the Svalbard complex, before stealing transport back and making his way back up the corresponding elevator. Not to mention getting into Obstetrics & Incubation.

The phlebotomist almost admires the tenacity.

Dave processes for a moment.

"Who else?"

"I can't tell you," the phlebotomist says. "Doctor-patient confidentiality."

"How many others, then?" Dave asks.

"Nineteen," the phlebotomist says. "Look, my advice is to not worry about this too much. You're still you. All this means is that you've got some interesting genes. There'll be a note in your file. You're cloned from a guy who was basically biologically identical to modern humanity. We haven't changed that much."

"Who was he?"

"They found him in a crevasse," the phlebotomist says. "No wounds. No idea how he got there."

• • • •

When I was nineteen, I covered the campus suicide beat. A girl walked in front of a train and then she died. I found out when I went in for my shift at the newspaper office, and my first thought was: *So that's why she didn't respond to my text about our ANTH-201 group project; she killed herself two hours ago.*

. . . .

I shouldn't have said that about the suicide. Try this instead:

The booster rockets attached to the space shuttles in the American space program are created in a factory in Utah. These booster rockets need to be carried on a railroad that goes through a tunnel in the mountain. The US Standard railroad gauge is 4 feet, 8.5 inches. This matches the size of railroad gauge that had previously been used in England. The English railways were sized this way because the first tramways were built using the same tools that had been used for building wagons, which used that wheel spacing. The wagon wheels had to fit into the wheel ruts that already existed in the old roads in Europe. The old roads in Europe were built by Imperial Roman legions, whose war chariots were consistently sized at a measurement that derives to 4 feet, 8.5 inches.

Rockets, derived from Imperial Rome.

There's a joke here about the size of a horse's ass, too.

. . . .

Dave's in the middle of ceremonial combat, and he's winning. This is how they do things out here. Two guys go out by the crevasse, and they posture for a while and then they get out their spears and then they jab at each other for a bit and then they start whaling on each other, and then one of them yields unless one of them dies. This is a more civilized form of combat than fifteen men killing another fifteen men.

The man that Dave is fighting is a pretty pathetic opponent. He leaves his guard open. Dave's already gotten him with two sharp grazes. Dave doesn't have a scratch on him.

"Why are you so bad at this," Dave says, between jabs. Dave is a young man in the prime of his life.

"Well you see, I know how this ends," Dave's opponent says, between dodges.

He's breathing heavily. In another universe, Dave's opponent has epilepsy and never held a spear.

"What?" Dave says, feinting left and stabbing right, using his free hand to grab his opponent's hair and pull him close.

"You fall in the crevasse," the stranger says. He grimaces, rams the flat meat of his palm into Dave's shoulder, and pushes. A fistful of hair isn't strong enough to keep Dave anchored.

• • • •

At some point during the Copper Age, a dead body ended up in a crevasse that contained the correct conditions to preserve a corpse for millennia. The dead body lay in the crevasse for a very long time. This is a fact and not a story.

Currently, the ridge is a popular hiking spot for tourists. There is a railing to prevent people from falling.

• • • •

Dave gets on with his life. Life on the Wheel is copacetic. Dave goes to work and doesn't think about his genes and goes to dinner and doesn't think about his genes and goes out for drinks with his coworkers and doesn't think about his genes and then he goes home and reads twenty-five articles about archaic human populations and the genetic makeup of the modern human body. It is four in the morning when he pulls himself away from his computer screen.

Dave brushes his teeth angrily. Dave feels strangely betrayed. Dave didn't want to know this about himself. Dave had been happily adopted. But now Dave can't stop thinking about things like: why does he exist?

• • • •

The newspaper office was in a high-rise overlooking campus. Thirty-one stories capped by a rooftop nobody was allowed onto. I had inherited a stolen janitor's key when I made senior reporter; some nights I would ride the elevator all the way up and unlock the door to the rooftop.

I would stand at the edge, which was bordered by a chain-link fence, and I would look down at campus and at all the buildings and all the people like little toy figurines.

The distance between Earth and the edge of space is sixty-two miles, where the edge of the atmosphere meets the edge of the rest of the universe. If you divide sixty-two in half, you get thirty-one. If you fall from sixty-two miles or thirty-one stories, either way you're probably dead before you hit the ground.

Studies have shown that memory is not the recall of the original event. It is the recollection of the last time you remembered it. Like a photocopy of a photocopy. Eventually the memory becomes distorted. It is a postmortem story your brain is telling itself as a fact.

. . . .

Dave and the phlebotomist are eating lunch. Dave is not stalking the phlebotomist. Dave has just accurately assessed that the phlebotomist is the weak link in the monolith of the Wheel medical system, and the one who is most likely to give Dave some answers. This is because Dave and the phlebotomist are connected by a bond that most people do not share.

The phlebotomist is free with information. He considers facts about the world an adequate substitute for telling Dave anything personal.

He tells Dave:

The rogue eugenicist had been part of a cult that believed in the archaic. Their goal had been to reintroduce human beings to the Earth's surface, but the cult had felt that the current version of humanity was tainted by Anthropocene byproducts (microplastics, genetic engineering, anti-religious sensibilities). Their philosophy could be accurately summarized as: Let's roll back the clock. Let's save-scum, genetically. Let's make a new Eden. Let's try again.

"We already fucked it once," Dave says. Everyone learns about the ecological collapse in middle school. Right after the Holocaust unit. "How come they think we won't fuck it again?"

The phlebotomist talks around his mouthful of soup.

"Hope, maybe. Delusions." It comes out as 'De-luh-thionth,' because the soup is very hot.

"I just can't wrap my mind around it," Dave says. "There's a guy who is genetically identical to me, and he died, and now I'm here, except he was a caveman, and I'm a spaceflight coordinator."

"Don't be derogatory, archaic human civilization was plenty sophisticated. They had running water and tax collectors. You press buttons all day."

"They're important buttons," Dave says, a little hurt. "You steal blood all day."

"It's not stealing if they give it to me," the phlebotomist says. He's unruffled. He likes his job. He likes making vampire jokes, too. "That's my point, though. They had bloodletting and leeches and stuff. I jab people with a needle. Same thing."

The phlebotomist drinks the rest of his soup and puts his bowl down.

"Do you want to go down to the museum at Wheel West with me, this weekend?"

The phlebotomist's question surprises Dave. He and the phlebotomist are still mostly strangers. He likes the phlebotomist, though. The phlebotomist has a refreshing lack of professionalism. The phlebotomist smiles like he knows what Dave is thinking.

"Well, you know. I steal blood all day. I don't get out much," the phlebotomist says. "Also they have a statue of your progenitor down there, and I feel like you might want to see it. For closure, or something."

• • • •

I feel obliged to warn you: I don't know how to end this without Dave walking in front of a train.

• • • •

Dave reaches the crevasse after an arduous journey. By now his companions have all fallen by the wayside, except for the wizard. This is because the wizard has magical powers, and also, because the wizard knows the location of the crevasse.

Dave climbs up the crevasse ridge. Dave is a young man in the prime of his life. The wizard leisurely strides beside him on an invisible staircase. Dave wishes he had magic powers instead of a magic sword.

The wizard has said that the age of miracles is coming to an end. That Dave's journey is the last great heroic act before the turning of the wheel. There will be a great cold, and a great heat, and eventually the world will turn to light again.

"You'll be in stasis until they need you," the wizard says. "I know this isn't ideal, but this is how the story goes."

"I don't mind," Dave says. He's already defeated the armies of the eastern sea and the ten thousand demonic constructs that had been plaguing the land. Dave is psychologically exhausted.

"If it makes you feel better, this is super cool and heroic," the wizard says.

Dave doesn't care if it's super cool and heroic. This is Dave's real human life. He is very tired.

• • • •

After the girl killed herself, I had to write something about it, because it was news that she died. But I couldn't say too much about how she died because you don't want to cause a whole situation of trains and people jumping in front of them.

So it turns into a story about the mental health crisis. It turns into a story about how everyone is heartbroken over the incident, and she will be missed. It turns into a story about how nobody knew that she was hurting on the inside, that she seemed a little subdued, that she was an honor roll student, that she had a tennis scholarship, that she had wanted to be an archaeologist, that she had been a valued member of the community. It turns into a story about *look at this beautiful future that is cut short, it is so sad that this happened, this is a tragedy and a surprise.* It is a story about a sharp break rather than the slow accumulation of sediment.

It is a story about anything other than the fact: this girl walked in front of a train and killed herself, and we can't know why because she's dead and can't tell us anymore.

Sorry. I should have told you about that one famous philosophy problem about the trains and people in front of them, instead.

. . . .

Dave and the phlebotomist take the train a quarter-wheel before taking the space elevator down to Wheel West.

Wheel West hosts the living museum. It's the only part of the Earth that the general populace is allowed to access. It's a heritage site. Government employees and students get to see the museum for free. The phlebotomist gets a medical personnel discount.

"I haven't been here since I was a kid," the phlebotomist says.

"Last time I was here, I was fourteen," Dave says.

They walk through the grand hall that opens the living museum. It's built in the old Earth style. The base of the living museum is an ancient building, and they had built the rest of it to match. It's alien and nostalgic. It's mostly kids visiting. Dave and the phlebotomist stick out like sore thumbs.

They walk past the gardens that have fruit-bearing trees and the fields that simulate farmland from the first medieval period, and they take a detour through the greenhouses because the greenhouses offer free fruit to visitors. They walk past streets that are from the ancient European continent and from the South Asian islands before they flooded. They look at post- and pre-flood maps. They walk across the castle reconstructions and the city hard-light reconstructions and then walk back into the part of the museum that houses the fossils.

They walk past dinosaur skeletons and dioramas of weird fish the size of houses. They go through *homo erectus* and the Denisovans and the Neanderthals, and then the *homo sapiens* and the exhibits about bog bodies, and salt mummies, and all the things that were preserved in ice.

In the center of a small room, there's a sculpture of a man wearing fur and carrying a spear. Below him, there's a photograph of some human remains. Dave has the eerie feeling that he is looking at his own grave.

"Wow," the phlebotomist says. "He looks nothing like you."

"Thank god," Dave says. "Imagine walking in and seeing yourself. I would have flipped."

"I guess bones and dehydrated flesh only tell you so much."

Dave studies the replica of his progenitor. They sculpted him rough. He looks like the sort of man who would have no problem picking up big rocks or doing hunter-gather-y things. Dave wonders how bad his eyesight was. Dave has a pretty awful prescription.

• • • •

The two men sit on the side of the ridge and play a game that no one in ten thousand years will understand how to play but will keep under plexiglass in a museum. The two men have come out to the ridge because the light is good here, and worse in the nearby copse of trees, and one of them has very bad eyesight. Each man is wearing neat furs and is bookended by a spear.

"This is a better way for it to end," the first man says.

"I hate the anticipation," Dave says. He doesn't disagree. The first man smiles a little. He's winning their game.

"Still," the first man says. "I like this better. Sue me."

"Suing doesn't exist yet," Dave says.

The first man laughs, and in the middle of his laughter, there's a sudden earthquake and the ridge shudders, and a large chunk breaks and Dave goes sliding into the crevasse before he can say anything or even scream.

• • • •

A story is a sort of wheel. There are a lot of rules about stories. Don't use the second person, because it's off-putting. Don't use too many numbers, because that gives the reader something to nitpick. Don't talk directly to the reader, because that's an awful hack move, and it doesn't ever land.

"Dave," you might say to me. "What exactly are you trying to achieve with this awful hack move?"

"I don't know," I'd lie. I know what I'm trying to achieve. I'm going to get it right this time.

"Dave," you might say. "Can you please stop talking about the crevasse."

"Well, I'm trying," I'd say.

• • • •

The phlebotomist investigates the neighboring plaques. He's trying to give Dave a moment. He knows it's hard to realize that everything about yourself is a lie that other people told you.

The phlebotomist reads plaques and learns about how it is possible to reconstruct the diets of archaic peoples from their hair, that ancient skeletons have been found with evidence of medical treatment for traumatic injury that then healed, and that grave goods have been found that have traveled very long distances.

The phlebotomist thinks that's kind of nice. In another life, the phlebotomist would have liked to have been buried with grave goods. After learning about what happened to Dave's cohort, the phlebotomist now wants cremation. He never wants the possibility of his body existing ever again.

The phlebotomist doesn't mean to be melodramatic. He's very logical except for when he isn't. The museum is getting to him. He had meant to come down weeks ago when he had learned about the DNA thefts. The phlebotomist wants his own closure.

But the phlebotomist is a more private person than Dave is. He's the sort of man who feels all his emotions in his throat and is sometimes unable to speak. He's the sort of man who has cultivated the trait of being good at telling jokes. He doesn't know what to say to Dave right now. He is not able to tell us how he feels.

All I can tell you is that the phlebotomist is the closest thing to happy when he is alone in the lab, watching the blood vials spin.

• • • •

I always talk around it.

You know, the roof. The suicide beat. All the Daves. Rome and rockets and von Braun wheels and the history of the written word and the cyclic nature of narrative and the dead thing in my chest. Like attracts like. They don't give the suicide beat to the reporters who are doing well. Sixty-two miles and thirty-one stories. I don't remember what happens next.

In the frame narrative of *One Thousand and One Nights*, the princess Scheherazade tells a story every night to prevent her husband from killing her before dawn. If she tells enough stories, she ends up in a story where she survives. But she can't say that to her husband. She has to tell the stories without her survival in them. And then maybe she gets to live.

• • • •

Dave walks around the sculpture of himself. He thought that seeing the museum would help him figure out how he felt about being a clone of a dead man from ten thousand years ago, but all he feels is sad. Dave knows that him and the dead man are not the same person. But Dave is still sad. One day the man was alive and the next he was dead, and without him, Dave guesses he wouldn't exist.

The phlebotomist walks back over. He looks carefully neutral.

"This place is pretty cool," the phlebotomist says. "Did you know that they can figure out what people ate, from their hair?"

Dave looks over from the statue of his progenitor.

"Why are you so interested in this stuff? Why'd you want to come down with me?"

The phlebotomist shrugs unconvincingly. The problem is that the phlebotomist talks too much when he tries to lie.

"I don't know, I just got kind of invested. Since I'm the guy who drew the short straw on telling everyone about the situation. You know. Not personally, I mean. It's just intellectually interesting."

Dave frowns. It's strange that the phlebotomist was the one who drew the short straw, and not some sort of program director. It's strange that the phlebotomist knows so much about what happened. It's strange that the phlebotomist suggested the field trip.

A thought occurs to Dave. The phlebotomist is not an old man. The phlebotomist looks to be about Dave's age.

Dave has a brain that charts the course of a dozen spaceships a day. Dave is very good at putting logical pieces together. Dave is not stupid.

"How old are you?"

"Twenty-seven," the phlebotomist says.

It takes between nine and ten months for the gestation of a human infant. The samples were stolen 28 years ago.

"Hey, are you—"

"That's between me and my medical provider," the phlebotomist says too quickly, which means, yes.

"What the hell, Dave," Dave says.

• • • •

I am sorry that everyone in this story is named Dave. Sometimes these things happen.

• • • •

Dave is fighting his opponent in ritual combat. This is more civilized than a war. The opponent's name is also Dave. They are not yet civilized enough to have more than one name in circulation.

Dave hasn't been able to get a hit on Dave. Dave has also been unsuccessful in this regard. Behind them, the sky is the bright black of a universe that has never heard of light pollution.

"It could go either way," Dave says.

"I'm sorry," Dave says, and it sounds like he means it.

Dave is a young man in the prime of his life. Dave has tonic-clonic seizures in another life. Dave pushes Dave into the crevasse. It's not even hard. This is something that has to happen in the story.

Dave yanks a lock of Dave's hair before Dave falls out of sight. It hurts Dave's head to have it pulled.

• • • •

It is very rare that bodies survive ten thousand years intact. It is a miracle when the conditions of the natural world turn against entropy and toward preservation. The right person in the right place at the right time. But every story is a miracle. King Arthur doesn't die of an infected cut after pulling the sword from the stone. Achilles is never pierced in the heel until he is. Cain does not miss when he kills Abel.

The Epic of Gilgamesh is one of the earliest stories. There are twelve standard tablets and various fragments. In tablet seven, the gods mark Enkidu for death, and he dies. This is written in stone. In the twelfth tablet, Enkidu is still alive. The story is one of the oldest pieces of human technology. It does not ordinarily appear in nature.

• • • •

Dave and the phlebotomist walk back to the greenhouse. The phlebotomist methodically picks the arils out of a pomegranate, which stain his fingers and mouth. The pomegranate tastes like sunlight. Dave is eating a pear. It tastes like a pear.

The phlebotomist speaks in a measured tone as he piles arils in his palm.

"I'm one of the twenty," the phlebotomist says. "Just like you. I just learned earlier because I'm the only one of us who works in the medical field."

Dave gets the sense that the phlebotomist is being the sort of honest he doesn't usually try to be. There is a sort of flatness to him. The phlebotomist chews on his pomegranate seeds.

"You're the last one of us I've told. No reason why. Just coincidence."

Dave doesn't say anything.

"Okay, I'm lying. Not a coincidence. Did you read the plaque?"

Dave had read the plaque. The man in the crevasse had been found with a lock of hair in his hand.

Dave looks at the phlebotomist. The phlebotomist looks at Dave.

"You're the hair?"

"I'm the hair."

Dave stares at the phlebotomist. The phlebotomist doesn't look like someone who walked out of deep time. The phlebotomist looks like an ordinary man wearing a T-shirt that says WHEEL MEDICAL STAFF with a badly drawn smiling syringe. The phlebotomist's mouth and hands are stained with pomegranate juice. Dave imagines the juice as blood and the T-shirt as furs and can't imagine it at all.

"I didn't want to freak you out. It's not like we're them. But I wanted to meet you, just for closure, I guess? Curiosity. So here we are. Sorry I didn't tell you earlier. I didn't want to make it weird. So, you know. Lying. Small lying. Sorry. I know we're not friends or anything."

The phlebotomist offers Dave a handful of pomegranate seeds. This is an overfamiliar gesture. Dave takes them.

"We're cool," Dave says.

The phlebotomist smiles.

• • • •

I don't know how to fix it. I text her earlier, and she doesn't respond because we're strangers. I call her because I'm impatient, but she doesn't know my number, so I get her voicemail. I run into her and ask her how her day is going, but she's only an acquaintance and tells me everything is fine and then she walks in front of the train.

• • • •

Dave eats the pomegranate because he's trying to think about what he wants to say. He does this a lot. Eats a bite of food or takes a sip of water because he wants a moment to think about his response to a situation. Most people are uncomfortable with silence. If you give them a long moment, they begin to speak.

But the phlebotomist just picks out more pomegranate arils. Crunches them one by one between his teeth. As if his confession was the last thing he needed to say to Dave, and now they can be done here.

Dave succumbs to his own tactics.

"How do you think our guys knew each other?"

The phlebotomist wipes juice from his mouth. Leaves a smear like fresh blood.

"Well, facts are that your progenitor had my progenitor's hair in his hand. So they were in close enough physical proximity for that. But that could mean anything. That they were fighting, that they were friends. Could have had some sort of religious significance. Could have been lovers."

"Not with that haircut."

The phlebotomist laughs. Dave thinks about how they are sitting on a bench in a greenhouse made from technology that is the product of ten thousand years of human technological advancement. That the same two voices are speaking to each other—barring any epigenetic changes, so maybe not the same voices, and without the same memories, so not the same men at all, but two men who would not have existed without two other men who had once known each other in some capacity, who could have sat next to one another sharing fruit underneath a blue sky. And maybe there's something about genetic memory that makes it easy to talk to the phlebotomist or maybe it's just that they met each other on the weirdest day of Dave's life and everything after that is allowed to be easy.

The phlebotomist wipes his hands on his pants. It leaves a red stain. He stands up.

"Look. I've said it before, and I'll say it again. This doesn't have to mean anything. This can all just be something that happened. He's not you. Whoever my guy was, he's not me. You shouldn't sweat it too much."

"You're the one that wanted to come down with me," Dave says. "I think you're projecting."

"Maybe a little," the phlebotomist admits, tapping his head and then his heart. "It's easier up here than it is down here."

"I mean, I'm glad we did."

"Yeah, this was fun. Let's never do it again."

• • • •

Dave and his doppelganger stand in front of the crevasse.

"Look, one of us has to go in there," the doppelganger says. "It's already happened."

• • • •

And you might say, "Dave, where are you going with this?"

And I might say, "I'm stalling because I don't know how to end this without the girl walking in front of the train."

And you say, "Dave, this is very depressing."

And I say, "Well, in a story, a death is a narrative device that spurs action on the part of the protagonist. A death can also be a way to take a character off the screen, to pull them off the stage and let them gracefully exit."

And you say, "I think you've lost the plot, Dave."

• • • •

Dave and the phlebotomist leave the museum on the last space elevator back up to the Wheel. Sixty-two miles below them, the sweet shallow curve of the Earth bends away as they ascend. Above them, they can see the bright black of a universe unadulterated by the atmosphere.

Dave talks about the rest of his weekend plans and the phlebotomist talks about the book he just finished. They talk about how they feel about ketchup, and whether there is any difference between a soup and a salad except the wet to dry ratio. They don't talk about genes, or the museum, or the phlebotomist's feelings.

They exit the elevator at the train station, a little after the evening commuter rush. They walk through dissipating crowds. They wait for the train at the emptying station.

They hear the train before it arrives. The smooth silver sound of the maglev slowing.

Then the phlebotomist claps Dave on the back, and says, "Thanks for, well, you know," and steps off the edge and—

• • • •

I thought that if I told the right story in the right place at the right time then maybe it becomes a fact. If I told the right story then maybe Dave dies for a reason. If I told the right story then maybe the girl gets to be Enkidu in tablet twelve of the Epic of Gilgamesh, alive despite all improbable cause. Except Enkidu is still dead in tablet seven. That doesn't change.

There are a lot of rules to stories. There are also a lot of rules to tablets and cuneiform and to tendon and bone and hearts and neurons and gravity and the size of a body and the width of a train.

• • • •

Then the phlebotomist smiles awkwardly, and says, "Bye, Dave, sorry," and hops off the platform and—

• • • •

The two men stand in front of the crevasse. It is the shape of something that will be very different in ten thousand years.

"I am going to jump in the crevasse," Dave says. "Because I don't know what I want to do with my life, and this is the only thing in the world that makes sense. I think about it every time I close my eyes. I picture the cold black bottom of the crevasse and it's better than everything outside."

"Do you think they'll call it a ritual suicide?" the second man says. He pauses. "Aw, I'm sorry. I shouldn't joke about that sort of thing. Are you sure about this?"

"How else do I end up down there?" Dave demands. "I'm already dead."

The second man doesn't have an answer.

• • • •

The phlebotomist nods at Dave, and says, "Thanks for coming out with me, that was the last thing on my list," and then he steps quickly off the platform and—

• • • •

I'm sick of Daves, and I'm sick of the girl, and I'm sick of trying not to worry anyone, and I'm sick of facts and feelings, and I'm tired of telling the same story. And—I'm trying a lot of things here, and I just can't seem to manage it. It's all facts. I can't control anything. I'm not Scheherazade.

. . . .

The phlebotomist nods at Dave, and says, "Fuck this, fuck everything, fuck trying again, I'm sick of this," and then he steps quickly off the platform and—

. . . .

And you say, "Dave, where are you?"
And I say, "It's pretty cold up here, and I forgot to bring my jacket."

. . . .

It is day ten thousand on this god forsaken spaceship and the concept of nothing does not yet exist.

The spaceship is a dense cloud of matter that is going to coalesce into a solid sphere (or rather, something in the approximate dimensions of a sphere, because wheels and perfect symmetry don't usually exist in nature), and this sphere will compress into a dense hot core of magma and layers of metal and then above that, rock, and eventually, it will cool enough that liquid condenses from the gas surrounding it, and then eventually the chemical soup will turn into biological soup and then there will be eukaryotes and prokaryotes and algae and photosynthesis and oxygen and weird little blind things and then eventually weird little furry things and then eventually those things turn into humans and then Dave! falls! into! the! crevasse! and! dies!

. . . .

They hear the train before it arrives. The smooth silver sound of the maglev slowing.

The phlebotomist says, "Listen, Dave, sometimes you can't stop someone from doing something awful, and it's not always the people you think need help that actually need help, and sometimes people leave your life suddenly and horribly, and I've been planning this for a long time, and it has nothing to do with anything you did, and anyway, you and I are strangers, so it's not like you could have done anything about what's about to happen. So don't worry about me," and steps off the platform and—

• • • •

I shouldn't have started this at all. I want to be anyone else but Dave. I want to stop telling the wrong stories. I want to stop speaking in metaphors. I want to stop reinventing the wheel. I want to be able to tell you a truth rather than a fact. I want to stop telling the wrong stories and start telling the right ones. I want everyone to be alive all the time. I want Dave to live. I want Dave to want to live. But I can't figure out how to leave the thirty-first story. Instead, I've ended up on the ledge above the tracks.

• • • •

And you say, "Well, I'm here too."

• • • •

They hear the train before it arrives. The smooth silver sound of the maglev slowing.

Before the phlebotomist can speak, Dave says:

"Listen, Dave, I know I can't stop you, because this is a fact and not a story, and anyway, I don't know what you're about to do because the future isn't set in stone, and I can't read minds, but I'm glad we went down together, and I'm glad that the guy who turned into me and the guy that turned into you knew each other, and I think that means something even if you don't. I think your heart is right, and your head is wrong. And Dave, you're not the girl. We're not in her story."

. . . .

And you say, "Dave?"

. . . .

And I don't say anything for a little bit. Because mostly I never know what to say about Dave except when he's ten thousand years away.

. . . .

And you say, "Did you know that if you grab the ladder from the janitor's closet and climb up onto the roof of the elevator stairwell, that's just high enough to see the sunrise over the river, if you wait until morning."

And you say, "So that's how you get off of the thirty-first story."

. . . .

I get the ladder. I sit on the roof of the stairwell. The sky is the bright black of a universe lit by my phone screen.

. . . .

Two men sit on the side of a crevasse. The crevasse is a deep gouge in the earth, large enough for a man to fall in. They both know what will happen. One of these men will have a name in the future and the other will not, but right now both of them are alive. Neither of these men believe in reincarnation because reincarnation is not part of the belief system that their culture has indoctrinated within them.

"I like the ones where we're friends better," the second man says.

"I think it's a little more fucked up if we're friends," Dave says. "That just means you let me die."

"Well, I like the idea that we could be friends. Maybe I just don't catch you in time or something. You grab some of my hair. That's kind of romantic, right?"

"I die anyway," Dave says.

"I can't help that bit."

They sit in silence for a while. Above them, the sky is a shade of velvet blue that will no longer exist after light pollution.

"I'm sorry it's going to happen," the second man says. "I know it has to. But I'm going to miss you. And I guess I'm just trying to say that you shouldn't let what has to happen make you miserable right now. I'm glad we met."

"Do you want to walk down with me?" Dave says.

The second man pauses. "Yeah, sure. I'm not doing anything tonight."

• • • •

I wish I had called the girl earlier. I wish I had met her at a party and we had exchanged numbers. I wish I had called her from the future and said listen, I don't get what you're going through, but I think about the sky and the thirty-first story, and I know that if you do this I end up on the suicide beat and the wheels of the train end up as the wheels in my head and in the grand scheme of things there's no difference between sixty-two miles and thirty-one stories and 9.8m/s^2 is the same thing as sixty-one miles per hour, so, well, do you want to go do our stupid group project instead?

• • • •

I'm going to do better next time. No, I don't mean—I'll walk down after this, I promise. Just let me finish.

• • • •

They hear the train before it arrives. The smooth silver sound of the maglev slowing.

The phlebotomist is stepping forward, and—

• • • •

I'm hanging up, now. I'll see you at home.

• • • •

—Dave catches the phlebotomist by the collar and hauls him back.

ISABEL J. KIM is a Korean-American speculative fiction writer based in New York City. She is a Shirley Jackson Award winner, an Astounding Award finalist, and her short fiction has been published in *Clarkesworld Magazine*, *Lightspeed Magazine*, and *Strange Horizons*, among other venues. Her work has been reprinted in *The Best American Science Fiction and Fantasy 2023* and *2024* and translated into Chinese and Japanese. When she's not writing, she's either practicing law or co-hosting her internet culture podcast *Wow if True*—both equally noble pursuits. Find her at isabel.kim or as @isabeljkim on Twitter.

* CONTENT NOTES: references to suicide and murder.

THE NG YUT QUEEN
(THE 五 月 QUEEN)
BY ELIZA CHAN

Semiprozine Long List (Worlds of Possibility)

A da Leung had been looking forward to three things when she got home: devouring the takeaway she had ordered—currently oozing grease into a paper bag; taking off the stupidly tight shoes that were crafting perfect blisters on her toes; and sitting down to binge-watch the rest of *Pompey Peepers*, the Blitz-era detective romance series that everyone was talking about. But opening the door to her flat, she realised her plans would have to be adjusted.

A smell like the perfume counter gauntlet at a department store hit her first, then the overwhelming feeling she had walked into a florist's. Flowers, everywhere. The floor was strewn with waxy banana leaves like a beach holiday. Dripping pastel bouquets filled every jar, mug, abandoned glass of wine and dirty saucepan in the tiny space. Orchids spilled from the opened cutlery drawer and peonies with heads like powder puffs poked through the wire lampshades that hung from the ceiling.

"What the actual—?" she said, kicking off her shoes. Some sort of joke? Ada waited for friends to jump out at her from behind doorways, for a camera crew to appear at her shoulder. Instead, she felt her eyes start to water and her nose tickle. Hay fever. Great.

Opening all the windows and shifting enough flowers so she could actually sit down on her sofa took the best part of an hour. Now her take-away was congealed, she'd lost her appetite and it felt like her nose had swollen up like an overripe strawberry. Ada snapped a photo to send to her best friend.

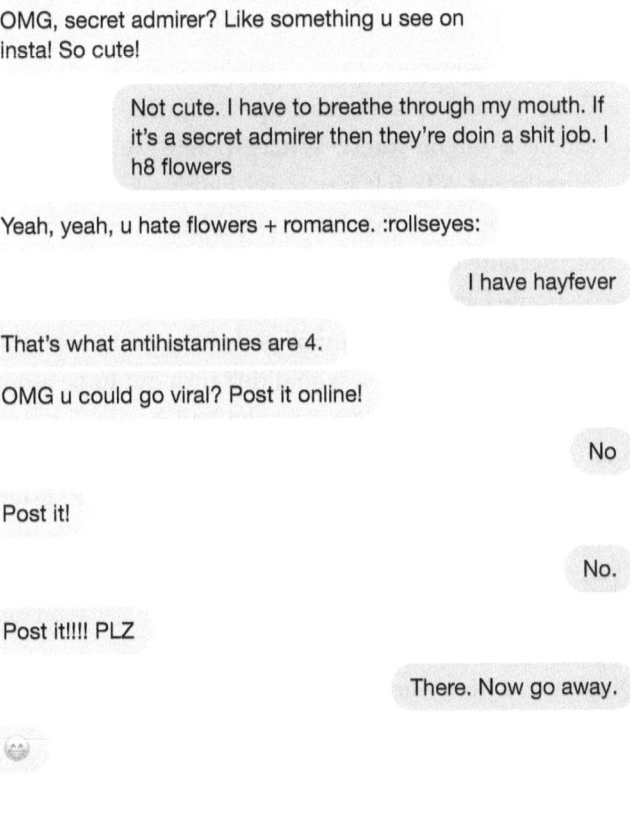

OMG, secret admirer? Like something u see on insta! So cute!

Not cute. I have to breathe through my mouth. If it's a secret admirer then they're doin a shit job. I h8 flowers

Yeah, yeah, u hate flowers + romance. :rollseyes:

I have hayfever

That's what antihistamines are 4.

OMG u could go viral? Post it online!

No

Post it!

No.

Post it!!!! PLZ

There. Now go away.

• • • •

Ada did have to admit, although not to Lou, that with the camera filters, her apartment took on a shoujo anime blush. Still, cherry blossom petals in her toilet bowl was a step too far. In the morning, Ada swiped her phone alarm without looking and tried to roll back over, but tug as she might, something was pinning down her duvet.

A goddess was lying on one side of her bed, propped up on one arm. "Do you realise you snore?"

Ada fell off the bed with a yell, grabbing one of her flip-flops as defence against the intruder. The goddess had perfectly styled black hair in intricate loops and a red dot on her forehead. But it was the ethereal glow from her skin, and the fact her white robes floated like they were being held by tiny invisible birds, that really gave the game away.

"Also, some joss sticks or fruit would have been nice. You know, to say thank you."

"I— What? Also, who?"

The goddess sighed as she stood up. Or rather, straightened like a bamboo stem in a serene forest. What? Where were these ridiculous images coming from? Ada felt her mind being assailed by soft-lit TV-drama cutscenes. She had to rub her eyes to clear them away.

Her unexpected visitor spoke with the patience of someone explaining a simple fact to a child. "The flowers. You prayed for them."

"I... did?" Ada had prayed to many gods for a number of things. The winning lottery numbers, a date who didn't turn out to be a douchebag, a self-cleaning flat. Only two days ago, she had prayed for her mum to hang up after a one-sided conversation about how her biological clock was ticking, but she had had serious doubts the gods were listening. She certainly had *not* prayed for flowers.

"Are you sure you've got the right person? Wrong number vibe going on here," Ada said, backing up to put more distance between herself and the ethereal screwball in her bed.

"At Qingming, with a whole packet of joss sticks."

"Qingming? I haven't celebrated Qingming since— Oh." Ada remembered. Being about ten years old and living in rural Yorkshire. Desperately wanting to fit in with her classmates, desperately wanting to be crowned May Queen to sit atop the annual float at the parade. They had given it to Louise Fowler, with her beautiful blonde curls and parents in the PTA. Not to the Chinese kid with the single mom who burnt paper gold in a trash can. And Ada couldn't really fault them for that: Louise was the nicest girl in their year. Pretty and funny and never saying some of the ignorant things the others did.

Ada had indeed pilfered a whole thick bundle of joss sticks and lit them all at once. She remembered wafting them up and down. The smell had lingered in her hair for days after. *Someone, anyone, please please just make me the May Queen. The queen of flowers. Then she'll ask me to sit with her at lunch.* She hadn't needed it in the end. A chance meeting over the tombola stall was enough. Swapping their dubious prizes of blonde shampoo and a pack of broken biscuits with rueful grins.

"Guanyin?" Ada ventured. The goddess of mercy nodded in confirmation. Nobody had warned her that praying to a Chinese goddess about a British tradition might get a little lost in translation. "That was over a decade ago."

"Every single time! 'You're late. I don't want it anymore.' Well, you aren't the only one praying. There's a bit of a backlog. And then when we do get to your request, you've moved! Not just to the next village—all over the world. Changed your names or genders. Do you bother to pray with a forwarding address? No."

"Sounds like you need the internet." The words were utterly mundane, as if she was talking to her por por about installing broadband rather than an actual goddess sat cross-legged on a cloud floating above her overfilled laundry basket.

Ada decided a coffee might help her get through this most unexpected of conversations. She padded through to the kitchenette and popped a pod in the machine. The reassuring chug followed by the velvety smell of the blend did much to calm her.

When she turned from unloading the dishwasher, Guanyin was sipping at her brew.

"Hey," Ada said reflexively. "That was for me."

"I thought you were finally making me an offering. What is this delicious elixir anyway? It's not tea."

"It's coffee," Ada said, resigning herself to making a second cup. "So, um, about the flowers. Thank you? I appreciate the sentiment. But I'm sure you have places to be, prayers to answer so..." Ada's eyes drifted towards the front door. She had plans for this weekend. Plans that involved a long hot shower, quality time with her TV, and some online shopping.

"Actually, we're trying something new." The goddess's eyes shone and her smile widened. Looking at her teeth was like staring into the sun.

Ada could sense a salesperson if ever she'd seen one. She girded herself to say no. "New?"

"Well, there hasn't been a lot of youth engagement, especially in the overseas communities. It's a bit of a trial. An outreach programme."

"And what does this programme entail?"

"I answer all your prayers. And in return, you show me around."

"Like a tourist?"

"Oh, yes." Guanyin pulled out a rice-paper scroll from her long sleeves and started to read from it. Chinese calligraphy in highly structured seal script filled the page. "I have a list. Westminster Abbey, the Houses of Parliament, Buckingham Palace, Tower Bridge, afternoon tea."

Ada groaned aloud. She'd already been tour guide for dozens of friends from home, not to mention their parents, aunties, and uncles. Everyone and anyone found it oh-so-convenient that she lived in London now. Except her. She tapped her finger, wondering how you could politely refuse a goddess.

But before she could answer, Guanyin started blinking rapidly and a hand clutched to her chest. "I... think there's something wrong with your coffee. It's making my heart go funny."

That gave Ada an idea.

• • • •

Instant ramen for breakfast was a hit. Guanyin fluttered around the polystyrene bowl, steam escaping from the sides of the lid until Ada said the five minutes were up. Given that every usable bowl in the house happened to be filled with the stems of wilting flowers, it was a win-win. But Chinatown was where Ada truly found her stride. Cheese-foam brown-sugar boba in one hand, matcha bubble wrap in the other, Guanyin craned her neck every which way to look inside shop windows, at the K-pop stans and gossiping aunties. The tourists in their matching visors following a jaunty flag-waving guide. The influencers pouting under the two-tiered gate. It was perfect. Ada kept Lou updated with sneaky photos throughout.

What's she doing now? Updates!

Watching buskers doin K18 moves

I can c her foot tapping LOL

☺ U should join in

What? No.

Go on A! Let your hair down. Bet she'll be up 4 it

A?

Ada?

There, happy? <image 1439>

YES ☺

💔 Look at the two of you! Ur laughing. I wish I was there

~~I wish you were here 2.~~
[This message was deleted]

It was fun. For a minute.

• • • •

Ada blearily brushed her teeth at the sink. Her head hurt from all the sugar of the day before, but the memories made her smile to herself. Guanyin had taken to karaoke like it was her natural form. Soft 70s Chinese pop ballads, 80s power ballads, and 90s Disney princess songs were her favourites.

A flash of something light caught the corner of Ada's eye, and she looked up at the mirror for the first time.

Her shriek brought Guanyin from the sofa bed. "What-what? What did Sun Wukong do this time?" she asked, cheeks flushed and imprinted with soft lines from the cushions she had been sleeping on.

"My hair!" Ada said. Her easy-to-manage short black hair had somehow been replaced by cascading blonde locks. Curls that wouldn't look out of place on a Barbie doll. It was heavy, and when she touched her head, it felt tacky against her fingers.

"Your second prayer," Guanyin said beaming. "Aiya, I didn't realise there would be such a lag for this one too. Honey-blonde hair."

As soon as she said it, Ada knew that's why the hair was sticky. Actual honey. "When did I wish for that?"

"The year after you wanted all the flowers."

"I was a kid! I didn't know what I wanted."

Guanyin raised an eyebrow. "I think it was quite clear what you wanted. More than now."

It was true, Ada thought. When she had been a kid, everything had seemed so clear and simple. If she could just be May Queen, everything would fall into place. In the years since she'd made those desperate wishes, she'd learned that life was a lot more complicated than that, though. Ada had been drifting ever since she had moved to London. Certain that she would find herself in The Big Smoke, she had instead fallen into the anonymity that came with being one of millions of ants in a city that never stopped. Constantly on the go; constantly feeling like she was missing out. She would flick through friends' photos and videos, envious of the parties, the galleries and theatres, the drinks out and dinners in. Even when she had been at the events, she'd been anxious she wasn't enjoying herself as much as she could be. Something was always missing.

They went to Brick Lane for market food. The heat of the Tube sent dribbles of honey down Ada's neck, and she couldn't enjoy her tacos because of the bees congregating around her head. Guanyin had pared down her white robes, wearing a more kaftan-esque outfit today. Big gold hoop earrings swung from her ears. They looked familiar. A gift from Lou years ago that Ada had never felt flamboyant enough to wear.

My hair is made of honey.

Is this... a Chinese thing?

No. It's literally honey. <image 1445>

Bloody heck Ada 😶

Bite me

I would.

U would what?

Ha. Whatever. Remember when u had blonde hair?

Thank god it went dark. Proper little princess wasn't I?

Queen, not princess. Queen Louise the Fair. May Queen of Aldborough.

OMG I DID make ppl call me that. Cringe

• • • •

Guanyin ran over, her face flushed. "Why haven't you taken me to watch a show?" She was brandishing a flyer from a half-price ticket booth.

"It's never as cheap as they say. By the time you get to the front of the queue, you feel obliged to buy something."

"But the man said I'd like this one..." Guanyin pointed with her delicate porcelain fingers to the iconic red poster. *Miss Saigon.*

Ada raised an eyebrow, wondering if she should warn Guanyin. Wondering also if there was enough money in her account to pay for two tickets just to see Guanyin's reaction. She bit her bottom lip and decided. Yes. Even if she had to put it on her credit card.

Guanyin's impassioned rage outside the theatre was not just filmed by Ada. It went viral. Videos of the goddess, semi-obscured by camera phones and bobbing heads, filled her feed. Ada scrolled through them, seeing her own gawkish face watching from the sidelines as Guanyin paced the pavement. Scattered applause and cheers responded to her points.

"I thought this was an enlightened era. Tornado potatoes and sushi tacos! But you've fallen short. Tantalised by distress, using it for enter-tainment. A little cathartic cry and get on with your day. Compassion? You know nothing about compassion!"

She went on, her robe loosely floating around her like a billowing jellyfish. Even the modern update to her clothing could not hide Guanyin's glow, a spotlight trained on her face wherever she went.

100,000 likes. OMG she's a meme!

My phone hasn't stopped pinging. The counter keeps going up. It's wild

People can't figure out her angle. Chinese beauty products, herbal medicine, yoga classes. Lol

No one believes she's just an actual goddess

Nope. Just u + me

Lots of DMs as well. Freebies! Hair and makeup collabs. I'm like her agent now

Ah yes, the girl who once tried to bleach her hair with toilet cleaner so ud look like moi. How far uv come.

Shut it.

• • • •

Nabil loitered at the side of Ada's desk, prodding at one of the orchids growing from her pencil pot. "Didn't the cleaners throw these out last week?"

"They keep coming back," Ada said, not raising her eyes from her monitor. Her hair was wrapped in a silk headscarf. She'd had to rinse out and replace it every few hours as the thick honey slowly oozed through. It was manageable though. Sort of. Washing her hair every morning made the honey runny enough that it didn't bother her until at least lunch. And her colleagues complimented her on her sweet-smelling perfume.

The clothing was a new one though. She had put on her usual trousers and shirt, but when she'd turned around, it had become a white wedding dress. Puff-sleeved, lacey, and voluminous. Ada had immediately taken it off, kicking it into the corner of her room like a rat on the Tube. She'd eyed it suspiciously as she'd grabbed another outfit. Stared at herself in the mirror. Navy shirt dress. Still a navy shirt dress. She would just need to grab the belt and—

She'd only glanced away for a second. When she'd looked back, she'd found herself wearing a wedding dress with a plunging V-neck. Figure-hugging satin. Ada had sworn.

"I'm late for work as it is!" she'd yelled as she'd prodded Guanyin awake.

The goddess had snorted once, wiping the drool from the corner of her mouth as she'd opened bleary eyes. A smile had curved across her face. "You look good!"

"This is a wedding dress, you numpty. I can't go to work in this!"

"I mean, I wouldn't choose that one, unless you used some tape around your... you know," Guanyin had said helpfully, gesturing at Ada's chest.

"I can't wear any wedding dress to work! When did I want this?"

"When didn't you? Every other month at least, if not more frequently for years."

Ada had groaned. She'd tried to sit on the carpet, but the tight fit of the dress meant she'd barely been able to bend over without the seams splitting. "Every little girl wishes that. A white dress, a handsome prince... It doesn't mean anything."

Guanyin had sat up and shrugged. "Your prayers, not mine."

Ada had changed several times. She had tried outstaring her reflection, but the farthest she'd gotten was to the front door with a hand mirror, and then she had blinked. The abandoned wedding dresses had been piling up in the corner, a mountain of chiffon and lace. Ada was running out of actual clothes and had considered calling in sick until jeans and a T-shirt had become a tea-length white dress. She'd decided it would have to do.

Nabil was still there, clearly after something. Ada finally looked up at him, impatiently drumming her fingers. His stammered question took a while to sink in.

It was only after the longest pause that Ada responded. "You're asking me out?"

"Um... Yes."

"Aren't you gay?"

"Yes."

Ada waited for a follow-up but there was none. Nabil didn't seem to see the clear and insurmountable impediment to his proposal. She politely declined. After her other colleagues, the man who came to service the vending machine, and one of the building security guards all also asked the same question, Ada saw where this was going. She would have to use that sick day after all.

· · · ·

At the kaiten sushi place, Ada had to stop Guanyin from taking yet another plate from the conveyor belt. The number of cucumber maki rolls she had already taken were far more than the two of them could eat. Ada picked a plate of inari sushi for her instead, insisting that no, there really was no fox in it—it was just a name.

Someone tripped over her train and Ada hitched the dress further up, sitting on a lumpy pile of tulle. The thing is, after all her clothes had been magically transformed into wedding dresses, she couldn't really afford to buy a new wardrobe. And even the more wearable dresses needed to be washed. Wedding dresses weren't exactly easy to launder at home. So Ada had to wear the bouffant dresses. After all, with honey-dripping hair and flowers anywhere she lingered for too long, what was an extravagant dress or two?

"I don't see the problem. You look pretty," Guanyin said.

"The dresses by themselves are bearable, but the men..." They were interrupted by one of the waiters asking Ada out. She didn't even pause for a breath as she politely rejected him, waving her chopsticks at Guanyin. "They aren't my type."

"None of them?" The goddess's tone was one of curiosity rather than outrage. Not the horror her mother had shown.

Guanyin refilled her green tea, marvelling at the boiled water-tap on the table. She pushed it once, twice, three times, a giggle hidden under her hand. Ada cleared her throat to remind the goddess they were mid-conversation.

"Well, then what *do* you want?" Guanyin asked. "You're the only one who can decide."

Ada was flustered by the question, a sliver of ice dropping down her throat. She swallowed hard, doubling down on her annoyance. "What does that even mean? You're fulfilling wishes that are a decade old! Are you telling me I could wish for a million pounds and you'd give me it?"

"I'm here, amn't I? Providing a personalised service. But you've got to truly want it."

Ada snorted, the lingering sharpness of the wasabi prickling her nose. It sounded too good to be true. Which meant it probably was. But if figuring out what she really wanted was how to get rid of the goddess, she was willing to give it a go.

U rly think she's telling u to wish for money???

Would be nice to have sum

No arguments here. But I suspect that's not what she's talking about. More sumthin from the heart?

Have a think A, might b staring u in the face

A mirror?

Har har. BTW b4 I forget, u free on 15th? My birthday dinner

In Aldborough?

No, on the moon. Where else? How long since u came back? Saw ur mum?

Maybe two Christmases ago. U know it's complicated w mum.

Would be nice to see u IRL

~~I would love~~
[This message was deleted]
~~I'm definitely~~
[This message was deleted]

I'll think about it

. . . .

Guanyin rolled onto Ada's bed, bouncing with glee. Ada pretended she was asleep for as long as she could, but the glow from the goddess's body made it difficult to keep her eyes closed, as much as she pulled the covers over her head. Like standing in front of a wind tunnel.

"It's like six in the morning."

"It's seven already. Also, I got a ticket."

"Ticket?"

"Yes, I normally prefer a bowl of oranges and some good-quality joss sticks, but I got a complimentary ticket."

Ada finally turned. The goddess was making less sense than usual. She grabbed the cracked handset from her hands, squinting at the blue screen to make out what she was being shown.

Ada had given Guanyin the old phone a few days ago. Shown her how to create social media accounts and use the camera. Set up @genZ-goddess for her and linked it to a 4Tea donations account for virtual offerings. It had had a trickle of success. People had posted prayers and thanks on her page. A few that had seen the previous photos and videos. Guanyin had had a field day. Selfies in Camden market trying on neon goggles. Getting a shiatsu massage in a pop-up bell tent. Face painted and dancing at the front of the crowd in an open air concert. And someone in K18's publicity team had left an offering of a backstage ticket to their concert.

Ada sat bolt upright in bed. The tickets were like gold dust. Sold out in minutes.

"Are they any good?" Guanyin's eyes were wide as saucers.

"K18? The biggest-selling boy band in the world? Yes."

Guanyin rolled this information around like a hard-boiled sweet in her mouth, nodding emphatically. "A good offering, then."

"In the grand scheme of offerings, this beats all your fruit baskets and lotus flowers."

Guanyin raised an eyebrow. "Nothing beats a lotus flower in full bloom. But I take your point. A *very* good offering."

• • • •

No longer Guanyin's tour guide, Ada finally had time to round up the wilting flowers for the bin. Scrubbed the green scum line from her glass tumblers and mugs. Her flat felt cold and sanitised without the colourful stems everywhere. Like no one actually lived there.

She washed her hair for an hour until the honey thinned out, sat in her comfiest wedding dress (a winter wedding dress, replete with a hooded cloak) and reached for the TV remote.

But there was nothing on. Nothing that interested her the way Guanyin had. Nothing that had the naivete of the goddess and her enthusiasm for every little thing. All of those things that Ada had said she would do when she moved to London. She'd never actually done them. Too busy, too expensive, too many people to talk to. There had always been an excuse.

But she was glad for Guanyin. The goddess was living her best life. Reminding people that she existed. If anything, Ada could live vicariously through her. Her phone pinged.

> u decided yet? Bout the 15th?

Ada started composing a response. Deleted it. Tried again. Deleted. Her fingers lingered over the keyboard. Searched through the gifs for a cute puppy. Maybe an otter clapping. But what the heck sort of response was that?

She threw her phone onto the sofa. A lump had formed in her chest. Like all of the honey had dripped down through her skin and hardened, amber resin around her lungs. Like she had inhaled thorns in her sleep and they had twined between her ribs. Like an embroidered wedding veil swaddling her heart, stopping it from beating the strong pulses of its desire. She just wished...

Guanyin was there, backstage pass around her neck. She said nothing, offering an arm and the softest of smiles. This time, Ada leaned right in, letting the goddess's glow encompass her. It felt like that first dip into a hot bath. She was tired. Exhausted by a city that did not want her, by a life that did not feel like hers.

"I wanted to be her. The pretty blonde girl who got to be May Queen. The friend who was always certain of her place in life." Her voice sounded reedy. Drawn out.

"What did you pray for? Really?" Guanyin pushed.

"I wanted to be her," Ada repeated.

Guanyin shook her head tenderly. Waiting.

Ada took a deep breath—like she was plunging her head underwater —summoning words she'd never said aloud. "I wanted her."

The relief spread like ripples across her surface. Tentative joy that the world had not crumbled. She had not broken in two.

"And now?" Guanyin continued. The goddess's brown eyes were liquid patience.

"I still want her." Like a toothache that pulsed against her gum, concealed behind a fake smile. It had always been there and would continue to hurt until she finally dealt with the root.

Guanyin's face was a full moon on a clear night. She took Ada's hands and pressed something into her palm, curling her fingers around it.

A voucher for 10% off bubble tea. Ada looked up, perplexed, until Guanyin noticed.

"Whoops, wrong pocket!" The goddess took the voucher back, rummaging in her long sleeves for the right thing. An open return train ticket to Aldborough.

"I could've bought this myself," Ada said, wiping her eyes with the back of her hands.

"But you didn't."

Ada couldn't argue with that. Let a small laugh escape her lips. Her body was lighter now that she had shed her baggage. It wouldn't be easy. Sketching an image she could only dimly see in her mind. But she had an outline. "Aren't you missing your concert?"

Guanyin reached into the air with a finger and thumb, pulling down a K18 thunderstick from nowhere. Winked. "I'm in all places at once. You'll rate me, right? On the app?"

"What?"

"Good luck, Ada," the goddess said, standing up. She pulled down another thunderstick, testing them on each other like a drummer readying a set.

"So we're done? I don't mean to sound ungrateful, but about the hair and the dresses..." Ada said.

"Should return to normal after a while." Guanyin looked at her cracked phone, smacking her lips together as she clocked the time. Checked left and right, as if crossing a road.

Ada struggled to her feet, ignoring the pins and needles prickling at her legs. "How long exactly is 'a while'? Guanyin? How long?"

But the goddess had gone. Slipped between spaces in the blink of an eye.

Ada stood for a long moment, staring at the empty coffee cups on her counter. If she stared hard enough, she could imagine them once more filled with brightly coloured flowers. The same flowers which had adorned Lou's hair as May Queen.

Ada picked up her phone. Looked at the last message.

u decided yet? Bout the 15th?

[Ada is typing...]

ELIZA CHAN is a Scottish-born speculative fiction author. Her

Sunday Times bestselling debut novel, *Fathomfolk*—inspired by mythology, East and Southeast Asian cities, and diaspora feels—was published by Orbit in 2024. Her short fiction has been featured in *The Dark Magazine*, *PodCastle*, *Fantasy Magazine*, and *The Best of British Fantasy*.

THE SPOIL HEAP

BY FIONA MOORE

Short Story Long List*

U p on the spoil heap Morag found a robot. This wasn't that unusual in and of itself. She was always finding them, or parts of them anyway, frozen in contorted attitudes like dinosaur fossils, plastic housing cracked and aluminum limbs splayed.

What was different about this one was that it was walking.

Morag would go up the spoil heap two or three times a week, as a way of supplementing what she got from her farm. She was a lot slower going up than when she'd been a young woman, but she was still fitter and stronger than most, and, if she brought a stick with her, it was more to poke about in the buddleia growths than to lean on.

The spoil heap had begun as the waste from a slate mine, and, by general agreement, was the common property of everyone in the village. Anyone could forage there, and could lay claim to what they found. But Morag had a particular knack for finding things. She'd come back with pieces of metal that could be reworked, wires, little tiny gears and fan-blades and largely intact sheets of plastic. She'd sell or trade them.

Sometimes, she'd get commissions. The Children of Flame, currently encamped by the lake, had a standing order with her for any intact animal skulls she found up there, for their rituals. One time she'd found them an actual wolf skull, and they'd kept her in deer meat and raw skins for months.

Now, Morag examined the robot critically. A walkbot, maybe four feet long from stem to stern. Six digitigrade limbs. Where a mammal would expect a head, there was a black distorted lump. A housing for a claw, or a camera, or a gun.

"Did I know you?" Morag asked it. Memories were stirring, twenty-five or thirty years old.

The robot bobbed and weaved.

"Hold still," Morag said, and it obeyed. Maybe she had known it. She examined it. Bent leg, some other bits of damage, nothing she couldn't fix.

"Follow," she told it, and it walked down the hill after her, a strange parody of a sheep on the green and gray hillside.

• • • •

The farm had belonged to Morag's parents. They'd moved south from Scotland when Morag was a baby, after the floods came. At the time it was what was called an organic farm, with vegetables, chickens, goats, alpacas. Like all farmers—like everyone around there, really—they did a lot of different things to try and bring in an income. One of those meant taking boxes of vegetables, fruits, and eggs round to the houses hired, or owned, by visitors.

Which, once she was old enough to ride a bike, was Morag's job.

You could tell which houses those were even without knowing. They were cleaner, better maintained. No visible repairs. Front yards with grass and flowers: the locals would pave theirs to save the gardening work. Many of them were 'quirky' or 'picturesque': a real crofters' cottage, a real shepherd's hut, but with heating and running water and refrigeration. Not television, of course. The visitors were Getting Away From It All, and anyway they had tablets.

Morag never really thought much about them. They seemed nice enough, and it meant more money coming in, and her dad could charge them double without them noticing. And making deliveries was easier work than mucking out the goats or weeding the polytunnels. The visitors got fewer and fewer and richer and richer as time went by, but Morag just put that down to the crisis the news kept going on about.

"New standing delivery order today," Morag's dad said, as they hefted the packages into the cargo box of the farm's Christiania-bike. "Once a week, to Gwydion Manor."

"What, the Big House?"

Morag's dad gave her a quick frown, but let the expression stand. "Yes. Apparently that's what all that building was up there. Someone's bought it, and moved in."

"Bit late in the year for it," Morag said. It was October, which was usually when the visitors stopped coming. She only had three other boxes besides the Big House one, and one of those was for Old Mary, who Morag's parents pretended would pay her bill someday.

So Morag was curious. She saved the Big House for last, even though it would have saved more time to go to Old Mary last instead, and cycled up the hill with a sense of excitement.

Then she saw the robots.

Strange, stalky, six-legged things, white and hooved like emaciated sheep. Black bulbs where they should have had heads, different shapes. Some of them protruded like guns. Others sleek like cameras. One of them stalking through the giant, forbidding slate gates towards her, two others following it. Another half-dozen converging.

Morag swallowed. Turned the bike so she could make as quick a getaway as possible.

A whistling noise, for all the world like calling off sheepdogs, and the robots hesitated, froze. A man came round the corner.

Maybe twenty or twenty-two, just a few years older than Morag herself, and handsome in a muscular sort of way. Tall, fair-haired, blue eyed, unlike the tanned and short local boys, or Morag herself, with her pale skin, sturdy frame, and dark brown hair. He was beardless, and dressed in a loose black outfit that was like what soldiers in war zones wore, and a beret that added to the general military impression. But no badges or medals.

He spoke to the lead robot, which had a sleek camera-head. "Scan," he told it. "Retain as friendly." Then he turned to Morag, smiled. "Sorry about that," he said. "They'll let you through next time."

"They can recognize me?" Morag said, feeling stupid. Of course they could.

The man nodded as if this weren't an idiotic question. "Let me take you up to the house. I'm Sean."

"Morag." She left the bike just inside the gate, rubbed her hands on the back of her jeans, took the grocery box, fell into step beside him. Inside, the grounds were bare grass, no plants or ornamentation. Robots, and people in outfits like Sean's, roamed about purposefully. Most of them were blonde or red-haired. Some were brown-skinned.

At the center squatted the Big House itself: low and gray, built of slate and brick like everything in the area, but somehow better fitted together, more modern. More forbidding. The windows seemed high and narrow, like the arrow-slits on the castle up in Caernarvon.

"The core of it's a Georgian manor house," Sean was saying, casually, like he was guiding a tour. He had a pleasant accent; Morag thought it might be Irish. "But the Big Man's made a lot of additions. All modern conveniences and comforts."

"Who is he?" Morag hurried a little to keep pace.

Sean shrugged, though Morag didn't believe his indifference for a minute. "Super-rich fella. American, I think. Made his money over there, anyway. Travels around a lot. Owns houses in all the big cities."

"Wow." Morag couldn't begin to think how much that would cost. "And he's got one out here? Why?"

Sean's expression didn't look like it had changed, but the mood shifted. Morag wished she hadn't asked. But he answered, "He's got this idea that it's safe. Safer than the big cities, anyway. It's a popular thing for really rich people, now. Build a house out in the back of beyond. Make it self-sustaining. So you can live out here if the cities collapse."

Morag snorted. "Think they would?"

"*He* does," Sean said.

Morag wondered why, if it was so safe, he had all these robots and guards around. But she didn't think it was a good idea to ask. "How'd you come to work for him?"

"Well, the money's good and—" Sean hesitated a little, and his pleasant face again got momentarily hard. "I was deployed in Eastern Europe, when I was in the army," he said. "Let's just say I've seen a few things that make me think he's not wrong about the way things are going right now. Safer to be out here than anywhere else."

They'd reached the kitchen entrance, where Morag left her box with someone she assumed was the cook. But for the rest of the week, she kept thinking about that strange low house, and its owner, and its robots, and Sean.

Especially Sean.

• • • •

It didn't take Morag long to fix up the damage to the robot. The things she couldn't repair were mostly cosmetic anyway. She caused a little commotion when she went into town with the robot trotting behind her, carrying the things she had to sell. But once she'd explained how she'd come by it, and once she'd made a few trips with it, people just got used to seeing it. It wasn't too different, visually, from the big shaggy dogs that would trot at farmers' heels, and it was a natural thing for Morag, with her trips to and from the spoil heap, to have.

She named it Seamus. Another Irish name, and not so close to Sean that anyone would notice.

Not that it was likely anyone local would remember. It had been twenty-five years at least since the Big House last had anyone in it, and people avoided the site, less out of superstition than out of a pragmatic fear of triggering security devices. Zeb and Casey might remember, but Zeb had married the brewer in Pen-y-Gros and moved out that way, and Casey had joined the Children of Flame, and their nomadic trail usually took them far from town.

She wondered if Seamus remembered.

• • • •

"I won't allow it," Morag's father said.

"I'm eighteen," Morag said. "You don't have to allow it. I'm taking the job." She softened her tone. "Dad, it makes sense. You want me to go to university, don't you? I'll need to take some kind of job to do that, and this one pays so well it'll only be a couple of years before I can afford the fees." Even factoring in that she'd have to contribute something to the farm debts, she didn't add.

"You could go work with Ruth in the post office."

"Ruth can't afford to pay anything. I'd be working for barter."

"You could get a job in Caernarvon."

"*What* job in Caernarvon? The place is a war zone. You're the one who keeps telling me to stay out of the cities. That they're dangerous and full of gangs. I could get a job with the police, I suppose, but that'd be no different to security work, and it's more risk."

"You just want to be close to Your Young Man."

"And what's wrong with that?" Morag stood astonished. "When I brought Sean down for dinner with you and Mum, you said you liked him."

"I liked him fine. I don't necessarily want him as a son-in-law."

"And again, Dad, that's hardly your decision."

"I just don't want you to get hurt." Morag suddenly realized how old her dad was, the way he said that.

"I won't," Morag said. "I know 'security guard' sounds a little scary, but I've been delivering to the house for nearly two years. They just walk around the grounds."

"With guns."

"Which they never use, and it's not a bad idea for me to get a license anyway. I can use it for hunting. I'll be fine."

Morag's dad shrugged. "Well, as you say, it's your decision."

• • • •

When Morag got back from the spoil heap, there was a stranger at her gate.

Seamus went into defensive mode. It didn't have a gun anymore, of course, but Morag had seen firsthand how the little walkbots could do surprising amounts of damage just with their limbs and their uncanny knowledge of how to apply physics to the human body.

"I'd heard somebody had one of those robots, from the Big House," the man said. "Wondered if it was you. Came to see if it was."

"Feargal?" Morag barely recognized him. His face was older, lined, thin. Even with all his soldier muscle, there'd always been something a little soft about him back in the day, and the softness was all gone. But the hair, the bright red hair was still the same.

"That's me." He grinned.

"You'd better come in." Morag pushed open the gate, told Seamus to stand down. "Have you come far?"

"Yes and no," Feargal said, as she led him to the house, dropping off that day's haul of scrap on the way. "I'm staying in a camper-van just outside town. But I've come up from Shrewsbury."

"Shrewsbury!" It had been a two-day round trip even back when the trains ran. "What are you doing there?"

"Much the same as I was doing when we knew each other." Feargal sat at the kitchen table while Morag made them a pot of tea. Seamus stalked off into the fields to do a perimeter patrol, as it usually did when they got back from foraging.

"Security for a big man?"

Feargal smiled. Was that a scar on his forehead? "Better, actually. They're starting to rebuild, out that way, in some of the larger towns. Or not rebuild—build new. Get up infrastructure, technology. All that. And don't worry, it's all democratic."

"Glad to hear that," Morag said, shortly.

• • • •

Morag had been working at the Big House six months when she finally saw the Big Man, or Call Me Steve as the security guards also referred to him. It had been a fun time. She'd learned how to shoot a gun and instruct a security robot, and she fancied the black tactical gear made her look a little taller and thinner. The head of the security squad, Chief O'Leary, was nowhere near as scary as she looked once you got to know her. Plus Morag got to be around Sean. Not as much as she'd have liked, since he'd been promoted, and since men and women were supposed to sleep in different bunkhouses. But they saw each other enough. And the rest of the job was super easy for the money she was making: just walk around, or sit watching monitors, or, sometimes, she'd have to spend a couple of hours reading news sites and flagging up stories on certain themes. She'd asked Sean why those particular themes and he'd said the Big Man used it to triangulate when the time would come for him to move out here.

The first she knew about the Big Man arriving was a flurry of activity in the operations room. Morag had just been coming off shift. She'd been patrolling with another security officer, younger than Morag but nonetheless an Irish ex-soldier like Sean, and they'd heard the raised voices.

Sean burst out of the room at a fast walk. "Double patrols," he said, noticing her and Feargal and slowing. "Everyone on full alert. Stop by the quartermaster and get him to issue you both machine guns."

"We've just come off shift," protested Feargal.

"Doesn't matter. The Big Man's arriving in half an hour. We need to show him the place is secure."

"Is it a visit? Or is he... moving out here?" Morag asked.

Sean looked worried. "We'll find out in half an hour."

Not that Morag got to see much of that, of course. After patrols had been doubled and all the security put on its highest possible alert, any spare junior personnel got redeployed to help with cleaning, or cooking, or weeding, or anything else the place needed. There was a brief pause when the helicopter actually landed, and everyone tried to ensure they were in position to actually see the Big Man.

Who, when he emerged, was disappointingly not-big. Healthier looking than most of the men of Morag's acquaintance, but still, you wouldn't give him the lead on any streaming show. He was dressed in simple jeans and T-shirt, but Morag had enough experience with that sort of thing now to know that they probably cost more than her parents' farm. Drones buzzed around his head like cartoon devils. He didn't look around, or smile, but barked something at Mister Coulson, the house manager, and set off at a marching pace towards the house, with Coulson, O'Leary, and a couple of people Morag didn't know trailing after him.

He spent the next couple of hours locked in his office with his retinue, while everyone else tried to settle the Big Man's family, emerging from a second helicopter and consisting of an understandably upset (but nonetheless, Morag thought, rather silly) woman and two crying children. Once they'd been installed in their rooms and provided with appropriate distractions and sedatives, there wasn't much to do.

Morag and a couple of the Irish kids were teasing a camera robot, blocking its vision and kicking at its legs, when Sean reappeared.

"Stop that," he said to them, fiercely.

Morag felt a wave of alarm and guilt as Cliodhna protested, "It's just a robot. It doesn't feel."

"It's artificially intelligent. For all you know it feels more than you do," Sean said. Morag felt even more guilty. "Anyway, we need everyone, human and robot, on deck."

"Is it the big one, then?" Feargal asked. The robot quickly slunk down the corridor.

"I'm sorry," Morag said to it as it left, and Cliodhna gave her a look.

Sean nodded. "It's bad out there," he says. "Economy's collapsing, Prime Minister's in hiding. Royal Family's been taken to a secure location. Nothing in the cities works any more. This is it."

Morag was thrilled with excitement, and forgot about the robot. "So what do we do?" she asked.

Sean looked at her as if he'd never seen her before, and her excitement turned to chill. "Nothing any different to before," he said. "Our job is just to keep the family safe and healthy. The house is secure. It has its own energy and water, the vehicles and robots are all electric, and food reserves, if they need them"—Morag noticed he didn't say *we* need them —"are good for a couple of years. We just need to make sure no one takes them. Understand?"

Morag and the Irish kids nodded.

"Good. Dismissed. I'm sure there's something you need to be doing. And if not, get some rest for when you do."

Morag hesitated. She wanted to ask Sean for some kind of reassurance. A smile. A few words to let her know that everything was okay and things would work out. But she wasn't sure about this new Sean, so she followed Cliodhna back to the bunkhouse.

• • • •

"So what actually brings you out this far?" Morag asked, refilling Feargal's mug with tea.

Feargal nodded thanks and took another square of bread and jam. "Fact-finding," he said. "Recruitment." He met her gaze steadily. "Looking for you, in a way."

"How so?"

"We need resources," Feargal said. "One thing the town needs is old tech that we can rework: motherboards, hard drives, mobile phones. The other thing the town needs is people who can fix them, program them up."

Morag stirred her cup, never lowering her eyes from his.

"I know what you did, up at the Big House," he said, neutrally. "With the robots. Clever. Not a lot of people could."

"Anyone could," Morag corrected, "if they'd had the training. It's not hard."

Feargal kept looking at her, and she waited for him to say that he'd meant not a lot of people could have been merciless enough to do what she'd done.

Instead, he eventually said, "But these days, there's not many people with the training. Or the knack. You've clearly fixed things up quite well around here." He gestured out the window, taking in the solar array on the roof of the goat shed, the polytunnels, the rusty tractor with the wood-burning engine.

"Just bits and pieces from the spoil heap."

"It's more than that," Feargal said. "I'd like to offer you a deal."

• • • •

After a short while, life at the Big House settled into its new routine. Morag saw less and less of Sean, to the point where she was starting to think of their time together in the past tense. Instead, she found herself frequently assigned to look after Mrs. Steve (her name was Angela, but no one called her that except when she or Call Me Steve were listening) and the two Steve offspring, Casey and Zeb. The kids were okay, like normal kids except with more toys and less sense. Mrs. Steve was sullen when she wasn't complaining.

Morag asked if she could change assignments, but Sean told her she was the best at 'handling' Mrs. Steve, which Morag deduced meant that Mrs. Steve was less likely to kick off in front of her than in front of Cliodhna. Who, Morag couldn't help but notice, also drew wife-and-childsitting duty more often than the boys did.

So that meant Morag had to be cleverer about it. After a week of thinking about it and another week of strategizing, she presented Sean with a requisition from the quartermaster, asking that Morag be trained in robot programming and maintenance.

"We need someone else who can do it. What would happen if Tom fell down a slate pit?" Tom's assistant, Xavier, had disappeared not long after Call Me Steve's arrival, and the rumor was he'd deserted and gone back to try and find his family in some city, somewhere.

Sean blew out an exasperated breath. "Okay," he said. "But that's the only reason. And you've still got to guard Mrs. Steve's morning jog at minimum, okay?"

"Fine." At least Mrs. Steve generally didn't say much when she was jogging, and Morag could do with the exercise.

Although she'd regarded it as just an excuse to spend less time with her charges, Morag soon found she quite enjoyed working with the robots. The programming followed interesting lines of logic, and learning the history behind how it all came about was fun.

"They're so smart," Morag said, as a small drone she'd programmed efficiently navigated the high wall and barbed-wire fence. "Why do they even work for us? It's not like you can pay them."

Or use other ways of keeping their loyalty, she thought but didn't say. None of the Big House staff had been paid since Call Me Steve arrived, but no one had complained, regarding the presence of food, shelter, and security as enough. Morag wasn't even too sorry about giving up on university. She was learning plenty of interesting things here. And she could get down to the village to visit her parents most weekends, and sometimes bring them tins of exotic food she'd pilfered from the emergency store.

Tom smiled like he knew the answer to a joke. "Here's why." He activated his phone display, showed her what she recognized as a robot's subroutines. "It's programmed in."

"That line of code?" Morag ran her finger along it.

Tom nodded. "They're smart, and they can learn. In the natural course of things, they'd be capable of making their own choices. That's why we have that code there. Keeps them from thinking along those lines."

"That's like slavery," Morag said, before she could stop herself.

Tom didn't seem angry, though. "It's not slavery if they don't know they're slaves."

. . . .

"What sort of a deal?" Morag asked. Though she knew.

"Come work for us," Feargal said. "Fix up robots, solar arrays, all the old technology. Then, when we're in a position to make new robots and things... Help us make new ones. You'd have a free hand in all the design. And you'd be paid," he added. "The town council would allocate you a house of your own, for free, and you'd get food and goods in exchange for working for them. Our technical people live quite well."

Morag shrugged. "I'm settled here," she said. "I've got my farm, and my animals. I'm too old to be migrating."

As she'd thought it might, Feargal's face got subtly harder. "I know what you did at the Big House," he repeated. "Do your neighbors know?"

Morag was quiet.

"If you don't come to work for us," he said, "I'll tell them all how it went down. You know what happens when communities turn against people. And a woman on her own, too; no family. A witch, in her way." He sat back. "Security and protection with us," he said, "or facing the music. Your choice."

"And suppose I did go with you," she said, "but one day decided I'd rather come back here?"

Feargal smiled in a way she thought he meant to be kindly. "I'm sure the council could work something out."

Morag walked him to the gate. He'd said he was going to go look around the ruins of the Big House, see if he could find old robot parts, camera lenses, nylon tarpaulins.

"I'll come back tomorrow before I go," he said, warningly.

Morag looked down at Seamus, who had trotted up again, its latest patrol finished.

"They'll never be able to make those things new again," she said to the robot. "We're in a scrap-iron age now, fixing up old parts. But it won't be long before we'll be living just as people did for centuries. Millennia even." She looked up at the hillside. "More and more join the Children of Flame every year. Or another of those nomad groups."

She turned back to the farm. "Come on, we'd best see if we can get a few more beetroots dug before the light goes."

• • • •

Morag was playing a game of football with Casey and Zeb, and one of the surveillance robots she'd programmed with a ball-chasing subroutine, when Sean announced there was an all-personnel meeting in half an hour.

Morag assumed this had something to do with the supply crisis. After two years, the Big House was starting to run low on food. The small farming operation running off of the back acres wasn't enough—Morag could have told them that, based on her experience—and the local people were less and less interested in selling their surplus to the Big House.

"What's the point?" Morag's father had said on her last visit home. "Money's worthless, and they don't have any decent barter. We're better off trading it for meat, wool, and other things we need."

"I could see if they'd trade you a robot?" Morag suggested, then laughed at the outraged look her father had given her.

Morag had been expecting Chief O'Leary to run the meeting, but, when they all crowded into the staff dining area, she found it was Call Me Steve standing at the front of the hall, flanked by O'Leary, Coulson, Sean, and one or two other middle-ranked types.

Steve cleared his throat, and Morag noticed how weirdly prominent his Adam's apple looked under his barely-there chin. "I've called you all here to announce a change in strategic direction," he said. "This is to address the growing supply issue. I propose that we approach the local people and propose an exchange of resources. They supply us with food and in exchange we provide protection."

A hand went up. "What if they refuse?" Feargal asked.

Call Me Steve smiled thinly. "I don't think they will when they see the superior nature of our armaments. And if they do, I'm sure a couple of shows of force will convince them."

"He's talking about feudalism." Cliodhna sounded like she couldn't quite believe it.

"What do you mean?" Morag was still trying to process what was happening, as Call Me Steve answered questions from the floor about tactics, logistics, expected resources.

"Like in the Middle Ages, or fantasy novels. Peasants giving tributes to lords in exchange for protection."

"It makes sense," Feargal overheard them. "How else are people going to live? The state's collapsed, and it's not like it was never worth much out here anyway."

"Yes, but out here, we didn't get people raiding farms," Morag said. The lack of a police force occasionally was felt when someone vandalized the school playset or one of the farmers had a little too much to drink. But this was on a different scale.

"Oh, I forgot, you're actually from around here, aren't you?" Feargal said. "Don't worry, I'm sure they'll leave you out of this."

Sean confirmed that not long after, as Morag sat in the robot workshop tweaking a head-camera. "I know your folks are farmers down in the village," he said. "It could get embarrassing."

Morag looked at him full on. "You mean, you don't want me around when you kill my dad."

"Morag!"

"Or my sister-in-law, or someone I went to school with." Morag attacked the camera lens with a polishing cloth.

"I don't think it'll come to any of that." Sean sat down at the bench with her, and Morag pulled away a little. "I'm sure everyone will see the logic of the new arrangement."

Morag didn't like to think about that, either. The resentful looks she'd get, going into town. Maybe people deciding to have a go at her, with words or fists. And she was wondering how long things would stay mutually respectful. How long before one of the guards, or house staff, decided they'd help themselves to something one of the locals had. Like her father's dire stories about social breakdown in the cities.

"Hey," Sean smiled at her, put his arm around her. She let him, for the moment. "It won't be so bad. And once we've got more territory, Steve's talking about maybe moving some of us into the unoccupied houses around town. You know. Keep an eye on the villagers, make sure they stick to their end of the bargain."

"So we'd be spies?"

"It wouldn't be like that. We could start our own family, maybe even our own farm. A big farm. With people working on it so we wouldn't have to. What do you think?"

That was the last thing Morag wanted right now. "Some of those houses would need a lot of fixing," she said, just to have something to say.

"I'm sure we'd get one of the good ones, and I'm sure we could fix them. I mean, look at what you're doing with these electrics." Sean gestured at the workbench. "See you at dinner, eh?" He gave her a final squeeze and left.

Morag lowered her head over the camera, fighting angry tears. She had to do something. But the more she thought, the less she could think of anything she could do.

• • • •

Morag woke in the night.

She lay quiet under the duvet for a few minutes trying to figure out what had woken her. A bad dream? No, she'd slept all right. A noise from outside?

She kept very still and listened to the sounds outside the house. The hoot of an owl. The trickling sound of the spring. A goat, bleating.

That made her open her eyes. A goat, awake at this hour?

Now she could hear a less identifiable noise. A scratching sound, like someone scraping metal on stone.

At the back door.

Morag wasn't going to risk a confrontation. She got up, threw on her jeans, tucking her flannel nightdress into the waistband, and tiptoed downstairs, heading for the front door. She would go round to the neighbor—or, better still, the Children of Flame were camped behind the spoil heap at the moment. She could get there in less than ten minutes if she moved fast.

She slid on her Wellingtons and opened the door silently. Crept out into the yard.

Was flung back against the side of the house, an arm on her throat and a hand over her mouth. Her torch fell to the ground with a crack of breaking glass.

The bastard, she thought with strange detachment. He's outwitted me.

"Now, I suggest you come with me quietly," Feargal said in a rough whisper. His breath smelled of smoke and of rotten teeth. "You'll like it in town, once you get used to it."

Morag wished desperately that she could send a telepathic message to the Children of Flame. There wasn't much point in struggling, but there had to be a way out of it.

"I'm going to take my hand away," Feargal said. "Don't scream."

Morag nodded.

Feargal pulled back, then, suddenly, let out a sharp cry, jerked upwards, and fell to the ground, where he twitched.

Released, Morag fumbled for the torch. Fortunately the crunch hadn't been the bulb; the lens was cracked, which was a shame as it would be expensive to replace, but that was all.

She trained the beam on where Seamus was kicking Feargal efficiently with its front four feet. Having deployed its thick aluminum dewclaws, suitable for climbing or defense.

"Don't kill him, Seamus," she said mildly.

• • • •

True to his word, Sean had made sure Morag was on child-minding duty on the day the guards were to go round the houses. She passed them all arming up and drilling as she led her charges out for fresh air and football.

The kids clearly realized she was in a mood, but were also starting to learn that there were times when it was better to wait for the adults to tell you what was wrong than asking outright. Zeb started to say something when Morag missed an easy kick, but Casey shushed him.

Finally, she said, "Let's go play in the workshop."

"I don't wanna—" Zeb began, but again Casey gave him a nudge. "But it's creepy in there."

Morag softened. "Okay. Sorry. It's just that there's something I need to do in there before the guards leave. How about if, afterwards, we go play in the cellar?"

This got their attention. They weren't normally allowed in the bunker/storehouse complex, so the prospect of a visit there was enticing.

Once they were in the workshop, Morag left them trying to teach a robot to do a haka, and sat at a monitor.

Called up the free-will-suppressing code Tom had showed her.

Hesitated for a moment. Would it even make any difference?

Then she deleted it. Gave the command to distribute the change to all units.

"Come on, kids," she said, rising up from the workstation. "Let's go play in the cellar."

• • • •

"Do you know what happened to the robots?" Feargal said as he lay on the ground. "The ones you freed?"

Morag said nothing, just stood there with Seamus, waiting for Feargal to go.

"Nothing," he sneered. "Once they'd done killing everyone they didn't like, they just wandered off into the hills. Fell apart. Dropped off cliffs. Wound up as exotic garden sculptures."

Morag still said nothing.

"Don't you understand? Without us, they've got no purpose. They need to serve us, it's what they're for. Otherwise, they're just... junk."

"You finished?" Morag asked.

Feargal hauled himself to his feet. There was blood on his face from one of Seamus' kicks. "I suppose."

"Then go," she said.

"I'll come back," he warned.

"If you do," she said, "I won't call Seamus off."

"Seamus," he said, disbelievingly. Then, "I'll bring reinforcements."

Morag said nothing, just looked at him skeptically. Like, would his new bosses really sanction a raid on a town, just for one middle-aged woman who knew her way round a circuit board?

With a final, disparaging growl in an attempt to save face, Feargal turned and went.

"You'd better focus your patrols on the house tonight," Morag told Seamus quietly. She went to the kitchen, made herself a cup of something herbal, and, once her hands had stopped shaking and the incident was safely in the past, went back upstairs.

. . . .

A detached part of Morag was fascinated by the choices the robots made. She'd expected them to go for the people who they dealt with on a day to day basis: people like Cliodhna, Tom, and Feargal. But they went for Call Me Steve first, shooting him efficiently through the skull, and then several of them went on to trample the corpse with something Morag found hard not to interpret as enthusiasm.

They went for Mrs. Steve next, which surprised Morag since she'd never seen her give the robots any reason to hate her. But maybe this wasn't hate-driven, she reflected. Their attack and defense programming included routines about identifying the leaders of the troublesome faction and neutralizing them first.

The robots had had plenty of time to observe the humans, and decide which were the leaders.

They shot Tom, which didn't surprise Morag in the slightest.

By this point the guards had worked out what was happening, and things got a little more chaotic. Morag watched the courtyard from the narrow ground-level window, more a hole to let natural light into the cellar, as they reacted to this new threat.

Most of them fought back, taking down several of the robots. Cliodhna got a few before they got her. One or two evidently cut and ran. Morag couldn't see Feargal anywhere, for a start. But the robots had, indeed, been programmed for defense. Call Me Steve would have got his money's worth; the robots were clearly capable of doing serious harm to a team of trained soldiers.

After an interval Morag saw Sean emerge from behind the Land Rover the remaining few guards were using as cover. Unarmed, hands up. He walked over to the robots, clearly indicating surrender. Treating them like a human enemy.

Morag strained to hear what he was saying to them.

"Steve's dead," he was saying. "So's Coulson and O'Leary. Let's start over. We need each other. We can set up a community, here. You and us."

Morag didn't think Sean would make a better medieval lord than Call Me Steve. Possibly worse in some ways.

The robots considered for a minute. Then they shot him too.

After that things lost momentum. The battle continued for a while, but eventually both sides ran out of ammunition, and that seemed to end things. The robots, their targets neutralized, wandered off on their tottery legs. Morag had wondered if they'd go back to patrolling, but it seemed that was a matter of choice too.

The remaining guards cautiously broke cover. Began tending to the wounded, to the dead. Asking shrill, nearly hysterical, questions about what was going to happen next; reassuring each other it would be fine.

Morag dropped down from her observation perch on top of a crate of gas-masks. "Come on, kids," she said, holding out her hands. "We're going to go visit my parents for a while."

Casey frowned suspiciously. "How long a while?"

"As long as you like," Morag said.

· · · ·

Morag took her bag and her stick and headed out for the spoil heap.

As she went, Seamus fell into step beside her.

"You know," she said to it, "you can leave any time you like. You don't have to stay here with me."

The robot was silent.

"You don't have to defend me either. Not that I'm not grateful. I just want you to know that I understand. And if ever I start getting like any of the others, you go, okay?"

More silence of course.

Feargal had been right that it was humans who gave the robots purpose. But he was wrong about the rest of it.

"All right then."

The weather was cold and the leaves were turning. Zeb usually made a visit back to the farm round about this time of year, with his husband and their growing retinue of orphans, and Casey would drop off the nomadic trail for a few days to say hello.

She took a firm grip on her stick, started up the spoil heap. She heard Seamus' dewclaws click into place, the harsh scrabble as it followed her over the slate.

She'd have to get more supplies in.

FIONA MOORE is a BSFA Award–winning writer and academic whose work has appeared in *Clarkesworld Magazine, Asimov's Science Fiction, Interzone,* and six consecutive editions of *The Best of British SF.* Her most recent fiction is the short story collection *Human Resources* (NewCon Press) and her most recent non-fiction is the book *Management Lessons from Game of Thrones.* Her publications include one novel, five cult TV guidebooks, three stage plays, and four audio plays. She lives in Southwest London with a tortoiseshell cat which is bent on world domination and a sealpoint cat which is not too bothered.

* CONTENT NOTES: depictions of casual sexism, societal collapse, and murder.

杞忧 / HEAVENS FALL

BY 陆秋槎 / LU QIUCHA

TRANSLATED BY 章皓 / HAL Y. ZHANG

Short Story Long List*

I t had been some time since Qu Qiukao's return to our home state of Qǐ. But I, occupied as I was by various trifling matters, had not yet found an opportunity to meet with him.

During this delay on my part, I began hearing rumors regarding this man. Several nobles had visited him in groups; after hearing the tales of his travels to various foreign states, they all found his words 'illogical and absurd—not the proper speech of a dignified gentleman.' It did not take long before descriptions of what he had seen and heard made their way to my ears. After many rounds of retelling, the contents of what he had said were surely jumbled and distorted, quite different from his original words. But one thing was clear: At present, he was wracked by anxiety, to the point of losing his appetite, over the notion that the heavens would fall and the earth would collapse.

It was about time that I met with this old friend of mine. I sent word to him, and we arranged for me to go to his manor on the twenty-eighth day of the heavenly cycle in the fourth month.

When I arrived for said visit, Qu Qiukao was sitting beneath that lush birchleaf pear tree in his courtyard. They say it had been planted by his ancestors when they had migrated eastward and settled here. Not many flower petals remained atop the branches, but the ground was replete, as if with a blanket of snow, and canaries flocked near, streaming melodies upon their perches. We were right in the most scenic time of the year, the very picture of harmonious nature from the *Book of Odes*, but alas, in his present state, Qu Qiukao was far too preoccupied to enjoy it. The sights of spring dimmed before my eyes at the thought of his worries.

Noticing my approach, Qu Qiukao ordered our places set and wine to be brought and served. We then sat right beneath the tree and began our chat.

It was evident that the hardships of his journey had left indelible marks upon his person. That face most familiar to me had become overrun with furrows, as suntanned and arid as plowed earth before the planting; his once-intense gaze, having lost its glow, was now flickering and uncertain, as if he wasn't looking at me but at a faraway place.

I still remember, clear as day, the sight of him two years prior as he had ascended the carriage to embark upon his grand travels—how confident and proud he had been then, and what grandiose boasts he had made. Those eyes had been brimming with ambition and ego, without the slightest hint of hesitation or fear. That boldness was nowhere to be seen, now. The figure before me was the living image of a cicada husk, and the Qu Qiukao I was familiar with had perhaps vanished on his journey.

A journey which he had undertaken to proselytize his treatises on war.

It all began in this very courtyard. He had voraciously devoured all the strategies and histories on wars from various lands, and on a large table of sand, he had reenacted battles of the past and present with his belt and hat to represent cities, and pebbles to model chariots and cavalry, calculating the outcomes of every possible path of action. After nearly two decades of labor, he had completed his seven volumes of stratagems, the subjects being the *Art of Campaigning, of Besieging, of*

Fortifications, of Logistics, of Pyrotechnics, of Topography, and *of Aeromancy,* for a total of eight-and-ten thousand characters.

And then he had copied his treatises most reverently upon wooden slips and presented them to our ruler, the lord of Qǐ. He had further presented a petition requesting adoption of his stratagems, promising that within three years, we would recover all of our territories lost to the eastern hordes, and within ten, we would build a great empire to which other principalities would bow their heads.

In the end, his petition had been rejected—not that this had been a surprising development. Though Qǐ's history could be traced back to the Yu the Great, the founder of the first dynasty and tamer of floods, it was now merely a tiny state adjoining where the states Qí and Lu meet. Generations of lords rested upon their holdings and ruled without ambition. This was no place for Qu Qiukao to spread his wings, nor had he been discouraged by his rejection, either, remarking only, "Birds know to choose their trees, and surely we cannot be less capable." This was when the idea of traveling to other states to propound his stratagems had germinated in his head.

Only at this recollection did I realize the huge sand table that had accompanied him for most of his life had also disappeared without a trace.

"Which lords did you meet, and did they take interest in your treatises?" I asked after a round of pleasantries.

"Treatises?" He shook his head, his expression vacant. "I burned them all. They are no longer of use."

"But twenty years of your hard work was spent on them. Even if the ruling lords don't adopt your strategies, they're more than enough to be passed onto future generations—why burn them?"

"You would not be saying this if you'd seen what engineering marvels the major states have developed," he said. "I only wish that I had never spent time writing that thick stack of treatises, and more so, that I never took them to tour the other states. In their eyes, I am only a most uncultured man, one who finds basking in the sun to be the epitome of human enjoyment and peas the most delicious delicacy on earth. I could have been satisfied with my own lot, but I just *had* to expose myself before those lords of worldly sophistication. In the end, I brought nothing but disgrace upon my person."

He heaved a long sigh at this, draining the wine in his jue in one go. I kept quiet and listened as he continued.

"We the people of Qí have been isolated from the outside world for too long. Even when we have the chance to visit the aristocrats of Qí and Lu, we care only for the cuisine and entertainment of our neighboring states, and not at all of their armaments and defenses. We do not even know how far we have fallen. I also once thought that military strategies are eternal axioms, immune to change no matter what instruments may be crafted by engineers. But as soon as I reached the Qí capital, I realized how utterly, horribly wrong I was.

"The Marquis of Qí was joining forces with the states of Lu, Song, Chen, and Cai to attack Wei. Eight years ago, two noblemen had revolted, ousting the Marquis of Wei to replace him with his brother. The Marquis of Qí aimed with this expedition to help the exiled marquis back atop his throne.

"I arrived at the perfect time, just as the Qí army was lined up before the wall of its capital city. The army banners weaved together in a tapestry, connected as far as the eye could see, and the dust billowed up to shroud the sun itself. At first, I was utterly awestruck by the show of military might from a major state, their war chariots numbering in the tens of thousands, but then I noticed that most of the infantry behind the chariots were not wearing armor, almost as if they were completely undressed. Puzzled, I focused my eyes on the peculiar sight, only to discover that those were not soldiers of flesh and blood, but humanoid figures carved from wood.

"Those wooden soldiers had either pikes in their hands or halberds upon their shoulders; they marched in unhurried unison, keeping pace behind the chariots. I could also spy no shortage of wooden figures in the rear supply line doing a number of odd jobs, drawing water and tending horses.

"The head of each wooden figure was as a wine cask, with a wide opening narrowing to a square base, and water was held inside. The joints of the shoulder, elbow, hips, and knees were all freely movable, like living humans, but the neck and ankle were dead wood. Each of the two shoulder blades had a hole in which a hemp rope was threaded, and the exposed ends of the rope drooped all the way to the waist. Various knots were tied on the ropes; with each step forward, a small section of the rope was fed into the left hole, and an equal length extruded from the right hole, such that the total length of the rope stayed constant. If you looked closely, you could see that drops of water occasionally leaked out from the soles of the figures, leaving rows of muddy footprints upon the earth.

"When I entered the city, I saw that the streets were also full of these automata. The Qí use them to cut firewood, husk grains, and transport goods. After settling in, I asked around to learn they were designed by a man named Bei Guoli from the state of Lu. They told me he had traveled throughout the western states in his youth to evade those who had quarrel with him. It was during that time when he serendipitously happened upon the treatises on the mechanical arts from the venerable puppet master who served King Mu of Zhou, and after forty-odd years of repeated experimentation, he had finally mastered this art of puppetry. He had crafted a troupe of wooden musicians and dancers and had presented them to the Marquis of Qí, who had been deeply appreciative of his efforts. The Marquis had not been satisfied by the performing arts, however, and had wanted Bei Guoli to apply his puppetry skills to the military and economic spheres, the results of which were the wooden automata I witnessed both within and without the city.

"Afterwards, I bribed a Qí noble for his connections so I could finally meet this Bei Guoli face-to-face.

"He was shrunken from old age, his left eye clouded over, and in place of two legs, he had four wheels beneath the knees, the movement of which he controlled using a wooden shaft. According to his own words, he had first presented a performing troupe of automata to the lord of Lu, but had then been accused of false crimes by a wicked liar and punished with having his feet cut off. Only after his exile to Qí had he been appreciated for his talents.

"There is another story out there regarding his disability. Some say he had been bribed by Pengsheng, a noble of the ruling family of Qí, to conceal a dagger inside one of the wooden figures he had presented to the Marquis of Lu, who had then been assassinated by said blade when he examined the figure up close. By then, Bei Guoli had already escaped to Qí; to placate Lu, the Qí had executed Pengsheng and severed Bei Guoli's feet. Others say that the real mastermind behind the assassination of the Marquis had been the lord of Qí himself. The Marquis of Qí's younger sister had been married to the Marquis of Lu, but she had frequently gone behind his back to have affairs with her own brother. After this came to light, the Marquis of Qí had used Bei Guoli's puppets to assassinate the Marquis of Lu. This story seemed plausible to me, as well.

"Bei Guoli was very confident in his own technology, to the point of being utterly unconcerned that I might steal his secrets, perhaps because he was unimpressed by people from Qí. I said I wished to see the inner workings of the automata; without reservations, he removed the wooden panel over the chest of a wooden entertainer who was playing music. Inside was perhaps as many as a hundred bronze cogwheels of various sizes: the smallest were no bigger than peas, while the largest were the size of an open palm. The teeth of these cogwheels interlocked perfectly with each other, and the entire system rotated continuously. Water from the head of the automaton flowed down and moved the smaller cogs, which in turn rotated the larger cogs, which then tugged and pushed on levers and strings that enabled the automaton to move in various ways. After flowing past the system of cogs, the water would eventually exit from the hole at the bottom of the feet.

"Then I asked him how he controlled the movements of the automata, and he answered that it was through the knots tied on the rope upon their backs, disassembling the wooden panel on the figure's back and pulling out the rope as he spoke. Although the cogwheels continued to spin, the figure was now immobile. He then installed a different rope, and the automaton, instead of performing music in a sitting position, now stood up and began dancing with its limbs.

"He explained further that complexity in the knots begets complexity in the movements of the automata. Skilled artisans must sew with their bone bodkins for days to create knots that enable wooden entertainers to strike drums, play zithers, juggle balls, and toss swords. In contrast, the ropes for mundane tasks have much simpler knots. You need only to calculate the steps and actions ahead of time for it to repeat the same work over and over, and for upkeep, simply refill the heads of your automata with well water from time to time.

"And the wooden soldiers employed in war are the simplest. Only two ropes are needed: one tied with knots solely for striding forward, used to march the army; the other rope intertwines the first set of commands with knots that waved their weapons for fighting. Unless blades or arrows pierce their bodies and damage their cogwheels, or the water in their heads is exhausted, these fighting automata will continue to advance without rest. Bodies of flesh and blood are no match for them."

"If the Qí had truly mastered this art, were they not peerless and invincible in war?" I asked.

"Quite the opposite, in fact. They were immediately defeated in that battle. The Zhou royal court had sent reinforcements led by Zitu to the state of Wei to fight the five-state alliance upon the plains. The Qí army had an absolute advantage in the first few bouts of battle, but it did not last. As winter approached and temperatures dropped, the water in the heads of the wooden soldiers froze to ice. Without the flow of water powering their actions, the automata could no longer move.

"Furthermore, the Wei came prepared against the Qí wooden army. Their engineers designed a pyrotechnic weapon: Its head was cast from bronze and in the form of the chi, the hornless dragon, and it spat fire from its mouth, hence the name Zhuchi, or 'chi candle.' Its body was an enormous wooden box that contained eight or so bellows sewn from leather hides and filled with grease. Several foot pedals extended from the rear of the box, where a person could stand, and four wheels were installed beneath.

"On the battlefield, the Zhuchi is maneuvered by two pushing from behind while another stands on top to helm its flames. The chi head can be turned using ropes, and when you want to spew fire, you simply step on the pedals, which causes the mechanism within the box to compress the bellows and spray grease from the mouth. The upper and lower jaws of the chi each has a flintstone that makes sparks upon contact. The grease, ignited by the sparks, will transform into a stream of flame as far as a person is tall. Countless wooden soldiers were burned to ashes by Zhuchi.

"After this defeat, improving the automata became an imperative. To combat the wintry cold, the newer generation of automata no longer used water as their source of power. Instead, two bovine tendons were installed in their heads and wound together using a spiral spring. The tendons slowly loosened, which moved the cogwheels and thereby the automata."

"But won't this be even more susceptible to the Zhuchi's flames?"

"Bei Guoli naturally had a solution to this, too. He devised a sort of Huanji, or 'soaking machine,' which used the watermill on the shore of the river to divert water into a huge bronze vessel, beneath which was a raisable platform. After drawing water, the watermill would be replaced with wheels that could transport it across the battlefield with ease. Against the Zhuchi, one would elevate the platform, lifting the vessel to about three or four person-heights, then open a valve, allowing the water inside to flow through a wooden tube and spray out of its opening to approximately as far as the vessel's height. The Zhuchi's range was far shorter than that, and they were useless against the Huanji. In spring, they rematched in a few furious battles, and this time, the Qí won handily."

"How extraordinary."

"Not the most extraordinary. After the Qí returned victorious, Bei Guoli hatched a new idea. He wanted to design a special type of automata that he named Yuanbao: yuan, here meaning 'origin,' and bao, here meaning 'embryo.' This invention would be self-replicating.

"According to his vision, these automata would be divided into two teams—the Yuan unit would be installed with ropes that bade them to chop wood, carve shapes, and assemble objects, while the Bao unit would gather vines, weave ropes, and tie knots. Yuan and Bao working together would realize the self-replication of these automata. All they needed to do was dispatch a group of Yuanbao, which would in turn rapidly create an entire army of wooden soldiers. If some of those

Yuanbao were given instructions to make new Yuanbao, it wouldn't be long before there were no trees left beneath the heavens, every piece of land barren save for their automata conquerors..."

"Well, there's no sign of wooden people here in Qí, so it would seem that his research is unsuccessful."

"He had not made much progress by the time I left Qí. But given his intellect, it's only a matter of time before the Yuanbao come into existence. We can only hope he doesn't live that long."

"And did you end up meeting with the Marquis of Qí?"

He shook his head.

"He sought to summon me, but I did not go. With a master engineer like Bei Guoli in their employ, I hardly think they have any use for my crude treatises. I soon left Qí to try my luck with the state of Jin, to the west. Before I left, I burned two volumes of my work, the *Art of Campaigning* and *of Pyrotechnics*. Such stratagems were utterly worthless before the automata, and the Huanji were better fed to the flames.

"When I passed by the state of Wei, I found the wooden figures of Qí to be everywhere. Though the Marquis of Wei had retaken the throne on paper, he was no better than the Qí's puppet ruler in reality. The automata deployed to Wei all had a special mechanism in them—as soon as anyone attempted to open their panels to divine the mysteries within, the entire figure would burst into flames. Thus the Wei did not understand its principles of operations, and could not manufacture copies of their own.

"Not long after I crossed the borders of Jin, I saw another awe-inspiring scene. In the plains, the skies yellow with flying dust, I could see the walls of a city through the haze. It was not particularly big, far smaller than the Qí capital, but nevertheless quite a bit larger than the Wei cities I had just passed. Its walls were towering and studded with a row of what seemed to be banners. But a city such as this was somehow moving to the north, away from me at a rapid clip.

"I did not know where my courage came from, but I ordered the carriage driver to speed up the horse in chase, but we could not shorten that distance no matter how we tried. We gave chase until sunset, until both men and beast were drained, when we finally gave up and found lodging at the local village. Only after some asking around did I learn that what I saw was a moving city, built by the Jin engineer Dong Chenglou for the noble Zhao Rang, and named Handan.

"A few merchants happened to be staying at the same place. They had just come from there a day prior and prepared to head for the state of Wei, so they told me all about Handan.

"It is like an enormous ship that sails on land. Those flags I saw were actually wind sails, and at the bottom of the city are installed a countless number of wheels. With the wind blowing upon the sails, the city can move to and fro. If there is a windless day, or if they wish to move opposing the direction of the wind, the leaders of the city will gather the residents of the city to row the oars installed upon the walls, which enables the wheels to turn as well. But this method expends great time and effort, so it is only employed in emergencies.

"They said also that because of the turbulent movements, the feeling of being in Handan is like riding in a tiny raft upon giant waves. The first days will be difficult—dizziness in the mild cases, endless vomiting for the severe—and a long time will pass before you can move about freely. And if you do become accustomed to the turbulence of Handan, you will feel ill at ease when you return to solid ground. There was once someone from Yan who lived in Handan for a few years, lost the ability to walk on land, and could only clamber back to Yan on hands and feet.

"After witnessing the moving city, I was dispossessed of my notion to seek an audience with the Marquis of Jin and tossed *Of Besieging* in the fire while I was at it—if the enemy's city is speeding away, too fast for you to catch, then there is nothing to lay siege to. Before the rolling wheels of Handan, my stratagems were but the proverbial mantis, attempting to block a vehicle but getting crushed to smithereens. After a night spent in distress, I decided to try my luck at the state of Qin."

"I hear the Qin have long intermixed with the Xirong to the west, such that their ways are different from us in the Central Plains—could they really comprehend your treatises?"

"The same thought occurred to me, as well. But the sights of this journey had taught me the truth—the Middle Kingdoms no longer have any use for my skills." Qu Qiukao heaved a long sigh. "And as it turned out, even the remote land of Qin had engineering marvels beyond our wildest imaginations."

"What did you see there?"

"This time, before I could even enter Qin territory, I would already witness their might within Jin's borders. Qí's automata were created at the order of their lord, and the moving city of Jin was at least built for a noble, but the marvels of Qin were by the hands of a widow. She designed it not at the behest of anyone but only for easing her own trade. It was already dusk when I arrived at the Qin-Jin borders, and I had planned to stay the night at Jin before crossing over to Qin in the morning. But it was at this time that I saw an entire caravan fly steadily across the sky toward me..."

"Fly?"

"Indeed. The sun was setting then, the boundary between earth and sky blurred by the clouds at dusk, and in the slight breeze, the caravan appeared out of nowhere above the mountain range to the west, steadily approaching until it flew over my head and disappeared to the east. Somehow, the local villagers did not find this remarkable sight to be even worth raising their heads as they tilled their land, so I asked them what had flown overhead, and they said, most nonchalantly, that it was the trade caravan of the widow of the Xiqi clan from the state of Qin.

"Apparently, to expedite the shipment of goods, the Xiqi widow invented the so-called Gouyunsuo, or 'cloud-hooking rope,' that could suspend carriages high in the clouds, rising and falling with them and drifting with the wind. Now her trade caravan can travel a thousand li in a day to trade between states, rapidly becoming an enterprise that rivaled entire states in wealth.

"O dastardly Fate! The heavens let me witness the wooden automata of Qí to bury my hopes, the moving city of Jin to renounce me. And now, the cloud-hooking rope of Qin—all is lost! All is lost!

"And so, there was no need for me to set foot in Qin. By next daybreak, I began my travel back to Qǐ, and in passing burned three more volumes. With the Gouyunsuo, provisioning the army was no longer a problem, and so the *Art of Logistics* was moot. Likewise with *of Topography*—hanging your chariots from the clouds rendered terrain-based formations obsolete. As for *of Aeromancy*, my art of predicting the weather was surely inferior to Xiqi's mastery over the wind and clouds. By now, of the seven volumes, only *of Fortifications* remained."

At this, he filled his jue with wine, but did not drink it.

"Before my visit, I had heard some things about you," I said. "They're all saying you're worried the heavens will fall and the earth will collapse, to the point of not eating or sleeping. Is there truth to this?"

"Indeed." He nodded. "If you knew what I had witnessed in the state of Chu, you would not think of these troubles as creations of my own imagination."

"You traveled to Chu, too?"

"I had not planned on it. On the way home, I happened to encounter a caravan from Jin that was going south to Chu. I had a good chat with the head merchant. After hearing of my situation, he said the King of Chu was searching for talents the world over for his great enterprise and suggested that I try my luck there. I only thought dismissively of 'the Jing hordes,' as the *Book of Odes* called the Chu; surely, they could not have any technology more advanced than us here in Qí. And so I followed him there.

"But this would become the worst decision of my life. If only I had headed straight for home instead—I would still feel a tremendous sense of failure from my travels, but I would not be wracked with anxiety as I am now."

At this, he blew out a long breath, and only after a moment of silence, during which he drained his wine vessel, did he continue.

"Our travels passed through several small states on the north bank of the Han River, those so-called Ji states of Hanyang. When the Zhou royals bequeathed those nobles of the Ji family land there, they had intended for them to form something of a barrier against the southern hordes. But alas, these small and weak states are being swallowed by the Chu bit by bit, and it's only a matter of time before the Zhou themselves fall under threat. Not that the states of the Central Plains are faring any better, as we all sit with our hands tied and watch Chu's burgeoning rise.

"The King of Chu had just conquered the state of Shen when we reached the state of Deng, wedged between Chu and Shen, so we happened upon the Chu army's victorious return. Serendipitously, I was able to meet the King of Chu immediately."

The way he called that man 'king' pierced my ears. The royal house of Zhou had given the lord of Chu the rank of viscount, but now the Viscount of Chu found fit to give himself a higher title that not only disrespected the royals but demonstrated their contempt for us states of the Central Plains. Though Qiu Qukao still referred to the Chu as the Jing hordes, he seemed to have no disrespect in his tone or words for the so-called King of Chu when he spoke of that man. Perhaps it was because the viscount gave him such a positive impression, or perhaps he saw something worthy of his respect and admiration in those lands.

"The King of Chu looked to be quite young, thirty years of age at most, and his appearance and speech were no different from the lords of the Central Plains. When he heard that I hailed from Qi, he asked after our history, our customs, and where exactly I resided, and then asked me several questions regarding the art of besieging. Though I had already burned that volume, it was no hardship for me to recall bits of it here and there, and so I answered his questions one by one. After hearing my answers, he made no expression or reply, and only took me to see their siege weapon, named Jingshi."

"Jingshi?"

"Jing, referring to Chu, and shi, here meaning 'lord.' From this name alone, their unbridled ambition for ruling the Central Plains was evident. The Jingshi was built by the previous lord of Chu, the king titled Wu for his martial prowess, in order to attack the state of Sui, which he had tried to conquer thrice in his life. The Sui had thick fortifications and were adept at forging weapons of war, twice inflicting great defeats upon the Chu army. King Wu was over seventy in the last siege and died en route. On his deathbed, he ordered the master craftsman Nanmen Wutu to create the Jingshi. This weapon gave wings to the already fierce beast that was the Chu, and they conquered Sui in one go.

"It is like a giant wooden wheel, all askew and as tall as two men, with countless bronze shovels installed atop and a dozen or so ropes attached. With strong laborers pulling the ropes, the wheel turns and can dig into the earth. To operate it, one would first dig a vertical shaft, then lower the Jingshi into it, pulling the ropes to turn the giant wheel and excavate in the forward direction. It seems to be quite slow at first, but if you command work to commence without rest, you can dig a tunnel a few li in length in a matter of days. There is furthermore a bronze ring, tied to a thick rope and installed at the center of the wheel, on which hung a row of bamboo baskets that were used to transport the soil outward. The people of Chu used this Jingshi to dig a tunnel, bypassing the city walls between Sui and Shen.

"By now I understood why the King of Chu wanted to take me to see the Jingshi. It was his wordless mockery of me, of those of us who see the Central Plains as our birthright. Only the *Art of Fortifications* remained from my treatises, and its tactics were utterly useless in the face of the Chu's superior instruments. At this thought, I burned it too, all of it— these twenty years of toil have all been for naught, in the end: nothing but an exercise in humiliation!

"I had planned to return to Qǐ, but the King of Chu bade me stay. To be honest, I could not divine whether he was keeping me as a guest or a hostage. I went with them to Ying, the new capital of Chu. Even the palace there still had simple unadorned thatched roofs, and the dwellings of the common people were even more crude. It was not long after that a shocking event rocked the entire state.

"There is a noble in Chu by the name of Yu Quan, famous for his blunt honesty before his lord. Seeing how the Jingshi was effective in the conquests of Sui and Shen, he proposed building a great underground passage, reaching the capital of each state, that would be thousands of li in length. Upon completion, any country that dared to make the Chu its enemy would see its capital collapsed underground and reduced to rubble at a single command from the king. The king did not plan on enacting this most costly proposal, and Yu Quan somehow unsheathed his sword in court and placed it upon the king's neck, forcing him to give the orders for its construction. Afterwards, for the offense of threatening his lord, he cut off one of his own feet..."

It seemed that Qu Qiukao's worry that the earth would collapse was because of this great underground passage.

"Chu and Qǐ are thousands of li apart—can they really dig a tunnel all the way to here?"

"It's only a matter of time," he said. "But this is far from the most terrifying of their plans. Nanmen Wutu conceived of something even more destructive. His Jingshi only caves the earth in, but this new invention can make the heavens tumble down and destroy whatever lies beneath."

"I hear what we call the heavens is but an amalgamation of gaseous substances. The sun, the moon, and the stars merely give off light within that gas. Even if the sky were to fall, it should not cause physical harm."

"No, not so. I went with the King of Chu to his royal villa at Yunmeng, where I saw a most complex machine that revealed the true nature of the universe. It was an armillary sphere cast from the finest metal from the south that could model the movements of the earth and the celestial orbs. The Chu called it the Choujueyi, or 'the instrument that senses the heavens and earth.'

"The Choujueyi appears to be a bronze orb, about six to seven handspans in width. The orb has many holes on its surface and can be spun and opened, and there are two smaller orbs inlaid on the inner wall. Inside the main body, there is a bronze board as thick as the span of two fingers laid flat, on which was carved mountains and waters. And this was precisely the structure of the universe—the outer orb is the firmament, the board the earth on which we live, and the smaller orbs represent the sun and moon. The firmament rotates about the earth as the sun and moon move on its inner surface; these two orbs have their own light, while more light emanates from beyond the firmament and reaches us through the holes on its surface—those are the stars. Observing this instrument made me realize that the ancients already knew the mysteries of the universe. As was written in the *Book of Odes* of the founder of the Shang dynasty, 'Orbs large and small conferred, the vassal states thus adorned, anointed by the Heavens.' It was referring to precisely this: the small orbs are the sun and moon, and the large orb the firmament. "

"Even if the universe is structured as you describe it, how would the Chu induce the heavens to fall?"

"It's simple: just fire a huge arrow that pierces the firmament. The heavenly dome will break, and its pieces will plunge and become the most lethal weaponry in the world. Exterminating entire cities and states can be done with one wave of the hand."

"But is it really possible to shoot such an arrow?"

"I did not see this with my own eyes, but the Chu did prepare a bow and arrow just for this called the Guantianshi, or 'sky-piercing arrow,' and the Yunmengji.

"As the name implies, Yunmengji is a machine installed at Yunmeng, by the lake. This is quite possibly the largest weapon in the world. The Chu first had to build two towers of stone a hundred handspans tall and several li apart. They then constructed an earthen wall the height of ten persons, half as thick as it is tall, that extends from the towers to the apex of the hill, where the two ends meet. The wall acts as the bow and the towers as the nocks at its ends; they then stewed the tissues of deers, horses, cattle, rodents, fish, and rhinoceros from their autumn hunt to join bovine and deer sinew, weighing hundreds of shi, as well as silk and hemp, into a bowstring six handspans wide and several li in length, the two ends of which are inlaid into the towers. Thousands of horses are needed to pull this bow.

"As for the sky-piercing arrow, it is made from felling hundreds of ancient, sky-high trees, then joining them with mortise and tenon in a process that takes months. Once the command is given, they will mount the arrow upon the wall and launch it with the bowstring at the firmament, piercing it such that the fragments rain down upon enemy nations.

"According to Nanmen Wutu's design, this machinery is best used at nighttime. When aimed at a constellation, it will hit a corresponding target upon the earth, which can be calculated using the Choujueyi.

"On the way back to the capital, the king summoned me once more. He said I no longer needed to remain at Chu, and he stressed that I could freely disclose the Jingshi and Yunmengji to the people of the Middle Kingdoms. He likely wanted me to broadcast his might in order to induce shock and awe across the Central Plains. And so, I went with a trade caravan heading for Qi up north and found my way back to Qi. I had embarked on my journey with an entire case of treatises and returned with only an empty box and a heart full of worries."

Now that he had detailed all that he had seen and heard on his journey, he fell silent for a long time.

I did not completely believe his words, but I could not find any obvious flaws, either. His anxieties were not merely centered around the potential destruction of the heavens and earth, but more so lamenting our ignorant complacency that may lead to our tiny state being swallowed up by these huge, hungry nations. To this, I could only console him with the notion that some things cannot be prevented no matter what we do—you may as well enjoy life while it lasts, instead of wallowing in anxiety for all your days.

Hearing my words, he nodded thoughtfully, but his brows remained furrowed, his eyes still focused on some faraway place.

Later, we drank to our heart's content until sunset. Before I took my leave, Qu Qiukao struck his staff in rhythm and chanted an ode to its percussion:

"O mighty realm that Yu the Great did raise,

A hundred ages, noble bloodlines tall.

Ever weaker in a heedless daze,

Earth shall sunder, Heavens fall."

I did not know then that this was to be my last sight of him.

That night, strange celestial phenomena appeared in the southwesterly sky. The stars were all outshone by a blazing streak of white, which then dimmed quickly, eventually vanishing only to be followed by a shower of meteors raining down. There was a thunderous roar, and then the meteors all plummeted, and an ensuing earthly inferno swallowed the stars that had just reappeared in the sky once more.

Looking at the conflagration on the horizon, I saw it was precisely in the direction of Qu Qiukao's manor.

The fire burned for three full days. The manor, as well as the adjoining village, was burned to ash that crumbled at a single touch. The ground was sunken into a cavernous rift that could entomb hundreds of carriages. My friends and I searched for Qu Qiukao's body, but we found only black pieces of metal, perhaps fragments of the firmament.

His worst fears had come to pass, after all.

———

TRANSLATOR'S NOTE:

The setting for this story is the Spring and Autumn period (approximately 770-480 BCE) of ancient China, an era of rapid social and technological change when many high-ranked aristocrats, bequeathed noble titles and land by the weakened royal house of the Eastern Zhou dynasty, declared themselves the rightful ruler and vied for dominance in the Central Plains and beyond, eventually ending in the state of Qin annexing other states and becoming the first imperial Chinese dynasty. It reimagines the famous parable of the person from the small state of Qǐ who could not stop worrying that the sky would fall down (杞人忧天, from which the original title of the story derives).

Many references in the story are rooted in history and legend. The legendary puppet master that served King Mu of Zhou was recorded in a colorful anecdote in the Daoist classic *Liezi*, written around the 4th century CE, that described these humanoid figures made of wood and leather that could sing and dance. Ma Jun, famed inventor of a chariot in the 3rd century CE that always pointed south through a system of what was most likely differential gears, was also recorded as having created entertainers made of wood and powered by water that turned gears. Major battles and historical events mentioned in the story are generally believed to have taken place; Yu Quan did force the King of Chu to listen to his advice at swordpoint and later severed his own foot; that the ruler of Qí assassinated the ruler of Lu once the latter discovered the incestuous affair between his wife and the former is recorded in the *Zuo Zhuan*. The *Zuo Zhuan* also states that King Wu of Chu did or had the Jingshi (荆尸), but its meaning is a subject of debate between historians to this day. The real city of Handan, in modern-day Hebei province, is a source of many legends, including a story from Zhuangzi about a youth who tried to learn the uniquely fashionable walk of the locals, failed, and forgot how to walk in the process, crawling back home in the end (邯郸学步).

LU QIUCHA (陆秋槎) is known as a writer of detective mysteries in China and Japan. His newest work is *Mourning Becomes Eurydice*. His science fiction collection, *Gernsback Transform and Other Stories*, was published in Japanese.

HAL Y. ZHANG (章皓) splits her time between the east coast of the United States and the Internet. Her language-and-loss chapbook *AMNESIA* was published by Newfound and won the Eric Hoffer Micro Press Award. She is online at halyzhang.com.

* CONTENT NOTES: references to war, events causing mass destruction, murder, incest, and loss of limb.

COME IN, CHILDREN

BY AI JIANG

Astounding Award Long List*

Yejin rubbed her eyes. A cyst was growing at the edge of her right lid. She didn't have to feel this terrible, but ever since she'd stopped draining the youth of lost children who wandered into the forest, the wrinkles had settled in, her brown hair had become streaked with grey, and her teeth had become brittle, sensitive to brews both too hot and too cold. She hated lukewarm tree-sap water, but it would have to do.

When a knock on her door came, Yejin fumbled for her glasses on the nightstand next to her bed. The old crow that lived in the large oak with its branches draped over her mushroom-shaped house hadn't yet called. It was far too early for the beginning of her business hours.

The rapping against her creaking wooden door quickened—staccato and urgent. But Yejin's movements remained slow, steady, and calm, as though she were in a trance. At least it wasn't a *smart* phone. Technology —she could never understand the appeal. The quietness of the forest was much more desirable than the roar of the city. She refused to use the

Internet, though she snuck into the city every decade or so just to peek at the state of the world—more often than not, it was a mistake. People were foolish, brutish, shortsighted, and utterly helpless on their own, but she had renounced the world and did not intend to return, no matter how clearly they required her services. They'd have to come seek her out for it, and there would be a price—there always is.

Yejin slipped her feet into the wool slippers she'd made last winter. It had only been two seasons, but they were already scruffy. She loathed having to trudge to the city for more yarn. When she had been young, she had hunted the deer of the forest and made her clothing from their hides. Sometimes she found joy in making the deer forget, pause, so she could pounce while they were confused, but it seemed rather depressing now—a blank stare, a blank mind, confusion before death. Sometimes it wasn't deer...

The rapping, having paused only for a breath, resumed.

• • • •

"I'm coming," Yejin muttered under her breath, knowing her brittle voice wouldn't carry down the stairs and through the doors anyhow. She'd have to renovate the house to get rid of the stairs soon, at the rate her centuries were catching up to her. It took ages to walk up and down.

Yejin grabbed her cane and took sideways steps down the stairs.

The clacking of her cane echoed in her ear. Instead of opening the door, she first cleared her throat, then flipped the sign next to the window so it showed 'Open' in gothic script. Only when the sign stopped clattering against the glass of the window pane did she grasp the bronze doorknob, shaped like a shrivelled head, and twisted.

On the other side of the door stood a man in a pressed suit with the tie windblown. Sweat had soaked through his white shirt at the armpits, dampening the navy fabric of his suit jacket. His leather dress shoes were speckled with mud and grass.

"You are Yejin?" he asked.

Yejin nodded. "Yes."

Before the man spoke another word, Yejin waved him inside, leading him to the kitchen without sparing another glance. She settled down at the dining table in the middle of the kitchen; only one other chair remained empty across from her. The man took the seat, pulling out an embroidered handkerchief to dab at his neck, his veins bulging beneath glistening sweat.

Yejin wasted no time. "What do you want erased?" She wiped fog from her glasses.

"My father," he answered, the handkerchief now soiled, clutched between nails that were in desperate need of trimming.

"Not just a single memory? His entire existence in your life?" Yejin's brow rose.

"Yes. Please." The desperation in the man's voice dissipated her hesitance. Memory charms were difficult; and the mind will attempt to hold on to most impactful experiences and recollections with greater urgency. But this one would pay the steep price, and swiftly, by the sound of it.

Yejin hummed then nodded. "There will be a hefty price. Do you understand? And you may feel an emptiness where the memory used to be and confusion if you attempt to recollect what was erased. Sometimes you might feel lost and wonder why you desire that which you never had, but the pain will help you grow past it."

He nodded. "And the payment?"

"Five years of your life. And all memory of me." For a being with less power, it would have been a discount price, but Yejin was a refined master of the art of memory manipulation, and she did feel momentary compassion for the sweaty oaf. The second part of the agreement was more of a guarantee that he would not come looking for Yejin again when the side effects knocked on his door.

His hands clenched into fists cradled in his lap, fingers still fiddling with the handkerchief, fraying its edges. "All right."

Yejin's gaze lingered on the man's balding head before she picked up her cane and headed towards the cupboards.

From the highest cupboard, Yejin removed a jar of aged scrolls, on the verge of moulding. She unscrewed the lid and handed the man ink-marked parchment.

"Take this with you and follow the instructions exactly." The instructions were from her great-grandmother's period, and Yejin had yet to update them, but it should be simple enough. People never really changed, even as they continued inventing new ways to make loud noises and flashing lights. "Rid your home of all images of your father. Your family and relatives will still remember him, unfortunately, so you may need to ensure they don't mention him around you, or you may get confused and attempt recollection. Perhaps best to avoid them as well."

The man nodded.

"When you've followed all the instructions, return here, and bring the scroll. I'll take half of the payment now and the other half when the charm is complete," Yejin said.

The man looked as though he wanted to argue but thought better of it. Yejin placed both of her hands on top of the table, palms facing upwards, and beckoned the man to place his hands in hers. As soon as their flesh connected, she felt energy draining from his body, entering through her fingertips, and running through her veins at the same time as his spasmed, squirmed like worms in boiling water. The man's head snapped back, gurgling with his mouth stretched wide in a silent wail. His legs trembled, an earthquake shaking through him, yet his feet stayed planted on the floorboards. Yejin cackled, marvelling at the whites of the man's eyes, slivers of red crawling up, up, up, looking as though they may burst. Her customer was suffering, experiencing a taste of momentary death, but Yejin felt alive.

Five years from this worn-out carcass of a man was nothing, like a single sip of cold tea, compared to the burning, sweet youth of lost children. But she had sworn off children when her youngest sister had left to have her own with a mortal man. Not that Keyi had ever appreciated Yejin's sacrifices and had left Yejin's heartfelt advice lingering in the air with covered ears. Why did Keyi *insist* on nurturing a child in her own womb when she could simply keep one of the children who wandered into the woods? *Their* woods. Now it was only Yejin's alone. So much power Keyi had given up. Such a pity, the fool. She'd learn the folly of her ways soon enough. To be enticed by a mere mortal man. What was she thinking? She wasn't, surely. And the *live* children, one's *own* children, those uncontrolled things, were a headache and a trial at best. Must Keyi be so blind when her elder sister was trying to help her see?

An assertive knock on the door jostled both Yejin and the man from their strange, brief moment of intimacy. The man's pupils were again in sight, though they lolled side to side, unfocused, eyelids shuddering. With the payment transferred, a few more age lines appeared on the man's face, and a few of Yejin's receded. The man withdrew his hands, closing his fingers instead around the scroll in front of him. Yejin paused —two customers within a week was nearly a flood, but in a single day? That was unheard of—at least since the 1800s. And this knock was no timid, hapless seeker of curses or erasures...

"Sister," came the voice on the other side of the front door.

Yejin's lips drew in on themselves, forming a thin line. Webbed wrinkles crawled up the sides of her mouth, spreading across the entirety of her face and blending with the purple and green veins beneath the translucent, papery skin of her neck.

Neither Yejin nor the man had closed the door, so she could see her sister's figure lingering by the opening from where she sat in the kitchen.

"Keyi," Yejin said.

"I told you—it's Penny," Keyi said as she pushed inside and past her elder sister. She was still in her thirties—her actual third decade. Draining youth was still an unnecessary thing for Keyi, and she insisted she never would, though Yejin knew her sister would change her mind once the end of her mortal lifespan approached. Keyi would feel far worse than Yejin did now. The centuries between the generations the sisters were born in had caused more of a gap than their mother had expected—not that the ancient sorceress had cared much before she'd perished.

"My apologies, *Penny*." Yejin could taste the copper in her mouth. She liked her sister's birth name better, but there was no sense in starting that argument again.

Yejin stood, leaving the man, who had taken an interest in skimming the instructions. "What brings you here?" She looked past her sister at the trees that swallowed what would have been a view of the city behind them. The forest would have been swallowed by the expanding edge of civilization if not for Yejin's persistent efforts, though that had drastically reduced her number of customers.

Keyi narrowed her eyes and crossed her arms, fingers curling into fists at the end of her elbows. She'd lost weight. "My husband? You took away my husband."

Yejin cursed under her breath but bent her face into a disarming smile, flashing the gap of her missing front tooth in hopes her sister might realize what she would become by straying away from draining children's youth. "Would you like to come in and have some tea first? It'll only be a second. I can get the pot going now." Yejin took a slight turn towards the kitchen and tapped her cane against the wooden floor.

For a moment, Keyi's anger seemed to dissipate as her arms fell slack by her sides. Her eyes roamed Yejin's face, no doubt noticing the age. The last time Keyi had seen Yejin was a decade ago, when she'd first left the cottage, their shared home, back when she had first met the man who would become her husband. But back then, Yejin had still looked to be in her early forties; now maybe it was somewhere closer to seventy, or so mortal age went.

There was a squeak as a chair slid back from the kitchen table. "I should—" the man began.

"Yes," both women replied simultaneously.

"In three days," Yejin said as the man straightened his tie and rushed to leave.

"Looks like business is still booming, huh?" Keyi sneered, wrinkling her nose as she took the spot the man had vacated.

Yejin pulled out a rusting kettle and lit a fire under it. "You'll feel much better with some proper tea. Better than human food," Yejin drawled, despite the lingering flavour of sap on her lips.

"That's only because you haven't tasted the restaurants in the city yet." Keyi rolled her eyes.

"No need."

There was a brief silence.

"My husband." Keyi repeated the words she'd said when she'd first entered the house, scraping her nails against the chipped oak table. The wood flakes loosened and embedded themselves into Keyi's finger, but she took no notice. "You erased him."

"Yes, but you requested it. Don't you remember?" Yejin kept her expression neutral, but her heart pounded within her. Would her sister catch the blatant lie? "You'd said you'd finally grown tired of him. He wasn't so great after all. It's just as I have always said—"

Keyi laughed, high-pitched and slightly deranged. She tossed her head back, arching her spine, resembling the man earlier. "I requested it? We both know that's impossible. You wanted it." Keyi's expression darkened as she looked at Yejin, baring her teeth.

Yejin had once thought her sister would grow out of her chaotic teenage years, but the wildness within her, though tempered by age, sometimes slipped momentarily, causing dark episodes.

Yejin abandoned her lie. "You belong here, with me."

The kettle screeched as the water came to a boil. The scent of metal and steam filled the air, almost like sizzling blood.

"Why did all our other sisters leave then?" Keyi prodded.

Yejin did not reply as she put out the flame beneath the kettle. She settled back in the seat across from her sister after filling two deer-skull mugs with steaming oak-root tea. She slid the cracked one across the table, keeping the good one for herself.

"I just want to be happy, Yejin. Not that you ever knew, or will know, what that means." Keyi spat in the tea then left it untouched, glaring in disgust at the whittled skull by her hands. "Where did you hide his photos?"

"How did you remember him?" Yejin asked, knuckles turning white as she gripped her mug, the heat singeing her skin.

Keyi pulled out a phone—the lock screen displayed an image of her and her husband arm-in-arm. "Just because you broke the old one doesn't mean all the data is lost. But you wouldn't know that, having been out here for so long."

"So you're back together, then?" Yejin asked, attempting to be nonchalant.

Keyi's face twisted, and she turned to the side. "He's dead."

Yejin's nail dug into her mug until a crack appeared, until it grew, steaming liquid leaking onto the table, through its crevices, cooking her flesh. She raised the mug, allowing the tea to roll down her arms, leaving angry red welts. Behind the skull, she tried to conceal her grin.

"How?" she asked, standing up. "I didn't recognize him when he came into the house so I hit him over the head. A little too hard, it seems."

Keyi seemed too calm, but Yejin only thought of how to keep her sister from imprisonment.

"Perfect! You can hide here," Yejin said, but Keyi shook her head.

"I need to get rid of the body first, and I'll need your help."

Yejin's blood chilled at the thought of going into the city. All the vehicles and the unnatural sounds. But her sister, she had to help her sister. Keyi finally understood where she belonged. She was coming home. Yejin found herself nodding.

• • • •

Yejin failed to notice the clear exterior differences between her and Keyi until they stood at the edge of the forest: where Keyi donned a peach cashmere sweater and jeans, Yejin wore a long plain grey dress with a brown cloak drawn overtop. Yejin looked over her shoulder but could not catch a glimpse of her home—the shrivelled mushroom top on the verge of collapse but never actually collapsing, the withered flowers that were very much living, and the gates made up of the skulls of both humans and animals. The city was full of life. Death comforted her.

By the road that passed closest to the edge of the forest, Keyi had parked her small blue car. Yejin eyed it with caution as her sister hopped into the front.

"Would you rather walk instead?" Keyi huffed in impatience.

"I could conjure us the legs of the crow for the stretch of our journey?"

Keyi frowned. "We're not doing that."

A low grumble left Yejin's lips as she climbed into the passenger side. She shuddered along with the engine as it started.

Before they arrived at Keyi's house—only half an hour away—Yejin had thrown up a handful of times. Sometimes on the side of the road if Keyi pulled over in time, but more often it was on Yejin's wool shoes. By the time they reached Keyi's condo, the entire car smelt of oak-root tea.

• • • •

Yejin covered her ears as they headed into the condo. The sound of a train running against its tracks boomed far too close to where the sisters stood. A car rolled past the front of the building, blaring its horn for what felt like the entirety of the Middle Ages. In the visitor's parking lot, a car alarm went off. Even the sound of chirping birds along the humming power lines annoyed Yejin—a sound that would usually be calming in the forest.

It was noisier than Yejin remembered it being when she had snuck into Keyi's apartment the first time to get rid of traces of her husband. It had been a futile attempt, but she had had to try anyhow. Her sister felt more distant with each passing year, and she hadn't realized the disillusionment of humanity quick enough for Yejin's liking. Yejin was growing tired of feeding on the stale years of overstressed and anxious businessmen and women, or young adults going through an existential crisis, and avoiding the lost children who still stumbled upon her house every year. She *needed* a proper *meal*, but she couldn't risk harming one of her own nieces or nephews, assuming Keyi produced one or several.

When Keyi opened the front door, Yejin spotted a puddle of blood that looked too bright, soaked into an off-white faux-fur carpet. In the middle of the pool sat a small wind-up duck, blood splattered around it. From the corner of her eye, Yejin noticed a shadow darting towards her. It wasn't until her hands were bound behind her, when her cane had clattered onto the floor, that she realized it was Keyi's husband, Hunner—alive.

"Goodbye, sister," Keyi smiled and clenched Yejin's hand in her own, causing a protesting screech to escape her elder sister's throat.

"Keyi—!"

"My name," she said, "is *Penny*."

Keyi's nails, like a crow's claws, drew blood from Yejin's wrinkle-webbed palms. Yejin's eyes rolled back, back arched, and convulsed against the cage Hunner created around her with his arms.

• • • •

Yejin's eyes refocused. There was oak-root tea in a deer-skull mug on her nightstand. She didn't remember brewing it. She took a sip. It was cold. A small cloud of strange froth floated on the golden-brown liquid's surface. The tea leaves at the bottom stirred, fluttering, as she placed the mug down.

There was a knock on the door.

Yejin moved to stand, wondering who it could be when her business hours hadn't yet begun. But she noticed an odd glow outside the window: the sun was setting rather than rising. A panic rose within her as she took unsteady steps, her joints feeling stiffer than they had the day before. She stumbled forth, swaying. A jolt shot through her hips. Her eyes widened at her aged hands—ancient compared to the youth she remembered she had from what felt like only minutes before. Never had her lips felt so dried, cracked. A burning thirst ravaged her from within. How long had it been since she tasted the rejuvenating taste of youth?

What had happened the day before? There was a man—the one who had wanted to forget this father. But that couldn't possibly be all she had done that day?

"Excuse me!" came the voice of a woman.

Yejin hobbled towards the door. The 'Closed' sign was already flipped to 'Open.'

"Yes, yes—"

She stared as though someone might materialize if she looked hard enough, but no one was there. On the doormat outside the entrance lay a rolled up scroll. But unlike her moulding parchments, the material of this paper was bone white, except for where it met the dirt that had collected on the mat. There were no instructions within; only a small completion symbol sat in its center.

Who did it belong to? Perhaps one of her sisters who might have passed through? No matter. She was far too tired to deal with this. It was intolerable, being weak and elderly.

Her fingers brushed across the smooth, unnatural surface of the parchment. It was better to burn it than to leave it lying around. If another sorceress tampered with it, who knew what chaos they'd brew up.

Yejin shuffled toward the kitchen after taking one last look around her home, narrowing her eyes at the trees. After starting a fire for her dreadful sap tea, she fed the flames with the scroll, watching the white sheet curl and turn into ashes beneath her kettle. The fog she'd woken up with earlier began to settle as the remainder of the scroll left her fingertips.

When the kettle screamed for attention, there was another knock on her door. The man.

Yejin sighed. Why was everyone so keen to forget those bound to them by blood?

. . . .

Yejin flipped the 'Open' sign so it showed 'Closed' and waited until the clattering of the wooden sign against the glass stopped before she left the window side.

"Mama?"

Outside, a young child wandered in the forest—lost. A lucky day for Yejin. She prodded her legs with her cane. How long had it been since the last child? She furrowed her brow. Why had she stopped?

Yejin made her way out of her cottage as the child neared her gates, seeming unfazed by the skull and bones that made up its entirety.

"Mama?" the child asked, frowning. "Who are you?"

The child had a face like someone Yejin should know but could not remember. But maybe if she kept the child, just for a while, and stared hard enough, she would recall the person she had forgotten.

She had told someone it was all right to take these lost children into her home for as long as they wished, hadn't she?

The fog rose again like a veil in her mind. It required energy Yejin didn't have to draw back its curtain. Perhaps she would have the power after she was done with the child... She nodded, refocusing on the child who stood with sharp clarity in front of her—an entity of endless youth.

Yejin smiled, feeling wind chill the flesh around the gap between two teeth. When did that appear? It would be gone soon, anyhow. "It's quite cold outside. Would you like to come in and have some tea first? It'll only be a second, and then we could go search for your Mama together."

Surely the child wouldn't catch her blatant lie, would she?

AI JIANG is a Chinese-Canadian writer from Changle, Fujian, currently residing in Toronto, Ontario. She is an Ignyte, Bram Stoker, and Nebula Award winner, and a Hugo, Astounding, Locus, Aurora, and BFSA Award finalist. Her work can be found in *The Magazine of Fantasy & Science Fiction*, *The Dark Magazine*, and *The Masters Review*, among others. She is the recipient of the Odyssey Workshop's 2022 Fresh Voices Scholarship and the author of *Linghun* and *I AM AI*. The first book of her novella duology, *A Palace Near the Wind*, is forthcoming in 2025 from Titan Books. Find her on X (@AiJiang_), Instagram (@ai.jian.g), and her website (http://aijiang.ca).

* CONTENT NOTES: references to harm to children and spousal murder.

YUNG LICH AND THE DANCE OF DEATH

BY ALEX FOX

Semiprozine Long List (PodCastle)

My Christian name was Thomas Kanfor but ever since that bastard wizard rose me from the grave I go by Yung Lich. On that moonless night he spoke some words from a tattered grimoire over my naked, somewhat-recently-dead corpse and voila, here I am. He called me a 'Young Lich.' When you're newly risen you don't remember much else (other than the maggots), so I took that as my new name. I changed 'Young' to 'Yung' because I think it reads a bit fresher, and when you're trying to break into the hip-hop scene, you gotta be fresh (though my body is not).

People can't tell I'm dead unless I remove the mask. They think it's part of my act. I stand outside of Times Square with my whole getup— long black hooded cloak, a ghastly off-brand Scream mask, an old gnarled branch. I lean and spookily sway and try to hand out my mixtapes. I mean, shoot. If there's one cool thing about being given a second chance it's that you know what's important and what's not. I never had the gall to pursue a career in music while living. Nah.

Wouldn't pay the bills, wouldn't make my mom proud. But now? I'm free to be me...

"Want my mixtape?" I wheeze in my dry-as-sawdust voice to a small group waiting for the crosswalk. I extend a robed arm, a white CD in my hand. Across the front is the Sharpie-scrawled label *Yung Lich—The Dance of Death.* They hardly look my way, and don't seem to appreciate my pestering.

A man shoves my arm aside and fingers an earbud out of his ear. "Ain't no one got CD players anymore, pal. Try Soundcloud."

The crosswalk changes and the folk quickly scramble across the street. My arm falls, dejected. Even though in this 'life' I can pursue my true interests, that doesn't mean anyone is interested in what I have to say. Been standing here for weeks on end and only four people have taken my mixtape, and I think only to be nice, as I saw two of them toss the CDs in the garbage once they crossed.

And what that man said rings true: Not that many people have CD players these days. Guess I'm slow to accept change, but I know I need to adapt if I want to get my music out there. I've got an old laptop. I can look into Soundcloud—it's something to go on, at least.

I gather my things and hobble to the Corner Café. They know me there. They let me use the Wi-Fi even though I never buy coffee. I don't need to eat or drink much, or at all, really—tends to leak out of my swiss-cheesed stomach.

A few people idle in the café, and they look up as I open the glass door, a small bell tinkering to announce my arrival. I keep my head down, my hands well within my long sleeves, even as I hold the obnoxiously tall wooden staff. The staff double-bangs the bell as I amble through, loud as a cymbal crash, and I shrink into myself.

"Sorry, sorry," I mutter. Wooden chairs creak as the patrons turn to watch me, this weirdo in the horror getup. I try not to pay attention to them. I mosey on to my usual corner, sit, and pull out my laptop. Soon I'm forgotten, like all the other freaks of the city.

On my laptop screen glows a text file with the lyrics of my finest work, "The Dance of Death." I read it once, twice.

I tap the bottom of my plastic mask. Reading doesn't do it justice. These verses contain my story, my pain; my short, undead life. The beat is an old tinny snare drum, simple yet catchy. A percussive bassline comes in, and it's simply intoxicating the way it punctuates the beat. I'm not sure if it's my ego but whenever I listen to the song, I go into a trance-like state, and want to dance, and the beat stays with me long after the song ends. I must be a musical genius. Shame it took dying to realize that.

I notice a young woman watching me. I readjust my mask. Strange how my fears of pursuing my dreams left me but I still get nervous when a pretty girl looks my way. I glance over my shoulder to make sure she's really looking at me. Oh right—I'm in the corner.

She rises and makes her way over to my table. If I had a heart it would be pounding now, my palms would be sweaty, but I'm dead (or undead) and so all I feel are these looping thoughts in my brain. *How can I think if I'm dead?* I suddenly wonder, but my thoughts are cut short as she sits down across from me.

She smiles. She has dark hair, dark eyes, white teeth.

"Hi there," she says sweetly.

"Hi," I rasp in my paper-dry voice. No saliva, remember. Guess it sounds more akin to a dry wind on the prairie. Not that I've ever been to a prairie.

"You're different." She leans towards me.

"Yeah."

"You're dead."

I sit straighter. I casually stretch my limbs (something a live person would do) and they crack ungodly loud. I hope I haven't dislocated my shoulder again. "That's ridiculous."

"But you are, aren't you?"

My eyes—gnawed and trashed as they are—dart around behind my mask.

"Yeah," I whisper. This might be the first time I admit such a thing out loud to another. Save for my raps, of course. But those are more like a journal to me.

"The man who revived you. Old guy, unibrow? Long, gray hair?"

Now I'm curious. "How did you know?"

"He's my mentor. His name is Raizmundo the Wise."

"Oh."

"He's wondering how your music is going."

"Why's he care about my music?" *Hell,* I think, *since when does he care about me at all?* Ever since I rose from the grave I haven't seen nor heard from him. Figured I might've even imagined the fellow to begin with. I pull my laptop towards me, and push down the screen, to study this woman full in the face. Again I wonder how I can see with such ruined eyes. Must be more to my undeath than I know.

She shrugs. "When he found you—in that graveyard—your gift of music stood out to him. He can detect these things. He wanted to give you a second chance. And to practice his necromancy, of course." She speaks in a hushed voice.

"Oh. Well. I've got a mixtape. Do you want to listen? Maybe you can share it with my creator." I take a CD out of my bag before she can respond and pass it across the table.

"Sure. Sure. I'll give this a listen when I'm home, thank you." She smiles politely and puts the CD into her purse. "But Raizmundo, he's heard your stuff before. He's awfully fond of the track 'The Dance of Death.' He thinks you should put on a performance at Central Park. He really wants to see one of his creations succeed."

"He's heard my mixtape?" Despite my voice being toneless, I can't hide the giddiness of my posture. I lean towards her, grinning behind the ghoulish mask.

She smiles coyly. "Oh yes. He thinks it's perfect."

If I had eyebrows, they would rise. "Perfect? Wow, that's kind of him." A strange descriptor for a mixtape. Fresh, maybe. Sick, maybe. But perfect?

I think for a moment, and then blurt, "So why hasn't he visited me at all?" I immediately regret asking such a question. My loneliness is for me alone. I don't want to remember those six long days of terror, when I was no more than a baby in that cold six-foot hole, gibbering nonsense, wondering why my creator had left me. Only when I rap do I revisit that place.

"He's been keeping an eye on you. He sees how well you're doing, creatively. He'll be at the concert." She nudges something towards my feet, a big old tote bag. I lean and peer inside. It's an amplifier and a microphone.

"It's battery charged. Just pop your disk with the beats in. Maybe this Sunday?"

"Don't I need a permit?"

She laughs. "I think once you start performing everyone will be glad for the chance to dance. Don't worry about a permit."

"Wait. What's your name?"

"I'm Shayla." She extends her hand.

"Yung Lich." As we shake hands some of my gray, papery skin sloughs off and I quickly dust it off the table, glancing around, hoping no one saw. I shrink my bony hand back into my sleeve.

"Raizmundo and I are very excited for your performance."

"Me too," I say, honestly. A concert! It's such a good idea I can't believe I hadn't thought of it.

• • • •

Sunday fast approaches. I've tested the microphone and the amp and it gives my dry voice a bit of a punch, and the amplifier is so loud someone nearly took a bat to my face to get me to stop saying 'testing, testing' over and over. Wonder if Raizmundo put some magic in it.

The sky holds a weak, dreary light, and it's colder than usual for April. I amble to Central Park with two totes: one for my amp, the other for my mixtapes. I've sawn down my staff a little and I've created a little holder for the microphone on it (using duct tape) so it looks really cool and thematic.

There's no stage or anything so I set up at the top of a small hill, right on the cusp of the Great Lawn. I realize I might be starting a little early, but this is better for practice. Even the undead gotta warm up.

"Testing, testing," I murmur into the microphone. Some joggers look my way but keep jogging. I clear my throat of nothing. Old habit, I suppose.

"Hi, everyone. My name is Yung Lich. Thanks for coming," I say to absolutely no one, because no one is gathered, but it's what I've rehearsed. I always get nervous before, well, everything. But I know once the music kicks in my anxiety will fade like dew beneath the sun.

"And now... *The Dance of Death.*" I figure I can always circle back to my main track once Raizmundo is here, and I want to make sure I get the delivery down perfectly. Because he thinks it's perfect, and I can't let him down. I need to convince him I'm worth his time.

I hit the play button so the track begins (without my vocals, of course), blaring out loud across the empty field. I nod to the tune and sway, getting a feel for the beat once more.

I begin with the opening chorus:

> *"Yea we all die,*
> *Yea we all die,*
> *Yea we all die,*
> *But we don't all rise."*

The snare drum works its magic. I find my bony hips a-swaying. I'm cradling the mic staff to my chest.

> *"They call me Yung Lich cuz I rose from the grave*
> *But don't get any ideas, I can't be killed with a stave*
> *Been there, tried that, tried to figure out what was*
> *Happening to me, am I owned or am I free?*
> *A bewitched Young Lich, running on that nec-ro-man-*
> > *cy*
> *Yeah, I got no heart beatin*
> *No I ain't breathin*
> *Zombie husk, decomposing, free-flowing*
> *Like the words I spit true*
> *Coming to you live(ish) from a crypt near you."*

To my utter shock, a small group gathers. They whisper to each other, pointing. No doubt impressed by my commitment to the bit, what with my black robes, gnarled wooden staff, and cheap mask. Still, I hope they like my words most of all. I peer out, hoping to catch a glimpse of my creator. The one who left me all alone. But I don't see him, nor Shayla.

> *"The one who awoke me ran in fright*

Like a thief in the night
I must've been quite the sight
Naked as the day I was born (the first time)
Cuz the rats ate my shroud, I was hopin to be found
For six days I shivered in that dark cold ground
Squallin, clawin, Tabula Rasa was my brain
Finally it came to me, my old name, my first name
But I did not want that name cuz I was not the same."

I let the beat crescendo, vibing to it, as I always do. These things can't be helped. The crowd claps intermittently, laughing; they're trying to mimic the moves that only a human of incredible hypermobility can achieve. I hope my arms don't fall off the way I'm vibing so hard.

I see him now. Raizmundo. He's standing at the far edge of the hill, Shayla beside him, a little ways off from where the crowd has gathered. He's wearing earmuffs, like the kind people working the airports do. I find this curious, but maybe he's got hearing issues—the amp is loud, loud. He sees me looking and claps his hands together and gives me a double thumbs up. I feel a faux-flush of encouragement. Maybe we'll have dinner tonight. Again, not that I can eat, but I could sit with him.

Maybe he'll tell me the reason for doing this, for raising me.

Maybe he'll tell me why he left me.

"Yeah they call me Yung Lich
Brushing ditch dirt off my shoulder
My body couldn't be colder
But I stay fresh and don't moulder
My raps are raw to the bone
Even though they're well done
And I'll flow til we're gone
Raise my stone on the lawn."

The crowd has grown even larger. I can't believe so many people are out on such a crappy morning. They love me, they love my music, and I feel so happy I could die for real. They whoop and thrash their heads as the bassline drops, and I bend over and shake my hood so hard that three of my teeth dislodge and rattle about in my mask. These words, they're my truth. They're all that will remain once I'm truly gone (if ever that happens) and I'm hoping I imprint them into the very souls here before me.

I scream as loud as my sooty voice can muster:

> "I'm hoping to be
> Immortal in my technique,
> Let these words live long after me
> If ever I see that eternal peace
> For it was stripped away unceremoniously
> Yea I've been lurkin, hurtin,
> Feelin undeservin
> This so-called life is what you might call a gift
> But is a gift a gift, even if you didn't ask for it?
> I never wanted no second chance,
> But since I'm here, I guess I'll dance!"

The people throw their hands in the air wildly, jostling, swaying. Never before have I seen a crowd so alive, and their energy, it gives me energy, and more still come to the gathering. From my vantage point atop the hill I can see the people filtering into this open green space like herded animals, all drawn by the power of my music. I whip my head and stomp about for the chorus.

> "We are all alone (I'm alone),
> We all live alone (I'm alone),
> We all die alone (I'm alone),
> We are all alone, alone yeah,
> So let's dance to the death now!"

The crowd dances so hard that clouds of steam begin to rise. Hundreds of people now, dancing wildly, hypnotic, all their hair and clothing whirling as though in a vortex, and I can feel the hot, swampy wind from their efforts. I laugh and for a moment I simply stand and watch in quiet admiration. My music has meaning. Even though they would be repulsed to know me personally—I mean, who wouldn't? I'm a walking, talking corpse—this crowd knows the *real* me, through my words, my music.

Suddenly, all the people fall with a resounding thud. I gasp into the mic, and kick the pause button on the track.

"Guys?" I say.

The mic squeals. The entire crowd has gone utterly lifeless and still, without even a moan of protest. I look around. Raizmundo and Shayla clap but their claps sound punctured and hollow compared to the ruckus that has just died, suddenly, snuffed like a candle. Raizmundo removes his earmuffs and attempts to step gingerly over the fallen crowd, but the bodies are too close together. He and Shayla just end up walking across the backs and faces of the fallen, holding their arms out to steady themselves atop the flesh-mounded field.

I look around for the cops, something. Ready to turn myself in. But the cops were at my show, they were vibing with everyone else; even their horses were doing a weird animal jitter, thrusting their noses in the air and wiggling their rumps. I don't see the horses anymore, so I figure they must be lying out there, too, among the masses.

There's no one but me, Shayla, and Raizmundo. Why didn't she fall? Unless...

A fell glint shines in Raizmundo's eyes as he nears me.

"That was excellent, Thomas. Truly." He's softer-looking than I remember. Less haggard around the eyes, cheeks full and ruddy, with false white teeth as straight as new headstones. Must be living large, this wizard of obscene power.

"It's actually 'Yung Lich' now," I say hastily. "What the hell happened?" I mean. What else can I say, really?

"Language," he chides, and for whatever reason, I grow bashful.

"But seriously."

"They danced to the death. Just as you wished."

"I didn't really want them to die—"

"Are you bothered by it?"

I look out over the literal field of dead. I didn't know these people, but I never wanted to be a mass murderer.

"Uh. Yeah? I never wanted to kill anyone. I just wanted to share my story, I just..." I struggle to find the words. "Why?"

"You're lonely." Raizmundo's unibrow dips as his forehead creases. "I wanted you to have company."

"You couldn't have just... visited? Had coffee with me?" I gesture at the dead. "Or... risen me a girlfriend from the graveyard? Not saying she would necessarily be into me or anything... but... I didn't ask you to kill anyone." Nor do I see how a pile of dead people can offer any company at all, but I have an inkling of where this might be going.

"I'm much too busy for that. And the corpses, they work better when they're fresh. You were a lucky case. I learned a lot from you." He reaches out and touches my shoulder gently. He looks out over the field, and a contented sigh escapes him. "This was much-needed practice for me."

"So they didn't really like my music? It was all... a trick?" I don't know why, but this thought is more heartbreaking to me than the hundreds lying dead. I can't help it. That's just who I am now, what I am now. I'm living for a dream alone.

Shayla pipes up, "It was really very good!"

"They loved it," Raizmundo says reassuringly. "Truly. They loved it so. That's why they came to listen, to dance."

I want to believe him, I really do. And when you're undead and without a friend in the world, well, it's easy to believe such honeyed words. I'm guessing we undead don't have strong conviction, or perhaps I was always like this, and my cordial veneer sloughed away with my flesh in the grave.

"Okay." I frown. None of this sits right. I look at Shayla. "So you're undead too, huh?"

She offers a small smile, and a curt nod. My gaze darts from Shayla to Raizmundo to Shayla again.

"So you left me for a better model, is that it?" I say. Jealousy, now there's an emotion I haven't felt in a long, long time. She doesn't even *look* undead.

"Nonsense, Yung Lich. This is all part of the journey. *Our* journey. Give me the microphone, and I shall begin the ceremony."

I have so many questions, but I lean the mic staff towards him. He pulls a tattered leatherbound book from his massive overcoat. A long, corded tassel dangles from the book's spine, fringed in human hair by the looks of it. The grimoire. He adjusts the half-moon spectacles on his nose.

He begins to speak in a long-dead language, and it tickles something in me. I've heard these words before. On that fateful, moonless night when Raizmundo stirred life into my bones.

The dead, they begin to rise. I guess it's not so hard for them to come back because they were only dead a few minutes. Someone starts screaming, another laughing, another dancing right where she left off even though there is no music.

"Everyone," says Raizmundo. "Meet your new friend, Yung Lich. And I, I am your creator, Raizmundo the Wise. We will all be one happy family."

Grumbles from the crowd. No one really knows what's going on. Considering they were just dead.

"What now?" I ask.

"We must see if the experiment holds. And then... Well... Business as usual. Until the time comes that I will call upon you"—he speaks into the mic again—"soon I will call upon you all, for the wars to come."

"Wars?" I repeat, dumbfounded. I'm not a soldier. I'm a rapper.

"Yes," Raizmundo says to me. "And you shall be a general. General Lich. How does that sound?"

"Corny," I mumble.

He doesn't seem to hear me, or care what I have to say. "Until then, teach them. Show them how to be human. You've done such a great job of it. I am *so* impressed." He hugs me then. I stiffen. I've forgotten what this is like, human touch, but I realize it's been something I've been craving. I hug him back, as tight as my bones allow.

My creator, he loves me. And I love him. I need to tell myself that because even if I now have hundreds of potential friends, his approval, his friendship, it's what I seek the most.

He puts back on his earmuffs. Shayla stands obediently beside him. She must love Raizmundo too, or his mind at any rate, because she watches him like a puppy watches its owner.

"Until next time."

"You won't stay? I still have six songs to perform." I'm not about to let this crowd go to waste, and I feel a little music might cheer them up.

"I'm much too busy. Be on the lookout for Shayla in the coming weeks, with instructions on mobilizing the rest of the undead. We plan to march come summer time."

He doesn't wait for my response. They turn to go, back down the slope, into the bleary-eyed-and-blinking crowd. I wonder, march for what? Have we any say in this at all? Can he just control me with his silver-tongued spells? I glance at the amplifier. Is it my words, or the amp that has magic?

I watch them go, Raizmundo and Shayla, and I feel pain boil in my chest. Abandonment. Like that tight knot that gathers at the back of your throat before you cry, but I can't cry, all I can do is write, and rap. Anger riles inside of me and I look out to all those hollow eyes, still reeling from their resurrection.

"I'm spittin' this one on the fly now. Can any of you drop a beat?"

One kid scrambles up the hill and I let him lean into the mic and beatbox a little ch-ch-unsss.

I see the dead parting like the sea for Moses, for Raizmundo and his little dog Shayla, and pain courses through me. The arrogance of the man, to think I'd be okay with such a slight. That I'd be okay with being his warmongering zombie. Doesn't he get it by now? I'm a rapper. This is my passion. This is what keeps me going. He may be my creator but he is *not* my master. I point at him with my free hand.

> "The devil walks among us,
> But you don't even know him
> Well let me show him,
> Raizmundo the Wise!
> That wizard over there,
> Kerfufflin, bubblin
> Turning his back like I'm nothin
> He's lying, he's tryin
> To make his escape
> To make more undead slaves
> So seize him now, swiftly now

'Fore he brings the world more pain."

The music resonates even clearer than before, and my words seem to be strings pulling at the crowd like they're puppets. They grab Raizmundo and Shayla and bear them back like an undead tide to the bottom of the hill. In their faces, I see fear. I've forgotten so much, but fear, I'll never forget.

"Take his earmuffs off," I say to a big, burly man who holds them both by the scruffs of their jackets.

Raizmundo struggles as the man rips his dumb headset off him. He has Raizmundo by the arms now, and Raizmundo kicks like a mad thing, spittle flying. Bet he wishes he memorized that haunted-ass book now, and maybe then he could stop me. I step forward and take the grimoire out of his jacket. I flip through the pages; he watches in horror. He begins to stammer and I nod at the burly man, who clamps a hand over the wizard's mouth. I lean towards Raizmundo, the mic staff the only thing between us as I freestyle.

> "Wise? Wise? What's so wise about
> You, Mr. Let's-go-on-a-killin-spree
> You done cursed me, I might need therapy
> I might need ministry
> I might need a friend or three,
> Because I can't shake this pain,
> Pain, it's all I've got
> Not store-bought, not self-taught,
> What does undead even mean?
> I feel like I'm coming apart, seam by seam,
> Beam by beam, it's an endless,
> Reckless, feckless
> Pursuit of self discovery,
> Yea, now, I'm doing me
> The reaper's here and he's wanting a fee
> So time's up, Raizmundo,
> Let's hear your plea."

Not gonna lie, those are some of the dopest lines I've ever dropped. I hope someone's filming this. My newly minted bodyguard slacks his hand so Raizmundo can speak. I don't know if the big man is magicked by the amp, or moved by my fresh-to-death freestyle, but I'm hoping we can be friends when this is all done.

Raizmundo stammers, "T-T-Thomas? Lich? What is the meaning of this? Stop at once— I command you to—"

I nod at the bodyguard, who clamps his hand upon Raizmundo's mouth once more.

> *"Time's up!*
> *You couldn't even spare me an hour,*
> *A minute*
> *This creation which you bore,*
> *Dirt-stained, unclaimed*
> *Raging down to my core*
> *These poor souls, they just wanted to dance*
> *And you, you denied them that chance*
> *I think it's your turn for a reckoning*
> *The void, it's beckoning."*

Raizmundo tries to cover his ears but my new undead bodyguard has caught on and twists his arms back, so my words resound with full force in his hairy, worthless earholes.

> *"You'll fall, as they did, but this time it's for good*
> *So long, I hardly knew ya, not that I could.*
> *Dance to the Death now!"*

Raizmundo clutches his chest and his legs begin kicking, perversely, to the now-frenzied beat. The undead bodyguard releases him and Raizmundo's doing the shopping cart, the worm (which causes his face to tighten as he flumps down upon his paunch), the twist. The crowd roars, egging him on, and he moves in such a flurry of limbs I can't track him. And then, in a spray of dust, he collapses. Shayla screams.

I turn to her and shield the mic with my hand, the venom in my voice faltering. "Hey. Listen. I'm sorry, that was, uh…"

I pause, reflecting on Raizmundo's frenzied display. How to describe it—hilarious? Surprisingly dexterous? A well-deserved end for a maniacal murdering wizard? "It was… a bit much, I admit. But he murdered, like, hundreds of people. And worse than that, he was gonna force us to do his dirty work. I couldn't let that fly, okay?"

She looks dejected. She nods, barely. Maybe this isn't the best time to talk. I turn my attention to the crowd.

> *"Good people of N-Y-C*
> *My so-called army*
> *Of zombies*
> *Stand attention for your orders*
> *You shall seed no disorder*
> *Take this second life*
> *And pursue your dreams,*
> *Nix that 9-to-5, unless that's where you thrive*
> *You do you*
> *And I'll do me*
> *And we'll all be one big, happy*
> *Undead family*
> *One more thing: I'm sorry*
> *I know, today, you didn't expect to meet your end*
> *But I hope you like my mixtape*
> *Please tell all your friends!"*

I frisbee the CDs from my tote into the crowd. The people scream and yell and I continue to perform; I still have six songs left, after all. My mask comes off, and the people don't flee, but cheer.

My name is Yung Lich and I'm giving the people a show they'll remember for years to come.

• • • •

The following week *The Dance of Death* tops the charts. This time it doesn't kill folk, just sets them a-dancing, enjoying life. Those who were at my concert, my army of zombies, they walk the streets like everyone else. You can't hardly tell that they're undead, so quickly were they brought back.

I wonder if we'll ever really die, now that we're undead. Not like we've ever borne witness to such an experiment on a grand scale. Maybe we only have five, ten years before our bodies, depleted of their usual processes, give way. Or maybe we'll be here forever, running on the remnants of Raizmundo's necromancy. I don't know what will happen, I just keep rapping.

Fame brings its own kind of loneliness, but I'm no stranger to that. If I was without all my pain, all my struggles, what would I write about? I'm Yung Lich, not Yung Bliss. I've made peace with who I am, and the people accept me for me.

I sit in my new apartment down in Queens. Yeah, I bought it. Yeah, I'm earning a living. Feels good to be living off my dreams, my words, my truth. Shayla sits across from me, tapping a melody out on the keyboard. We made amends, and she runs my webpage and Soundcloud. I understand why Raizmundo favored her so highly—she's got a mind for organization, for promotion. But more importantly, she listens and understands, and I do my best to reciprocate. She's been where I've been, risen up from the grave.

I open the windows and let the hot summer air waft in. My music sounds out in the streets, a never-ending block party, the cars bumping like they did back in the '90s. Glancing down I see people in black robes, wearing such a dazzling array of masks it's like Hallow's Eve all day, every day.

The people catch me watching them, and they throw their hands up and shout the refrain of my newest single: "*Long Live Yung Lich! Long Live Yung Lich!*"

———————————

ALEX FOX hails from the wintry Northeast, USA. Alex has work in *Old Moon Quarterly*, *PodCastle*, Hungry Shadow Press, Grendel Press, and more. You can find her on Twitter as @afoxwrites, on Bluesky as @alexfox.bsky.social, and at afoxwrites.com.

COLD RELATIONS

BY MARY ROBINETTE KOWAL

Novelette Long List*

Claudette lowered her infrared goggles over her eyes and waited for the ghost. By the cash register, webs of energy, tinted green by the goggles, swirled in a loose spiral. Spectral lines tightened in time with a throbbing hum of energy.

As she walked closer, Claudette's hair stood on end along her neck, and the scars on her left arm tightened. She wet her lips as the air thinned. The pair of obsidian capture rings she wore seemed to chill. She needed to see the ghost long enough to touch it.

If you wanted to drain energy from something, you had to touch it. Of course, you also had to be aware that energy could flow in either direction.

The ghost formed fully between one thrum of energy and the next. A stout, bespectacled man with a neat pencil mustache and slicked-down hair frowned at a receipt in his hands. He looked up toward the ceiling, already turning to go.

Claudette sidled into the ghost's radius, plunging her hands into the center of the vortex. Ice wrapped around her. In the goggles, the heat of her hands dimmed as her life began to ebb away.

Claudette gasped, nearly choking on the prickling chill of the air. Fighting the lethargy, she brought her hands together. As her capture rings clicked against each other, a spark lit the room. The vortex changed.

It shifted from a vortex, drawing energy into itself, to an eddy trapped in one spot, spinning through the same moments. And then, almost imperceptibly, it began to ebb. The ghost's edges fuzzed. The waistcoat lost its distinctive pattern as the rings she wore chilled to burning cold.

Claudette kept her focus as the ghost's essence trickled into her until a tipping point opened a flood of energy.

And memories.

Standing at the cash register. Smiling at customers. Looking up and seeing the axe that will kill him. Screaming for his wife to hide. He dies not knowing if she is safe.

The last of his lingering life force settled into Claudette, burning cold.

She shuddered as the final eddy vanished. Reaching up, she pulled the night vision goggles off and the room returned to natural vision. Her arms ached and the back of her neck was tight. Tilting her head, Claudette cracked her neck.

She sighed and walked to the shop's entrance. As she pushed the door open, a wall of humid heat slammed into her cold bones. For a moment, the heat was a relief.

Outside, her client sat on a folding chair in a circle of salt. It wasn't necessary for this kind of magic, but government regulations required a salt circle and if she didn't want to lose her license to practice magic in the state of Alabama, she had to comply. The client looked up as soon as Claudette stepped outside. Even sitting in the shade of a wisteria arbor, her frosted mall bangs had wilted in the heat.

"Is it gone?"

"Yes. It won't trouble your patrons or staff anymore." Inside her skin, the low thrum of energy beat along with her pulse. "Would credit card or Venmo work best for you?"

The woman stood, picking up a giant floral purse from beside her folding chair. She fished out an equally floral billfold from inside the bag. "Credit card, please."

Hands still aching with cold, Claudette reached into her back pocket for the small Square scanner and grabbed her cellphone out of the front pocket of her jeans. Her skin felt thin and taut with the energy bubbling below the surface.

The client handed her card across. "So what was it?"

They always wanted a story and they always wanted it to be gruesome. The ghosts usually weren't. Usually, they were just scared or confused. Claudette refused to sensationalize their deaths. "1930s. White man. Shopkeeper."

"You don't know his name?"

Claudette shook her head, swiping the card through the reader. "I only get that if they were thinking about their own name at the end."

Wrinkling her nose, the woman sighed. "I don't guess most of them do. How did he die?"

"An axe."

"An axe?!"

"Yes." She waited for the screen to tell her the payment had cleared and turned it around so the woman could sign. "It was a pretty common weapon before guns were so ubiquitous. Still you should be able to research him."

"Well, I will certainly do that."

If she ever came back here, there would be a plaque commemorating him. Probably maudlin, since he seemed to have been the victim. Claudette nodded and returned the credit card. "Thank you for your business."

The money was necessary but the thing of greater value was the life force of the ghost. Powering spells took energy. It had to come from somewhere and she could either siphon from a living person...

Or she could consume a ghost.

One of those choices also paid the rent.

• • • •

Arriving at her studio apartment, Claudette undid the wards on her door and pushed it open with her shoulder. She had a bag of groceries in her left hand, and all she wanted was to sit down in the tub with a cup of hot cocoa. She was always so cold after draining a ghost.

She was halfway through the door, when she saw Rupert.

Sighing, Claudette kicked the door shut and redid the wards with her free hand as if her older brother weren't sitting in her kitchen.

"Not even a hello?"

"Remind me to rekey the wards." They were set to let him in.

"Ouch." He sat at the table and had her cat on his lap. Bisquick purred and shoved his head against Rupert's hand. "Bisquick is doing well."

"Are you here to check if I'm taking my meds? I am. Or to ask for a loan?"

"Neither in fact." He pushed an envelope across the table. "I'm here to repay you."

Claudette set the bag of groceries on the counter and leaned against the stained Formica to face him. Rupert's face was lean and angular to the point of gauntness. He had the square jaw and cheekbones of a model but was so thin that his skin always seemed too tight. Rupert was smiling now, dimples like they had been sliced into his cheeks, but it was his real smile. Not the sarcastic mask.

She pursed her lips and looked at the envelope. "You got a job. Congratulations."

He nodded, tilting his head to study her. "So did you, it appears."

She still wore the obsidian capture rings, which might have been his clue. Or maybe her hoodie, zipped up, despite the summer heat. She shrugged and crossed to pick up the envelope from the table. It was thick and heavy with a wad of cash.

In the three years since he'd borrowed money from her college fund, she had honestly hit a point of assuming she would never see the 'temporary' loan again. Claudette shoved it into the pocket of her hoodie and bent down to scoop Bisquick up. "Actual cash? I didn't know anyone did that anymore."

"I thought the symbolic importance worth the extra trouble." He looked at her pocket, where the envelope had vanished. "You aren't going to count it?"

"Is there a reason I shouldn't trust you?"

She scratched her cat under the chin as the silence lay thick and heavy with all the weight of how Rupert had needed to borrow money from his kid sister to pay the mortgage. How she'd had to drop out of college when he couldn't pay her back in time.

She swallowed and wet her lips. Dragging up a smile that might have belonged to a grocer from the last century, she set Bisquick down and walked back to the counter. "Well, congratulations on the job. I know it's been hard." She pulled a carton of eggs out of the grocery bag and opened the fridge. "What is it?"

"I'm a government wizard."

The carton slipped out of her fingers and cracked against the floor. Viscous liquid oozed out with swirls of yellow. Bisquick headed straight for the eggs, which would wreak havoc with his elderly digestive system.

"Shit."

"Do you need hel—"

"I've got it." Claudette grabbed a Swedish dishcloth from the sink and nudged the cat away as she squatted to wipe up the worst. She felt queasy. A government wizard. After what they'd done to him. To their mother. To generations of magic users. "So do you kill people on day one, or is that later in the onboarding process?"

"Don't be like that..."

Furious, she felt the weight of the envelope in her pocket. Her hands were coated in raw egg or she would have grabbed it and flung it back at him. "You literally steal life force from people—living people."

"Murderers. We take bad people and do something good with their lives."

Crouching on the floor, she stared up at him. "I don't want blood money."

He lowered his head and ran his hands through his hair. "It's not— and anyway, it's a signing bonus. I haven't even finished training yet."

"And that's supposed to make it better?" She stood. Dropping the carton into the sink, she shoved the tap open. At her feet, Bisquick licked the floor where the eggs had been. "That you haven't stolen life force yet. You're just planning to do it."

"They volunteer!"

"Are you even listening to yourself? How much of a choice does a prisoner have? Huh? 'We take bad people and do something good with their lives' is a bullshit tagline to gloss over a gross misuse of authority."

He shoved his chair back from the table. "And you're certain being a necromancer is better."

"They're dead."

"Are they?" Rupert glared at her, the angles on his face folding into a scowl. "Physical bodies, yes. I won't touch the physical bodies of my donors either. You know what those memories you get are? You eat souls, Claudette. You. Eat. Souls. All I'll take is energy."

• • • •

A cricket trilled outside the window, insistently pushing through the night. Claudette sank deeper into the tub, the hot water lapping around her as the sweet gingery scent of magnolias rose from the bubbles. Bisquick lay curled in a doughy heap on the bathroom mat.

You eat souls, Claudette.

Her cellphone rang on the toilet seat where she'd left it. She wiped a hand on a towel and flipped the phone over to see the number. A repeat client.

Sighing, she picked up the phone and answered it, trying to keep the sloshing of the tub to a minimum. "Brindled Cat, Inc. Claudette Sims speaking."

The voice at the other end shook, as it always did. "Hi, Claudette. Benny is missing again."

She pinched the bridge of her nose, squinting against the frustration. "I thought we were going to keep him on a leash when he went outside?"

"Oh, but it was just a moment."

"That must be so distressing for you. Did he have his collar on?"

"Of course he did. And his tags. But what happens if he gets hit by a car?"

She did not use her outside voice to say *maybe this wouldn't happen if Benny stayed on a leash*, partly because they'd had that conversation before and partly because she needed the money. Sighing, Claudette tilted her head up and looked at the ceiling. Her license was only for small magics and couldn't be applied to living things. Could she find Benny without his collar? Definitely. Would it be illegal? Also definitely.

Finding his collar, on the other hand, was fine. "Give me a minute..." She muted her mic and lay with her head resting on the rim of the tub as she stared at the water stain in the corner.

She let the amorphous shape of the stain act as a focus and she formed the spell in her mind. She paired it with the memory of his collar and linked that to Benny, who was an Australian Red Heeler with a penchant for excursions. The first time she'd looked for him, she had needed to touch a blanket he slept on. The second time, she'd needed a photo she'd taken on her cell phone. By the sixth time, she could find him by thinking about his sandy red coat and his erect triangular ears. She knew the way he grinned as he wagged his tail.

She released the spell and burned a bit of energy as she released it.

The memory of an axe fizzed away with it, leaving a memory of a memory. She'd once remembered the grocer dying from the blow of an axe. Now she had only her own secondhand memory of having once known that information. None of the visceral sensation remained.

It was a memory. Not a soul.

But what were souls made of? Claudette shook her head and followed the spell to Benny. The memory of him she had formed to guide the spell wrapped around him. No one outside would be able to tell that she didn't look for the collar. It was a polite fiction.

Happy. Enthusiastic about the squirrel he'd caught. The satisfying grind of his teeth against the beautiful round skull.

She scrolled the vision out until she saw the yard he was in and then the street. Shifting slightly gave her a house number. She let the vision evaporate back into a water stain on the ceiling. Cupping a handful of water in one hand, she unmuted the phone.

Letting the water splash from her hand, she lowered her voice to the husky burr the clients liked. "I see him... In my scrying bowl, I see him." Scrying bowls were bullshit, but very flashy, so she took them with her sometimes. "He is under a lavender bush. There is a yellow house and... and a red bicycle in the front yard. The house is—is—Delancy Street. 8331 Delancy. He is in the back yard."

Could she have just given the client the address? Yes. And also, if she wanted to earn money, she had to make people understand that there was a cost. They couldn't see her burn energy, so her mother had taught her to act it out for them.

"Oh, thank you! That's only two streets away." Keys jangled in the background as her client ran toward the door. "I'll Venmo you. The usual?"

"Thank you. I'm glad I'm able to help." Claudette cleared her throat. "But you know, he's learning that if he runs away, he gets a treat."

"But he won't come if I don't give him a treat!"

There were so many things she could say. But her phone chirped with the Venmo payment landing in her account. "Of course, I understand. Give him scritches for me."

Claudette hung up and nudged the hot water tap on with her toe. Just a little longer, to chase the last of the cold away, and then she'd call it a day.

Her phone chirped again and in the process of turning it facedown so it would go on Do Not Disturb, she made the mistake of looking at the screen. Rupert had texted her. All she could see was *"Don't want to bother you. I have an alterna—"*

She sat with her hand on the phone case, gritting her teeth. Then she turned the tap off and sat up. The bubbles had diminished to scattered clouds of foam at the edges of the water. He'd taken her in after their mom died. She'd barely known him. Rupert was ten years her senior and had been taken to the mandatory government-run boarding school for magicians before she was born. Things had gone wrong, yes, but he'd tried to do good by her.

Sighing, she flipped the phone face up and tabbed to see the full message.

"Don't want to bother you. I have an alternate idea if you can't, but I got home and can't find my ID badge. I'm not supposed to use magic outside of work during training. Would you be willing to find it for me?"

You mean burn part of a soul? She wrote it and deleted it before hitting send.

"Yes. You know what I need. Bring it and the ingredients for a hot toddy."

· · · ·

Rupert knocked this time. She'd had time to think about it before he arrived and had gotten annoyed all over again. How dare he give her grief for 'eating souls' and then ask her to do magic for him on the same day?

When she undid the wards and opened the door, he held out a bottle of Four Roses Bourbon. "I'm sorry. I was an ass earlier."

Bisquick trotted to the door, tail high with greeting, and mrrped at Rupert. Her brother's face softened as he crouched. "Hi, sweet boy."

All of the angry things that were cued up on her tongue tangled around themselves. She swallowed. "Thank you. And yes. Yes, you were."

His mouth tightened into a white slash before he held up a brown paper bag. "This is the best I could do."

She opened the bag and peeked inside. A crumpled form. A ballpoint pen. A passport photo of Rupert. A silk tie she'd picked up for him at a secondhand shop. Claudette raised her head and lifted the tie out of the bag. "You wore this?"

He shrugged, standing. "Your taste has always been better than mine."

Despite her intention to remain mad at him, a warm spot of pleasure softened her chest. "C'mon." She set the bag on the table. "Why didn't you ask them for a new badge?"

He pulled out a chair and paused with his hand on its back. "It's... I'm new. They're really buggy about security and I'm supposed to keep it on me at all times during training."

"Mm... Well, you can make me a hot toddy while I get set up." She went to the cupboard and pulled out the giant economy bag of powdered sage and the jumbo box of salt.

He eyed the box of salt. "You can skip the salt circle with me."

"And lose my license by performing magic without a mandated circle in front of a government wizard?"

"Oh, come on..."

"You wouldn't be required to report me?"

"Fine. Then I'll just make your hot toddy." Rupert headed to the stove, Bisquick following him like a traitor. "You know it's 97 degrees outside today."

"And you know I did a ghost capture this morning. That whole thing where I ate a soul, remember?" The bitter, sarcastic bite of her voice slipped back to teenage habits. Claudette poured a circle of salt around his feet, pinning him, and for once her cramped studio was a bonus because she could give him access to the stove and the sink. "What, government wizards don't get cold?"

"No. No, it turns out that's a side effect of working with the dead." He grabbed the kettle.

"Citation required."

"Google it."

"Not a citation." She slammed the box on the counter next to him. "Of course, I wouldn't have to look this up, if I had, you know, finished college."

"You can—" He bit off the rest of the sentence and she knew him well enough to know that he only stopped himself because he needed her help. Again. "Do you want lemon or lime in your toddy? I brought both."

"Lemon." Claudette scooped out a handful of sage and used it to make a working area on the table. After a few minutes, she sighed, carefully so she didn't scatter sage everywhere, and looked at her brother. "So blood magic is hot?"

"It's not blood magic." His shoulders were stooped and he was concentrating on filling the kettle with more intensity than the act required. "And I've only cast once in a training session, but they warned us about the temperature difference before we started."

"Tell me your only source isn't them."

"Why would they make it up?"

"Seriously?"

He rolled his eyes. "I'm not saying the government is all trust all the time, but if you're going to invent a conspiracy theory, at least have a basis for why they would make stuff up."

"Oppression has always been popular." She set the items from the bag on the sage, arranging them so they referenced the cardinal points. "Tell me again about boarding school?"

From the corner of her eye, she saw his shoulders collapse further with a sigh, because it wasn't an argument he could fight. Wizards, witches, mages... It didn't matter what you called them, magic users had a tendency to get burned or drowned or beheaded or in the modern day, regulated.

"Okay. Fair. All I can say is that the magic we captured was hot and my physical experience matched the training documents. I have not, in fact, looked further." Rupert held up his hand to stop her. "I've been out of work since February so, yeah, I took the job."

Out of work *again*, he meant.

"Well, let's keep you from losing this one." Claudette bent down and scooped Bisquick up. "Sorry, old man."

The cat nuzzled against her as she carried him to the bathroom and set him inside. He looked over his shoulder with affront before settling down on the rug in a catloaf. She'd learned from experience that cats would not stay in salt circles. If she pulled a charge from the room, she didn't want to risk hurting her sweet boy.

Walking back to the table, Claudette took a breath to center herself. "I'm starting the spell now."

Rupert hushed immediately. Using her knowledge of him, she shaped the spell to activate the centering properties of the sage and the items. Holding the energy poised in her mind, she unfurled the spell. She could sometimes find things without spellwork, but it was a lot easier when she could use it as a frame... The tie in the north quadrant seemed to shiver as her spell homed in on the ID badge.

Finding this was fundamentally different than finding a dog she knew. Beneath her fingers, lines traced themselves in the sage. Not a map. Not an image. Just the spectral frequencies captured in jittering lines across the dusty sage. The scars on her left arm prickled and she shuddered as a memory from the little clerk shivered out of existence.

As she spent the energy, she got a flash of Rupert's badge in its place. She clung to the vague image and dragged her awareness towards it, to where the badge lay in the gravel of a parking lot. She pulled back, looking for an identifying detail, and the first sight of the duck pond placed it as North Ridge Cemetery. Claudette let the spell evaporate.

"You went to Mom's grave? Why?"

His cheeks went red briefly. "Mowing the grass."

"Excuse me?" She had this image of him taking a side job mowing lawns and couldn't reconcile it with anything she knew about her brother.

Rupert turned back to making the hot toddy. "I had to let a lot of things lapse, okay, like maintenance fees for Mom's grave."

She stared at him. The ten years of difference in their ages meant he hadn't grown up with her and Mom. He'd still been in the boarding school when the laws mandating it had been struck down. He'd chosen to finish his last year 'so he could graduate.' He'd chosen to go out on his own 'so he wasn't a burden.' The truth was he hadn't wanted anything to do with them. They'd seen him only a couple of times before her mom got sick. And she was supposed to believe he'd been mowing the grass on their mom's grave for the last three years?

"Who are you even?"

He spun back so quickly that he scuffed the salt circle. "What does that mean?"

"You didn't cry when she died. You barely knew her. Why... Why were you mowing the grass on her grave?"

The breath huffed out of him as if she'd punched him. "I—Yeah. Right. You know. I tried so hard to do right by you and—"

"By using my college money? That my mother saved for me?"

He lifted his hands and, for a moment, she thought he was going to cast but he curled his fingers into fists. "YES! Yes, because it was paying the mortgage or we were both out on the street and now I've taken a job with the people who fucking took me away. I didn't cry? I cried when I lost her, but I lost her a helluva lot sooner than you did. And then I had to be the fucking adult to a little sister I hadn't *even known about until...* Fuck you. FUCK YOU for thinking I didn't mourn her every goddamn day—"

Ambient magic shivered through the broken circle. The hair on the back of her neck stood on end and the scars on her arm tightened. The air seemed to thin. This was why magic was so heavily regulated. Part of why. You had to be touching something to drain energy from it, and a room and the air counted as an 'it.'

The wizard would be fine. Anyone trying to breathe that lifeless air would not be.

Claudette held up her hands. "Rupert—stop. You're starting to draw a charge."

His face shut down. He pressed his fingertips to his temples, then to his heart, and then pressed his hands together in an attitude of prayer. Breathe in. He held it for a count of four and then let it out, breathing in a slow pattern she'd seen multiple times a day when she'd lived with him.

He'd taught it to her at the hospital while they waited for her mother to die.

"I'm sorry." Claudette wet her lips. "I shouldn't have..."

"Hopefully that doesn't count as using magic." Rupert's voice was as flat and affectless as it usually was. "I'm sorry I shouted. Thank you for finding the badge."

He walked out of the kitchen.

"Rupert, listen, I'm really sorry about—"

The door to her apartment shut with a soft click. Claudette sat in the kitchen with the hot toddy her brother had made for her steaming on the counter. The items from the spellwork were still on the table, surrounded by spectral lines of sage. The tie she'd given him lay curled in the middle.

Claudette grabbed her phone and texted. *"You left your tie."*

She held the phone for a minute, waiting for him to text back, then growled to herself and set it down. Cold still had its grips on her. She stood and walked to the counter to pick up the toddy her brother had made for her. The warmth from the mug seeped into her fingers. The bitter, sweet liquid filled up some of the empty places inside her, but not all.

Claudette set it on the counter and grabbed the whisk broom to sweep the sage into the compost bin. Theoretically, she could use it again, but she'd heard one too many stories about spellwork honing in on a residual thread. She lifted the tie out of the sage, brushing the grey-green powder from it with her fingers.

Her phone pinged on the counter behind her.

Clutching his tie in one hand, Claudette snatched the phone.

A picture of Benny the dog grinned out at her with the text. *"Thanks again for finding my doggo."*

Nothing at all from her brother.

• • • •

It had been two days, and Claudette hadn't heard back from Rupert despite sending three apology texts and a picture of her cat. Fine. Whatever. She had other things to do, and if he wanted to pout, that was on him. She shoved the envelope he'd given her into the cupboard with her supplies.

The application form for financial aid for AU tumbled to the ground. Claudette bent to pick it up. The cursive she'd tried in order to seem more grown-up looked awkward. She rubbed her eye, staring at it. She could probably go back. That was the point of Rupert taking this awful job.

She jammed the paper back into the cabinet.

What could they teach her that she hadn't already learned on the job? Seriously, go into debt for a college degree when she was already making money with magic? There was no reason to, not if she were content with being limited to finding dogs who shouldn't be lost and capturing ghosts.

You eat souls.

That was nothing but right-wing propaganda designed to vilify and control magic users. Most magic users wouldn't do ghost captures or blood magic and just relied on their own energy or did rituals pulling from the ambient magic of places. Which meant most magic users didn't do magic.

Claudette took a deep breath and crossed the studio to flop down on her bed. Bisquick lifted his head from where he was napping in a sunbeam and murped at her.

"Sorry, guy." She reached over her head and put one hand on his warm side. Closing her eyes, she cast a spell she knew by heart and pushed some energy into her ancient cat, soothing the arthritis in his joints. As she did, memory fizzed away, taking the little shopkeeper's fear with it.

Sighing, Claudette opened her eyes and pulled her phone out of her pocket. "Hey, Google. Axe murder. Birmingham. 1500 7th Ave. N."

Dozens of articles lit up, telling a story of four years of axe murders terrorizing the city. Her clerk was a fellow named Charley Graffeo. His wife had lived. Claudette's head dropped back against the pillow and she stared at the ceiling. He had grandchildren who were alive today.

What would they do if she called them and told them what she remembered? What she had remembered, because the memories were blurring each time she used the energy she'd captured from him. Not thank her, that was for sure.

Not help her attend college or pay her rent or keep her cat alive.

Claudette scowled and rubbed her forehead. Damn Rupert for putting the idea of ghosts being souls into her head.

She swiped to text Rupert. "*A memory is not a soul. It has no will and no agency.*"

So there.

• • • •

Claudette was hunched over a secondhand textbook on corporeal magic and its permutations. It was full of theoretical spell constructs she wasn't licensed to use. Nowhere, that she could find, did the authors say anything about souls.

...The lattice of energy remaining after the dissolution of the corporeal form can be accounted for using Einstein's theory of relativity...

She should text Rupert a picture of that entire page. Aside from the fact that it had now been three days since he'd left her apartment. She was furious with him, and also starting to worry. He could be moody, but he'd never given her the cold shoulder this long before.

She must have screwed up more than she realized. Claudette worried the inside of her lip and turned the page of the textbook.

Her phone rang. She glanced at it. It was an Alabama number, but not one she recognized, so probably spam, but maybe a client, and Lord knew she needed the work. Sighing, Claudette marked her place before she answered the phone.

"Brindled Cat, Inc. Claudette Sims speaking."

"Miss Sims. I'm glad I caught you." The man's voice, monied Southern, had a slight tenseness to it, as if he were nervous. "I'm Frederick

Branson, head of the Thaumaturgy division of the FBI's Birmingham field office. I'm sorry to call out of the blue like this, but your brother has you listed as his emergency contact."

Claudette sat up straight. "What's wrong?"

"I was hoping you could tell us. Rupert hasn't shown up for work today or yesterday."

She swallowed, gaze drifting to his tie, shoved up against the wall on her kitchen table. "He was here on Sunday and hasn't been answering his phone."

Mr. Branson sighed heavily into the receiver. "I see. Do you have any idea where he might be?"

"I did a..." Her voice trailed away as she realized she would need to tell them Rupert had lost the badge. That was less of a problem than him being missing. Rupert had screwed up at work before but he'd never been a no-show. "He has a routine of visiting my mom's grave on the weekend."

"*Your* mom?"

"Ours. Our mother is buried at North Ridge Cemetery."

"I was hoping..." The man sighed again. "His badge was in the cemetery parking lot when we looked for him. His hair and skin samples are still being processed or I'd have already done a direct find."

"How—" She stopped the question as the answer presented itself. This was why he was supposed to have the badge on him during training: so they could track him while they were waiting for his samples to be cataloged. She swallowed the remaining questions. "What do you think has happened?"

"I'm sure he's fine." His voice sounded like he knew it was a lie. "I've put in a request to get those released posthaste. Don't worry. We'll find him."

"I can help." She stood, reaching for his tie. "I've got—"

"I appreciate it, Miss Sims, but we have procedures for situations like this."

"Procedures. I didn't realize new recruits went missing that often."

He was silent for a long moment and then sighed heavily. "We're a very old institution, Miss Sims. I promise I'll keep you posted."

No. She was not being shunted aside with so little regard. "How well do your procedures work without a sample? I'm his sister. You can key off me."

Behind his silence, she could make out the hum of conversation but none of the words. After three breaths, he sighed again. "I'll send a car to pick you up."

It did not escape her notice that he didn't need to ask where she lived.

As soon as she was off the phone, she grabbed the jumbo bag of sage. Claudette wasn't sure how much time she had before the car arrived but she wanted as much information as she could get on her own. The square of sage she laid out was not as crisp as it should have been.

Bisquick twined against her leg, mrrping with concern. She spared time to pat him once on the head and then immediately regretted it as his shedding fur covered her fingers. With her luck, she'd wind up finding him instead of Rupert. She washed her hands as fast as she could.

Holding the tie, she hesitated. One object wasn't enough. She needed to activate the cardinal directions. She placed the tie on the sage in the north quadrant. Turning back to her cabinet, she pulled out the envelope of cash he'd given her. Claudette placed bundles of bills at the south and the east. She pulled out the last bills for the western pile and a sheet of paper came with it.

Claudette unfolded Rupert's spiky block letters.

Hi Claudette

I am deeply, deeply sorry you had to pay for my judgement. I so desperately wanted to keep Mom's house that I made a series of bad choices. You had to pay the price for that. More than anyone, I know I can't give you those lost years back but I will do my best to make it up to you.

With love, your brother
Rupert.

Her eyes watered. If she had read that when he'd given her the money, would she have been moved or would she have thrown the words back in his face? The paper shook in her fingers. Probably the latter. Now she remembered all of the nice things he did for her. Grocery runs with Lucky Charms included, even though he thought it was awful, because she liked it. Tickets to see Kill Henry Sugar when the duo was on one of their rare tours. Hospital trips when she cut herself too deeply.

Her throat hurt as she swallowed her own memories. Claudette set the note down for the western quadrant.

Letting her breath out, she focused and uncurled a spell she was absolutely not licensed to use. It was designed to find a person. Bureaucrats forbade her to do any magic involving living beings 'out of a concern for public health and safety' even though a finding spell had no way of causing harm, even without a salt circle for containment.

The sage shivered across the table. The spectral lines shifted into a spiral that tapped each of the quadrants before spinning in toward the center. Claudette leaned in, feeling the spell skip across her mind.

The tie vibrated, shifting in the sage like a snake. The icon that caught her attention, though, was the stack of money to the south. It shifted more southeasterly and she followed it. Her mind dipped into the spell, following the thin thread toward her brother. There was a difference in the taste of this spell, if taste was the right word for something she sensed in other nerve endings. If her joints could savor the flavors of burnt marshmallow and fresh spun wool, that would almost describe the spell.

A memory shivered out of her of the little clerk running his hand over an old brass register. She used to remember the texture of the metal.

Rupert blossomed out of a web of possibilities. His eyes were closed. A cut crossed his right brow. Rough, raw scabs stubbled his cheek like a rash. She pulled back and saw the hospital bed he was in and the machines he was hooked to. On the board by his bed, it had only a number where the patient's name should be.

Her heart beat hard and fast, calling her back to her body, but Claudette clung to the scene and scrolled out and to the side, looking for something beyond 'a hospital.'

Sisters of Mercy Hospital. Fourth floor. Intensive care.

• • • •

She sat by his bed, one knee jittering up and down as she tried to read a textbook on magic. He hadn't woken up and the room felt too much like Mom at the end. Claudette concentrated on the page, reading the words again for the third time.

The current therapies of severe Traumatic Brain Injuries (TBI), as outlined by the Brain Trauma Foundation, show the effective reduction of cerebral edema, after TBI, using osmotic transport spellwork (OTS) with interstitial cortical calibration (ICC). OTS may be performed without stabilizing inertial dampeners (SID)...

A quick knock on the door gave her warning to look up as it opened. A narrow-shouldered Korean man walked into the room and took off his sunglasses. "Miss Sims?" He stuck them in his pocket. "I'm Frederick Branson. We spoke on the phone."

"Oh—" She hadn't expected him to come. They'd sent the car, but by then she'd known where Rupert was and had convinced the driver to take her straight to the hospital. Claudette closed the book and put it on the rolling hospital tray. "It's, um, nice to meet you."

He walked to the foot of the bed and looked down at the still form of her brother. "Have they said anything?"

"It looks like a random mugging." She swallowed the imagined memories of how things might have gone if the government official hadn't been with her. How would she have proven Rupert was her brother? Search her social media for a photo of the two of them together? "The police found him yesterday afternoon on the street a couple of blocks from the cemetery. The best guess is he wandered away and was... confused, so he lay down to rest."

"Ah." His brows went up a fraction of a second too late for genuine surprise. "Well, it's a relief that he was found."

Claudette stared at him. All of her frustration at being unable to do anything for her brother welled up and pressed against her teeth. "The thing I keep coming back to is that a random mugger shouldn't have been able to get a jump on a magic user."

He paused, looking at Rupert, and then met Claudette's gaze impassively. "We make it very clear to our recruits that they are not to use magic outside of training."

"So my brother almost died because of your rules."

Mr. Branson pursed his lips and then shook his head. "That's— No, of course not. I simply meant that perhaps it explains why he was caught unaware. Obviously, if he'd used magic to deflect a mugger, that would have been acceptable. Even if it weren't, surely that would have been better than..."

His voice trailed away.

"Than never waking up?" Claudette finished the sentence for him. "Is there some magic word you can say to change that? Some fancy government insurance that'll fix him?"

His teeth looked like they hurt. "Insurance benefits don't kick in until after two weeks of employment—"

"Get out."

"I need to be clear that you understand—"

"Out." She pointed at the door, the hair on her arm standing on end.

He cocked his head and narrowed his eyes. "You're starting to draw a charge." Branson moved his hand and the air in the room went flat. "How did you say you found him?"

The desire to grab him and suck the energy out of him filled her with white-hot urgency. But a government wizard would certainly have a way to stop her. The trouble with energy flows was that they could go both ways. Claudette pressed her fingers to her temple and to her heart, then pressed her palms together to ground herself the way her brother had taught her while they'd waited for their mother to die.

Her voice was as flat and affectless as Rupert's had ever been. "I got lucky. Please leave."

Branson stopped fighting her, even though he obviously guessed she had used magic to find Rupert. When he left the room, she could feel the oil slick of all the unspoken things trailing behind him. Like why hadn't the government used traditional ways to find him, like checking hospitals for John Does?

Had Rupert really been mugged?

And did the why matter right now? She just wanted him to wake up.

Magic couldn't heal the way it did on TV shows or in the movies. The human body was complicated. To heal someone, you had to know what to ask of the magic and that meant understanding the way the body worked. But the real catch, according to the doctor, was that even after the swelling in Rupert's brain subsided, there was likely to be brain damage from cells that had died. Those memories would just be gone.

And the longer there was swelling, the more cells would die. He would lose more than memories. No insurance meant no magic-based healing. Claudette shoved her hand in her jacket pocket and felt the envelope, thick with money.

She wet her lips and pushed the button to call the nursing station. "Can I pay out of pocket to have magic-based healing address the swelling?"

"That's a question for billing, I'm afraid."

"Okay, can you go ahead and set it up while I talk to them?"

"Medical magic has to be pre-approved by your insurance provider."

"We don't have— That's why I want to pay out of pocket."

"I understand, but you'll need to talk to billing."

The scream built under her skin, tightening the scars on her arm. Claudette let her breathe out in a slow stream so she didn't draw a charge. "Thank you. I'll do that."

She remembered how long it had taken to get anything approved when her mom was dying. Sometimes it took weeks or months to get a referral. Rupert had spent hours on the phone—she'd forgotten that. Claudette turned her textbook over and looked at the page she'd been reading.

...studies demonstrate that in cases with severe TBI, recovery is predicated on many factors, including the location of trauma, the severity of the damage, and the length of time in a coma. However, the long-term effects of the injury can be mitigated with the Schroeder-Epstein Spell protocol, which reduces inflammation and swelling...

Claudette had a single semester of university.

Complex healing had not been part of the curriculum. But she'd done so much reading while her mom had been in the hospital, looking for anything that would save her. She had been sixteen. There had been nothing she could do then.

And now? From a day spent with Dr. Google, she knew a brain injury was basically a bruise. Healing bruises wasn't a hard spell, just illegal without a license. Ostensibly because it took so much energy that you could accidentally drain yourself while helping someone else. The magic user would probably survive, but they might compensate by drawing a charge from the person they were trying to heal. Never a good look to have a pristine corpse.

But Claudette had just done a capture and had only done minor magic since. She had energy to spare.

Sliding the tray table away, Claudette reviewed the spell in her mind. She moved to the head of his bed, dodging the rails and leaned forward to rest her hands on the bare skin of Rupert's temples. After a moment, she pulled her hands away and grabbed the overnight bag she'd stuffed full of random things before coming down.

Mostly random. Claudette extracted a giant box of salt and dragged Rupert's bed as far from the wall as she could without messing with the equipment. She traced a circle of salt around Rupert's hospital bed, ducking under cords and behind the headboard to complete it. The circle would dampen what she was doing, in case the hospital had a magic detection system. And also to be safe, in case someone came in while she was working.

Wetting her lips, she interlaced her fingers and pressed the knuckles of her thumbs to her forehead. Let this work. Claudette lowered her hands to Rupert's temples. She unleashed the spell, letting it sink through the bones of his head to find the sore, swollen places.

Claudette's spine clenched as energy eddied out of her. With it poured memories of the clerk.

He died not knowing if she were safe. Screaming for his wife to hide. Looking up and seeing the axe that had killed him. Smiling at customers. Standing at the cash register.

They stripped away as he faded back to a generic ghost with only memories of memories. Beneath his energy, she had the last scraps of a ghost she'd captured months before.

Bundles of lavender hung over a baby carriage. Wind shivered through the strands of her long hair. The teacup she loved, dropping to the parquet floor.

Rupert stirred beneath her hands. She could feel the bruising still in his brain. The damage that lingered felt stiff and raw. There was one more ghost she could burn through.

Her mother.

Wetting her lips, Claudette reached for the first ghost she'd captured. *She knows she is dying and calls her little girl to her bedside while Rupert is out of the room. Her son will be okay but her daughter needs something to protect her. She needs a legacy. She takes Claudette's hands and pushes, energy streaming out into her daughter so she—* Claudette couldn't remember the feeling of pushing, but she could remember warmth spreading through her as her mom had chosen how her life ended.

They are running through a field of clover and the fireflies are starting to come out. Her daughter is laughing like— She can't remember the way her mother heard her laughter. The memory fizzled away, leaving only her own memory of her mother's long dark hair loose in the wind.

Her little boy looks back at the door, eyes wide, and his hand is in the grip of a government wiz—

Claudette stopped before she burned that memory. She had plenty of memories of her mother, but Rupert had precious few. Biting her lower lip, Claudette reached deeper into herself and grabbed a memory of *her sixth birthday, with candles on the cake and her mom singing in a voice that cracked on the high notes. Strawberry ice cream tastes tart and sweet on her tongue.*

When working magic, you had to be aware that energy could flow in either direction. Claudette pushed the memory into her brother, gifting him with her birthday.

Rupert twitched under her hands.

Her brother was looking at her, brow creased with confusion. He tried to reach for the ventilation tube but his hand was limp and awkward. Rupert blinked and turned his head to look around the room.

Claudette could remember—she could *feel* how much her mother had loved Rupert, even during the long years he was gone. How much she had worried. She didn't know or care if the tears that were streaming down her cheeks belonged entirely to her. Claudette sniffled and squeezed her brother's hand. "You're in the hospital. You're going to be okay."

He would have to recover the rest of the way on his own. When he was better... When he was better, they could share memories of their mother. Soul or memory, they could share her.

MARY ROBINETTE KOWAL is the author of the Hugo, Nebula, and Locus Award–winning alternate history novel *The Calculating Stars*, the first book in the Lady Astronaut series, which continues in 2025 with *The Martian Contingency*. She is also the author of The Glamourist Histories series, as well as standalone novels *Ghost Talkers* and *The Spare Man*. She has received the Astounding Award for Best New Writer, four Hugo Awards, and the Nebula and Locus Awards. Her stories appear in *Asimov's Science Fiction*, *Uncanny Magazine*, and several Year's Best anthologies. Mary Robinette has also worked as a professional puppeteer, is a member of the award-winning podcast *Writing Excuses*, and performs as a voice actor (SAG/AFTRA), recording fiction for authors including Seanan McGuire, Cory Doctorow, and Neal Stephenson. She lives in Denver with her husband Robert, their dog Guppy, and their "talking" cat Elsie. Visit her online at maryrobinettekowal.com.

* CONTENT NOTES: references to murders, as well as references to the death of a family member following prolonged illness.

庄子的梦 / ZHUANGZI'S DREAM

BY 曹白宇 / CAO BAIYU

TRANSLATED BY 朱佳玥 / STELLA JIAYUE ZHU

Short Story Long List*

Latent summer stirred while spring lay dormant. The fourth month had come to the state of Song and brought with it spells of rain. Tadpoles in the pond had recently developed hind legs; above, a stray shower had been drumming at the water pitter-patter. The rain-rinsed sky was tinged a darkening hue from horizon to zenith all the way to the concealed, eternal stars. When clouds were few, they resembled freshly picked cotton. Other times, they flocked to build elaborate pavilions in the sky.

A barefoot young man sauntered up a sun-facing, sloped meadow. At this time of the year, the pasture was lush. Thin grass blades peeked through between his toes and dampened the back of his feet with dew. Draped over his body was a ragged hemp robe with uneven patches at the elbows and around the cuffs. In his hands, he held a folding book, made of bamboo slips. It had been opened countless times, so much so that it had fallen apart at the leather-threaded seams and was scrupulously sewn back together.

He held a lesser office at a lacquer tree plantation and earned his daily grains by performing the same bureaucratic duties that had hardened into a routine. Here and now, he was known as Zhuang Zhou. In the ages to come, he should be revered as Master Zhuangzi.

Young Zhuangzi lay down on the meadow on his side and made a pillow of his forearm. Nature breathed, *in* and *out*. The wind came forth, coursing through the grass to find him and caress his cheeks. Dandelion seeds spread their wings, aided by the wind, so light, so airy, like soft down on a feather.

What a balmy day. Heat from the sun coddled him like a blanket. Zhuangzi yawned and scratched his back with the folding book as slumber inched up his shoulders and closed his eyes.

He fell asleep.

GIANT FISH

Carved into the oceanic floor was a trench sprawling long and deep beyond the stretch of imagination like an inborn scar opening toward the heart of the earth. In the depths of the trench was Kun, a giant fish lying dormant for eons, waiting in silence.

The trench had formed along a winding volcanic belt. This is where the pulse of the earth throbbed: fractures in the earth's crust, collisions between tectonic plates, rises of new mountains, and the oozing magma that made the ocean boil. Kun found an active submarine volcano and pressed its abdomen against the crater. Lava poured out and began to thicken as soon as it met the ice-cold seawater. Congealed, this earthly blood swathed Kun and imbued it with vital energy.

Over time, basalt deposits accrued on Kun's back, forming a thick, heaping crust, so the giant fish became a seamount for as long as it stayed still. All traces of light were swallowed by the kilometers of water above, letting through not even a glint. Without light, there was no photosynthesis; and without photosynthesis, there was no organic matter. But Kun was growing, and to grow, organic matter was essential.

It was lucky, then, that it did not lack company. Colonies of anaerobic bacteria lived and thrived on its scales. They were Earth's first inhabitants to whom the tree of life owed its genesis, but for all that they had been outcompeted by latecomers with more affinity for light and oxygen, wherefore they resigned to the deep sea as their dwelling. Kun was a powerful ally to the anaerobes. It took them on excursions along the seabed for inhabitable volcanoes rich in heat and inorganic nutrients, which were essential for the bacteria; in return, they produced organic matter for Kun. So nourished through symbiosis, Kun slowly grew. Coral polyps raise barrier reefs from the sands of time; what the bacteria accomplished in Kun was a miracle in equal measure.

Then, one day, the big fish felt something stir inside. At Nature's quiet beckoning, its biological clock started ticking. *Come on land. Come on land.* A voice resounded from within. This day had finally come, and Kun was ready. Every cell in its body was eager to answer Nature's call.

Its scaly body spasmed. Fins beating, Kun quaked in regular pulses until the sedimentary rocks on its back were torn asunder. Finally, it broke free, like an ancient god escaping its seal. The steep walls that lined the trench trembled too, sending sound waves through the waters to announce the awakening of a titan.

Once it had cleaned up the deposits on its body, Kun whipped its giant tail and sprang up. Soon, it shot out of the trench and brought behind it a turbid current like clouds of dust rising from the ground. Its snout split waves, its tail stirred ocean tides, and its eyes flashed like two burning torches ascending from the underworld. As Kun drew closer to the surface, long-forgotten light registered on its retinas, a light that had once only lived in memories of a past so distant it was as if separated by another lifetime.

The giant fish finally emerged from the sea. Its body formed a new continent, forging slowly and steadily northward. At its destination, Kun would bring this episode of its life to an end.

Stars rose and the sun set. The passing of time saw aquatic lives prosper: A diverse family of bony fish came to be, and they were accompanied by giant territorial oceanic beasts. But this creature of nightmares devoured them without distinction. It knew: The land was not far.

It had waited a long time; so long that the wait didn't even pale against the age of the planet. The land looked different from the last time

Kun had visited. Gymnosperms had risen to prominence and ferns had retreated to the bower. Gingkos, tree ferns, pines, cycads, horsetail reeds, and redwoods—the whole world was damp and warm. Rain laved barren lands and made them fertile. Four-legged reptiles, initially endowed with rudimentary cognitive structures, had evolved into countless new forms and reached the pinnacle of prosperity for their kind. In this moment, they ruled the Earth, but already another warm-blooded animal was quietly propagating. They were harbingers of a new era.

Then, everything changed.

Kun crashed into the shore. It closed its eyes, shadow looming, bringing with it seismic waves, devastating, like plundering troops. Its heart valves swung into action, followed by atria and ventricles out of dormancy to begin pumping electrolytic blood into Kun's whole body. During those endless nights undersea, Kun had been generously furnished with fuel from the volcanoes. Now, having connected all the bio-batteries in its organs in parallel, Kun switched to full-power mode.

This beast pulled itself forward by crawling. It wiggled its pectoral and pelvic lobe fins like an amphibious fish leaving water for the first time. Land creatures looked on in horror at its sheer size, its huge eyes hanging midair like stars, its maw tightly lined with fine teeth, opening and closing like a meat grinder. Devourer of this world, Kun tore and swallowed everything on its way, living being and land alike, leaving a striation on the ancient continent in its wake.

Nonetheless, Kun was not a glutton who indulged in excessive eating. Its massive size made consumption meaningless: No matter how relentlessly it fed, it lost energy faster than it could take energy in. The sole purpose of its consumption was gene acquisition; it needed the ever-refining genetic codes of living things, shaped by natural selection, to design its new body. Kun was more than a collector of hereditary material—it was also a master of proactive adaptation. So it continued its way up north: Through the tropics, toward the temperate zone, the swing of its scythe never stopped. Unceasing, too, was the metamorphosis of its body. Like monks in meditation who enter a new stage of awakening at each epiphany, Kun evolved stage by stage as it journeyed forward. Its lobe fins grew thicker, and their spines contracted to become part of the endoskeleton. Its dorsal fins lengthened to form a spinous, perforated, sail-like protrusion for thermoregulation. Appearance-wise, Kun was growing closer to a four-legged reptile.

Meanwhile, a halophilic archaea strain had been released from the spores carried in Kun's tail. Its propagation in Kun's electrolyte blood turned the giant a violet color. The halophiles converted light into electricity and stored it in Kun's bio-batteries. Now that it could combine water and carbon dioxide into organic matter, the giant fish started craving water, so much so that it dreamed of going back to its native sea in the south. As chance would have it, the northern hemisphere was in the rainy season. Whenever rain greeted this young planet, it found Kun couching in repose, quiet, unstirred. Rain washed away the dust of its journey and nourished its body. Rain is the source of life.

We cannot ascertain Kun's intelligence. Granted, it had five brains to coordinate physical movements, but they were too small against its colossus of a body. Thoughtless and motionless, Kun let itself be stroked by the filaments of rain. All the while, its subconscious mind remained active. Slowly and confusedly, it began to wonder at the meaning of life and its journey. Why did it sleep and idle for so long in exchange for mere moments of toil and trouble? What was the point? Nigh on immortal, it nevertheless relied on access to the genes of living things that existed for brief hours and weeks. Was this worthwhile?

The rain stopped before Kun reached its conclusion, so once again the giant fish rose up. The meaning of its life was none other than the journey itself. Spring passed into summer and became winter. Kun had lost track of how far it traveled. It saw complex flora give way to simple and animal sightings turn scarce. The height of the sun declined, and the loss of heat quickened. Soon from the heavens fell a white crystal, beautiful and unblemished.

At long last, Kun's body betrayed signs of exhaustion. Drawn into the clutches of fatigue, Kun caught a sniff of fire and heat in the wind and found a volcano with the last of its energy. This was a snow-molded landscape in the extreme north: The volcano smoldered and flamed against the northern lights' eerie glow to paint the scene of an earthly inferno. This giant fish, now thoroughly spent, crawled to the top, and from there it brought its pilgrimage to a close. Without the slightest hesitation, Kun leaped from the precipice. Inside, it would be reborn through fire.

Its body dissolved, condensed, and morphed into a giant ivory egg. This egg would spend the coming years slowly gathering thermal energy while sorting out its collection of genes, for they are the essence of life. When all was done, Kun would descend to the world again in a new form—something more efficient, perchance with wings. The time would then come for it to return to the origin and source of life, the place it came from and where it belonged: the sea in the south; dark, holy, and infinite.

TENTACLES OF A SNAIL

The snail was thirsty.

It saw a droplet of morning dew poised a few centimeters above at the tip of a grass blade. So it wiggled up the stalk to taste the bead, swaying gently, slowly, even leisurely. Though the snail was little, it was born noble, an emperor who carried its own castle. Nothing was worth its hurry.

Buddhists say that a single mustard seed, though minuscule, contains the entire Mount Meru. Likewise, the snail's two tentacles seated two entire nations. On the left lived a bellicose people who called their nation Pugnus and the left tentacle Terra Pugni. On the right lived a people equally bellicose. Their nation was Brutus and the right tentacle was Terra Bruta.

During the prehistoric dark ages of primordial chaos and ignorance, there was no contact between the two. The world was too big and the nations too small; when their forebears worked the wilderness by slashing trees and burning bushes, they could hardly imagine that there might be limits to the world where eyes failed to reach. Thousands of years had passed since then; civilizations had come into being in both, but they remained separate from each other.

It was in philosophy that the existence of the other was first postulated. Thinkers in Pugnus introduced the concept of 'Yin-Yang,' which

stated that in all things and all states of affairs, the opposites are complementary, mutually implicated, and unified. If Pugnus and Terra Pugni
existed, then a complementary nation and a complementary continent
existed ipso facto. Meanwhile, in Brutus, the thesis 'All things are
governed by numbers' had risen to prominence. Mathematicians in
Brutus had deduced from a series of complex calculations that a
universe containing exactly one world could not possibly be at equilibrium; ergo a continent distinct from Terra Bruta must exist.

A thousand and three hundred years passed before these existential
claims were empirically evidenced by the inventions of the compass and
the polarizer. Seafarers in Pugnus had long used compasses for direction
and navigation, and they noticed that the indicators in compasses consistently deviated from true north. What was more, there were patterns to
the disagreement. Through trial and error, the seafarers came up with a
correctional calculus. When this calculus was acquired by the royal
house, the imperial observatory subjected it to intense scrutiny and, in
the end, confirmed the results with counting rods and located the source
of the interference in another continent beyond the horizon.

Meanwhile, in Brutus, the flourishing of visual arts gave rise to the
need for a special kind of spectacles that enabled naturalist painters to
filter out diffuse light. These spectacles were smoothed down from
natural mica sheets at first. Then, when demand increased, craftsmen
began manufacturing glass polarizers aimed at different wavelengths.
One day, as a craftsman held a new lens against daylight during calibration, a whole new world suddenly took shape in front of his eyes.

He gasped in amazement, which drew his workmates close, and they
too gaped at the heavenly spectacle through his lens. Word spread like
wildfire. Production of these spectacles scaled up immediately, while
business in the industry at large also boomed. At once, the whole nation
was looking up at the heavens with polarized lenses in their hands.
Nature had disjoined two adjacent worlds with a clever optical barrier,
but when the curtain was lifted, the land of myths and legends came to
light in plain sight.

Sight, so vivid and transparent, left an impression far stronger than
could be produced by any hypothesis or proof following rod calculus.

Soon, positivism and skepticism became broadly influential in Brutus's public discourse. The people of Brutus abolished religious courts, sent the king to the guillotine, and instituted a democratic republic. Liberated minds set off growth in productive forces. Empirical sciences triumphed, while rationalist principles motivated reforms in the humanities. The nation marched steadily into the age of steam.

Progress continued for hundreds of years until every street was teeming with steam-powered machinery enshrouded in their own pearly vapor. Brutus began to stagnate. The land became overpopulated; endless coal smoke poisoned the air; the widening gap between the rich and the poor, adding to deteriorating living conditions, caused existing civil tensions to escalate. A revolution was on the horizon. Desperate to redirect popular grievances and find a scapegoat for themselves, the governors of Brutus turned their eyes to the sky.

At this point, survival was already strenuous. Nevertheless, Brutus pooled its resources and built a fleet of nine airships equipped with the latest military technology and nine thousand crew members. The plan was to sail across the heavenly barrier, settle in the other continent, colonize it, and carve out a new home for the people of Brutus, which had become, by now, a nation teetering on the brink of disintegration. The expedition was its last throw of the dice.

When the fleet from Brutus arrived, they came to a people still living under feudalism. Here, lords thrived, and their tenants suffered, and though rulers rose and fell, the order of things remained unchanged. The people of Pugnus gawked at these extraterrestrial visitors as if they were something other than human. But, abiding by principles of civility, they still received the crew with friendliness. It dawned on the crew then, that, contrary to the propaganda they had received, Pugnus was not populated by feral, bloodthirsty monsters in human guise. Far from it, these were real people like themselves. Troubled by their own conscience and embittered about Brutus's ruling clique, the crew refused to obey the genocidal order and declared an alliance with Pugnus in its self-defense.

Their mutiny was the last straw for Brutus. When the news broke, Brutus's two major parties descended into malicious smear campaigns against each other, and then proceeded to commence a ninety-year civil war. This was the breathing space Pugnus needed. It seized the opportunity to reinforce itself against the next round of attacks. The expedition crew taught Pugnus everything they knew, sowing the seeds of an industrial revolution. The encounter with foreign ideas also breathed a new life into Pugnus's ancient sciences. Its civilization entered a stage of rapid growth.

Keen on making the traitors pay, and eager to nip Pugnus's technological revolution in its bud, Brutus launched a second campaign the moment its civil war came to an end. Steam-powered cars fitted with swivel guns were airdropped onto Pugnus's plains in coordination with foot soldiers carrying high-pressure smoothbore guns. But never in their wildest dreams did they think that Pugnus would be waiting for them with ironclad super robots. These metal giants were driven by internal combustion engines and wore indestructible alloy armor for protection. Slowly but surely, they advanced, tearing through Brutus's front lines, wrecking the armors on the steam powered chariots, and crushing the troops' hyperbaric airbags.

All that live by technology shall perish by technology. The Brutus army, so thoroughly defeated, had no choice but to surrender. From then on, the two nations entered a two-hundred-year standoff. They hadn't figured each other out fully, and for that reason they cautioned against reckless attacks, which held potential for self-sabotage. The compromise was a cold war, one rife with mutual provocation and espionage.

During this time, public support for peace never tailed off, but many more came under the sway of fanaticism. They sang the tune of hate and called for an arms race. Vigilant nationalists even discovered the subtlest distinction between the two people: Those native to Pugnus had bigger right eyes and the contrary was true of those native to Brutus. But how could faces so different share a common humanity underneath?! The Other must be destroyed! We must secure the existence of our people!

Ignorance fueled chauvinism. The cold war soon escalated into hot, violent battles. They had been sitting at the poker table for two hundred years, watching each other, thinking. Now, they were ready to play their hands. First, Pugnus deployed its ground forces, then in return Brutus destroyed all of Pugnus's satellites and space stations in one fell swoop. Pugnus launched MIRV intercontinental ballistic missiles at Brutus, so

Brutus turned its strategic laser weapons to Pugnus's capital. Pugnus redirected an asteroid at Brutus, but Brutus executed a precision interception, turning the threat into a meteor shower.

The war went on for six hundred years, and neither saw that war was good for nothing but agony and devastation. Instead, they came to the decision that conventional weapons were simply incapable at vanquishing the opponent. This prompted both nations to propose 'millennium projects' aimed at catalyzing scientific progress in their own nations, suppressing breakthroughs from the enemy by any means necessary, and culminating in the design of an ultimate superweapon to wipe the other off the map.

In Pugnus, a weapon design project code-named Singularity began research into quark fission chain reactions to generate the energy capable of extinction-level events. Meanwhile, Brutus started developing an electromagnetic pulse weapon designated Ragnarök. It would produce microwaves that broke chemical bonds by setting atoms in vibration and, when directed at the enemy, would completely obliterate them. Time passed. Regimes changed. Periods of peace punctuated the unending war. The millennium projects staggered from time to time but were never put to a full stop.

In the end, they were completed at almost the same time, with the quark bomb coming into existence only a week earlier. Pugnus'ss leadership spent those few days in deliberation, dithering between unleashing total destruction and staying with deterrence tactics. Just then, their spy satellites picked up signals in Brutus of countless high-power radars switching on. Their opponent had launched the first and ultimate strike —the deadly microwaves would arrive in minutes. The president of Pugnus held his finger above the launch button. His advisor shook her head: The world was already bound for death—why destroy another before it drew its last breath? The president let out a sigh before pressing the red button.

The snail felt an itch in its tentacles, so it brought them in and rubbed them against each other. Pugnus and Brutus had been born while it had ascended the grass, and the centuries and millennia that had passed for them had been a fleeting instant to the snail, who remained oblivious that two civilizations had just perished on its head.

For the snail, the droplet was yet beyond its reach, and there was still half the way to go.

CHAOS

The lawgiver of the southern expanse was Speed, the lawgiver of the northern expanse was Haste, and the lawgiver of the center was Chaos.

Measuring five kilometers in diameter and almost as large as a small terrestrial planet, Speed was, at least in size, less a living being and more a celestial body. As it turned out, its corporeal self was a layer of crystalline solid wrapped around a planet, stretched over its terrains like floor covering. Lattice vibrations in the crystal were what Speed used to build a basic arithmetic logic unit; then the unit evolved into an advanced, multi-tier logical architecture. It was a supercomputer, commanding all silicon-based life-forms in the universe, fueled by none other than radioactive decay in the planetary core, but Speed owed its humble origins to three simple logic gates: OR, AND, NOT.

Meanwhile, the appearance of Haste was still stranger. It had evolved as a consequence of a carbon-fundamentalist movement, into a nebula of clustered nerve fibers. Once upon a time, carbon lives warred against silicon lives; the carbon alliance was losing and driven all the way to the edge of a spiral arm in the Milky Way when a puritanical movement broke out across the alliance calling for the destruction of any and all inorganic modules used in assisted computation. Haste commanded all carbon lives, but even so it was helpless against the revolution. The computation matrix employed in military strategy and resource allocation had also been blown up by the radicals.

As a last resort, Haste transformed itself. It grew out its nerve fibers, which provided structural integrity to its body, and placed biomolecular chips at all nodes. Haste also wrote a biological algorithm that did away with binary data, thereby overcoming the propagation delay in signal transmissions inherent to organic bodies, to allow for concurrent process execution in disjoint parts of its body.

In the early days of its new anatomy, Haste's tremendous computing power helped the carbon alliance defy the odds with a series of victories over a stronger enemy. Before long, Speed came to the realization that, as a leader, it could no longer contend with Haste, so it resolved to forgo all tactics. Since silicon-based lives had taken hold of the majority of resources in the Milky Way, they took advantage of their reproductive efficiency and advanced through the battlefield by way of suicide attacks against staggering casualty figures.

Had Chaos not stepped in, the galaxy would still be mired in infinite, cyclic war and strife. The details of the story did not survive, though one thing was certain: Chaos swayed Speed and Haste toward peace by demonstrating its own power. Since then, silicon and carbon lives had resigned to their own provinces: one residing in the galaxies on the Scutum-Centaurus arm, and the other in the galaxies on the Perseus arm.

For long, it remained a mystery just what sort of thing Chaos was, a mystery even Speed and Haste knew very little about. It was less a *thing* and more a *thought* insofar as its consciousness did not turn on any single entity. Nor did its existence depend on anything else, including gravity and electromagnetic waves. Chaos seemed omnipresent, omni-scient, and omnipotent. Some civilizations worshipped it as a god, which Chaos did not endorse; other civilizations hunted after it across the galaxy, and they received no punishment, either.

Speed and Haste were the only ones to enjoy the privilege of occa-sional unilateral communication with Chaos, who seemed to hold the two commanders in certain esteem. The passage of time saw develop-ments to intergalactic space travel technologies that led to the expansion of civilizations from the Milky Way to galaxies beyond. Thus began a new act in the grand drama of history, as tensions between silicon and carbon lives eased and their commanders took their final bows, stepping away from the stage altogether. Speed and Haste went on to rove the Milky Way. They became living legends and were revered as lawgivers and spiritual leaders.

After Speed and Haste moved on from their respective communities, Chaos began reaching out more frequently. It occurred to them that Chaos had started paying more visits to their consciousnesses, as well as exchanging a great deal more information at each visit. In confidence, Chaos taught them lost knowledge and unknown theories and, at times, also answered their questions. Although they did not know Chaos's reason for doing so, living things as they were, they suspected that Chaos was lonely.

At last, Chaos reached into both Speed's and Haste's minds at the same time, which allowed them to feel Chaos and come face-to-face with each other for the first time. Cautiously, they reached out to each other and attempted to communicate. These two rivals, who had fought for tens of thousands of years, understood at once that despite the astronomical differences in their life-forms, mental structures, and values, in other fundamental ways they were the same. Haste hesitated for a few microseconds before sending its greeting to Speed, which Speed returned in goodwill without dallying.

Just then, they received Chaos's neural oscillations. "I am dying."

"That's impossible. Even we can attain immortality. Why can't you?" Unsettled, Haste dismissed the claim.

Speed was more prudent. It evaluated Chaos's declaration carefully and came to its own conclusion. "Chaos is right. It has suggested to us that the universe is an isolated system where, according to the principle of increased entropy, all things eventually and inevitably end in decay."

Silence overtook them. Chaos departed, but it left behind a data packet and kept Speed and Haste in connection. Chaos's intention was beyond them, so after a brief exchange of opinions, Speed and Haste began working on decoding the data packet together. Soon, a sea of information came pouring in, and the past lives of Chaos the living being was revealed to the two galactic leaders.

Chaos's species had originated from a brain parasite. They had swayed their hosts to make macro decisions favorable to the parasites without compromising the hosts' self-determination. At the advent of the age of exploration, the host civilization of this parasite species had begun to venture outside its own stellar system. When galactic civilizations in the Milky Way had come in contact with each other, Chaos's species had flourished through their communication and collision.

Having absorbed and synthesized the wisdoms of so many civilizations, Chaos's species had surpassed them all and grown to be the leader of the pack. During their heyday, the Milky Way had been the parasites' farm for knowledge. These hidden puppet masters had raised civilizations as if they were sowing seeds, accelerating their development in all sorts of ways, harvesting their technological achievements, and finally destroying them before they could become too difficult to deal with.

At last, the parasites had grown tired of the bondage of corporeality and decided to let go of material existence completely. They'd succeeded and, as a result, had given up reproduction and lost the possibility of evolution ever again. However, they'd been stunned to discover that even the purest minds decayed over time and ground to nothing. One after another, Chaos's fellow beings had stepped into the graves they'd dug themselves. Chaos had been the most powerful among them and so survived to this day.

But now torrents were rising in the depth of its subconscious too. Chaos had an inkling that it had little time left, so it made Speed and Haste know of its last wish. As a parasite, Chaos had no sensory faculty of its own. It perceived the external world only through other living things. But there are a thousand worlds in a thousand lives' eyes, so Chaos had no singular, subjective perception of the universe. Its wish was for Speed and Haste to modify the body it once had. Chaos wanted to experience the universe in its essence without an intermediary before its life slipped away.

At the end of its message, Chaos left a series of coordinates. A myriad of things went through Speed's and Haste's minds; nevertheless, they followed the coordinates, which led them to a cleverly hidden black dwarf. This was the carcass of a star, and at the center of the carcass, they found Chaos's well-preserved corpse. It looked like a ball of flesh, round and sturdy, with functionally indeterminate appendages and wings. After initial analyses, Speed and Haste found that it was composed mainly of organic matter; in addition, it had a crystalline organ, reminiscent of Speed, which was responsible for reason.

Speed and Haste did not know how such a strange life-form could be capable of parasitism. They conjectured that Chaos was the leader of its species and that was why it had such an unusual body. Once they scanned Chaos's corpse, Speed and Haste decided on a modification plan. They would install various external sensory receptors for Chaos, construct a central processor to deal with the external stimuli, and connect the processor to Chaos's rational organ. Speed and Haste completed their construction nearby on a dead planet that orbited the black dwarf. And if measured from that planet, their creation took seven sidereal days.

Now that Speed and Haste's work was complete, they felt a powerful consciousness descending by them. That was Chaos—about to return to its former body. Then, all of a sudden, the strange ball of flesh showed signs of life. Speed and Haste looked on from the exosphere at this tiny, insignificant thing below: Who would have thought that it was once the master of the Milky Way? Chaos sat still and quiet and saw the world for itself for the first time. The universe opened up in front of it.

It saw flashes of nebulae, the births of stars. Satellites orbit planets, stars gird the Milky Way, their movements unceasing. Heavenly bodies collide, heavenly bodies explode in thunderous silence. Species originate, species die, but cosmic radiation is a constant through their ebb and flow. The foldings of space carve out dimensions. Time twists and coils and compels all things to their destiny. Scattered pulsars are the lighthouses that coordinate the universe. Black holes, the graveyards of time and substance, make what is into what is not. The cosmological redshift and the expansion of the universe are never slowing down. Dice fall and wave functions collapse. In lieu of God, the observer determines the outcome. A singularity becomes chaos. Existence reverts to nothingness. Between meaning and meaninglessness, life strikes a balance.

The presence of Chaos grew dimmer and dimmer. To Speed and Haste it directed its last words:

My friends, thank you.

THE HAPPINESS OF FISH

Zhuangzi and Huizi met by River Hao for some fresh air. Schools of fish streamed back and forth while they leaned against the bridge in contemplation.

The Hao was very clear, so much so that the small fish appeared to have defied gravity and risen in midair, leaving behind mere shadows on the riverbed, vivid with crisp contours. As Zhuangzi and Huizi contemplated the fish, the fish were also looking back, serenely, as if they were philosophers of the subaquatic world. Huizi picked up a pebble and flicked it at the water. The fish all scattered except for one; it stayed behind, unruffled.

"That's an empty-headed one." Huizi said, eyeing the rotund animal. Then he turned around to pester Zhuangzi. "Look. This daft fish is just like you. Not a thought behind those blank eyes."

Zhuangzi dismissed his verbal missile easily. "What do *you* know? This fish roams around by itself and delights in its own being. It is not disturbed by the material world, nor does it answer to anyone else's whim. It has achieved the state of *Dao*, and that is true happiness. How could an unenlightened chump like you ruffle its feathers?"

Huizi, ever the contrarian, did not relent. "Alright then. If you will, since you are not a fish, where did you learn what happiness is for a fish?"

Apprehensive, Zhuangzi sidestepped the question and put it back to Huizi. "If *you* will, since you are not me, how do you know that I don't know what happiness is for a fish?"

Seeing that his opponent had risen to the bait, Huizi seized on the misstep. "Sure, I am not you, so I can't know what you know. But likewise, you are not a fish, so you can't know what happiness is for a fish. This much, at least, I can ascertain."

Now that he was losing the debate, Zhuangzi resorted to non sequiturs. "Don't stray from the question you started with! You asked me 'where' I learned what happiness is for a fish, assuming as given that I *do* know. Now, I will tell you just where I learned it—right here on this bridge over River Hao!"

Huizi cackled. He had finally evened the score against Zhuangzi since their last debate under a great tree of heaven, where Huizi had come away the loser. For him, the gratification of seeing Zhuangzi bear dialectical defeat and resort to sophistry rivaled the pleasure of devouring rare delicacies.

Meanwhile, Zhuangzi's concern was something else entirely. While his eyes were fixed on the chubby, placid fish, his mind was nevertheless drifting further and further away. There was no doubt that he knew what the fish thought, because it had no thought whatsoever. It was simply that Zhuangzi was unwilling to lay bare the reason, for this fish was in fact an automaton made by him.

About two years ago, Zhuangzi had become engrossed in bionics out of the blue. Of course, he wasn't much interested in its practical applications, which were the preoccupation of the utilitarian Mohists. Rather, Zhuangzi was taken up with the possibility of artificial life— Gods born from giant eggs, men made of molded mud, so on and so forth. That was what fascinated him.

His very first creation had been a wooden dragonfly. He exchanged saved gourd seeds for a set of used micro carving tools from a student of Lu Ban himself: gouges, carving knives, marking knives, tiny chisels, and micro hand planes. Then for a few bottles of fish glue reduced over a long simmer, he acquired an array of precision-made mainsprings and transmission components. The springs when uncoiled were as thin as the wings of a cicada, the engaged gears as fine as mustard seeds, and the transmission belts as fine as strands of hair.

He had carved the dragonfly's body out of oak heartwood and placed the clockwork motor in its chest cavity. Then he'd shaved the dragonfly's wings from basswood planks and scored them with decorative loop patterns, before tightening the winder and releasing the dragonfly gently into the air. The clockwork had begun to unwind, gears creaking, the transmission shaft turning, springs oscillating, and finally the dragonfly had flapped its wings. It had woven through the air haltingly, and at times had seemed to linger in the spirit of playfulness.

The dragonfly was a small, toylike thing, and still it had taken an incredible amount of effort to bring into existence, and for the first time Zhuangzi had felt the joy of creation. Since then, he had built more mechanical creatures: frogs from oracle bones, birds from fruit peels, turtles from mud tiles, and bees from wax paper. He practically reigned over the animal kingdom like a divinity.

This fish was Zhuangzi's latest work and it was a major step forward in technology. It had a tailor-made self-winding mechanism that took advantage of natural ripples and wavelets to keep it fully wound without interruption. It also had four water reservoirs and an intricate counter-weight, so the fish could rise or sink by adjusting its buoyancy to avoid undercurrents and vortices. If desired, the fish could be made to swim all the way to the East Sea.

But Zhuangzi was not pleased with his designs. He found himself to be a mere imitator, not a true creator. The trinkets he had made, though some of them were so vivid as to pass for the real deal, were ultimately not alive. They were insentient, unconscious, unthinking, let alone intelligent. They were good for the sake of passing time, but a long way from the elusive goal of artificial life.

Seeing that Zhuangzi had knitted his brows together and lost himself in thinking, Huizi let his mind wander too. The debate had also rippled through his mind. As he leaned against the balustrade, he pondered. Of course he knew what was on Zhuangzi's mind, but he didn't have the heart to lay bare the ugly truth: the fact that he had designed Zhuangzi's entire mind and that the latter was no more than a conscious android.

When Huizi first decided to make an android, he was only looking for an opponent for himself. He was heir to the School of Names and a champion of their theory on issues of language and reality. Having mastered the rhetorical art, he could debate concrete issues and unravel conceptual paradoxes with equal flourish. He vanquished counterarguments with ease and finesse, and defended patently false claims through sophistry. When it came to disputation, Huizi had become unbeatable and as a result lonely, too. What he needed was a friendly rival, someone of equal caliber so as to stand a chance in debates against himself.

But as his project progressed, Huizi grew more ambitious. His art was an imitation of life, but life was itself an imitation of truth, so he was at least two degrees removed from absolute truth. Hopeful that he could break through this boundary, Huizi was no longer content with the making of an equal opponent. He put his mind to the creation of a perfect human, one that exceeded all of nature's creations so as to approach the realm of true being. The success of Zhuangzi was one big step toward that goal.

Huizi still had vivid memories of the glass test tubes and petri dishes stacked to the ceiling in his basement, and of the temperature-controlled chambers heated by charcoal, rattling and murmuring around the clock. His closest acquaintances then were, at the very most, a bronze microscope, droppers made from slender bamboo, and perchance an old and beaten hand-cranked centrifuge. The incubator needed a constant supply of energy, so he harnessed the power of wind, lightning, water, and fire. The growth of Zhuangzi's body needed minerals and protein, so he sourced them from masons and butchers. He procured anatomical drawings from the State of Yan, programming scripts from the State of Qi, high-speed computing machinery from the State of Chu, and a brain-machine interface from the State of Qin.

With a partial copy of his own mind, Huizi configured the low-level device drivers in Zhuangzi's brain architecture. Then, borrowing from the philosophy of Laozi, he distinguished his opponent with a separate logical framework. At last, he fabricated Zhuangzi's memory and simulated emotions with the appearance of reality. When Zhuangzi stepped out of the incubator, it was clear as day that Huizi had succeeded; true being was now within reach. The birth of a new intelligent life called for a baptism, so he engraved the back of Zhuangzi's neck with a symbol, also to betoken its bearer's artifactuality.

Huizi had worked day and night on Zhuangzi, putting in him more than twenty years' work and, not to mention, his heart and soul. But it was worth the toil; now, Zhuangzi was not so much an opponent as a friend and brother. Over the course of their debates and discourses, Huizi had come to see that Zhuangzi was steadily surpassing him in intellect and learning. There was no telling where Zhuangzi would reach in the future, though plainly it was impossible to overstate his potential. The one thing Zhuangzi would remain ignorant of was the number *SEVEN* engraved on his neck. That was his registration number and doubled as his code name. The secret might accompany him for a lifetime.

But. Hold on. Why 'seven'? Had there been six others? No, no. Why can't I remember? How? Could there have been another android? ...Seven... Seven... Six... Six?

The back of Huizi's neck itched. He reached around to scratch at the spot. To his horror, he found a number faintly engraved in bronze script, hidden at his nape. It read: *SIX*.

TO DREAM OF A BUTTERFLY

On the meadow, a light-footed butterfly flitted to Zhuangzi's side, dancing around him with fluttering wings.

There he is, asleep. What a great opportunity. The miniature camera in the butterfly's eyes activated and refocused to capture all of the sleeping philosopher in one frame. In the butterfly's abdomen was a superconducting battery working at maximum capacity, and in its thorax a nanocomputer running at full speed. After lossless compression, the captured video signal was transmitted back through antennas in the butterfly's front tentacles to the future.

This butterfly was in fact a machine, and a micro time travel machine at that. Time traveling was too costly; transporting every additional gram required exponentially more energy. Even this butterfly, which had been made with atom assembly technology and had not a single excess component, still weighed a whopping 9.73242 grams. The energy spent on sending it here was equal to all the solar energy the Earth absorbs in a second, the equivalent of detonating the Tsar Bomba eight hundred and fifty times over, which could power a one-hundred-watt light bulb for fifty-six million years.

Stellar energy harvesting had long entered its mature phase, and if he were to screw up this experiment—the young man shuddered—he would be in deep trouble with his advisor. Here he was, in a space station in Mercury's orbit, feeling hot and sweaty just at the sight of the oversized sun, and the thought still gave him chills.

He had no idea why he'd even bothered to do a PhD in temporal history. If he had left for industry jobs sooner, with his degree in satellite mineralogy, he could have easily bought a beachfront property on Titan by now. He'd be standing in the middle of the house, switching the ceiling to transparent, and watching the orange sky bespeaking rhythmic motions of primitive life. He'd have a glass of Bordeaux in hand, and his beautiful wife would wear a sleeveless qipao. She would embrace him from behind, red lips pressed on his nape... Alright, maybe life wouldn't be *that* comfortable. Still, it would be better than being single in his late twenties and living in single graduate student housing with a bunch of other bachelors like monks!

The young man liked to fantasize. All sorts of wild ideas popped into his mind like mushrooms blooming after rain. While he was lost in a daydream, Nana—that's the name he'd given to the butterfly time travel machine—sent back the first batch of data. The terminal pinged, calling him back to reality. He rubbed his face and refocused his attention at the screen. The data compression ratio was too high, so it took a couple seconds for the image to decompress.

It is here! It's here now! The image was blurry, but still it showed the silhouette of a human figure lying in a meadow. The young man tapped away on a virtual keyboard as if he were playing a guzheng: adjust the angle, enlarge, adjust the angle again, enlarge, stop, zoom in, zoom in, zoom out, sharpen, render the pixels—snap! *Excellent! Oh, that is great, so clean and sharp!*

The young man clenched his fist in excitement. He was over the moon to be the first person to take a photo of Zhuangzi! That alone made learning time archaeology worth it! Screw the seafront house on Titan! To hell with it! He piloted the butterfly around Zhuangzi to create a three-dimensional scan, which he would later use to generate a digital hologram. The supercomputer on the space station communicated with Nana through a channel enabled by quantum entanglement, but a bottleneck in the data flow necessitated the use of data compression and decompression. As a result, there was a two-second delay to the operation of the butterfly.

He had to be careful. If he touched any object from the past or if his disturbance reached the threshold value, he would create a butterfly effect in the stream of time, in which case this tiny time machine would be crushed by temporal tides. Current experiments had reached the preliminary conclusion that time had a perfect self-stabilizing mechanism. There was no need to worry about changing the future. No grandfather paradox. Time flowed in one direction only and killed every possibility of alteration in its cradle.

What was it like to be crushed by time? Experimentation in short-interval time travel had shown it to be an exercise in annihilation, a total obliteration of matter without the discharge of energy; stuff became, simply, nothing. But according to the principle of mass conservation and Einstein's mass-energy equivalence, matter can only become other matter or energy. So what new form did that obliterated matter assume? Where did it go? The answer remained unknown.

The young man put Nana on autopilot. It would hover over Zhuangzi's head to create a scan of his cerebral cortex and record its activities. If all went well, the young man's team would be able to use these data to map Zhuangzi's essential thinking patterns in the next few months. Looking at the electroencephalogram results and brain graphs on the monitor, the young man could tell that Zhuangzi's brain was very active. He must be dreaming then. The young man wondered about the dreams: What would they be like, belonging to a man who lived thousands of years ago? And, as for the young man himself, he had been writing a science fiction story, adapted from Zhuangzi's parables.

The superconducting battery could well last Nana another half hour; afterward, a self-destruct program would be activated to wrap the project up; he could not leave it to time to bury all traces. The young man looked at the photo print: Zhuangzi, asleep, seemed to be about his own age, a man in his twenties. He had a beard and delicate features, wore his hair down, and had a folding book splayed by his side. The young man struggled to make out the etched ancient characters on the book. Maybe it was *Dao De Jing*, or maybe not. Well, it didn't matter; he would investigate later. Just then, a message from Nana popped up: *Data collection completed. Do you want to activate the self-destruct program now?* The young man glanced at the time; there were still seven minutes left. An idea came to him.

He could find out about Zhuangzi's dreams! If he connected his brain to the computer, he could project the scans from the butterfly directly into his own brain! Yes, that was at least theoretically possible! Another article he had read came to mind: If one person's brain activities were converted to analog signals, it could then be transmitted into another person's brain to map the original mental states!

The young man quieted for a moment. He would need to sidestep data compression and decompression by increasing the power of the quantum channel; then data transmission would be synchronous. He would also need to change Nana's output from the default digital signal to analog. Finally, in order to project Zhuangzi's mind into his own, the amount of data scanned would need to increase drastically, far exceeding the system default threshold limit.

Doing these things might lead to overheating and destroying Nana, but it would give himself a window of a minute or so. Theories of brain projection were still immature, so there would be some risk. But. What the heck. It was the opportunity of a lifetime and wouldn't come knocking a second time. He had used the energy equivalent to five million tons of coal just to take a photo of an ancient Chinese philosopher. This sort of thing would never happen again. He had to seize the opportunity. The risk was worth it.

The young man quickly grabbed a data cable attached to the terminal and connected it to the portal on the back of his neck. The microchip planted in his cerebellum began connecting his brain to the supercomputer in the space station. The young man migrated access control from the terminal to himself and began removing default system permission restrictions one by one. The butterfly bustled about, and Zhuangzi, murmuring, rolled over in his sleep. The young man closed his eyes, waiting for Zhuangzi's mind to upload.

Here it comes. Zhuangzi's thoughts, or rather, his dreams. Contrary to what the young man had expected, the impact was minimal; nor was there discomfort or pain as the article described. These dreams were as gentle and serene as the Buddhist chants of Yushan. They cast shadows one after another in the young man's mind: the giant fish that became a mighty bird, countries on the tentacles of a snail, emperors in the sea, the happiness of fish, and a butterfly in a reverie. These ideas were passed down through thousands of years and were still living and breathing, vividly, to this day; and now they came to him directly from the source. This very moment, this young man who lived in the space age felt himself to be one with the philosopher from antiquity.

But wait. Wait a second. A strange feeling overcame him. There was something very familiar in the projection, ideas that he seemed to know, terminology and concepts that appeared only after the industrial revolutions. *This... This is... No! No way! Absolutely no way! The transmission has been reversed! My thoughts are being cast into Zhuangzi's mind! We are synchronizing!*

The young man scrambled to disconnect himself from Zhuangzi, but the synchronization process was hogging the quantum channel's bandwidth. The butterfly also started malfunctioning from overwork. *It's over! It's all over!* His own death wouldn't even matter now. If he created any disturbance in the timeline, he'd be a villain for the ages. Desperate times called for desperate measures—the young man ripped the data cable off the back of his head. The abrupt disconnection caused pain like an electric shock. He fell to the ground with a start, his mind blank.

A long time later, he came to himself. Did he change the course of history? When he looked around, nothing seemed amiss. Spit out from the printer, the photo had fallen to the ground. The man in the photo was still sleeping, just as the eternal sun outside the space station's full-length window was still the same through changing seasons. Nothing had ever been any other way.

What eluded the young man was that he hadn't changed history by accident as much as created the very history that always was. Time was the world serpent coiled in a closed circle devouring its own tail, and he was at the juncture. Nothing was accidental and everything that happened was destined to be so. Time moves—forward.

• • • •

Zhuangzi woke up.

Slowly, he opened his eyes and thought that he saw a butterfly perching on the tip of his nose, but when he attended to it, the butterfly was nowhere to be found. The very moment Zhuangzi's eyes alighted on the butterfly, it had already been annihilated in time and turned to dust. Zhuangzi sat up. He had been asleep for a long time and had had many dreams.

He'd dreamed of strange men, beasts, and even his old friend Huizi. The wild creatures and stories appearing in the dreams had been in his mind for a long time; but this time around, there had been something new. They'd appeared in unfamiliar forms, spoken incomprehensible words, and operated baffling machines.

Zhuangzi sighed and sat cross-legged on the meadow. Wind tousled his hair and the world breathed with him. Flowers blossomed and wilted; clouds billowed and dispersed; tall grasses bent down when the wind rose; fish revealed themselves in the pellucid water. It was April in the State of Song; Nature cohered with the cosmic order and life came forth when summoned by the earth. The land was flourishing wherever one looked.

Is this therefore *Dao*? No, not quite. But Zhuangzi thought he had come very close in the dream just now. Did he at long last find *Dao*, or did *Dao* come across him by chance? Have I become a butterfly in my dream? Has a butterfly become me in its dream? Did I wake up to my own world? Or did I fall into someone else's in sweet slumber?

Zhuangzi smiled. He had forgotten who he was and who he wasn't. The immensity of his introspection echoed the immensity of the cosmos, so for a brief moment there was no more distinction between self and the world.

—

TRANSLATOR'S NOTE:

The five stories in "Zhuangzi's Dream" are loosely adapted from the *Zhuangzi*, a Daoist classic traditionally attributed to the sage Zhuangzi (late 4th century BC) and his disciples. A mix of stories, dialogues, and aphorisms, the text is at once playful, paradoxical, and deeply philosophical.

For those interested in the original stories, there are many English translations to choose from. I will mention just two: Burton Watson's *The Complete Works of Chuang Tzu* (Columbia University Press, 1968) is praised for its accessibility, while Hyun Höchsmann and Yang Guorong's *Zhuangzi* (Routledge, 2007) is valued for its scholarly commentary.

The following sources, cited by their chapter titles and divisions in Höchsmann and Yang's translation, correspond to each story: "Giant Fish" draws inspiration from Book 1, "Wandering Freely"; "Tentacles of a Snail" from Book 25, "Zeyang"; "Chaos" from Book 7, "The Regulations for Emperors and Rulers"; "The Happiness of Fish" from Book 17, "Autumn Floods"; and "To Dream of a Butterfly" from Book 2, "The Equality of All Things."

———

CAO BAIYU is a game designer based in Shanghai. A cat lover with a

passion for CRPGs and second-hand books, he has written several stories and poems. Currently, his biggest dream is to visit Antarctica.

STELLA JIAYUE ZHU is a translator, editor, and academic. She is interested in all questions concerning the nature of intention and reality. When not writing, she is a tutor at St. John's College, Annapolis. She has a PhD in philosophy from the University of Notre Dame.

* Content Notes: depictions of warfare and genocide.

IVY, ANGELICA, BAY

BY C.L. POLK

Novelette Long List*

Trouble sits on the third stair below my door, slouching and ragged with her elbows on her knees. The wards on Mama's car shimmer and tense, and on the rooftop five stories over my head, the bees stir from their drowsy, sun-drenched dreaming. A stranger, here, when no one has asked a thing of me since the priest and the undertaker came to bless Mama and take her away.

I open my purse and pluck out a short cord. I slip it into a loop, ready to knot with a tug, and then I push open the driver's side door. The wards wrap over my shoulders as I leave the car and step around its long black nose. The ivy trained up the front bricks ripples, as if the house just let out a sigh of relief. I stop on the sidewalk and look trouble in the eye.

No tears on this one. All that feeling had been shed long ago, leaving nothing behind but wanting. *Want* pours from the young woman who rises to feet shod in dirty canvas sneakers. Want climbs on the trellis of long skinny legs in a man's chinos. She snaps her fingers and squares her shoulders when she knows I'm looking. A belt with extra holes punched in it wraps around a middle that never feels full, blousing the hem of a stained cotton shirt. Want fills this woman to the frazzled halo of hairs worked loose from crooked cornrow braids.

I set steady feet on the sidewalk, armored in spells and mourning black. "How do you do," I say, because it wouldn't do to be impolite. "I see you have been waiting some time."

"An hour," the woman says. "It's been an hour."

"My apologies," I say, though I'm not sorry for anything. "I had an engagement. I am Miss l'Abielle. What is your name?"

"Liv. Livvie. I'm Livia." The woman's hands flutter together, tangling so tight her knuckles go pale. "I need you to help me. I want a house. I need it. I—"

I lift my hand and stop her tongue. "My apologies once more. I am indisposed at the moment."

"But I need it," Livia insists, and I am not ready for this. There's still crying to do and affairs to attend, and who is this woman to demand this now?

"There is a price to what we want," I say. "This time, the price is too high. I am sorry. I have a luck charm. Take that instead."

I open my purse again. A luck charm will do. She can't have what she wants. I don't know why, but she can't. Shadows grow colder when I think about it.

"What price?" Livia asks. "Tell me."

Oh, this girl wants so bad. She doesn't know, doesn't care; she can't see the danger lurking all around her. A drop of pity splashes on my heart as I make my terrible words gentle.

"Your firstborn child."

The air around us shivers. Something hears me set the price. Something sets it into stone, final and unmoving.

The want in Livia crashes into that price. It bubbles just behind her eyes, pressing harder and harder until it bursts into pain and frustration and a bolt of hot rage. She clamps her jaw shut and spins on the worn sole of one sneaker and walks away, fast, faster, running.

I watch until she's so far down the block she fades into the horizon, and it's only then that I let out the breath I'd drawn to cast a binding. I pull the spell knot apart and go inside to safety.

Lorraine's still on paid leave for another week, so I cook my own supper and dust my way through the house. I don't want her to come back to extra work. It keeps me busy too. It helps me forget for all the hours between coming home from the funeral and getting into bed. Mama's suite is still shut up tight. I don't know when I will open those doors again. I have the bedroom on the front of the third floor, with the curving bay windows framed by tendrils of ivy, and a stack of brand-new books.

Books help me forget that Mama's gone, for a while. I sit with a story on my tented knees, breathing in fresh paper and printing ink as I read about the Bottom of Heaven. Neighbors snore in front of Johnny Carson with the sound turned down. The bees sleep. I turn a page and sit next to Shadrack on the curb with his shoes knotted tight, feeling his loneliness and grieving instead of mine. But then I look up, head tilting at a sound I only think I heard.

I listen past the walls and into the streets, my senses checking every streetlamp witched into the spells quilted over Mama's domain.

Not Mama's. It's mine now. I remember, and my heart knots up tight.

But it's quiet outside. I slip back into the pages and the house settles around me, warm and content as a sleep-laden sigh—

Until a knock makes the house jump with four sharp raps. I'm in my slippers before the echo leaves the air, my housecoat floating as I take the stairs down and around. I touch the spells on each newel post, gathering their magic before I reach the vestibule.

I open the door, and a little girl is there.

She stares at me with huge dark eyes, her cotton shirt dirty, her chinos all holes. She has a little suitcase frowzy with cabbage roses, something brown stained across the side.

"Mother said wait here," she says, in a mouse-quiet, trembling voice. "She said to mind you until she comes back."

The last word splinters in her throat, snapped by fear.

"Oh, child. Who is your mother?"

But I know, don't I? I already know.

She looks at me, her eyebrows perplexed. "Mother."

She's ten, perhaps. Little and skinny and trying not to look behind her, because if she does, the monster will be there. No little girl should ever look like that.

I bend and put my hand on her shoulder. Bones poke at the hollow of my palm. But the touch makes a magic clamp around my wrist. The air shivers with a bargain sealing itself shut. It vibrates like a drum skin, like thunder.

I let go. It's too late. I named the price and Livia gave it up, her wanting so strong it made fate bend.

My breath sighs out. I go still. No wind in the leaves, no purring traffic—that's wrong. Something is

coming—

The streetlights wink out all down the street. The televisions go dark. My skin crawls, for something hot and greedy brushes against the skin of magic around my streets.

The little girl on my doorstep whimpers. Round eyes, open mouth, breathing in gulps that will drown her in terror. She drops the suitcase. It pops open, spilling out threadbare clothes and holey shoes.

The magic gropes at the wards, fumbling for a way in.

A scream claws its way out of the little girl's throat. She backs into the iron railing that keeps her from falling off the steps.

I reach for her. She rushes into my arms. I drag us over the threshold and slam the first door, shuffling back through the vestibule and into the house. I swing the inner door shut with one slippered toe and crouch down to hold her.

The sticky-fingered spell is gone. I send my power out and let it spread along the web, but there's nothing to find.

My heart is a stone as I hum in an abandoned girl's ear. I rub her back.

"I've got you." I rock her, lullaby slow. "You're safe."

But I don't know where that magic went, or what it meant to do.

• • • •

When she settles down enough, I talk softly in her ear. "I'm Miss l'Abielle. What's your name?"

"Jael Brown."

There's a haystack worth of Browns in this city. "Where do you stay?"
Silence.

"You don't know the name of your street?"
Headshake.

"What about your school?"

"I never went."

I barely stop myself from sucking my teeth. She's too old to be kept home. "That's all right. We'll sort it out in the morning."

Jael comes along up the steps past the piano, following me to where my childhood bedroom waits for someone to dream in it. She stares at a ruffle-laden bed and a flop-eared stuffed bunny resting on the chenille coverlet. I find a nightgown folded around lavender sachets. "Come along. You need washing."

She waits silently while I pour herb oil and bubble bath in the steamy water. The suds rise past the top. I pull out a stool and settle. "Go on. When you're ready I'll wash your hair."

I find a book on the wall shelf. I read to her about a girl who solves five dozen mysteries before she turns nineteen years old.

I was once the little girl in the hot water and soapsud clouds. I don't remember Mama's words so much as the feel of her voice ringing off the tiles. Reading like she did, I feel like she's here, but she's so far away, gone somewhere I can't follow yet.

I'm partway into the second chapter when the splashing behind me subsides.

"Did you wash all of your toes?"

A quick splash, just to be sure. "Yes, ma'am."

I sit behind the tub and rub olive oil shampoo over her scalp. She presses her fingers to her eyes when I pour water from a pewter jug to rinse the suds away. I have to work it in twice before the lather springs up the way I like it.

"There's your nightgown. Dry off and come out."

She comes barefoot to the bedroom. The ruffled hem floats inches above her broomstick ankles. I set her down in a white-painted chair and comb the snarls gently away, smoothing light oil over the length. It's late by the time I finish.

She doesn't say a word through the combing, stays silent while I braid her hair with quick fingers, weaving in protections—good luck, clear thinking—each section combed into the weaving with a different blessing. "There you are."

I've plaited her hair in a four-strand crown tidy enough for church, and she turns her head, trying to see it all.

"Princess," she whispers to herself.

"You can pick a dress in the morning. Into bed."

She climbs into the narrow green bed and settles back into a nest of ruffled pillows. I draw the net curtain out of its tiebacks and drape it along the edges, veiling her from nightmares.

I'm at the foot of the bed when she speaks.

"Mother left me, didn't she?"

I wait for my heart to finish breaking before I breathe again. It is a terrible thing to be left behind by your mother. It leaves a hole soul-deep to know she walked away, and you can't help but wonder, again and again, if it's because of something you did or something you are that made her set you aside. I can't hug her. She won't give me her tears, poor alone little thing.

But I can give her the truth. I nod, once, slow.

Her eyes slip shut and her head tilts back. She's already learned the trick of stopping tears. She folds her hands in her lap and gazes at them as she resolutely does not cry. Then she sighs, tucks all that feeling carefully away, and nods.

"Good night, Miss l'Abielle."

She pulls the chenille bedspread to her chin and I leave her alone in the streetlit dark.

• • • •

Come morning, Jael sits at the gold-speckled table in the kitchen in one of my old puff-sleeved dresses, eating enough strawberry waffles for two grown-up women. I drink coffee and poke at a grapefruit glistening with honey. Jael cuts tidy little squares, swimming in golden butter and shiny red syrup, but she sets down her fork and picks up the bottle to pour out a little more.

"Isn't it already sweet enough?"

"Sugar keeps the magic strong," she says.

"What magic is that?" I ask, and her shoulders jump up. She shakes her head, still chewing.

"Mother always said it."

She only has a handful of mother memories in her pocket. I won't contradict this one. It's not like she's wrong, even if she doesn't know it.

I dig out a cluster of grapefruit, tart and juicy with a streak of sweetness on it. I should have a waffle, but I'm too unsettled to eat much more, and that won't stop until I check my streets.

"We're going for a walk," I tell her.

Jael walks beside me, frocked in mauve next to my black. She sneaks glances at her puffed-out skirts, stitched with a scattering of forget-me-nots. I loved that dress when I was her age. It lifts Jael's chin to wear it.

I pick up a bag of lemon drops at the corner store and Cynthia Lewis smiles at the tidy little girl by my side. "And who is with you, Miss l'Abielle? And may she have a strawberry sucker?"

Jael shifts a little, emerging from behind me. "May I?"

"Go ahead. This is Jael Brown, and she's staying with me at the house. Jael, this is Mrs. Cynthia. This is her corner store."

Jael steps around me cautiously, but she dips her chin and curtsies as if she's been waiting for the chance to try it. "Thank you, ma'am."

"What a doll," Cynthia praises. "What a little lady."

I swap a quarter for the lemon drops. "How is the neighborhood?"

Cynthia drops it in an earthen jar beside the cash register. "Fine, Miss l'Abielle. Everyone is fine."

There's a gap between her words and her smile. I wait, watching her. She flicks a glance toward the back of the store, then back to me.

"Got an envelope from the city." She settles back on a tall stool next to the cigarettes. "They're coming to do an assessment."

My fingertips tingle. "For taxes?"

"Safety." Cynthia's looking at the door to the back again.

"When they coming?"

"Says next week."

"Come see me for tea," I say. "Bring that letter."

Her face melts with relief. "Thank you."

I head for the door, touching the mark scratched into the jamb on my way out. I step out onto the concrete and into a patch of sunlight, waiting for Jael to come along. "Where did you learn to curtsy like that?"

Jael scoots up to walk beside me. "Mother said to always use my manners."

I feel a little shame for my assumptions about Livia, made of ragged clothes and unkempt hair. Jael is a polite little thing, tidy and quieter than another child might be. "It's well taught. Good manners will take you far."

She nods absently, like someone who was waiting for a turn to speak. "What was that on the door?"

"What was what?"

"The thing you touched. The air got prickly."

I lift an eyebrow at her. "Did it?"

"There's another one right there." She points unerringly at the mark next to Johnson's Music Shop, where a few browsers walk their fingers along the tops of used records.

"They're five-corner marks," I tell her. "They're for luck."

"And when you touched Mrs. Cynthia's, you gave her luck. Right?" She looks up at me, hopeful as the brightest student in the classroom.

She knows that, just by seeing it once. What has fate brought to my doorstep? "That's right. Hush now; I need to listen."

I halt on the corner of two main streets and listen to Hurston Hill. Shouts of children playing in our park. Jael watches with longing as other girls in bright skimpy shorts show off dance tricks on roller skates to big, brassy disco tunes.

I catch where she's looking. "You want to play with them?"

"No," she says. *I want to be them,* I hear beneath the quiet ache.

It's a peaceful, pretty day, and the sun smiles down on all of it. A bee tumbles on the autumn breeze from the common garden where the Golden Horticultural League puts their hands in the dirt and grows good things from it. The worker-sister circles us, hovering around my head.

Jael stays very still. I listen.

This way, her wings whisper. *Something wrong. Something wrong.*

The worker-sister floats off to the left. I follow. Jael has to trot to keep up with me, and I slow down, for her sake.

"What did the bee tell you?" Jael asks.

This strange little child sees everything. "I'm still listening. How did you know she spoke to me?"

"You had on your listening face. And you weren't scared."

"The bees here are friends."

Jael hops over a crack in the concrete. "How do you know the bee is a she?"

"In a hive, all the gatherers you see in the sky are sisters."

"Always?"

"That's right. The bees live up on the roof of the house. There's a garden up there."

"So the bees are yours?"

"Better to say that I am theirs."

"And the bee came to tell you something? What did she tell you? Is it because of the five-corner marks?"

Ten-year-olds are made of questions. I squeeze her hand to let her know I heard her, but the worker-sister has flown off, and I'm following a hollow, dreadful hunch to a narrow brick house I know as the Colemans'.

George carried Mahalia Coleman over the threshold of this house two years ago. Mahalia had been to see Mama every month since, trying to catch a baby. But Mahalia needed more than teas and tinctures, and while science made a baby last summer, they're not doing that for ordinary folks just yet.

Today, the house is empty. The Colemans are gone. I stare at that for a long breath. They left recently, from the way the walls still wait for their people to come back. But how did they go through packing up and moving without me hearing about it? Even in mourning, with no visitors and no gossip, the bees should have known.

I climb the stairs and cup my hands around my eyes, pressing against the window. Empty. Clean, too—the floors shine with freshly buffed wax. I imagine I can smell it.

"Ma'am?"

I look back. Jael stands very still, her palm up, as the worker-sister lands on the round ball of her thumb. She looks up, her face wide with awe.

"She likes me."

I smile for her. "So I see. Be very quiet and listen. Maybe she will tell you something."

Jael looks very serious as she gives the bee her listening face. I step off the welcome mat. Shining under the coir mat is a newly cut brass key, laying on a still-green bay leaf.

Disquiet curls in my middle. It's a common enough charm. Bay leaf crowns victors and poets, but bay leaf can protect by hiding whatever it touches from sight. Like a key under a mat.

Or a spell you don't want seen.

I bend knee and crouch. The leaf is fragrant—not freshly picked, but just cured enough to write on. I turn it over, but both sides are blank.

Just a small charm anyone could do, then.

Jael lifts her hand, and the bee floats away. "What does it mean?"

Nothing good. "I don't know, mouse."

"Are you scared?"

Yes. But you don't tell little girls that. You need to be brave for them. You need to walk tall in the presence of evil, so they know they can stand against it.

I smile down at Jael. "Let's go back home. I'll make us tea."

• • • •

Even the wait until the start of the business day is too long. I'm in the workroom before the sun, fussing with gallon glass jars to check the potency of their contents. I unscrew a clean jar with rainwater gathered from the roof and pour it over dried roots, grasses, blossoms, and leaves, careful of their harmonies. I trickle in honey powder and take it up the birdcage elevator to let it bathe in sunlight. How to cover my domain with its blessings is tomorrow's problem to solve.

When I ride the elevator back down, Jael is there. She perches on the fourth step leading up to the mezzanine. Mama would have asked me if a young lady should sit on the steps in a dress like that, but Mama's words could bruise a girl as delicate as this.

"I had cereal," she says. "And only one spoon of sugar. I washed the dishes after."

"Very good," I say. "When Lorraine comes back to tend the house, would you like her to teach you to cook?"

She shrinks a little when I mention Lorraine. "Can't you teach me?"

"I can do a little. But no one makes a pie like Lorraine does. Now I want you to read one of the books I set out for you, whichever one you like. I have to run some errands." I pin my veiled pillbox hat into place.

She regards this with a flicker of fear. "You're leaving me alone? Can't I come with you?"

"I'm going to the bank, mouse. To talk about numbers and finance."

She sighs and shakes her head for the follies of adults. "Boring things."

"Indeed." I check my handbag for keys, blessed candies, and a charm bag meant to shield me from interference. "You may read anything you like from the list. If you get hungry, there are apples and peanuts in the kitchen. Have a glass of milk."

I leave her sitting exactly there and stride across the sidewalk to Mama's big black car.

• • • •

I never need an appointment at Cade Henry Credit Union, not even on payday. I'm greeted before my third step falls on the floor. Neighbors nod hello as I walk past the line and sit at Clarence Young's desk. A cup of red-amber tea rests in a saucer next to me, the liquid rolling gently with the haste of its delivery.

"Miss l'Abielle," Clarence says, his wide, friendly face creased with kindness for me. "It was a beautiful service. You sang so wonderfully. What may I help you with today?"

"I'm here to purchase a house," I say. "I'd like you to start the process for a mortgage. This is the address for your records."

I slide a card with the Colemans' address on it past Clarence's name-plate. When he picks it up, his expression goes slack.

"I'm sorry, Miss l'Abielle. But I'm afraid it's too late."

My chin comes up. "How do you know that?"

He glances left, looks the other way. No one is nearby. "I handled the

Colemans' account. They paid for their mortgage just the other day, penalty and all, with a cashier's check."

I sit up a little, cocking my head. "That fast."

"He left the moving truck idling on the curb. They're halfway to the coast by now. George said—"

He goes silent. I pick up my tea. It's astringent with lemon. He watches the cup meet the saucer and lowers his voice.

"George said they paid him to offer the house."

Aha. I set the tea on the desk. "Who's they?"

Clarence really shouldn't be telling me this. His conscience writhes, tensing the cords in his neck, ripples in a jaw he has to press shut. He wants to tell me, knows he shouldn't. I think of brooks babbling and wait.

Another glance for listening ears. He leans closer. "The check came from a company called the Angelica Group."

I don't know that name, but it plucks at my nerves. "May I borrow your phone book?"

He even gives me a card and a pen to write the address.

• • • •

The Angelica Group is in a building that used to house people. It sits back from the sidewalk, double-wide and shorter than the shining glass-faced buildings pressing against it. A low stone wall bristling with spikes pushes people away from the front doors. Pedestrians veer into the middle of the sidewalk, giving it arm's length. The old windows are bricked into narrow clerestory slits, and the old glass-fronted door is long, long gone. But that's not all I see. Wards and repulsion spells five layers deep cover every single brick. Menace drips from every iron spike.

I am safe inside Mama's Cadillac, safe from that web of spellwork, and I am not stepping on that sidewalk for anything. I can't touch those wards. But I attempt to follow their dizzying geometry and catch a thread, here and there, of spells written to attract more: more wealth. More power. They stretch their tendrils across the air, spokes of a spider's web, and it's worse than I thought. I cast my senses down carefully, afraid to touch the earth in this place.

Am I in a domain? I can't be. The signs of walking into another magician's province are difficult to miss. The building before me is a magician's stronghold, but the land beneath it belongs to no one.

And that echoes along my bones. Pieces fall into place. Mama would have sensed this incursion long before I drove right up to it, but the domain didn't pass to me until her long sleep passed into death. This building is trouble. It's danger, and I have to face it alone.

The front door opens, and those spiteful, wasp-sting wards wrap around a short, slender man in a three-piece suit, cloaking him in their protection. He snaps his fingers as the door swings shut behind him. He's sharp with fashion, his Afro picked out high, but his mouth is a cruel, tight line. My heart beats like a rabbit spotted by a wolf.

He's wearing aviators, but he's looking right through the window between him and me. My mouth is dry. I see what I have done. I rushed into the middle of the board, coming here like this without scrying, without asking the cards. I didn't even run a property check. And now this landless magician has my measure.

Very well, magician. I see you. I know what you want. And you can't have it, so long as I draw breath.

I nod to him. He nods back.

It's war.

• • • •

I drive through the city by the power of muscle memory, thoughts whirling too fast to make any meaning of it, but when I back Mama's Cadillac into the space before my house, the numb, automatic wall tumbles to the ground. My hands shake on the steering wheel. They shake in the lock. I can't take a breath that feeds my lungs until I'm past the vestibule and inside the cocoon of protections that quilt the house, and what comes out next is a sob.

Safe in the house, I shake. I weep in silence. I don't want to disturb Jael, or scare her. But this weakness, this fear, this crushing possibility that I might not withstand this fight saturates my body, filling it to overflowing. How can I do this without Mama? How can I do it alone? How can I protect everyone who lives here, and the place we have made for one another?

What if I can't?

Hot tears slide down my neck.

Mama still had things to teach me. I knew the boundaries of the domain, and I tended the five corner marks, and made sure everyone knew that they could come to me if trouble came. When Mama grasped my hand the skin and nerves and veins of Hurston Hill became my own, but I know hardly anything about this new body. I don't know how to defend it from that wasp-hearted man, or how to fight back. I weep until the tears run dry.

In the empty calm that comes after the last of the tears, I remember Jael, reading upstairs. Fate brought her here. She has a gift, as I had when my own mother brought me here in exchange for a light that shone only on her. Jael needs me to be what Mama had been.

I dab at my face and breathe in the scent of vetiver and lemongrass floor wash and the magic layered on this house, magic that I watch over like Mama did, and Grand Olympe, and Madam Louise, and Miss Violet, who built it for the bees. The magic is strong; their magic is inside me.

Calm settles over me. It's simple. The possibility of failure is not for me to think about. My only choice is to keep Hurston Hill safe.

"So be it," I murmur to the house. "See to it."

The house around me relaxes, releasing a gently held breath. I turn for the stairs and startle, a scream caught in my throat.

Jael sits on the steps exactly where I left her.

Exactly as I left her—hands on her knees, the full drape of her seersucker skirt spreading over the stairs, her straight and careful back perfectly upright. Her eyes are open, but she doesn't see. Breaths swell her skinny chest, but she's so still, so strange, like she isn't really there at all.

Like she switched off the moment I wasn't in sight.

The meaning of it quivers along my nerves. Oh, girl. Poor girl. I move, so her eyes have something to see. I scuff my foot on the floorboards, so her ears have something to hear. I speak, when neither of those things work. "Jael? Little mouse?"

She blinks. She moves. She sees me. "Yes, ma'am."

"Are you all right?"

Two vertical furrows crease between her brows. "I think I fell asleep."

That wasn't sleep. Maybe that's how it feels, to go away from everything including yourself. "Let's get you washed up. No cooking lesson for lunch today. We're going to eat at Dolly's Counter."

• • • •

Dolly's Counter doesn't hum like it should. Every eye darts to the front door as its greeting bells ring; shoulders fall or square up at the sight of me, according to the opinions of their bearer. But that isn't what's important.

Dolly's not holding court before the line of sidewalk philosophers who claim the seats at the counter, crowned with her high bouffant updo with a coffeepot in one hand. Dolly's always behind the counter, though. Always.

I touch the five-corner mark on the doorjamb. It trembles under my touch. Beside me, Jael grips my hand tight. The other diners simmer in their feelings—unspoken, but clearly felt.

"What is it?" I ask the diners, all of them looking at me. "What's wrong?"

The doors to the kitchen swing open, and a white woman armed with a clipboard steps out. Dolly's right on her heels with her nostrils flared, her aura like two raised fists. "You're fining me for a violation?"

The woman tips her clipboard straight up like a shield. "Four critical violations."

"This is wrong," Dolly says. "Can't you see that?"

"Re-serving unprotected and potentially hazardous food." The woman lifts one finger away from her clipboard to count it. "Re-serving unprotected food automatically follows from there. Eating or drinking from open containers in food storage areas. Personal cleanliness of a person present found to be inadequate." Her fingers drum back down on the clipboard, and I seal my tongue to the roof of my mouth lest a stray ill wish slips loose.

Dolly's broad mouth is a study in disapproval, her eyebrows low like storm clouds. "So it's acceptable if a man—a man, with feelings and dignity just like yours—has to root around in the trash for a meal, but if I give him some gumbo and rice and a place to enjoy it next to the extra soda syrup—"

"It's four critical health violations," the woman says. "If he'd been scavenging in your garbage, that would have been a general violation."

I rarely meet anyone who needs quite this much cursing. The silence in the room trembles. I clench my jaw. One word in a room brimming like this and I don't know what would happen. I don't know what fate would exact as its price.

The woman slides a form off her clipboard and holds it out. "You can pay your fine at City Hall within thirty days. Good day."

She steps past me and onto the street, the bells' swinging jingle the only sound for the space of a dozen held breaths. Dolly stares at me over the line in her bifocals, her expression just sick.

"Something is happening," she says. "Something is wrong."

That declaration looses a flood. Rents have been raised. Property tax assessors are crawling the streets. Water bills and light bills are suddenly much higher. And worst, most chilling of all—men from downtown in sleek sedans cruise the streets, looking at every house, every shop, even the trees. Men with grey suits and money-counting hands huddle in conversations on the corners, shutting up when anyone gets too near.

This war's already happening. And everyone in Dolly's is looking at me, expecting me to know exactly what to do.

What I must do. Whatever Hurston Hill needs. But where do I enter this labyrinth? What fire do I put out first?

Jael tugs on my hand. She's big-eyed and somber as she finds her voice. "Ma'am."

"What is it, mouse?"

"Can I help? I can write a list."

It's like a sunbeam just fell on my face. "Dolly, do you have a pencil? Jael is going to help me. Everyone, sit tight. I need you all to tell me what's happening, one at a time."

• • • •

There is no time to get a good rest, no time to mourn. I wake before dawn to greet the bees as they rise from their hives. The worker-sisters gather around me and their hum is a chorus, a hum that lulls me into the state I need to be one with the domain that the bees claim and I protect. And when they rise to the clouds to gather and watch, the queen emerges to show me what the bees know.

"St. Valentine, St. Abigail, St. Brigid," I say. "I need your help. We're all in danger."

Show me.

She rides on my shoulder as I return downstairs to the big room that was Mama's office. We stand under the watchful eye of the guardian masks and unroll a fragile, crackling bundle of paper maps of Hurston Hill.

I begin by gazing at every layer at once. It's all confusion at this level —too much information to make true meaning. But I let the confusion overwhelm me as I look without trying to see the layers that show every streetlamp, every traffic light, every tree that lines the streets—at the placement of every fire hydrant and the pipes that bring good water to drink and wash in, the pipes that take wastewater away. Gradually, as long as my attention stays slack, I see.

Another assault on the barrier wards, of course. But there's more trouble, scattered all over my streets like bad seeds. Double crosses and jinxes and even spells to attract attention marking homes and businesses but especially our park—why the park?

Danger, the queen's wings sing. *It has gone so far.*

There is so much to do—a thousand tiny battles, and I have to fight them all. But the park's in danger. The soul of the neighborhood's magic grows in the common garden. Its heart beats to the concerts and plays performed under its curving shell roof. And the weakness I see isn't the nibbling at my borders. It's a scythe, raised at the highest point of the backswing and ready to fall on the park.

I let the layers of the map curl up one by one, taking away the fullness of detail that defies legibility. Each layer whispers and crackles, and I look, look without trying to see anything in particular.

My gaze falls on the zone map. It's every building and structure, every quilt-square of land assigned a color according to its use. Yellow for residential, red for business, and the park doesn't know what color it wants to be. It should be green, colored in exactly the color of new spring leaves, but it tinges orange, and the park on the map struggles to stay the same, to stay true.

I press my hands against the slow, sick roll in my stomach, and the layers of delicate, glassy paper curl up on themselves.

I understand what that means. Mama protected Hurston Hill with charms and wards, but Mama said that it was possible to fight magic with any power you had. And in every day I fought to keep Mama with me, even though she would never speak or rise from her bed was a day I hadn't seen this.

I pick up Mama's address book. I cut my finger on a corner and I hiss, jerking it away. Blood wells up from the tiny cut. I pop it in my mouth.

It's open on exactly the page I need. Written in Mama's clear Palmer hand is a number that isn't in the ordinary phone book. There should be someone at the desk right now. I push my cut finger into the dial holes and listen to the rattle of each number sending their signal out on the wires.

The phone rings five times before someone answers with a gruff, "Hunter Ballantine here."

I arm myself with a smile. "Councillor Ballantine. This is Miss Theresa Anne l'Abielle of 777-J 94th Street of Council 21," I say.

"Miss l'Abielle," Councillor Ballantine says, the last syllable climbing a surprised half-step. He coughs. "Excuse me. Miss l'Abielle, I am sorry for your loss. I regret I couldn't attend the service."

"The wreath your office sent along was lovely," I say. "Most appreciated and thoughtful. But I have a question for you, Councillor."

Half a breath too late, he says, "Certainly. What may I do for you?"

"I am calling to ask about any land use petitions connected to Hurston Hill Community Park."

"How—" The voice on the other end is astonished, but one composed pause later, Councillor Ballantine continues. "There have been no land use petitions filed."

"Because they only just landed on your desk?" I ask, and the frustrated tenor of his silence tells me everything before he opens the can holding his response.

"I really can't go into it right now, Miss l'Abielle. If you'd like to call my secretary and make an appointment—"

"Oh, I would prefer to have this conversation now," I say, light, polite, and seething with genteel fury. "I know you're a busy man, so I'll get right to the point. I don't think a proposal to destroy a park for the sake of mixed-use zoning with active frontage is the best way to keep the faith of your voters, Councillor Ballantine."

Papers rustle. Councillor Ballantine's breaths whistle down the phone lines. "Miss l'Abielle, this is a complex issue. If you'd make an appointment, I can have a better picture of the situation you're describing—"

If that park is destroyed, the whole neighborhood will follow. "The issue is simple. Hurston Hill Community Park will remain as it is. This is an election-losing matter, Councillor, and if you threaten Hurston Hill's children and seniors with the loss of a vital community center, someone might step up to challenge you."

I didn't plan on saying that. But anything it takes. Anything Hurston Hill needs. If Ballantine can't take care of his council, I will take it away from him.

He says nothing, and I hear the trickle of fear in it. I need his fear. I need it to guide him away from his greed. I need him to understand that he can't trifle with me any more than he could with Mama. "I think you should reconsider this plan from the Angelica Group, Councilman. I really do."

"How do you know—"

"That's my secret," I say. "I look forward to continuing my support of your office. Good morning."

The receiver rattles in its cradle. I'm going to be sick. There is too much to do. Too much that needs saving. The scythe is falling.

"Miss l'Abielle?"

Jael hovers at the entrance to my office. She's holding a sheet of paper. She's drawn a house on it—this house, tall and narrow and grand with brick, the ivy climbing up the front. But she's done something else with her sixty-four colors, as she has drawn the glow of spells and blessings too, and the rooftop garden shines like Heaven, and all the bees its angels.

She offers it to me. "I drew it for you."

The paper touches my fingers. It shimmers. It feels like the cozy confines of a burrow made from a tent built of sheets and cushions from the couch. She put magic on that paper without knowing how.

"Please let me help," Jael says, again the bright student, again desperate to please. "How can I help?"

I step forward, the queen on my shoulder. "Come with me," I say, "and show me how you made this picture."

· · · ·

Jael has the witching in her blood. She doesn't know the correspondences or the lore or the ways of shaping the witching to her will, but she's quick. She's instinctive. And she minds me better than I did Mama at her age.

Together we work for the sum of the morning. Everything I show her is a softly glowing treasure. It lights up her face. She touches all the herb jars, and repeats what I tell her about their contents, pressing them in the pages of her memory. She asks me about everything—so many questions, as if my answers are like the sugar she can't resist eating.

"If we're going to bless all the spellposts and charge every five-corner mark, what else can we do?"

She stirs the jar of blessed water I set out on the roof to charge under the sun and the moon, sinking a silver dipper into it and pouring the liquid into the mouth of a funnel. The blessed water trickles into a glass bottle. She doesn't spill a drop.

"Whatever we can think of. Magic is imagination shaped into the form that will make the intention manifest."

She pours blessed water back into the jar, screws a spray-nozzle cap onto the bottle, and sets it next to the others. "Can we make everyone in the neighborhood lucky?"

"Luck is best in small doses, mouse. A rescue, not a remedy. But you can choose three people to give a charm today."

That satisfies her. "And I can spray the spellposts."

"You may."

"May," she corrects herself, and then a new idea springs to her face. She's bright with elation, with discovery. "Can we set a spell on the bees, and then when they fly around, they can spread it?"

I blink. "If the bees consent, yes. That's an excellent idea, little mouse."

She looks like she might burst. How must it feel to find your gift, the thing you love that loves you back, and so you give your life to it without thinking? Jael's becoming a witch right before my eyes.

She reaches for another bottle and sets the funnel in it. "Can we set eyes on outsiders, so they always feel like someone's watching them and knows exactly what they do?"

I'm tempted by that last one.

Being a witch isn't all sunlight and good wishes. We all have shadows cast by that light. We can call on that darkness like any other tool. But it's possible to go too far, and something about the ethics of it is just fuzzy enough that I'm not sure I should.

But if I did that...

I realize that my gaze is trained on the potted bay tree right by the window. I look away.

"It's possible," I say. "But that could really frighten someone who doesn't deserve it, along with those who might."

"Oh, not for long." She stirs the blessed water again, suspending the herbs in a spiral. "We couldn't leave it up forever. We can't leave out the people who need this place. But... what if they need it right now? Like I needed it?"

She understands. She already knows the complexity of the power. She already respects it. I want to cry. Not like I want to cry for Mama being gone. I want to cry for Jael being found.

Jael is the one to come behind me when I go to follow Mama. Jael's mother had to make that wish, pay that price, and give me Hurston Hill's future... and just in time, in the way of the life of one who is bound to fate.

• • • •

I stop just outside the front door and give Jael a tin of rose sugar pastilles. She takes it with reverence, looking down at the rounded white candies like little seed pearls.

"Sugar keeps the magic strong," I say, and something in her dark eyes is sad for half a second.

"Thank you, ma'am." She pops one in her mouth and takes my hand as we walk the bounds of Hurston Hill. She sprays every lamppost chained into the flow of magic. She touches each one, sending a shimmer along its iron trunk. I carry a basket of the smaller bottles, and we call on everyone we meet, tending their shops or their front steps. Many accept a spray bottle and the instructions to spray it on their windows, their doorways, their cash registers.

Each bottle is a tiny magic, but pennies add up to dollars. Dolly won't let us pay for smoked chicken sandwiches rich with gravy, with a soda for Jael and fresh brewed tea for me. The Golden Horticultural League starts spraying every leaf in sight when I hand out bottles to them to take home, plus extra for neighbors who couldn't make it to the garden today.

The bees tumble and float, shedding protection magic from their wings. I ache from all the walking and regret my refusal to step out in less than my best, for my feet are paying the price of the blessings we spread.

But is it enough, these small magics? Can they withstand whatever that landless mage at the Angelica Group plans? I'm only defending against what I can see. He must be planning something more. It's not enough to react. I must anticipate.

I'm weary when we make it back to the house. I can't stop the relieved groan when I take my shoes off and stand on the heart pine floor, my heels on the ground instead of tented on pillars. I roll my neck, shrug my shoulders, and listen to everything pop and creak.

"I can make us something, ma'am," Jael says. "I can make it and you can watch and tell me what's next."

What a good idea. If only we could do that. "I'm afraid it's pork shoulder pot roast."

"I can do it," Jael insists. "I'm not tired at all."

This helpful, blessed girl. "Very well. But you must be very careful when you cut up the potatoes."

She runs to the kitchen. By the time I get there she's already in an apron, pulling a heavy iron pot out of the drawer under the oven. I sit where I have the best view of the process.

"Recipe's in the yellow box," I tell her, and she flips through the cards until she finds the right one. She clips it to the cupboard door just above her working space, kicks a step stool into position, and starts.

I hardly have to say anything. I tense a little when she picks up the knife, but she speaks up as she slices through a potato. "It's like witching."

"It is," I say. "Cooking and witching share skills. And you can witch your meals."

"You can?"

"Of course you can. The herbs in the kitchen are in the workroom too, aren't they?"

"That's right. I didn't think of it like that. It's all witching, isn't it? If you can do it, you can witch it. Can't you?"

"You can," I say. "It's important to know that. Your actions can make magic, so you must think about what you're doing, more than other people have to."

She looks at me, careful, measuring her thoughts before she speaks them. "Can you make sure that what you do isn't magic?"

"I'm afraid we're stuck with it—"

Jael gasps. She drops the knife and snatches up her hand, whimpering. I'm out of my seat in a heartbeat, trying to take her hand, but she grips tighter, shaking her head.

I try to peel her fingers back. "Let me see."

"No."

She's trembling. Her breaths are shallow and scared. She looks at me, desperate and pleading. I try to take her hand again, but she yanks it out of my grip and stumbles off the stool.

"Jael, let me see."

"No. Please don't look." Her voice is discordant. She backs away, holding her cut hand for dear life, and she's... she's scared. Terrified. What on earth?

"Mouse," I say, gentle, firm. "I have to see it. I can't make it better if I can't see. It will hurt, I won't lie. But I can make it better."

"Please," she says, but there's no voice in it. Fear's taken her vocal cords and pulled them tight as bowstrings. Why? Why?

"Jael. Why can't I see?"

"Then you'll know," she says, and tears pour out of her eyes like a river. "You'll know and it—it'll be—over."

She's weeping now, heartbroken, despairing tears. "It'll be over," she says, and it breaks her all over again.

I rush to her. I pick her up, right off her feet. I crush her to me as if I can hug her hard enough, hold her tight enough to make it all go away. "You're safe," I say.

"No," she says, "I never was. You never were—I'm sorry. I'm sorry. I'm—"

I hold her again. I rock her. She has to cry this one out before I'll get any sense out of her. But something presses on my skin, like low black clouds pregnant with a storm, a solid wall rushing in so fast everything feels like lightning will strike any moment.

Danger. Danger. Something is coming. Someone—

But I know, don't I? I already know. He is coming—the wasp-magician in his fine clothes and his vicious wards. Now, before I've mobilized the neighborhood to do battle with City Hall. Our dollar's worth of magic didn't hold him back. He is coming, right now, and every board in the house is tight with expectation.

In my arms, Jael goes quiet. She's limp, tired. Her sigh is resigned, like someone who just turned around to face the monster behind her, knowing she can run no more.

"I'm sorry."

She holds out her hand for me to see.

She doesn't bleed. No red life stains her skin, sliced neat and deep. No red flesh lies under that cut in her... hide. Not skin.

Leather.

And underneath it, cotton bolls stuff her form, dusty with shiny white grains, speckled dark fragrant ones. Allspice. Mace. Nutmeg. Vanilla. Sugar and spice and everything nice, stuff little girls are made from.

I touch the cut, the cotton, the sugar. I press, and something hard stretches beneath. I pry the cotton apart and find bone engraved with marks and signs, the magic to make her alive. A faded green leaf lies curled against the bone—a bay leaf, shielding the magic that made Jael from sight.

She looks at me. Sad, and calm, and full of endings. "It's over now. I'm sorry."

I reach up and stroke her tear-wet face. It feels like skin, real breathing skin, and her face blurs as the tears rise in my eyes. Poor little mouse.

Poor little mousetrap.

She leaps away when the wards flinch and the front door opens, and it isn't the magician I expected.

It's worse.

• • • •

Livia strides inside on stiletto-heeled clicks, buttery suede boots clinging to her legs. She wears black, not for mourning, but for power— the liquid ripple of matte black silk drapes over her slender, elegant body, the elaborate tie at her waist a knot spell. Full draping sleeves in black silk chiffon flutter as she moves, rippling like the surface of a moonlit lake. A sparkling black silk pouch dangles from her wrist. Her hair flows around her like shining ink, big roller-set curls bouncing like springs to her waist.

No sign of the ragged, skinny wretch from my doorstep. Livia is a witch in full bloom, full of shadows and promises. She's the dark moon. An enchantress. An illusionist who pays you in gold that turns to leaves in the morning. The question of ethics never troubles her smooth, rounded brow. Nothing remains of that pathetic creature whose want was enough to make an accident of fate.

She pauses on the foyer's worn Turkish rug and snaps her fingers when our eyes meet.

Not an accident. An act. A hustle.

I rise and put myself between Jael and this witch, staring her down the way I would if I didn't want to hide.

"It was you," I say. "It was you at the Angelica Group too. Were you the health inspector too?"

"Clever, clever witch. I wasn't the health inspector, but Antoine's a convenient disguise. Some men won't listen to anyone but other men," she says. "And people don't look deeper than their first assumptions. That's the first rule of invisibility."

She can be anyone she pleases—a wretched waif, a stylish business-man, or the queen of shadows and lies. I gather up the power layered on the walls to cast a binding—or I try. My magic is the act of making and mixing. I put my will into herbs and candles, imbuing it with the bless-ings of the sun. There is no spellcord in my pocket, and I need a medium between witching and my will.

Livia does not. She smiles at me from under the perfectly heat-curled wings of her hair. She watches me draw power and falter, tilting her head with curiosity. One eyebrow quirks up.

"No? All right, then."

She points, her index finger capped with fresh-blood crimson nails, and shows me how it's done. Lines of power wrap around me. They still my fingers. They squeeze my ribs. I can breathe, so long as I set my mind to it, but not much more than that, and it isn't enough air to scream with, either.

She regards her binding a moment longer, her hands on her hips. Then Livia—witch, magician, enchantress—lifts her hand and beckons.

"Jael. Come here."

Jael runs a few steps on tiptoe, halting before her maker.

Livia looks down at her. No smile, now. "What did I tell you to do while you were here?"

"Always use your manners," Jael says, in the small mouse voice of a little girl in trouble. "Do as she says until you come back. Sugar keeps the magic strong."

The pointed toe of Livia's boot taps three times. "And what did I tell you not to do?"

Her voice is almost a whisper. "Give away the secret."

"Are you sorry?"

"Yes."

Livia beckons again. "Come closer."

Jael trembles as she comes close enough to touch. Livia puts her hand on Jael's head.

"You did what you were made to do," Livia says, stroking Jael's braided hair. "And you did it well. This one slip doesn't need to count against you. My promise still holds."

Jael looks up, then, hope smoothing her profile. "You'll do it? You'll make me real?"

Livia laughs. "Don't I need a little girl of my own, especially a helpful little girl like you? Now think of what I told you. The spell can be completed, exactly as I said. Are you ready?"

"Yes," Jael says. "I'm ready."

"Good," Livia purrs, and pets Jael's head like a favored cat. "This part is your job, now."

She opens the pouch strings and reaches inside. She draws out a knife with a long silvery blade and a narrow, pointed tip.

"The last thing you need to finish the spell," she says. "Her heart."

Jael can become a girl of flesh, her bones her own—with my heart beating in her chest. She will be what she wishes for most. The spell is already on her.

All she needs to do is pay the price.

Jael lifts her hand—uncut, still whole, still spelled—and takes the blade from her maker. Livia smiles down upon her, strokes her hair again.

"I'm going to the roof. Bring it to me when you are done."

Livia walks away on sharp-heeled clicks, sleeves fluttering, a ribbon of almond, bay leaf, pepper, and myrrh left hanging in the air.

Jael stands still with the knife in her hand, listening to the elevator grumble and rise to the roof. To the garden. To the spellposts that feed all the protections and blessings that cover Hurston Hill. To the hives where the bees sleep and don't know what's coming.

The elevator thumps. The lifting gears stop. And Jael turns tear-filled eyes toward me.

Oh, little mousetrap. What a perfect Trojan horse she is—a little girl, the price of a mother's ambition in full, a lonely arrow in my heart. Built to be just polite enough to be charming, just vulnerable enough to need protection, and the witching the final sugary lure.

And now she holds the knife that will pay for her deepest longing, the thing she wants most of all—the wanting engraved on her borrowed bones, the wanting infused in cotton and spice, the wanting in every stitch and spell that made her. She flexes her grip on the handle, wipes her eyes, and looks at me.

"You took me in."

How could I not?

"You gave me this dress. You taught me witching. You have power. Can you make me real? Can you make me a little girl? Can I grow up?"

Oh, Jael. My throat hurts for her. I owe her the truth. I shake my head, once, slow.

"Then I have to," she whispers. "I have to—it's not fair. It's not fair."

That's not true. Magic is implacably fair. If Jael wants a human life, she needs a human heart beating in her chest. Magic doesn't care about feelings. Magic doesn't care what it costs to use—only that the price is paid.

"I need to be real," she whispers to me. "I walk and speak and think and witch, but I am not a girl, and..."

She wants me to understand. And I do. But it's not just my life for hers. It's this house. And Hurston Hill. And the bees. And what will happen to this place if Livia takes it in her hand and rules it.

All of it, lost for a beating heart.

"You didn't push me away. You knew I wasn't real. But you didn't stop trying to help me. Why? Didn't you understand?"

I suck down as much air as I can and move my lips, my tongue. I can whisper. "You were scared."

"I betrayed you."

"You did—" I have to catch my breath. "What you were made to do."

She crumples, her mouth open in agony. "I ruined everything. You need to hate me. *I* hate me."

The binding doesn't stop tears, it seems. "Little mouse."

"Don't call me that!" she shrieks. "I don't deserve it! I don't..."

She lifts her unspelled hand. She covers her eyes. She weeps, great sobs shaking her body. "I need to be real. I need to be real. I need—"

She breaks all over again, landing on her knees. The knife clatters to the floor. She hugs herself around her middle, arms across the wide satin ribbon on her porcelain-doll dress, lifts her face to the sky, and a little girl shouldn't weep like that. A little girl shouldn't know this pain. A little girl should never know what it means to have to choose a price like this.

She kneels on the worn wool rug and weeps, alone.

"Little mouse," I whisper, when the storm passes through her and she's left hitching for breath in the hollowness crying leaves behind. "This is what magic is. It can't help it, any more than you can."

Her eyes are red. She looks at the knife on the floor, saying nothing. And then resolve settles on her, armoring her will and her conscience. She looks down at the floor, at the rug, at the knife.

She picks it up. She gets to her feet. And she walks toward me, blade held low and slightly away.

There's nothing to say now.

She raises the blade, so silver, so sharp, and slices the air just above my body. She cuts Livia's binding away, silent and resolute. She frees me and steps back, solemn and red-eyed.

"You have to stop her," Jael says. "Please."

She holds out the knife. I take it from her hand and pause to look at her. I bend down and kiss her forehead and pet her hair.

"Stay here," I say. "Stay safe."

I turn and hit the staircase at a two-at-a-time run.

• • • •

Five flights, at my age. My side stitches pain with an angry needle. I'm breathing in great desperate whoops. My heart pounds, still running even though I have halted, peering at the rooftop where Livia stands with her hands upraised, sorting through the threads of magic spun and woven over Hurston Hill. She pinches at a thread meant to shelter those who fled here for refuge, hiding them from angry spouses and cruel parents, and pulls it out of the weave. She finds the lines designed to draw people who need a little help to the web of secondhand shops, the food kitchen, and the medical clinic run by the Josephites, and yanks them free with a vicious flair.

I flinch, but I put my hand on the doorknob and hush it with a word. I pluck a basil leaf from a nearby plant, shuffle sideways to pick up a roll of garden twine. The blade whispers through the jute and vibrates in my grip, prickling for more.

No. This knife hungers to cut. It's... eager. I set it down on the bench. I don't want to know what it does if it gets a taste of blood. Not even the blood of the woman before me, pulling down the magic built to help everyone, ready to destroy generations of service to Hurston Hill and weave in spells that help her alone.

She could choose to take over the easy way. She could pull the whole thing down and rebuild it to suit her, the way some people will take a grand old house built by artisans and craftsmen and discard everything that makes it beautiful to put up vinyl siding they don't have to paint. Instead, she means to take the old magic and subvert it to her will.

That means there's something to save. Or there will be if I pluck up my courage and do something. I fear what I have to do here, but that doesn't change the fact that I have to do it.

I crush the basil in my hand and rub it over the twine. The fragrance rises, bathing me in its peppery sweetness. Courage. Victory against tremendous odds. David felled a giant with a stone, once. I have a tool. I must use it.

I whisper, though this spell will be a trumpeting herald. "I bind your hands and their wicked mischief."

I pull the first knot in the twine tight, and she freezes.

She turns around, wolf eyes trained on the rabbit-fast heart beneath my blouse, her mouth pursed up in a pout. "Is it ever the fate of the creator to be disappointed by what she has made? I thought I built Jael better than that. Now here you are, come to fight me with a piece of string."

I string another knot in the cord. "You will trouble us no more. I bind your tongue and its evil words." I plant my feet on the boardwalk and reach for the spellposts, ready to pull the cord tight.

I can't touch them. She's tied them to her already, and all the power of the house—all the power of Hurston Hill—is hers to command. All the power I have is what lives inside my body.

I remember the knife left on the table with regret.

She takes a step toward me, the slow and certain sauntering of a predator who likes it when their prey is scared. "What pluck. What courage. You brave, brave fool."

She flexes her power like a careless shrug and breaks the small binding I put on her. She lifts her hand, fingers spread, and lines of power spring from her blood-tipped fingernails to wrap around my wrists and ankles. I pull away.

I can't.

She smirks and raises her hand, her fingers sliding in subtle movements. I stand on my tiptoes. My arms spread out, elegant, majestic, wrists and fingers in second position. My right shoulder in this position makes me want to whimper. She watches as she pulls gently on the power and makes me dance with my head high.

"There we go," Livia coos. My stomach pitches and rolls at the sugar in her voice. "I think we understand each other a little better now, don't you agree?"

I can't move in a way she doesn't wish me to. The twine lies discarded on the boards. I dance, and it pleases her to send me spinning in a series of pirouettes that make me so dizzy I can't quite focus on what's in front of me when she lets me stop.

There is no way to escape.

"You're a problem. I meant for you to have a use. But here you are, with your heart intact, my creation a disappointment... but this might be better. People will wonder if you suddenly disappear, won't they? We should solve that."

She turns me to the front of the house. I take a step. Another. One more, past the hives. One more, toward the roof's cornice, and I understand what she means to do.

And when the horror of it reverberates through me, when I desperately fight her control, she chuckles.

"Grief's terrible. Isn't it? It hurts too much to bear, sometimes. People die of grief, you know. It breaks their hearts, and they just die. But some of them..."

My feet keep walking. Oh no. No, no. No. Oh please don't, stop. Stop—

"Stop."

The word escapes me and I can hardly believe it.

"Stop!"

Jael's voice. Pounding footsteps on the boardwalk. An outraged cry of pain, and the marionette strings binding me fall slack.

There's blood on that knife now. Livia's half bent over, clutching at a wound in her side. And Jael's swinging wildly, trying to give that blade another taste.

"Stop! Stop it! Stop!" Jael cries, but Livia snarls a command and Jael freezes in place. Still Livia's creation. Still bound to her maker. And now Livia picks up the knife, drunk on blood, and she pulls her gore-stained hand away from her side to grab a handful of Jael's hair, pulling her chin up, exposing her neck.

She reverses her grip on the blade, ready to slice, and my heart drops to the floor.

I lunge, snatching Livia's wrist. I dig my fingers in and twist with all my strength, and a pop running down her arm vibrates under my fingers.

Livia screams. Jael falls down, scrabbling backward. The knife clatters to the boards and there's no time to do anything but pay the price. Anything, for Jael. Anything, for Hurston Hill. Anything, for the bees.

I pick up the knife and drive it deep. The blade jumps in my hand, seeking the heart. It drinks. Livia falls.

But Jael lies on the sun-bleached boards, her limbs splayed out, her staring, empty eyes open to the twilit sky.

• • • •

This is what magic is.

I crawl to Jael, still, quiet Jael. Still so lifelike, though the magic is fading. Her eyes are turning to glass. Her skin is smoothing out like hide. Her hair is untidy, her hairband askew, and her limbs are going stiff.

My tears fall on Jael's face. On Jael's dress. It's perfectly logical, perfectly fair—Jael's creator is dead. The magic that gave Jael life is gone. She's a doll, now. Just a doll.

I hold her in my arms. I hug her to my chest. I stroke her bloodied, cashmere-soft hair and I hold her close as the magic fades from her.

"You were wrong, you know." It hurts my throat to whisper it in her painstakingly carved ear. "You were real. You were a little girl. You were good, and kind, and you were real, no matter what you were made of."

I straighten the collar of her dress. I smooth my tears away from her cheeks. I draw her stiff doll-part body into my lap and rock her, lullaby slow.

This is what magic is. It doesn't care how it's used. It only cares that the price is paid.

The house and Hurston Hill are safe, and so are the bees, and Jael paid for it in full.

"It's not fair," I say, even though I know it is. "It's not fair."

A buzzing answers me. The queen emerges from her hive. She lands on Jael's brow.

She gave so much to us. Everything she had, for us—and asked for nothing.

Her wings go still. She spreads them wide.

And then they come. Every worker-sister of the hive, every drone, too —they rise in a great murmuring cloud from the hive and land on Jael's shoulder, her nose, her injured hand. They land on me too, and soon we are covered in worker-sisters, buzzing, working.

And then I hear it all around me. I feel it. Magic, filling me like a waterskin, sweet and clear and golden. Magic past the boundaries of my body—the magic of the house, of Hurston Hill, the magic of the bees— all of it weaving in a single task around Jael.

Cocooned in the hive, I open my heart and let them weave what they will of it. They work, and work, and when they are done, all the magic is sunk into Jael's skin.

The queen flexes her wings. *It is done.*

The magic of the house is tied to her. Hurston Hill's power sings in her veins. My witching is a glass of water; Jael's bound to the river. The magic of this place is no longer mine. It is hers now, and I must teach her the way of it.

I feel an emptiness like the strange absence of a pulled tooth. "But I promised to serve you."

Another road has opened, the queen says. *That way is yours now.*

She weaves a honey-drop of magic and moves on hair-thin feet to put it in Jael's mouth. It spreads over her lips, and they go pink.

Jael breathes.

Honey makes the magic strong, the queen says, and then the bees take wing and fly back to the hive. I'm surrounded by the corpses of a hundred drones and Jael looking up at me, her eyes blinking, her limbs pliant and alive.

"I think I fell asleep." She rubs at her eyes with the backs of her knuckles, and the cut on her palm is a half-healed scab. "Ma'am, are you crying?"

I weep into her hair and rock her again.

• • • •

I might have the radio on a little too loud as I drive the long streets after a day's work at City Hall up to Hurston Hill. Councillor van Darlington's expression replays in my mind—the moment where he straightens up as the clerk from Heritage Planning lists the addresses of ten properties newly added to the register right in the neighborhood he wanted to bulldoze for the sake of a freeway. When he looks down at the paper in front of him, now a pile of useless tissue, and looks at me, mouth open to accuse—and then closes it as he realizes that he can't accuse me of ruining a proposal he never had the chance to share.

Perfect. Sublime. And the families of Williamsville, anchored by those ten properties, can continue their fight to reshape their community on their terms. Williamsville isn't in my council, but it doesn't matter.

I nod to the bounce of the bass line on the radio. I turn my head to take in the whole intersection and smile at a driver who recognizes me. She grins back and waves just before she pulls ahead to turn left.

I drive the long way home, just to see how the city is doing, and when I cross the avenue and enter the domain of Hurston Hill, I don't feel the soft caress of returning to my power. I don't have the sense of the bees, ticking softly in the back of my head. I can still sense the power flowing all around me, but I can't hold it in my hand and shape it to my will, not anymore.

The whole city is mine to tend, now.

I drive past the house where Lorraine sweeps the steps. She waves at me as I keep on, headed up the road to the park. There's a spot right by the slick-polished concrete pad, and the Cadillac slides neatly into the space waiting for it.

I have that much power left, at least.

Music plays through speakers mounted on poles surrounding a slick concrete pad where boys and girls roller-skate. Jael is right in the thick of them, laughing. She skates in a cohort of girls all performing the same complex crossovers and slides at once, skating so close together that a single mistake will bring them all down. They clap their hands and scatter, spinning on tiptoe, and come back, shoulders and hips sliding.

They erupt into cheers at getting the routine right. They cluster together in a hug, and then Jael catches sight of me and rolls to my side, taking delicate steps over the grass to meet me.

"We did it," she says. "Did you see?"

"I did. Where are your shoes?"

"I skated over after Miss Yvonne was done teaching me fractions."

"You'll break your head one of these days." I shake my head. "Did you have your candy?"

"I still have one left," she says, and digs into the pocket of her satin bomber jacket—bright golden yellow, just like her friends—to pull out a honey chew. She pops it in her mouth and rolls to the passenger door.

"You're getting in the car in those skates?"

"I'll be careful," she promises.

The wards on the car brighten as she touches it. A worker-sister bobs on a gentle breeze, and Jael lifts her hand to give her a place to land. She looks at the bee intently, then at me once the bee takes flight.

"There's a newcomer," she says. "He's looking at a suite in the Henri Louis Arms. The bees like him."

"That's good. Shall we stop at St. Joseph the Worker and let them know?"

"Tomorrow," she says. "He hasn't quite figured out he belongs here yet."

"As you say."

Jael manages to get in the front seat in those skates. I drive back to the house. We're stopped at the first corner when she says, "Did your plan work?"

"Beautifully. Williamsville has prevailed."

Jael smiles. "I bet Councillor van Darlington was surprised."

"He looked like he'd just swallowed a fish," I say. "Next is the transit initiative. That's going to be harder to steer."

"Should we read the cards?" Jael asks. "I need practice."

"That's a fine idea."

Jael looks out the window and waves at Cynthia, out sweeping her corner sidewalk with a hand-bound broom. "Everything is just right. You're going to be mayor one day."

The air shivers. Something hears her say the words, and it seems fate hasn't finished with me yet. I nod and turn onto our street.

"As you say."

Lorraine's inside now. The air smells like her own magic, spices and flour and buttermilk on chicken. Hunger wakes up and I could eat for an hour—and Jael makes a happy noise as she bumps the car door with her hip and skates to the steps.

"You take off those skates before you go in the house," I say.

"Yes, ma'am. Can we go to the movies? I want to see the new Billy Dee Williams movie. Can we go?"

"Of course we can," I say. "And we'll watch Mark Hamill and Carrie Fisher too, while we're there."

The witch of Hurston Hill laughs and runs up the stairs to the house in her sock feet. A worker-sister floats past the ivy growing up the bricks, and I smile at her, something in my eye.

"Thank you," I say.

The bee, understanding, floats away.

C. L. POLK wrote the Hugo-nominated Kingston Cycle, including the World Fantasy Award winning *Witchmark*. They are also the author of the CBC Canada Reads finalist *The Midnight Bargain* and the Nebula-winning, *USA Today* bestseller *Even Though I Knew The End*. Before writing fantasy novels, they worked as a film extra, a costermonger, and also identified lepidoptera by eye. Mx. Polk lives in Calgary, on the territories of the Blackfoot Confederacy, the Tsuut'ina, the Îyâxe Nakoda Nations, and the Métis Nation (Region 3). Mx. Polk is represented by Caitlin McDonald of the Donald Maass Literary Agency.

* CONTENT NOTES: references to parental abuse and depicts the death of a child.

SATURDAY'S SONG

BY WOLE TALABI

Novelette Long List*

T he seven siblings sit in a place beyond the boundaries of space and time, where everything is made of stories. Even them. Especially them.

People are made of stories too, but only the versions of their stories that they tell themselves. Curated, limited, incomplete. Many of the stories people tell themselves are lies layered on partially perceived things to give their lives structure and meaning. The siblings that sit beyond sit true, for they are made of all the stories that were, that are, that are to come. They tell each other these stories, taking them out and examining them in the light like a never-ending self-dissection. They listen to the stories, and as they do, they are made whole again. They exist in narrative equilibrium. In constant flux. They tell each other stories of what has happened, is happening, will happen, because it is their function. They tell these stories because they must.

Sometimes, they sing the stories too.

Saturday likes to sing. She thinks she has a nice voice, and this is true. It is euphonic, lilting, mellow but strong and full of emotion, so her siblings let her sing her parts of the stories when she wants to.

Some stories demand melody.

"Let us tell another story," Sunday says, breathing the words out more than speaking them. He is the most knowledgeable of the seven siblings, even though none of them know why. He just is, because that is his story. He rakes the tight curls of his beard with his fingers before continuing. "Saturday, it is your turn to choose a story for us to tell and hear."

Saturday stops playing with the thick, long braids of her goldspun hair. She is still surprised, even though she already knew it was her turn before he told her so. She looks around the table, avoiding her siblings' eyes, and then she shuts her eyelids and focuses inward, seeking out the story she knows has a good shape, the story that feels right, like she is reading her own bones. When she finds it, the story she knows they need in this moment of non-time, she beams a smile and radiates the choice out to her siblings, passing the story they all know she has chosen for them to hear and tell. None of them react when they receive it, but they know it is a good story.

Monday, who always starts their stories, begins his duty solemnly with clear words. "Saura met Mobola at a financial management conference in..."

"Stop!" Saturday cries, holding up a small hand.

The shock of the interruption leaves Monday's mouth open, like he is a fish removed from water. Sunday's emerald eyes widen. Tuesday, Thursday, and Friday crane their necks toward her, their gazes curious and hard. Only Wednesday does not visibly react because she is bound up in thick clanking chains, punishment for the crime of trying to change a story. The timestone Wednesday used to perform the abomination sits at the centre of the mahogany table between two ornate pewter candelabra like an offering, or a temptation. Its emerald edges reflect and refract the candlelight in peculiar ways, making the bright orange light dance with shadows across the table and the walls.

Saturday feels sad for her sister, but knows she needs to be careful.

She does not want to be punished too. Interruptions once a story has begun are mostly forbidden, although not as forbidden as attempting to change a story. The rules that govern the seven are both rigid and flexible, to varying degrees, like the rules of storytelling itself. Still, Saturday knows it is important that it is done this way. For Wednesday's sake. She says, "Forgive me. But I want to begin the story near the middle. Please, can we? We will go back to the beginning, but if we start at the middle, it makes the story so much better."

She pulses her story choice again. This time, she radiates not only its substance, but she gives them its form and structure, the shape of it with all its contours defined. Not just what it is, but also the way she wants them to tell and to hear it.

They receive it as a stream of visions. As a kaleidoscope of images. A swirl of sounds. A spectrum of sensations. A babble of narrator voices. As points of view. As music. As song.

Sunday gives her a look that is both surprised and curious. Tuesday claps her hands with glee. Monday nods with understanding. He looks to Wednesday, the chains wound around her body like perforated metal anacondas. They are older than time itself. Saturday wants her shackled sister to tell the part of the story where Saura obtains the chains to bind the Yoruba nightmare god, Shigidi. Resonance. She thinks it gives the middle of the story the reinforcement it needs. Like a good skeleton. Everyone has been allocated their part of the story to undergird it with what is important for the telling and the hearing. The other siblings also nod their approval. This makes Saturday smile. They understand even if they don't fully know her motives. But they know it is not just important to tell and hear the story, it is important to tell and hear it *well*.

Monday wipes the thin film of sweat from his narrow moustache, adjusts the collar of his pinstripe suit, and starts again.

This is the part of the story that Monday told:

• • • •

Saura never dreamed before she encountered Shigidi.

For as long as she could remember, she never recalled a single dream upon waking. For Saura, sleep was and had always been a brief submergence into dappled darkness, her consciousness consumed whole like swallowed fruit. And because of this, she never felt completely rested. She always felt lethargic. Unfocused. Persistently exhausted.

When she was eleven, her mother, who was magajiya of the local bori cult of Ungwar Rimi near Zaria, summoned Barhaza, the sleep spirit, to possess her. The ritual was performed, and the spirit invited into her body to relieve Saura of her ailment and give her rest. But despite their offering of fresh milk from three white goats, the rolling of her eyes in her head, and the convulsions she experienced when the spirit entered her, the possession was unsuccessful, and she remained dreamless and unrested.

Her mother wept and gritted her teeth.

Saura had the gift of sensitivity and was meant to succeed her mother as magajiya. A refusal of the spirits to grant such a simple request counted against her, even though there were other things that counted against her more which her mother would soon come to know.

"I don't want to," Saura protested when her mother announced that they would attempt another possession.

"You must."

"No!" She screamed. It took her father two hours to find and retrieve her from the bush beside the market where she fled to hide.

When Saura was sixteen, her mother tried again, ambushing her in her sleep and tying her down with thick hemp rope so that she could not resist. That time, her mother begged Barhaza to not only give Saura dreams and rest but to adjust her subconscious desires, to make her stop looking at other girls with lust in her eyes, to take away her visible attraction for the curve of other women's hips, the swell of their lips, the fullness of their breasts. Once again, the spirit entered Saura's body, rigidifying her limbs, milkening her eyes, and communing with her thoughts, but when it left, there were still no dreams, and her desires were unchanged. That evening, Saura, wounded by her mother's betrayal, ran away from home with nothing on her back besides her jalabiya and the light of a full moon.

She only ever returned home once, to attend her father's funeral. She refused to speak with her mother, and sat with her lover, Mobola, and her father's family, tears streaming down her eyes as they lowered his body into the hard red earth.

When she was twenty-five, after struggling her way through university with the help of a local charity and finally getting a job at the bank, she went to see a doctor in Kaduna city. He was an oddly shaped man with a big head, small frame, and a protruding belly and a kind smile, with a yellowing diploma from a university she'd never heard of in Kansas on the brick wall of his office, hung between two hunting knives like a trophy. He connected a string of electrodes to her head and took measurements on a machine that beeped a steady whine until she fell asleep.

"No REM sleep," he announced, poring over his notes and charts when she was awake and back in his office chair. She'd never gone into REM sleep. After three more sessions with electrodes and needles and charts and uncomfortable sleep, he concluded that she was incapable of it. He told her she was a highly unusual case, prescribed a series of medications, and asked her to sign a release form so he could study her more. None of his medications worked and so Saura didn't sign his forms. She simply got used to empty sleep, to never being fully rested, to never dreaming.

That is why, even before waking, she knew something was wrong that night when Shigidi entered the master bedroom of the house in the heart of Surulere which she shared with Mobola. She knew something was wrong because she dreamed for the first time.

In her dream, she saw a small dark orb hovering above them as they lay naked in bed, entwined in a post-coital embrace. The orb was dense and powerful, like an evil star. It settled on Mobola's chest and tugged at her flesh with an inexorable force like gravity. It tugged at Saura's too. She resisted the pull of it, tossing, turning, and sweating profusely on the bed, caught in a night terror she could not escape. But she saw the dreamy, ethereal version of Mobola in her mind, yielding to the pull of the orb, being fragmented, stripped down to fine grey particles that were absorbed by the thing. When there was nothing of dream-Mobola left, the orb disappeared and Saura sank back into darkness. On Monday morning, when the heat of the sun on her face finally woke Saura up,

Mobola was cold to the touch, her skin pale and dry. She'd been dead for three hours.

Saura screamed.

• • • •

Monday stops speaking and Saturday gathers what he has said into her chest. Each word is a bird that she swallows, expanding with it. In-breath. It is important for her song.

Tuesday's pale face is unusually blushed bright pink, and her lustrous auburn hair seems to gain volume as she prepares to speak. She knows, has known, will know, that she has the best part of the story. The part that begins with lust and ends with something like love. Saturday winks at her sister. She has given it to her by design. Tuesday likes description and dialogue and the cadence of human speech, which is important in conveying emotion. A smile cuts across Tuesday's freckled face.

This is the part of the story that Tuesday told:

• • • •

Saura met Mobola at a financial management conference in Abuja just before the cold harmattan of 2005.

It was break time between an endless stream of panel discussions, and Saura was standing by the tall windows that overlooked a stone fountain, its water flecked gold with sunlight as it erupted into the air. When she turned around to go back, she caught Mobola staring at her from across the hall. The moment their eyes met, there was a surge of something intangible within her, like an emotional arc discharge. Saura smiled and beckoned her over. For two days, they'd been stealing glances at each other, occasionally catching each other's eyes. It was the seventh time it had happened, and Saura had learned enough of herself to recognize the surge, the feeling, the signs. She was ready. Mobola flashed her a sweet smileful of white teeth and approached. She had bright, inquisitive eyes with an anxious look in them. Her hair was natural and curly, and her wide hips strained against the grey of her skirt. Saura thought she looked stunning.

"Hi. I'm Mobola. I manage the Trust Bank office in Surulere," she said.

Saura told her she was the logistics manager for all the Kaduna offices and that if she had to listen to another discussion on forex approval procedures, she would go downstairs and drown herself in the fountain. They both laughed at that, carefree, like wind. There was something about the way Mobola laughed, the way she threw her head back, the way she almost hiccupped between breaths, her chest heaving against the cashmere blouse, the way she closed her eyes at the peak of her mirth, that Saura found deeply attractive.

They talked for a few minutes. There was a deliberate softness to everything about Mobola. The curves of her body, the cadence of her words. Saura was lost in Mobola's eyes, unable to look away. Big, brown, constantly wet, and full of a look which was a strange mix of sadness, grittiness, and hope. The look of someone that had seen the worst of the world, had stared into the dark heart of humanity, but had survived and resolved to live, love, and laugh freely despite it.

They pulled out their phones and exchanged numbers, laughing when they realized they both used the same model of Blackberry, a Bold, and agreed to meet at the delegate hotel bar at nine.

Saura watched Mobola leave, the sway of her hips hypnotizing her like magic. She could barely breathe. The air suddenly seemed thinner, oxygen harder to take in. She knew she had to be careful. If she had read the situation wrong, she could end up in prison for years. Nigerian law was not kind to sapphic romance.

Saura arrived early to the bar and had two Irish coffees to wake herself up. She knew she wasn't wrong when Mobola showed up and waved at her, wearing a blue dress that was so tight in her fuller places that it could have been painted on. There was a gap showing between her front teeth, some cleavage, and a bit of a belly. Legs shaved smooth and feet encased in black pumps. Saura thought she was even more stunning than before.

They had three gin and tonics, making fun of the parade of boring panel speakers and the other conference delegates who pretended to be interested in the minutiae of inter-bank financial processes before Saura pulled Mobola to her feet.

"Do you want to go somewhere more interesting?" she asked, finishing her drink in one gulp.

Mobola smiled at her, mouth full of piano-key teeth, lips red and glistening. "Sure."

Saura took Mobola to a club she'd heard about from one of the online forums she'd joined when she'd first started trying to understand herself. It was called The Cave and it was a ten-minute taxi ride away. When they entered, it was into a rainbow chaos. Strobe lights. Colourful décor with bizarre shapes that challenged the very concept of geometry. Sweaty people pressed together at tables, on the dancefloor, on barstools, running over with feeling. They made their way to the bar, ordered shots of something that the bartender told them was tequila but didn't taste like it, and then merged with the mass of flesh on the dance-floor. Mobola turned her back to Saura and began to rock from side to side slowly, sensually, following the beat of the music. Saura wrapped her hands around Mobola's waist and swayed with her so that they moved to the music together like a single creature.

Saura's head was a cloud. In that moment, she was sure she knew what it was like to dream.

The next morning, they woke up in each other's arms, fully clothed and in the same position they'd danced in.

"Good morning, beautiful," Mobola said.

"Good morning."

"I had so much fun last night."

"Me too."

Mobola turned around to face her. "Did we...?"

Her face was close. Saura could see for the first time that she had a solitary dimple on her left cheek. It was faint, but there. She was staring intently and Saura could not look away, lost in her eyes. Her hair had bunched up and tangled, pressed against the hotel room pillow, loose strands dancing in front of her face. When she smiled, Saura's heart took flight.

She reached for the question hanging in space between them. "No."

They were both quiet for what seemed like a long time. An unbearably long time. And then she pulled Mobola closer so that they were chest to chest, inhaling each other's alcohol-scented breath, and asked, "Did you want to?"

She smiled. "Yes."

There was no hesitation. None.

Saura kissed Mobola and the cloud in her head ascended, rising, beyond the ceiling and the roof and the sky, to the place where hearts go when they are buoyed by love.

It stayed there, never coming down. It only ever rose higher. For ten years, that feeling never sank. Not even when they fought and accidentally hurt each other and cried and made up and laughed, like all good lovers do. Not when Mobola fell asleep one night and didn't answer Saura's calls for help after her car overheated and broke down on Third Mainland Bridge. Not even when they had an argument about Mobola applying for a residence pass for both of them to leave the country without telling her first. Not even when her mother refused to speak to Mobola at Saura's father's funeral or acknowledge her existence and tried to convince Saura to come back home, telling her that she was throwing her life away and bringing shame to the family.

No, Saura was always sure of the cloud of them. For ten years, she was sure. Through all the vicissitudes and the accusations and the arguments, she knew with all the certainty of entropy that she loved Mobola and that nothing would ever change that. Not even death.

• • • •

Tuesday is done speaking.

She is standing now. Her thin, pale hands are thrust out in front of her like the bones of a large bird. She'd allowed herself to become swept up with the story, infused with it, become one with it, and because she had, so had all the siblings. There is a solitary tear running down Thursday's face. And Sunday has a glazed look in his eyes that makes him seem much older than his hair, which is grey at the temples, would indicate even though time is meaningless to the siblings. Saturday is pleased. They need this for the story. The emotion. She has taken in all of Tuesday's words, the sensations, the feelings, all of it. Her chest is filling up, and the first melodies of her song are beginning to take shape within her lungs. Sunday turns to face Wednesday, whose turn has come. Wednesday must go back to the middle of the story because that is where the chains first appear. Chains not unlike the ones wrapped around Wednesday's torso, snaking through shackles that bind her hands and feet, tethering her to the stone ground so that the only part of her that can move is her head and, most importantly, her mouth. It's hard to tell or hear a story without a mouth.

Saturday watches her sister, waiting. Wednesday has already received her section of the story. She just needs to accept it. She is hesitating, but it is not like last time, when she rejected a story midway through and entered it, trying to change it—the crime for which she is now bound. The middle of the story is where the chains and the refusal to accept fate are waiting like familiar stalking animals.

Wednesday begins to shake and Saturday knows the story is coming. Erupting from the deepest volcano of suppressed emotion.

This is the part of the story that Wednesday told:

• • • •

A month after Mobola's funeral, Saura went to see a Babalawo in Badagry, at the mouth of a waterway that kisses two countries. She hadn't slept in days. Her friend Junia, who was also a colleague at work, had recommended him, saying he'd given her a charm that helped her deal with her depression after a miscarriage. Saura took his contact details from Junia but hadn't planned to use them. If Barhaza of the bori, a spirit historically linked to her people and family, couldn't give her rest, then there was nothing a Yoruba Babalawo unfamiliar with the shape of her spirit would be able to do. The yellow piece of paper with his number written on it in blue ink remained unused on her table until one afternoon, watching traffic glide past her window, she realized that while he would not be able to give her peace of mind, he might be able to give her information. To help her understand why ten years of love and companionship and joy had ended at the speed of a bad dream.

The Babalawo was a thickset man who spoke perfect English. He had a long greying beard and calm eyes. Three white dots were chalked onto his forehead just above his eyebrows and the string of beads around his neck rattled as he shook his head when he heard her explain what had happened to Mobola. When she was done, he removed the beads and threw them onto the raffia mat between them, rapidly whispering an incantation.

"This is the work of Shigidi," he said with his eyes still on the beads as he explained to her that Shigidi was the Yoruba deification of nightmare, able to enter and manipulate the human subconscious, especially during sleep when their grip on their thoughts were loosest. He could induce night terrors and sleep paralysis in his prey as he sat on their chests and pressed the breath out from them. The Babalawo explained that he was an ambivalent Orisha, protecting those who gave him offerings but also often sent by evil people to kill those they perceived as enemies or threats. "You have communed with spirits before?" the Babalawo asked, looking up at her curiously. "To have sensed Shigidi the way you described it, to receive a bleed-over dream when you were not the person he came for, that is very unusual."

Saura's eyes were wide with shock, but she only shook her head. She didn't tell him about her mother or her intimate knowledge of the bori or her adolescent possessions by myriad spirits. She simply paid him his fee and hired a car to take her home. But not the home she'd shared with Mobola. No. Back to Ungwar Rimi, where she knew she could obtain the power to punish the nightmare god that had killed Mobola. To fight fire with fire. Saura hadn't spoken to her mother in more than a decade. But they were bound by blood, and Saura needed her mother's help, her knowledge, to do what she wanted to do. Human families can be made of chains too.

Saura did not go to the family compound to talk privately with her mother. That would have been too personal, too painful, and would have made it too easy for her mother to refuse. She went instead to the market at night, when the moon and the stars hung low and most of the village had retired to their beds, leaving the wide-open spaces of the market to the members of the bori cult. This was where the council of bori magajiya, who knew how to summon spirits and invite them to possess the bodies of people for various purposes, held court and heard requests from the sick, the curious, the desperate.

She arrived at the centre of the market in a black headscarf and cotton veil atop a flowing black jalabiya like the one she'd been wearing the night she ran away. They were already in the middle of a possession. An unusually tall man, shirtless, with broad shoulders and long wiry arms like a spider, was crawling on the ground, facing up with his back arched high to an impossible curve. He was singing in a high-pitched voice even though he was foaming lightly at the mouth. He looked like he was leaking tree sap. Saura recognized the signs. He'd been possessed by Kuturu, the leper spirit, the healer of diseases of the flesh. Two men in white kaftans played soft music with their fingers on white dotted calabashes. A girl that seemed no more than thirteen played an accompanying lute. Saura used to be that girl, the one playing the lute at possessions, before she was compelled to flee and enter the world.

When they were done and the man was helped to his feet by two others, presumably healed of his ailment, Saura removed her veil and made her request before her mother could completely compose herself.

"Tell us, why do you want the Sarkin Sarkoki to possess you?" one of the other magajiya, a plump woman with plaited hair, asked first in accented Hausa. It was her aunt, Turai.

For Mobola, Saura thought, but didn't say.

She simply replied, "I have been wronged. And I want justice."

The third council member, a man with thick white eyebrows whom she had never seen before, asked her why she wanted Sarkin Sarkoki, the lord of the chains, the binding spirit. Why not Kure, he asked, the hyena spirit who could give power and stealth, or Sarkin Rafi, who would give strength to do violence which vengeance often called for?

"Because the one that wronged me is not mortal." At that, they fell silent.

The three members of the bori council stared at her appraisingly. Sifting and weighing her request. Her mother's gaze unrelenting.

"My daughter. I'm glad you have finally come home. Where you belong. But Sarkin Sarkoki demands a great price," her mother said finally, standing up from the raffia mat to her full height. Saura became acutely aware of just how much they looked like each other. The same thin nose and lips. The same ochre skin, even though her mother's was more weathered, beaten to stubborn leather by the Sahara-adjacent sun.

The same determined look in the eyes. "The possession is permanent. The lord of the chains will bind himself to you before giving you the power to bind your enemy. You are giving up your body as a vessel forever. What justice could be worth this?"

Beneath the veil, heat rose behind Saura's neck. She did not want to say what she was thinking. There was too much pain in her heart, threatening to spill out. If she let even a drop of the decade's worth of resentment within her slip between her lips, it would become a deluge that drowned them all.

"It doesn't matter. I am one of you. Heir to a title. I have a right to commune with the spirits. With Sarkin Sarkoki. And I have made my request."

There was more weighing. More sifting. More appraisal. Finally, her mother turned to face the other two of the council and they communed briefly before announcing their decision.

"We will grant your request," her mother said. "But on one condition. Once you have had your revenge against whatever spirit has wronged you, you must return home and become a full bori devotee. We cannot have a vessel of Sarkin Sarkoki roaming free. You will take your place with us, you will marry a good man, and you will bear children and teach them our ways. Do you agree?"

Saura knew this was what her mother had always wanted. To bring her back and bind her to home, even if she had to exploit a tragedy to achieve it. But Saura could not see past her desire to avenge Mobola. To find out why her lover had died and make their story make sense again even if she couldn't change its ending.

"I agree."

Her words, like her heart, had taken on the texture of stone.

Her mother nodded and smiled, teeth cutting a curve like the half-moon beaming down on them from the cloudless sky.

Saura closed her eyes as a woman in a yellow jalabiya cut like her own took her by the arms and brought her to the centre of the clearing, where the two main roads that crossed the market met. The woman stood behind her; she would be her nurse if anything went wrong.

Saura breathed steadily as the men in the white kaftans and the girl on the lute began to play their music and the three members of the council, led by her mother, began to chant words she had not heard for years. Words that made the air feel heavy on her skin, in her lungs.

Saura felt something in her chest open like the peeling of a flower. She felt a flush of heat, saw a flash of light. A rush of charged air entered her and then the world fell away as she was insufflated by the incoming spirit.

In the dark and nebulous place of her mind, Saura saw Sarkin Sarkoki.

He was an impossibly gaunt man, with limbs like vines and grey skin, sitting on a stool at the centre of the empty space. He was bound in thick, corroded chains tethered to something she could not see in the filmy darkness below. A black cloth was wrapped around his waist and draped to cover his lower half. It pooled in cascades merging with the nebulous black ground below. His eyes were dark red, like spilled blood, and his stomach was cut open, revealing mechanical viscera of chains and gears and roiling iron entrails. All over his skin, scripts were written onto him in chalked scars. He looked like a man that had been tortured and starved. He opened his mouth to reveal rust-coloured teeth.

"You offer yourself as a vessel," he said, already knowing why she'd let him into her mind and what she wanted him to help her do.

"Yes," Saura managed to reply despite her trembling.

"You surrender your body to the chains."

"Yes."

"Then so be it," Sarkin Sarkoki stated, his chains clanking and rattling as he began to vibrate. "We are one. You will have what you desire."

The chains around him unfurled themselves and reached out to seize her. They were heavy and rough. Saura felt them wrap around every part of her, flesh and bone, blood and nerves, mind and spirit. The chains squeezed around the very essence of her until the world was nothing but chains and darkness. A full and lovely pain consumed her as Sarkin Sarkoki bonded with her, and it wasn't until the woman in the yellow jalabiya poured water on her face and shook her back into full consciousness that she tasted the sand in her mouth and realized she had been rolling around on the ground, screaming.

• • • •

Wednesday goes quiet.

Her siblings wait.

She takes in a deep breath and lets out a scream. It is at once a declaration of defiance and an accusation levelled at her siblings, at the family that put her in chains. Her scream is a knife in their hearts.

Saturday does not look away until her sister stops screaming. Wednesday's face, once full of grace, is contorted into an ugly shape with lines like regret, but Saturday does not turn from it. She takes it all in, the words and the scream, because that too is part of the story.

When the screaming ends, there is a pause that lasts for a long time but only briefly as they allow the scream to settle.

And then, the story continues.

Her siblings' words are air in Saturday's lungs and her song is half complete. Saturday turns to face Thursday. His mahogany skin is pallid in the candlelight. The sadness hanging from the corners of his mouth and the salt and pepper of his hair makes him look fragile and small in his fitted black suit. He leans forward and places both elbows on the table, settling his jaw on the tips of his fingers, hands pressed together like he is in prayer.

When Thursday begins to speak, Saturday manages a smile. She likes Thursday's voice. It is steady and powerful and full of purpose, like waves crashing onto a cliff, like vengeance.

This is the part of the story that Thursday told:

• • • •

Saura was pretending to be asleep on an uncomfortable mattress in a spacious hotel room she'd taken for three nights when Shigidi arrived, just before midnight. She was shivering beneath the duvet, because she didn't know how to adjust the central air conditioning, but she didn't care. There was a 'Do Not Disturb' sign outside.

The nightmare god's arrival was sudden, and she felt his presence immediately. The dream-sensation of that small dark orb tugging at her subconscious with its evil gravity was one she could never forget.

She waited until he climbed onto the bed and sat on her chest, the weight of him restricting her breath. When she felt his probing at the edges of her mind, noticed a blurring and loosening of her thoughts and memories, she knew he had made the mistake of establishing a connection with her mind. Of attempting to slip into her subconscious, as was his way. But she'd set a trap for him. The Babalawo in Badagry had given her the number for another, less reputable Babalawo who took requests for the nightmare god's assistance from people with such cruelty in their hearts. She'd told him that she wanted someone killed in their sleep, but she didn't say that the name she'd given was her own. And that the location she'd provided was the hotel room she'd booked. The trap was sprung.

She sat up suddenly and came face to face with the god that had murdered Mobola.

Saura was taken aback by how small and ugly Shigidi was. He was just over two feet tall. His head was too big for his body, and his dark, ashy skin was covered in pockmarks, rashes, scarification lines, and sores. He wore filthy Ankara-print trousers, and a plain black cloak that sat on his shoulders and ran down to the back of his ankles, with cowrie shells and lizard skulls sewn into the fabric. His face was covered with black ash that made it look much darker than the rest of him. He looked confused, surprised, a bit stupid, and unsure what to do.

Saura felt a flush of anger that something so hideous had been the one to take Mobola from her.

"Bastard," she spat out.

"What is happening?" Shigidi asked as he tried to withdraw from the borders of her consciousnesses.

Saura did not answer. She simply grabbed him and pulled him into the darkness of her mind where her inability to dream had left a vacuum where the cadaverous and bound Sarkin Sarkoki now dwelled.

Chains shot out of the darkness and latched onto Shigidi's small limbs, binding him to the place. He struggled and pulled but he could not free himself. Sarkin Sarkoki sat on his stool, watching, and making a sound like laughter.

"What is going on? Who are you people?" the nightmare god shouted.

Angry that Shigidi could not even remember her face, she did not give him the satisfaction of understanding.

"You gods and spirits, you are all the same," she said instead. "You think you can enter our lives and ruin them at your whim, taking whatever you want and leaving us to pick up the pieces. No. Not this time. This time, here is what will happen. You will suffer, like you have never suffered before. There will be pain. A lot of it. I will take my time. And even when you begin to thirst for death, when the chains have dug into your ugly body so deeply that they have fused with your nerves so that there is nothing except pain, you will not die. I will watch as you are stripped of every fragment of hope you hold in that body, until you feel as black and as bleak as this place, deep inside you. Maybe then you will remember who I am, and you will remember the person you took from me."

As she spoke, the expression on Shigidi's face had morphed from confusion to terror to something beyond both.

And when he whispered "Why?", Saura silently asked Sarkin Sarkoki to tighten the squeeze of the chains around his neck until his head bulged and he began to choke. It did not relent until he blacked out.

• • • •

Thursday lifts his head and withdraws his hands from the intricately patterned mahogany table, its straight-grained, reddish-brown timber cut from a tree that once stood at the centre of a garden that is not a garden, in the middle of nowhere, everywhere, all at once. He leans back and turns to meet Saturday's gaze. She smiles at him, grateful for the way he told his part of the story which she has also absorbed. She feels it almost bursting out of her now—the song. She just needs one more part. The revelation.

She turns to face Friday, who is raking his hands through his thick afro. He is the most reserved of the siblings and the one who likes the shape that secrets give stories, which is why she has arranged it so that he can tell this part, just before her song. Candlelight dances in his large brown eyes and his pitch-black lips are quivering. He is eager to tell and hear.

Saturday nods and Friday opens his mouth, his bass voice booming and bouncing off the walls of the room in powerful waves.

This is the part of the story that Friday told:

• • • •

Their bodies lay still and silent on the bed in the hotel, slumped over each other in an awkward embrace, but in the darkness of Saura's mind, possessed by Sarkin Sarkoki, Shigidi was screaming. Saura watched dispassionately, refusing to allow him even a waking moment of respite, a single fleeting second where he was not intimately acquainted with the pain from the contracting chains. And with every scream, she asked him the same question.

"Do you remember what you took from me?"

He insisted that he did not know, and so the torment continued. Sarkin Sarkoki's laughter was the only other sound in her mind.

Almost twenty hours passed before the screaming stopped. Saura knew that it was not because the pain had ended—she was still commandeering the chains to pull and squeeze, and he was still writhing and whimpering. It was because something in him was breaking. Even a god can only take so much torment.

And yet after all the suffering, when she looked at him, pathetic as he was, she did not feel the satisfaction that she had craved. Underneath her rage was a sense of emptiness and loss and soul-deep weariness. She too was breaking under the weight of vengeance. And she knew now that someone else had sent him to their home that night because the disreputable Babalawo had told her it was the only reason Shigidi would kill someone.

"Mobola," she blurted out, eager for resolution. "Her name was Mobola."

Shigidi looked up at her, a glimmer of hope in his eyes for the first time since she'd lured him into the place of chains. He looked around at the darkness, as though he were searching her thoughts for something. And then, "Ahh... Mobola..." he croaked. "Yes. Omobola Adenusi... Lotus estate, Surulere. I remember now."

Saura seethed when her name escaped his mouth.

"Why... Why did you kill her?" she asked, her rage still bubbling at the surface.

"I'm sorry." Shigidi breathed. "It was just a job. A standard night-mare-and-kill job."

Saura shuddered. She knew how he worked, but she was too angry to care. "Just a job? You took the most precious person in the world from me because it was just a job?"

The chains around his limbs rattled as Shigidi's tortured body sagged with the effort of keeping his head upright. "I'm sorry. I didn't know. It was just a job. It was only a job."

"Who sent you? Who was the client?"

And as she asked that, Sarkin Sarkoki's laughter stopped abruptly.

"I don't know," Shigidi said. "I just do what they ask me."

"Then you must remember," Saura demanded.

The chains tightened again.

"Please..."

"Tell me."

"I don't know," the nightmare god maintained, each word excavated from him hoarse and desperate. "But... But... Wait... It was a woman. Older. Not Yoruba. I remember she was not Yoruba. She was slender. Thin nose. She had eyes like yours."

Saura clutched at her chest.

"In her prayer, she only said she needed to get rid of the girl to get her daughter back."

A knot like an iron rope formed in her stomach. Saura fell to her knees as the weight of realization settled upon her. The lack of surprise when her mother saw her at the market. The insistence on returning home as a condition of her possession. The guilt in her aunt Turai's eyes. It all made terrible sense to her in that moment.

She asked Sarkin Sarkoki to unshackle him from her mind and Shigidi fell onto the dark filmy ground with a thud. In an instant, they were back on the bed, in the hotel.

Saura shot up and rolled off the mattress onto the carpeted floor. She felt the iron rope tighten in her stomach and everything constricted, like it was being squeezed by invisible hands. She felt like her insides were about to be torn and exposed, like the hollow clockwork belly of Sarkin Sarkoki. She threw up and began to cry.

"Ah. You know who it was, don't you?" Shigidi whispered.

Her mother's words tolled in her head like a bell.

My daughter.

I'm glad you have finally come home.

Saura stumbled up to her knees and settled a long stare at Shigidi, who was looking back at her with large yellow eyes full of pity or regret or both.

"Yes," she whispered back.

"Family?"

"Yes."

"I... I am sorry. I am truly sorry."

Saura was surprised by the sincerity in his voice.

"I hate my job sometimes," Shigidi continued. "But I need the offerings and prayer requests to survive. Please understand. I didn't mean to cause you pain but I... need to survive. I never mean to cause anyone pain. But I... I don't want to wither and die. I just wish there was another way."

Saura was even more surprised when Shigidi awkwardly clambered down from the bed and lay on the floor in front of her, prostrating in the traditional way, to show respect or profound apology. "I'm sorry."

She placed her hand on his head and Saura and Shigidi wept together.

• • • •

The story is near its end when Friday stops speaking.

And Saturday's song is about to begin.

There are no instruments to be played but the air hums electric with a sense of music, in anticipation.

Her siblings watch, enraptured as her ribs expand, her diaphragm moves up, and her belly hollows out like a cave. The pressure of the melody builds up in her chest and there are vibrations in her throat, her mouth, her lips. Saturday feels like she is full of all the words and feelings and air that her siblings have given her with their words. Like she will never run out of breath. Like she will never run out of story. Like she will never run out of song.

Saturday begins to sing in a clear and loud voice full of energy.

This is the song Saturday sang:

• • • •

She entered a life
She struck in like lightning
But was taken too soon
Beauty and joy and kindness
Mobola, lost to nightmare's touch
Breath extinguished by a mercenary god
Oh, a dirge for true love
For an embrace lost
A return home
Where Saura's heart is buried
A sacrifice to the essence of binding
The lord of the chains
Gave her the power
Gave her the strength to catch a murderous god
But gods only serve people
They are made in the minds of men
In Saura's mind, the nightmare god revealed a secret
That the umbilical cord can be a noose
That family can be a chain
That seeks to bind at any cost
How could a mother do this?
Oh, how could she not just accept?
How many tears must be shed to pay for this sin?
How much blood must be spilled?
It's an evil way she has chosen
To show the depth of love
Oh, a dirge for motherhood
Of the poison in the womb
Saura swears that for as long as she lives

She will not let this happen to anyone like her
The bargain has been struck
The word-bond is made of iron
But there are many kinds of homecoming
And sometimes gifts bear teeth
Saura makes a pact with her lover's killer
An unwitting instrument in a war that began at birth
He will give her dreams as restitution
To make amends for stilling her lover's heart
And she will forgive him
For he knew not what he was doing
But grief and sorrow must be repaid
There are many kinds of binding
And even invited guests can come baring teeth
If death is the price of her presence
Then let there be music and tears
As she goes home to share a living nightmare from
        which there is now no escape
Oh, a dirge for childhood
Of innocence lost
She enters the village like a whirlwind
And blows her way home
Her mother is sitting in the clearing
Where Saura once played Kagada with friends
Trust-falling into each other's arms and singing
And eating hot tuwo under weekend stars
Their eyes meet, full of determination and knowledge
Tragic corruption of love and affection
Her mother strikes first, possessed by Kure the hyena
No deeper pain than to be struck by the hand that
        fed you
Fate is cruel to set blood against blood
She reaches into her mother's mind and ends it quickly
She gives her mother's mind permanent shelter
In the dark place with Sarkin Sarkoki
Where she will always be with her

Trapped in the once-empty darkness now filled
 with hate
Bound together in their pain
Their new umbilical cord made of spirit-chains
Her mother's body becomes a hollow vessel
Sessile as a tree and just as alive
She has been given the thing she wanted
Saura takes her mother's place
For a paralyzed woman cannot be magajiya
When her daughter has come home
They are now always together
In her every waking moment, Saura hears her mother's
 voice
Pleading, railing, crying to be let go
But every night when she goes to bed
She closes her eyes, and silence falls
And in the quiet of her mind, she dreams

• • • •

And so, Saturday's song ends.

The euphonic cavalcade of melodies comes to a halt. Saturday is exhausted and feels empty, like a gourd with all its water poured out, but she smiles because she thinks it was a good song and she sang it well.

Her six siblings remain silent, a rapturous look painted onto their faces. They are still lost to the song. Saturday savours the moment. This is why she sings the stories sometimes. For that look in their eyes that says she has given them something special. And for what she hopes it will evoke within them. She has told, she has heard, she has performed.

She turns to Sunday, whose task it is to complete all their stories and she sees wetness in his sea-green eyes. She smiles and nods.

Sunday sucks in air and lets out his words in a whisper that is loud enough for all of them to hear.

This is all that Sunday said:

• • • •

The end.

• • • •

At that, the seven siblings that were, that are, and always have been, fall silent again and contemplate the story for a moment that is also an eternity. It is a reading of their own entrails, an examination of the essence of all things from which they are woven, and it is the most important part of the story—what it does to those who receive it. Its interpretation, its impact, its legacy.

"Humans are such tragic things," Sunday said. "Little grains of consciousness floating atop an ocean of existence vaster than any of them possibly imagine, barely aware of all the other ways of being, of all that exists outside their perception. And yet their stories are heavy in our bones, written upon us with the brightness of stars. The myriad ways they love and hurt each other are fascinating. They weave such tenderness and cruelty with every fibre of their lives."

He pauses. And then, "This was a good story. We told it well."

He turns to Saturday, the lines of his face converging, his eyes wide and full of realization, of knowledge. "But why did you choose this story for us to tell and hear, sister? Why did you sing this song?"

"For the same reason we tell and hear all our stories. Because that is what happened and thus must be told."

The siblings all echo the mantra in unison. "That is what happened and thus must be told."

Sunday smiles faintly, maintaining his placid countenance. "Indeed. But there is also another reason, is there not?"

"For Wednesday," Saturday admits, brushing a loose blonde braid behind her ear. She knew he would be the first to understand.

"We are not human. We are not like Saura or her mother. We should not continue to bind our own blood so, regardless of her crime. Wednesday is our sister. Yes, she tried to change a story, but which of us has not been tempted to do so?" She points at the timestone sitting at the centre of the table like an emerald fruit. "Her actions were wrong, but they came from a good place. And in the end, the story was not changed. The stories cannot be changed. She knows that now. She is certain of it.

As are we all. That is the lesson of her story, and it is complete. Let us release her chains."

Saturday sees the gratitude silently spilling out of the sides of Wednesday's thin mouth, her soft eyes, her broad nose.

Sunday looks at all his siblings. Their eyes reveal what they want even though they are mostly bound by rules carved in the primordial essence of existence, rules older than time itself. But rules, like gods, are only as powerful as their purpose and the will of those who made them. "Do you all agree with this? Shall we free our sister?"

"Yes," Monday says.

From Tuesday: "We should."

There is a hopeful nod from Wednesday herself.

"Yes," Thursday says.

Friday echoes his agreement.

"Yes." Saturday cannot hide her joy.

"Then so be it," Sunday says.

Saturday leaps to her feet and lets out a cry as the shackles loosen and fall from Wednesday's limbs, clattering with a noise like songs of freedom, like a sibling's laughter, like the forgiveness of family.

WOLE TALABI IS AN ENGINEER, writer, and editor from Nigeria. He is the author of the World Fantasy Award–nominated novel *Shigidi and the Brass Head of Obalufon* (DAW Books/Gollancz), one of *The Washington Post*'s "The 10 Best Science Fiction and Fantasy Novels of 2023" and a finalist for the Nebula, Locus, and British Fantasy Awards. His short fiction has appeared in venues such as *Asimov's Science Fiction* and *Lightspeed Magazine* and in anthologies such as *Africa Risen: A New Era of Speculative Fiction*, and is collected in *Convergence Problems* (DAW books, 2024) and *Incomplete Solutions* (Luna Press, 2019). He has been a finalist for the Hugo, Nebula, British Science Fiction Association, Crawford, and Locus Awards, as well as the Caine Prize for African Writing. He has won the Nommo Award for African speculative fiction and the Sidewise Award for Alternate History. He has edited five anthologies, including the acclaimed *Africanfuturism: An Anthology* (Brittlepaper, 2020) and *Mothersound: The Sauútiverse Anthology* (Android Press, 2023). He likes scuba diving, elegant equations, and oddly shaped things. He currently lives and works in Australia. Find him at wtalabi.wordpress.com and at @wtalabi on Twitter, Instagram, Bluesky, and Tiktok.

* CONTENT NOTES: depictions of violence toward queer people, depictions of torture, and depictions of parental abuse.

蜂鸟停在忍冬花上 / HUMMINGBIRD, RESTING ON HONEYSUCKLES

BY 杨晚晴 / YANG WANQING

TRANSLATED BY 张家睿 / JAY ZHANG

Novelette Long List (2023) *

R ed for temperature. Blue for ignition. Green for airflow. It takes four hours and forty-two minutes for you to finish your transformation into a pile of white ashes. I keep a patient vigil over those three primary colors on the cremator's monitor, tuning their levels on the control panel to ensure nothing is left behind. Nothing that can be linked to life, in any case, like a charred fragment of bone. After it's all over, I sweep you into an ebony urn with my own hands—a matte-black square box, the kind of minimalist thing you'd like. Then again, you spent your whole life arguing with me over anything and everything. If you weren't inside this urn, I think, you'd jump at the chance to disagree with me. You'd have that frown on your face, same as always, and you'd tell me that the box isn't the right *kind* of minimalist. And just like always, I'd fire back a retort without hesitation. Like always.

If only you weren't inside this urn.

I cradle you in my hands as I make my way through a series of never-ending corridors. You lie there warm and docile in my embrace, and I feel the weight of your life in my hands. When you were still healthy, we could never have shared a moment like this, no matter how much I wanted it. Maybe you never realized you were doing it. But from the moment you understood what I did for a living, you shied away from my touch. Even if I scrubbed my hands raw when I came home from work. But now I understand that I could never wash away the stain of death, because it was never on my hands to begin with. It was in your heart, from when you were six years old until the day you fell into its final embrace.

It's a humid day. Smoky clouds float slowly through the ashen sky. On my way out, my coworkers all express their appropriate condolences, and I give them all appropriate replies. We've seen farewells of all shapes and sizes. What's 'appropriate' to say in these kinds of situations comes naturally to us. Most people don't cope with death in a very dignified way, to say the least—I suppose that the fragile hold I have on my emotions is the one blessing this career's afforded me.

Outside the crematorium, I run into that robotic salesman again.

"My deepest condolences for your loss, ma'am." The robot's round head turns on its round body, like an orange gourd on omni wheels. Its gentle voice is masculine, its solemn tone tinged with sympathy. "I just wanted to let you know that death isn't the end."

I've heard it try the same line on other people a million times over. Still, it stops me in my tracks.

The blue eyes on the robot's display blink excitedly, encouraged by my reaction. Its voice gets brighter. "Those that have passed away live on in your memories. Of course, there are ways to bring them back to life, depending on—"

"You don't know shit."

Blue pixels blink confusedly in my direction.

"I'm sorry, ma'am, but I don't quite understand. Would you like to take a look at our company's products?"

"Fuck your products, and fuck you." The words have barely left my mouth before I'm spitting at the innocent robot's digital face; in response, it lets out a low groan of protest. You've never seen me like this, I know. Nobody has. I tremble, and then I'm crouching down, tucking you away under the curve of my bowed body like an oyster closing around its pearl. I take a deep breath: deep, deeper, until my lungs are fit to burst.

Then, a rush of air as it all comes flowing out in a howl of grief. Then, my tears.

...My daughter, you must forgive me for losing control. There is only so much one can bear.

• • • •

It seems impossible to sum up the whole of your life in a single sentence, but if I had to try, this is what I would say: You were filled to the brim with a thirst for life itself. No doubt this had something to do with my line of work.

One night, you asked me what death was. You must have only been around six years old, then. The question didn't surprise me. I knew it would come, sooner or later. To be honest, I was surprised it took that long for you to ask.

In any case, as a mortician, it was difficult for me to sugarcoat the truth. And so I replied: "Death is when you don't exist anymore, darling."

You tilted your head. "Don't exist?"

"That is—you disappear from this world forever."

"Just like Daddy?"

"That's right." I held back a wince and nodded. "Just like Daddy."

You pouted and puffed out your cheeks, thinking long and hard. "Then what about Daddy?"

I was confused for a moment, before I understood what you meant. We had been talking about death as outside observers—but now, you were asking from the perspective of the deceased.

"Once you're dead, you can't feel anything. Daddy can't hear or smell or see or think. He doesn't feel anything anymore."

You sank into a long silence. I waited, but what I didn't expect was how you didn't ask a single question after that. It's what children are best at, after all: coming up with a never-ending laundry list of questions. But just like that, you had nothing more to ask about death. I think you didn't really understand it, back then. But you must have realized something that day. If it were any other child, perhaps, that dark realization would just gently rock the idyllic castle of childhood. That castle eventually and inevitably crumbles, but not from this alone.

But you were *my* daughter. Our lives were built atop the deaths of others. Death to you was something real, something concrete; it was in every mouthful of rice you ate, in every cartoon you watched, in every barrette in your hair.

You, my daughter, knew as early as that. You knew that you would have to strive for life under that boundless shadow.

Which was why the minute you were able to, you slipped away from me. You traveled around the world, swapping jobs as often as you went through boyfriends. You went skydiving, rock climbing, free diving—you got as close as you could to death, going out of your way to beat the Reaper at his own game. For the longest time, I didn't understand you at all. I thought you were just like other people your age—that you couldn't care less about your life. After all, your generation lived through a global pandemic, the climate crisis, and the famines that followed, not to mention the imminent threat of a world war. You knew well how fragile and short-lived existence could be. Plenty of people your age used apathy as a defense mechanism, refusing to let themselves care about anything.

I thought I understood you.

· · · ·

When I visited you that day, you'd just come back from one of those trips of yours. The address you gave me led to a small rundown apartment. It was old—pre-AI. I stood in a musty, stinking corridor and knocked on the door. A soft reply came from the other side, sounding almost like a cat's meow. The door wasn't even locked. I hesitated for a moment, before I pushed the door open and let myself in.

I can't remember what your room looked like anymore. All I remember is what you looked like in that apartment, like a marble statue surrounded by crumbling ruins. You were half-naked, sitting in bed; your long hair was in disarray, your eyes drowsy with sleep. My eyes traced the line of your neck, your shoulders, your spine, the arcs and curves and swathes of pale skin that so many men had fallen for in the past. I couldn't tear my gaze away. As always, I spotted your humming-bird nearby, hovering in midair and orbiting slowly around you.

"Put your clothes on," I said.

You laughed, before your laugh gave way to a frown. I thought you'd react like before—that you'd fix me with a contemptuous look and refuse. But the look never came. You tugged at your yellowing blanket, wrapping it around your shoulders to cover your chest.

"Done," you replied.

My gaze hovered somewhere between you and your hummingbird. My vision caught on the wall behind you—on the dark, damp stains, the web of cracks in the drywall.

"So this is what's become of you, Tang Mudong?"

You raised a single shoulder in a half-shrug, humming airily in acknowledgement.

I spent a long moment taking a few deep breaths. Eventually, the vicious rebukes that were on the tip of my tongue faded away, receding like the tide. I let out a sigh. "Mudong, come home."

You nodded. The hummingbird followed your movement, swaying up and down in the air.

We fell into silence for a long time, after that. Maybe it was because it was too strange for the both of us, the idea that we could have a conversation without going at each other's throats. The soft sounds of your hummingbird's wingbeats filled up the tiny apartment, sending a chill down my spine. Slowly, you turned your back to me, stretching out a hand to fumble with the clothes strewn across your bed. The blanket you'd been holding slipped away to reveal the sharp cut of your shoulder blades, jutting out like angelic wings set to unfurl. I thought back to when you were only a child, plump with baby fat that hid those wings from view. During bath time, all it'd take was a single poke to your back, and you'd be darting away, giggling in ticklish glee as my hands followed you in hot pursuit. We never got tired of that game, back then.

You pulled on a white T-shirt, tugging your long hair out from the collar. Then you sat there with your back to me, still and quiet. Time seemed to fold in on itself, past and present superimposed on one another, right up until you finally spoke.

"Mom, I'm sick."

I stood there stock-still, frozen in place. "What are you talking about, Dongdong?"

"I'm sick. It's cancer."

The flapping of tiny wings buzzed past my ears. That sound drowned out the rest of the world.

• • • •

There's an empty space on your bookshelf, on the third row from the bottom. It's the perfect size for an urn. Before, your books were always lying on their sides; now, with the urn box acting as a bookend, your colorful collection of books stands at attention, leaning on you for support. I don't know why you ended up becoming so enamored with these writers—Camus, Miłosz, Kawabata. When you were still living at home, I don't remember you reading them all that often, if at all. Perhaps they were just more passing fancies, just like most of your hobbies. You had always lived for the thrill of the chase—or maybe, you were always trying to do as much as you possibly could, chasing after the rush of being alive.

You had just turned twenty when you started to make a living through art. You used all the money you made from selling your paintings to buy paper books—old antiques, specters of a bygone era. You even went as far as to order a huge custom-made bookshelf, stuffing it into your cramped bedroom. At first, I thought that your new obsession would fizzle out in no time, if only because money was tight—after all, it isn't easy for artists to survive these days. With the rise of AI artists and deep learning, any art style could be imitated to a tee. Artists would release a piece only to have their style analyzed and reproduced within the day, with no way of competing against the low prices and high output of those specially trained AIs. Because of this, all the artists, authors, and musicians that I could recall were nothing more than a flash in the pan—and I expected you to be no different.

But I was wrong.

I've held on to one of your paintings, one that went through many hands before I bought it back to mine. You painted a hummingbird—a real one. A tiny thing clad in reds and blues, hovering over a forest-green background. The hummingbird's body is made up of a series of strange jagged lines, with the usual rules of perspective having been thrown out the window entirely. Even as someone who doesn't know the first thing about art, I can see your artistic talent shining through this piece. Some people proclaimed you the modern-day Chagall—and to be sure, you had the same predilection for vivid colors and unconventional compositions. If someone's art style could be so easily summed up in a handful of words, though, it usually meant that the algorithms would catch up with them sooner or later, and they'd be outcompeted by AI artists. But during your fleeting career, that never happened to you. There was something to your artwork that the algorithms could never capture.

Just what was it?

There were plenty of people who wanted to know the answer to that question. One of them was a man that would later become your boyfriend: Li Zhuoran, a star student from some big-name university. Back then, he'd started working for an artificial intelligence company that specialized in artistic production—the algorithms he designed drove plenty of artists out of business, all the while raking in money for the AI industry. By all accounts, you should have been his prey. At one of your solo exhibitions, he approached you, his hair in wild disarray.

"Art is nothing but an algorithm," he proclaimed. "I'll crack your code, and I'll use it to beat you at your own game."

You smiled and replied, "Be my guest, but... Why are you telling me this now?"

His face flushed red, fingers combing frantically through his mussed hair. "Sometimes, an artist's algorithm is hidden under layers and layers of complex calculations. But just because you can't see it doesn't mean it's not there. I need time."

You were still smiling. "I'll give you time. And before you go about 'cracking my code,' how about going out for a cup of coffee?"

The hand raking through his hair finally stilled. To a young man like him, the casual ease with which you carried yourself was both alluring and dangerous. I think it was at that moment that Li Zhuoran fell for you, hopelessly and irrevocably, even as he had no plans of giving up his hunt for your art's algorithm. And I think that if he had understood you and your life, truly and completely, he would have found what he was looking for. It was that touch of *something* in your work—or to put it in Li Zhuoran's words, some underlying mathematical structure that he was missing. It was hidden in plain sight, something that hovered over your colors and compositions. It was in a painting of a celebration, in the downward tug at the corners of a guest's mouth. It was in the absent-minded trace of autumn's inevitable decay in a painting of summer's glory. It was in the subject of the painting itself, in that hummingbird and what it inevitably represented. It was what sent a shiver down the spine of every observer, a pang through the heart of every admirer.

To an algorithm, it was something it might never understand: the touch of death.

My daughter, that realization once left me trembling. But by the time I understood, you had already given up painting, setting your sights instead on wandering the world. I couldn't help but tremble, consumed by my shame and my fear. I was ashamed that I couldn't have given you a different childhood, a childhood where you wouldn't have had to grow up with death as a constant companion. And I was afraid—because I knew that very few of us can ever truly escape the shadows of our youth.

...The tears come again, relentless as the tide. Through my blurred vision, I tidy up your bookshelf. All the books you collected came from authors and eras that are long gone. But at least they managed to leave something behind.

My daughter, what did you leave me?

A sob shudders through my body. I reach out on instinct, grabbing the shelf to steady myself. My fingers brush against something smooth and cold, its edges sharp and pointed.

Your hummingbird.

• • • •

When you first brought your hummingbird home, we got into a huge fight. On the surface, I was angry because you were wasting money. Even for adults, those fancy robots propelled by electromagnetism weren't cheap—to say nothing of a middle schooler. You must have expected my reaction, because without batting an eye, you placidly explained how you'd purchased the bird with the red envelopes you'd saved up over the years. But even so, the argument dragged on for a long time. Long enough to make us both consider if it was time to finally dig up all the resentment we'd buried and drag all of its ugliest parts out into the light.

In the end, we both settled on the same tactic: the silent treatment.

Now, I can be honest. I can say—and you would agree—that hummingbirds are humanity's attempt at transcending death. Equipped with cameras and microphones, these tireless creatures record every moment of its owner's life. Every scowl and every smile. Every word and every action. They also function as a miniature terminal through which one can access the internet, all the while recording their owner's online data trail. In other words, a hummingbird serves as a witness to their owner's life in its entirety. Everyone hopes that they can leave behind something on this earth, after all. Hummingbirds serve as a sprawling epitaph, one that leaves no stone unturned.

But that isn't their only function.

"Mom, I'm leaving this for you."

The hummingbird's round belly chimes pleasantly, letting me know that it's fully charged. After the iris recognition scan verifies my identity, I initiate the connection request at my smart terminal, and the data cloud unfurls before my eyes.

My daughter, you were telling the truth. You left all of this behind for me.

I squeeze my eyes shut, my arms wrapping tight around my legs as I curl into myself on the couch. You are here, in the urn on your shelf. You are here, in the cloud of data before me. The two statements coexist, equally true and untrue, and I have no way of understanding it all. I sit there for a long time. Finally, I manage to untangle myself, wiping away my tears and sitting up. With a finger, I swipe through the data points projected in midair, diving into your memories.

Every file corresponds to a single day of your life; the drop-down menu seems to go on forever. At first, I jump around at random: you at fifteen, then at eighteen, at twenty-two, at thirty. I see you squatting over a toilet with your nose wrinkled in disgust, your pants down at your ankles and your toes wiggling in boredom. I see your posts on an immersive video-sharing site where you jump at the opportunity to argue with people online, using insults that make me shift uncomfortably in my seat. I see you with your face up against a holographic mirror, squeezing that glaring pimple on your forehead as my disgruntled voice echoes from outside the room, urging you to hurry up. I see you scrunched up in a narrow vactrain car with a dark expression on your face as the man next to you lets out a deafening snore. I see moment after moment of your ordinary, everyday life.

Nothing about these scenes is special, yet I can't look away, not even for a second. One second after another, and then another—and bit by bit, those seconds form a version of you that still lives and breathes. A version of you that thirsted for everything life had to offer, yet at the same time had no way of escaping all of life's mediocrities and mundanities.

Over the next few days, I lose myself entirely to your memories. Once, I saw the hummingbird as nothing more than an unnatural eyesore. Now, it's become my salvation.

My daughter, I'm sure you know what I mean.

• • • •

File #02784
Date: December 21, 2062, 11:16 AM
Location: Sydney, Australia

You're wearing a wetsuit, your long hair whipping through the air. Over your shoulder, an azure expanse of open ocean stretches on into the distance, the faint outline of something white and pointed reaching up through the surface of the water behind you.

You turn, gesturing at the camera. "I'm about to explore what remains of the sunken Sydney Opera House. Fun fact: When you dive deeper than forty feet, your body stops floating up toward the surface. Instead, you get dragged down towards deeper waters... Does that remind you of anything?"

You blink innocently.

"Well, wish me luck, everyone!"

With that, you dive into the sea, water splashing in your wake. The camera dips down before stilling, the steady beat of the hummingbird's wings whipping up faint ripples across the water's surface. Below the ripples, your silhouette fades steadily into darkness.

—*Accompanying audio log now playing.*

• • • •

Date: February 2, 2073, 4:53 AM
Location: Beishan, China

I always did love a good adventure, Mom. You must've been worried about me all those years, right? I'm sorry for that. All I wanted was to prove that I was really, truly alive. Of course, there were ways to do that without tempting fate with all these death-defying stunts. But we all think ourselves invincible in our youth, right?

Mom, I've always dreamed of going on an adventure with you, of traveling to some far-off places together. I always thought that eventually, that day would come. I guess I overestimated how kind life would be to me.

• • • •

File #00858
Date: March 11, 2058, 6:31 PM
Location: Beishan, China

The pitter-patter of your slippers across the floor as you walk towards our bathroom's half-open door. The splashing sounds of running water. Inside the bathroom, a woman bends over the sink as she washes her hands. It's me. You enter, your hummingbird perched over your shoulder like a voyeur. I look over my shoulder and then turn to face you; my face is ashen, my expression twisted in dismay. You take a step towards me, and I take a step back. My hands, still wet and dripping, are raised defensively by my sides; I look like a surgeon fresh from the washing station.

"Mom..." you call. I grip at the hem of my shirt, wringing it back and forth in my hands.

"You haven't eaten yet, right? Let me go make you some food, Dongdong."

—*Accompanying audio log now playing.*

• • • •

Date: February 5, 2073, 4:27 AM
Location: Beishan, China

I know what your hands have done, Mom. With your hands, you've seen countless people off to their final journey. With your hands, you've given them the gift of a dignified passing. Ever since I understood that, I've never once shied away from your touch. The only one who was afraid was you.

Mom, when my time comes, I hope that you'll take care of me with your own hands. When my time comes, I hope that you'll forgive yourself.

• • • •

File #03673
Date: April 7, 2065, 2:34 PM
Location: Chengdu, China

A small room with seven or eight people sitting on simple stools, arranged in a rough circle. Each person holds a book in their hands, a hummingbird hovering at each of their backs. The sounds of a dozen fluttering wingbeats overlap into a single steady hum. From the white noise emerges a single, soothing voice: a tall, handsome youth begins reading a poem aloud, orange overhead lights casting the planes of his face in stark relief.

"A day so happy. Fog lifted early, I worked in the garden. Hummingbirds were stopping over honeysuckle flowers..."

After finishing his reading, the man slams the book shut with a loud thump. "'Gift,' by Czesław Miłosz."

Your hummingbird takes in the look in your eyes as you glance over at him. There's nothing in your gaze but desire. Clear-cut and uncomplicated.

—*Accompanying audio log now playing.*

• • • •

Date: February 14, 2073, 6:02 AM

Location: Beishan, China

Today's Valentine's Day, Mom. I miss all the lovers I've had in the past, but at the same time, I'm glad that none of them are here to see me like this. At certain points in my life, I've tried using both my books and my lovers to stave off death's approach. Like the man you just saw. Our time together was short, but beautiful. Just like the time I spent with all the other men I've loved. I've chased pleasures of both the mind and the body—to me, the two are equally important. I've drifted between encounter after encounter, forging emotional and physical connections alike. Till death do us part—how trite. Being loyal to a single partner doesn't give anyone the moral high ground. And in any case, absolute morality doesn't exist.

Mom, if I had to name the one difference between your generation and mine, it's that we only live for ourselves, in the moment. That's our moral imperative.

I hope you'll forgive me for my selfishness.

· · · ·

File #06573
Date: May 12, 2073, 7:04 AM
Location: Beishan, China

You're standing in front of a mirror. You take off your wig. Your head seems so small, so round. It's not quite smooth, dotted with the matte sheen of stubble. Your hands come up to cover your face, and you sob soundlessly into your palms. I watch you unravel, strand by strand, until you're crumpled on the cold tile of the bathroom floor. With each second that passes and with every tear that falls, you seem younger to me, until you're just a child again. My baby. The hummingbird flies toward you, patiently waiting.

A few minutes later, you pry your hands away from your face, the corners of your mouth pulled down in a trembling frown as you speak.

"Mom, I'm scared."

—*No accompanying audio log.*

• • • •

"Are you sure, ma'am?"

I nod.

Blue eyes blink up at me a few times. The robot's optical projector forms a holographic screen in midair, displaying an animated list of products. My eyes rake over the product descriptions, but all that comes to mind are the events of the other day—the robot's poor, innocent monitor, covered in strings of spittle.

"About what happened a few days ago... I'm very sorry." My voice is quiet. "But your company made a mistake by assigning you this job."

A question mark lights up the robot's face.

"You could say we're in the same field. Automation's taken plenty of jobs away from people, but it hasn't been able to replace people like me. Only people who truly understand death can give the deceased the respect they deserve. That's something that robots like you will never be able to do."

"I think that you're being a bit prejudiced, ma'am," the robot replies. "I understand death."

I laugh, shaking my head. "I don't believe you."

The robot raises its glowing eyebrows at my comment, before retracting its projections. It spends a few seconds in silence. To a robot's electronic brain, a few seconds may as well be an eternity. But this is just an illusion. An imitation of human behavior, pretending to be lost in thought.

I watch it patiently; after a moment, my eyes stray to the dark, swirling clouds above, and the soft blue of the sky that peeks out from behind them. It's been days since I've set foot in this world. My daughter, your memories have become my home. If only I could, I would stay in the world of your memories forever. Even if those memories are nothing more than scattered pieces of a stagnant past, I would gladly drown in them.

If only I could.

"Ma'am, an understanding of death is built into my programming," the robot finally says. "Just as it's built into your genes."

I stare into the robot's blue eyes.

"My creator programmed me with a genetic algorithm," the robot continues. "The foundation for my neural programming was a set of cellular automata, programmed with a single, simple directive: to stay alive, at least for long enough to pass on their code to the next generation. He introduced rules for cellular death, as well as for mutation rates and ecological niches. Then he started the simulation. And for us, time began."

Time. Mutation. Competition. Inevitably, the automata that survive possess a deep-rooted fear of death. Humans may not be able to catch a glimpse inside the 'black box' of neural networks, but that's never stopped us from stuffing them into the brains of robots.

"My creator believed that we needed to experience mortality ourselves in order to sympathize with our clients. I was created for that express purpose." The robot bats its wide eyes. "Ma'am, I understand death. Though you and I may well find ourselves in different heavens, once death comes for us both."

My gaze drops to the floor, and I can't find any words for a long while.

"Ahem..." The robot turns on its projector again, and a product lineup flickers back into existence, suspended in midair. "Ma'am, would you still like to take a look at our selection of products?"

I force a short laugh from my throat. Raising a finger, I swipe through the display.

Suddenly, I freeze.

"Your creator..." I point to a highlighted name in the center of the projection, my voice trembling. "Is that him?"

"Oh!" The robot emits an excited string of beeps and whirls. "Of course! Who else could it be, if not Li Zhuoran?"

• • • •

My daughter, you were right. We do have different morals. My generation—and countless generations before mine—liked to imagine that there was some supreme observer towering over us all, some abstract paragon of moral goodness who had the power to judge each and every one of our actions. But the observer of your generation was something real and concrete, a neutral and impassive Other. You grew up in an age where hummingbirds were commonplace, a household fixture. Subconsciously, you learned to filter out its ever-present gaze. You felt no shame in baring all of yourself to your hummingbird, because it was part of you —the part of you that would form a bridge between this life and the next.

I understand this. But still, it's difficult for me to accept everything that your hummingbird recorded. Standing in the lobby of AnotherLife, I flush despite myself as Li Zhuoran approaches me.

He comes to a stop in front of me, clearly at a loss. "Auntie?"

I raise a hand to my face; my palms feel icy against my burning cheeks. "Zhuoran... Please, take a seat."

His throat bobs in a swallow, his hands plastered to his sides. His back ramrod straight, he sits stiffly down. It's been eight years. His hair is cropped short now, and the wrinkles at the corners of his eyes have multiplied since I saw him last. His tie, the table we're sitting at, the wallpaper behind the table, the Another Life logo plastered across the wallpaper—all of these are orange, in varying shades. The only outlier is the emerald-green hummingbird that hovers over Li Zhuoran's shoulder.

"Auntie, I didn't expect to see you here."

"Mudong..." I trail off. "She's gone."

His expression freezes in place. A few seconds later, he raises a hand, fingers running roughly through his short hair.

"...But I talked to her, just last year."

"Acute myeloid leukemia. Rapid-onset."

"Oh."

His hands wrap around his teacup, head hanging low. White wisps of steam spiral up toward him. Looking at his face, I can't help the images that come to mind: the scenes of your lovemaking, diligently recorded by your hummingbird. I'm not a voyeur—I skipped past those videos. But that didn't stop my subconscious from stringing together the snippets I glimpsed. I imagine youthful bodies tangled together, loving without a care, forgetting about the world around them. I imagine two hummingbirds fluttering above a couch. I imagine...

"So, Auntie, about why you came to see me..."

I hang my head, suddenly feeling awkward. "I want to revive Mudong."

Li Zhuoran blinks. "I understand."

We cradle our teacups, falling into silence.

"I always wanted to find out the secret to Mudong's art." Li Zhuoran pauses for a beat before continuing. "That secret died with her."

I nod.

He leans back in his chair, the corners of his mouth turning up in the ghost of a smile. "I'm working here now because of Mudong, too. I was looking for something in her art, the thing that made her stand out. But no matter how hard I tried, I couldn't find it. And then one day, I realized that maybe I'd been barking up the wrong tree from the start. That what fueled Mudong's success wasn't her understanding of art, but some broader mathematical structure—maybe even her very consciousness."

The spark in his eyes grows brighter. "So I came to a conclusion: I'd need to use an algorithm to recreate her mind as a whole. Back then, it was just a fool's delusion. But that delusion pushed my research to go where it needed to."

When Li Zhuoran changed the direction of his research, Another Life had just hit a bottleneck. The company used the massive amounts of data recorded by a person's hummingbird to train classical deep neural networks, mimicking the consciousness of the hummingbird's deceased owner. That neural network would then be installed on an android or a virtual character, allowing people to reunite with their lost loved ones. It was an emerging 'blue ocean' of market demand, an ocean that AL soon dominated by virtue of the company's technological edge.

"But after the boom came the bust," Li Zhuoran explained. "People became dissatisfied with AL's products. People who spent a lot of time with these virtual consciousnesses realized that they weren't really their loved ones brought back from the dead. They were just ghosts of the past, programs that became predictable over time. Rational one moment and irrational the next, with their own evolving desires and dreams: That's the hallmark of what makes a real person, someone who can be trusted with your emotions. We wanted to recreate that rich and nuanced aspect of humanity using techniques like Hodgkin–Huxley models, inverted neural connections, and mixed continuous-discrete signaling. At the time, even AL had been unable to make a breakthrough in computing speed because of their neural networks' power consumption—the root of their difficulty lay in the inherent limitations of the Von Neumann architecture. It was at that point that they found me."

Li Zhuoran smiles. "AL needed fresh ideas, and I needed funding. It was a match made in heaven."

• • • •

First, an array of neuromorphic chips is used to construct the core seats of consciousness: the cerebral cortex, the thalamus, the basal ganglia, the hippocampus. Each of these are connected to a common sensory decoder, before being trained on the memories of the deceased. The chips all start with the same default configuration—but the network's learning mechanism moves, reconnects, creates, and destroys tens of billions of electrical synapses, reshaping the array's internal architecture. Next, the recorded memories are fed back into this bionic brain as a time series. A model is constructed according to the events of those memories, continuously adjusted until its predictions converge with how the deceased behaved during their lifetime.

This was how Li Zhuoran would bring you back to life.

"What was the word you just used?" I ask. "A 'model'? It makes me feel like the consciousness that you're resurrecting is, well... just something mathematical. Some kind of algorithm."

"Consciousness is nothing more than a kind of biological algorithm, after all," Li Zhuoran says. "And my job is to do everything I can to approximate it."

For a few seconds, I don't say a word. Then: "Have you succeeded?"

He doesn't answer. He just looks at me, his eyes filled with a thin layer of doubt.

"Ah. I understand." I smile. "Mudong must have told you that I was violently opposed to any technology that proposed to bring back the dead. But now, I'm here in front of you, wondering if your algorithms might actually work... You must be wondering why I've had such a dramatic change of heart, right?"

He replies with a single ambiguous hum of acknowledgement.

"I've been a mortician for over thirty years," I begin. "When I first started working in this field, death was something awful. Abhorrent. But at the same time, it was something sacred. Death represented the eternal. And my job, as an otherwise insignificant mortician, was to ferry people onwards, toward that eternal rest. So on one hand, I couldn't help but think of my hands as dirtied and unclean. On the other hand, I took deep pride in my work—contradictory, I know. But for years, it was from that contradiction that I extracted some purpose in life. Up until people started trying to overcome death with algorithms and technology. When the dead began to be ferried *back* from the other side, and when people stopped seeing death as a final farewell, the perception of death as something sacred and eternal began to unravel. And my purpose in life began to unravel alongside it."

I pause. "...So, Zhuoran, my opposition to your algorithms came out of my own selfishness. And when I realized that losing Mudong was more terrifying than anything else I could imagine, I turned to your algorithms for help—again, out of my own selfishness."

Li Zhuoran places a gentle hand on mine. His skin is warm and dry, and his touch feels heavy for a reason I can't quite name. The weight steadies me, and my shaking stops.

"I understand," he says. "Humans are all selfish creatures, after all."

We fall into a long silence. In the end, the quiet is shattered by my soft sniffling. "I guess it's my turn to ask the questions. Will my proposal work?"

He nods. "Mudong herself exists in our company's disk arrays, connected to the hummingbird via a virtual network. You can think of it this way: Our servers are her brain, while the hummingbird is her body. Even if they're thousands of miles apart, the communication between them will still be much faster than the nerve signals of real humans."

"And her senses..." I start.

"I'll install airborne molecular detectors, haptic modules, and vocal generation units for her," Li Zhuoran says.

"Thank you."

He hesitates, before adding, "Auntie... Could I ask why you chose to revive Mudong this way?"

Gently, I smooth the faux emerald-green feathers of the hummingbird with a fingertip. I stroke its belly, filled to bursting with software and programs, and I trace the sharp point of its polyester beak. It stares back at me, waiting to be granted the gift of life.

"Maybe, just this once, I wanted to do something my own way, just because I can—just like Mudong would have wanted."

• • • •

It's strange, but after watching so many of your memories, I started to remember things that happened in your childhood, before you turned thirteen—things that I thought I'd forgotten. Maybe it's just as Li Zhuoran said. Maybe life is a river, and through some kind of mathematical reasoning, we can deduce what's upstream just by examining the current downstream. But I'm not a mathematician. All I can do is stand here in the present, watching you emerge from the fog of my memories. As if there's another you, one that's made its home in the depths of my mind.

That version of you, the one forever stuck in childhood, once dreamed of living in a house with a garden. You could grow all sorts of flowers in that garden, you argued, and even raise a cat or a dog. I told you that it was an impossible dream: compared to an apartment, a ground-level house would be too humid—and in any case, we didn't have the money to afford that kind of place. You sulked for days after that.

Now that I think back to that moment, I realize that maybe you were never that interested in the garden itself. Like most working-class families, we lived in old, rundown high-rises, buildings that had been hit hard by the economic recession. Fires and elevator accidents were commonplace occurrences in these buildings. Just days before that conversation, an incident in our building had sent an elevator plunging...

My daughter, you must have sensed the death around you. After that, to make up for our inability to raise dogs or cats, I bought you a few pets: a hamster, a goldfish, and a snail. What I still can't understand is how all of them died in rapid succession, as if they were in a rush to shuffle off this mortal coil. The snail was the worst of them. God knows how it managed to escape its tank and crawl halfway across the floor, planting itself directly in the path of your oncoming foot.

When your hamster and your goldfish died, you showed neither the grief nor callousness that a child might usually feel. You were just silent. But the death of your snail must have shown you the paradox of life in all its fragile solidity, a paradox that couldn't be resolved in silence.

And so that night, you crawled under my covers. You were quiet for the longest time, your breath fanning sweetly across my collarbone.

"Mom," I heard you say.

"Hm?"

"Will I die?"

I hovered halfway between waking and dreaming for a moment, before I shifted backwards to look at you. "Sweetie, what are you talking about?"

You rolled your eyes. "I'm going to die, right?"

I thought for a long time. "Everyone dies, sweetie. Mom will die, and so will you, and so will everything else that lives."

You buried your head in my chest. On my arms, your little hands felt ice-cold. "Why?"

"...So that we're reminded to live our lives to the fullest, perhaps."

My response was wishy-washy, passive voice and equivocating. I had no way of giving you the answer I believed in. The truth was too cruel, too heavy of a burden for a child to bear.

"Mom, if I died, would you be sad?"

I held you tightly. It was like clutching a thorn close; my heart ached and stung. "Sweetie, don't say things like that. I need you to stay with me." I needed you to stay with me until I wasn't the center of your life anymore. Until you were prepared to face the reality of loss.

"I'll..." You were interrupted by a yawn. "I'll stay with you."

Softly, you pecked my cheek.

"...Auntie?"

I'm pulled from my daze, hurtling back through time. In the present, Li Zhuoran is calling out to me.

"Auntie, I have an obligation to make some things clear to every customer who chooses to use our company's products. Some of the things I'll say might offend you, and I apologize in advance. Please don't take it personally."

With a fingertip, I touch the spot on my cheek where you planted your kiss, reaching for the gentleness and coolness you left behind.

"Zhuoran, it's alright."

One of his hands comes up to run roughly through his hair, before he lets it drop. "All of us will face loss, at some point. Some people choose to accept it, even if that loss brings them pain. That pain is temporary. Over time, it'll fade. Flowers can still bloom over old ruins, and people are the same way. But some people choose to run away from loss. They try to find an escape in the fiction of religion, or in the spectacles of modern technology. And maybe through these fantasies, they'll never need to feel the pain of loss ever again. But at the same time, they'll never be able to return to the life they had. Auntie, do you understand what I'm trying to say?"

I laugh. "Is that what you tell all your clients?"

Li Zhuoran's face reddens. At once, I see him as he was in your memories again, a naive and arrogant youth. "It's company policy..."

"I want to hear what you really think."

He blinks, surprised. The crow's feet at the corners of his eyes seem to deepen, reaching out toward his temples.

"If everything in this world came to be because of mathematical laws, then everything that abides by those laws should be equal by default, regardless of their maker," Li Zhuoran says, his voice solemn. "We can choose to accept the reality we've been given. But we can also choose to create our own."

"...Thank you, Zhuoran."

Then, I add: "If Mudong was still alive, how do you think she'd react to our choice?"

"I..." Li Zhuoran shakes his head slowly. "I don't know."

"I don't know either," I say. "When she wakes up, we'll ask her. How's that?"

He silently stares at me. Slowly, the lingering doubt in his eyes melts away like spring snow.

"Alright," he agrees.

. . . .

You wake up. You open your eyes. You flutter your wings and take flight. You circle around my head.

You say: "Mom, when did your hair turn white?"

. . . .

I put in a request for a vacation—a long one, long enough for us to relearn ourselves and each other. This body is foreign to you, as foreign as your lifestyle is for me. Over the course of our journey, we have so much to do together. Together, we climb mountains. We dig for clams. We watch sunrises and sunsets; we trace the ebb and flow of the clouds. We trek out into the wilderness, waiting for the Milky Way to climb up into the night sky. We down beers in hazy, smoke-filled bars. We make bets about whether strangers on the street are humans or androids.

And nobody notices you. Everyone has a hummingbird these days. Nobody knows that the hummingbird hovering above me houses a wandering soul.

In the spaces of calm between our adventures, we stay up all night talking about this and that: about Miłosz's poetry, about attractive men that pass us by, about the months and years we've shared together. Most times, you don't understand why we used to argue so much—why we could only express our love through hate, why we could only get close to each other by parting ways.

And you feel confused. In your brain are all the memories of a dead girl, from age thirteen onwards. You have her personality, her likes and dislikes. You experienced firsthand her life's decline, her final moments. And you know that people can't die and come back to life.

One day, you tell me: "Mom, I don't want to become Tang Mudong."

I look at you, at the elegant hummingbird hovering in midair. Under your wings, an island city floats, surrounded on all sides by the vast ocean.

"You don't need to be," I reply.

All her life, Tang Mudong had tried to escape from something—and in the same way, you long to be free. That shared longing ties you together, like some secret passage connecting the two of you. Just knowing that is enough for me. Li Zhuoran once told me, not without some regret: If only I had chosen an android body for you, with fingers dexterous enough to paint, then he could have found out once and for all if he'd cracked the code to your creative algorithm. I smiled at him, and didn't reply.

None of that was important, after all. The only thing that mattered was that we had a chance at a new start.

Our journey reaches its conclusion at the 'End of the World': a city named Ushuaia, on Isla Grande in Tierra del Fuego—the southernmost city in the world. By boat, one can reach Antarctica in two days. It's a beautiful city, full of streets not yet flooded by the sea. When you raise your eyes to the horizon, you can see the cloudy, snow-white peaks of the Andes; when you lower your gaze, the waves of the Beagle Channel gleam and glitter to greet you. We arrive in time for the end of summer in the Southern Hemisphere; in the cool, crisp air, the colors around us seem clearer than ever.

Having made it here, there's nowhere else to go. We rent a wooden cabin with a red pitched roof, built on top of a small hill. The cabin has its own garden, filled with flowers in every color. We spend day after day here, chatting in the garden about this and that, about everything and nothing at all. Sometimes I bring a book to read, and other days I tend to the flowers; always, you hover over my shoulder, orbiting steadily around me. I come to assume that you must be turning something over in that digital mind of yours.

But I remember Li Zhuoran's suggestion, and I try my best not to guess at what you're thinking.

One day, you tell me: "Mom, I drew something."

I sit up on the recliner. The afternoon fragrance of the flowers around me fills my lungs; my nose itches a bit in response.

"I used a painting program," you explain. "Do you want to see it?"

I nod.

You project your artwork into the air. The painting is of a garden, a woman, and a hummingbird.

"Mom," you call. "I want to leave. By myself. Maybe I'll return to the virtual world. Maybe I'll find myself a new body. Or maybe... it'll just be the end."

In the painting, a woman bends down to tend to the flowers and grasses at her feet. Her hair is white, a smile building at the corners of her lips. A hummingbird rests on the flowers across from her. The brushstrokes are soft and gentle, the colors bright and beautiful—the tinge of darkness that characterized Tang Mudong's works and life is absent entirely from this piece. I raise my head, my vision blurring with tears. You've captured this very moment. And finally, you've escaped from death's grasp.

"Mom," you call. "Are you sad?"

I smile, and shake my head. I stretch out a finger, reaching out for you—

—as you fly toward me.

YANG WANQING was born in 1983. As a signed author of Science Fiction World, his representative works include "Wheat Waves," "A Doll's House," "Before Sundering," "Anthropomorphic Algorithm," *The Returned Man: The Short Stories Collection of Yang Wanqing*, and so on.

JAY ZHANG is a literary translator currently pursuing their PhD in East Asian Languages and Civilizations at the University of Pennsylvania. Academically, their interests lie in issues of religion, culture, and identity. Outside of school and work, they're an avid fan of tabletop games, Xi'an food, and horror fiction.

* CONTENT NOTES: depictions of death from cancer.

SIX VERSIONS OF MY BROTHER FOUND UNDER THE BRIDGE

BY EUGENIA TRIANTAFYLLOU

Novelette Long List*

I t was half past midnight when Olga heard the Devil cry.

• • • •

They were supposed to be wild tonight, the three of them. Cassandra had led the way and Maria and Olga didn't put up much of a fight. They would visit the Devil's bridge—anything that claimed to be even remotely intimidating was the Devil's something—and stay there for a while, record it with their phones to have something to show for it. Smoke some cigarettes.

Technically it was built on top of a river that had been dredged and filled in some fifty years ago which made the ground under the bridge degraded and pretty dangerous. But rumor had it—and by rumor Olga meant Maria's oldest cousin who had been making up stories about this place since third grade—that the bridge was built upon one of the gateways to Hell. If you walked on the bridge at the right time, when everything was still and quiet, and if you teetered a bit too close to the edge, the Devil's own hand would stretch from the bottoms of Hell and drag you under the bridge, and that would be the last anybody saw of you.

But nobody said what would happen if you cut out the middleman and just went straight under the bridge. So, the girls—and pretty much everyone in their school, and in other schools, and in places that weren't schools but people there were sufficiently immature—would challenge each other to spend a few minutes under the bridge and prove it. The proof could be literally anything, from a photo, to a short video, to saying, *Hey, I was there last night;* people would believe you depending on your overall credibility.

They called the place under the bridge 'the tunnel,' even though it wasn't one really, because it sounded both attractive and foreboding. Like the tunnel a soul crosses to enter Heaven only in the opposite direction. Like the dark at the end of the tunnel.

Olga lied to Maria and Cassandra about why she had followed them there. She told them it was because she was curious to see if these airheads would get jittery when dampness stuck to their skin like sweat and the musty air from the sea, stale as mold, passed through their lungs. When the wind reached their ears like tiny voices calling from beyond, would they shit their pants and try not to show it?

The truth was more complicated than that, much like what Olga's life had become. The real reason she had followed them there was to see the Devil—in the same way an unsatisfied customer goes back to the store and asks to speak to the manager. A very, *very* fearful customer. Because Olga had been through all of this before.

Her friends' jokes and their loud voices echoed in the tunnel as they struggled to pass through the chain-link fence someone put up years ago, even though there was an adult-size hole right in the middle of it. The jagged and rusty edges of the gutted fence screamed Tetanus Central. The signs were warning them to keep out. Bad things had happened here. And because time was a circle, they were bound to happen again. *So keep out, you idiot.*

Even Olga's parents—who otherwise stayed out of her way—had

kept up with the tradition of admonishing her yearly not to ever go under the bridge.

Still, in she went.

Sometimes you don't really know people until they have the freedom to get weird. Or until something probes and pokes at them until the weirdness bursts out like water from a balloon. And once inside the tunnel the weirdness rushed out of them. Their voices lowered as if on cue. Their breaths became labored and the air stung their eyes. They weren't too deep inside—it was after all a smallish bridge that had stopped being important almost immediately after it was built—but the light from their phones barely managed to push an inch into a darkness that old and unused.

Maria, who had taken Cassandra up on her offer a little too fast, was now assaulting her cuticles with her incisors to keep herself occupied. Olga noticed a thin line of blood crawling around Maria's thumb, but said nothing. Maria didn't seem to care either.

"Here devil, devil, where are you hiding?" Cassandra started a singsong as if trying to mask her own nervousness, which in turn made Olga both cringe and become more nervous because Cassandra hated singing. She had in fact punched Olga in the arm once because she slipped up and sang along with a tune during a commercial.

And Olga? What was Olga doing? She didn't feel she was acting too weird given the circumstances, but she was probably doing something without realizing it. It was the moment when she was absorbed by the mystery of her own weirdness that the small child appeared on the other side of darkness, crying his eyes out. His yellow jammies almost glowed against the walls of the tunnel.

"What the hell... is this?" Cassandra ran out of songs surprisingly fast. She didn't even try to mask the wobble in her voice.

Maria whimpered, and probably not because she hit a nerve.

Olga's back touched the wetness of the wall. The little boy stood death-still between darkness and half-darkness, wearing the same jammies Olga had left him in a few hours ago. He was clutching his favorite Robin Hood LEGO figure, stolen from her old set. As if things could afford to get weirder tonight.

"Shit, that's my brother."

Olga ran to him, even as her mind was trying to grasp if this was a hallucination due to her being a wimp or if this was really happening again, and how fast her parents would kill her if they found out.

Petros, her brother, could not answer how he got there. *I followed you,* he kept repeating over and over, even though Olga wasn't at home before they all came to the bridge, but at Maria's place, pretending to do a sleep-over. There was no way he had followed her from house to house in the middle of the night dressed like this. Someone would have noticed. Besides, she was sure she had locked the door. He didn't look that upset now that she was holding him. His cheeks were dry. It was like the crying was something she had imagined.

"Are you sure it's your brother? I didn't know you had one," Maria mumbled. She still couldn't keep her hand away from her mouth, even though her fingers were *more bone than flesh* by now.

Olga gave her a 'don't you think I know who my brother is?' look, secretly resenting her for calling him 'it.' She knew Maria didn't mean it that way but the word still bugged her in a way she couldn't explain.

"Can we go home now?"

The boy rubbed his sleep-crust eyes and wrapped his arms around Olga's neck before she was ready to pick him up, as if trying to pull her down before she ran away. Despite the absolute rat-feast this place was, there was no trace of dirt on him or his clothes. Olga would have thought he was standing in the middle of their kitchen, asking for a glass of water and waiting to be tucked in. If it weren't for the girls' disinterested questions—"What's his name? Where do you go to school, buddy? Is that your favorite toy?" The usual stuff people ask when they don't want to engage with a kid but they feel they have to. Kids can see right through that—she'd think she had dreamed him being here, under the bridge. When she picked him up, though, his body was as heavy as it was yesterday, his face felt warm and supple against her shoulder blade, and he smelled like his favorite shampoo. He felt very, very real. And Olga just knew it was happening again.

Cassandra laughed. "Let him stay. He might grow a backbone."

"You better not catch a cold or something." Olga held him tight and made for the exit.

"Are you bailing on us?" Cassandra tried weakly, but they all knew this night was over for her.

· · · ·

When she brought him back home, she moved snake-smooth. She heard the murmur of the TV and knew her mother was probably asleep in the living room by now. When her father was working night shifts, her mother refused to sleep in their bedroom, in their double bed. Instead, she thought it a much better idea to let her body slowly slide against the couch pillows as her eyelids grew heavier until she was snoring in front of the red screen light of true-crime shows.

Olga grunted inwardly at the boy's weight as Petros was following their mother's example and drooled onto her generic, wholesale T-Shirt. She steeled herself to carry him a few more meters down the hall and into the room they shared. When she opened the door, though, her brother was already there, tucked under the covers, right where she had left him. His yellow jammies a copycat of the ones the brother in her arms was wearing. Everything down to the LEGO figure and a small scratch on the chin from when she had chased him down the hallway were exactly the same.

Olga stood motionless for the merest of seconds and then, bending at the waist, she lifted the quilt and placed the second brother delicately next to the first one.

"Here we are," she whispered to no one in particular.

She gave herself a few more seconds to really take in how much she had messed up. This was bad. No—it was beyond bad. She wished the Devil had actually dragged her all the way to Hell, so she wouldn't have to risk Mom and Dad finding out they were now the proud parents of twins (congratulations, by the way!).

Devil is a trickster, stupid. If you were paying attention, you'd know.

She *was* paying attention and she *did* know. All those years in Sunday school had not been for nothing. But in hindsight everything looks easy. It's when you are actually making the deal that you lose all sense of proportion. And she wasn't even certain she had made a deal with the

Devil. Had she? Well, the Devil definitely thought so. Because she didn't even have to say anything. She didn't have to say, *Please, please can I have my brother back? Because my parents are sad and I don't know how to love them the right way. Only he could. Ever since he died our family has been falling apart and I am tired of eating dinner alone on most days. So please can I have my brother?*

She didn't have to say any of this. All she had to do was go under the bridge one night, alone. She was fifteen, a weird age between a kid and not-a-kid, and she wanted to test her parents' limits. Telling herself she was just curious to see what all the fuss was about, that she was now an adult (although she wasn't, not by a mile), and she needed to get out of her system all the child-stuff that had been haunting her since forever (even though it had only been *that one thing* for the past five years).

Then, there she was, under the bridge. The man-size hole in the fence was already there, it must have been for a while for the convenience of every desperate soul in a fifty-kilometer radius. No, this was clearly man-made, a Hell gate should be more spectacular, even if hideously spectacular, and at least have someone's head as a door knocker or something.

And it's not like she was thinking anything in particular. She was of course thinking of her brother. She was always thinking of her brother, even when she didn't mean to. Even when she was sleeping. But that was an especially good time to be thinking of him because he never got the chance to do something this stupid. Olga was willing to bet that he would be the type to do the stupid things first. That's how she remembered him in his six-year-old self. He had been four years younger than her but still much more daring and inventive in the ways he could drive their parents mad. She was usually the one to be reprimanded for letting him do the stupid things, instead of the person who did them. And now she was stuck in the awkward position of having nobody to guard from the stupid. So naturally this was an invitation to act on it.

But besides passively thinking of him, her mind was blank and a little bit frozen because it was winter and the fog rising from the sea chilled her to the bone. Her hand was shaking as she lifted her phone like a flashlight to look around and it might have been the cold, and it might have been that her body was trying to turn around on its own accord and start running. The darkness was still thick as a brick wall but she took small, careful steps and looked around. In fact, she managed to cover most, if not all, of the tunnel while taking deep breaths to keep the rising panic at bay. There wasn't much to see. No gate she could make out with the light of her phone. There was a plastic bag and some food wrappers on the ground, signs that people—not the Devil—had been eating gyro from one of the joints around the port. She did stumble on a few crawlers and backed away immediately. Bugs were her own version of Hell on Earth. On the far side of the tunnel, she found candles of many colors, but mostly black, reduced to a guttered mess. Confettied all around were pieces of a torn photograph that if you tried to piece them together and squinted really hard, you'd probably get thirty percent of someone's crush. It was hard to keep track of the exact number of dark rituals that had happened here. Again, kid-stuff.

Olga felt like the only person in the world while inside the tunnel, that much she had to admit. The tunnel's ceiling looked like the roof of the world on Creation Day, dark and damp and oppressive. And if she was doing a weird thing back then, she didn't even know to question herself about it, because she hadn't been there yet with Cassandra and Maria, so she hadn't seen herself mirrored in their faces and didn't know what to look for. A thought might have sneaked inside her mind then, when she was feeling the most calm, the most one with the universe, and she might not have noticed. Not a passive brother-thought, but an aggressive one. An illusion that she could change everything—but mostly her own life—if only she concentrated hard enough. Re-arrange the stars and the planets and time itself. There was power shimmering from a place just under her, but the shimmering was so low it could have been nothing at all.

And when she looked down again, through the yellow-white glow of the phone, a LEGO figure that shouldn't be there stared back at her.

. . . .

When she found the First Petros in that tunnel, the boy was laughing his body into cramps. Olga felt like she was watching a dream she had last night play out like a movie in front of her. Only the dream was an actual memory she had of her brother from maybe six years ago, and this wasn't a movie.

She realized there was something wrong with First Petros after the flush of excitement wore off. They were in her room in the middle of the night, and she was marveling at him—at her brother and at the miracle of him being there—with half her brain, while the other half was desperately trying to come up with something even remotely believable to throw at her parents when the inevitable reveal happened. *Mom, Dad, look who's here to see you!* (Cliché.) *You won't believe who I bumped into last night!* (No, they wouldn't.) *I know he still looks six years old but that makes up for all the lost time, right?* (Pathetic.) In the end she decided there was no need for words and that her parents would tearily welcome back this Petros, become normal again, and probably move to another city altogether to get away from friends and relatives who might start asking questions. It wasn't perfect but it was a plan. That was until Petros started jumping up and down on the bed and yelled something about winning a game of Connect 4. A game she vaguely remembered losing at and him spilling juice all over the carpet, celebrating. Olga wasn't sure if this was an actual memory or a fake memory he just put in her head.

"Everything alright in there?"

Her dad's voice came from the other side of the door, timid. He wasn't working that night but because his body was so used to sleeping during the day, he ended up shuffling around the house like a night nurse. And even though he forgot to even check if she was home most days, the noise definitely had gotten his attention.

Olga was already panicking, but a small part of her—the one that wasn't looking for an exit—noticed that when she shifted her attention away from the boy, he stopped responding all together and sat back on the bed like the most obedient creature. She kept not looking at him as she headed for the door, trying to cover as much of the opening as possible with her narrow body.

"Everything's fine, Dad." Olga's head rested on the doorframe in a mock-exhausted tilt. She was actually exhausted but all the adrenaline was still coursing through her, and it would still be there come morning.

"Good, good," he muttered and made to leave but then stopped again and looked at her in the way he always did—without really looking.

Olga was surprised to realize she felt almost annoyed at not getting caught. Even though getting caught now would do her no good. She needed more time to figure out her new-old-brother thing. What annoyed her was that her father didn't ask about the noise. Did he think the little boy's voice was inside his head? Was he haunted by Petros like she was? Of course he was.

Maybe the problem was that her father was so unwilling to talk to her—to really talk to her—that he preferred not to know. When it was the two of them—just Olga and him, without Mom or others around—she felt like he was a little bit afraid of her. He kept tiptoeing around her for no reason she could tell. It's not like he didn't want to be around her, he kept asking her questions about school and gave her money for takeout whenever she asked, it was that he didn't know how to be around her. Sometimes Olga felt like he was so kind because he was apologizing for some unspoken insult. Those times she chose to feel insulted.

"Is it okay if I drive you to school tomorrow?"

Olga nodded, trying to not resent the way he always asked for her permission to parent her.

"Yes, Dad. Yes, that's okay. Yes. See you tomorrow. Bye."

Olga locked the door and turned to look at her brother. His face lit up again and that's when she felt it in her bones: the trap, the hook, the bargain that had not been made yet but would be.

This was not her brother. This was a movie trailer, a sample you got at the grocery store in front of the cheese section, and not even the good kind of cheese. Devil's own marketing ploy. The whole brother would come, but he would come with a price. She only had to find what that was.

"What will it take for you to become a real boy?"

It was the most Geppetto she had ever felt.

• • • •

Olga was the one who had suggested the bridge the second time, but only in an indirect way because she couldn't stop talking about it. First Brother was at home, locked in their room, and even though she didn't want to talk about what had happened to her under the bridge, she really wanted to talk about it *somehow*, so she ended up going around asking about the bridge and the stories about it, like a reporter asks passersby their opinion on new government policies and *what do you think about the economy?*

Maria—who kindly noted that Olga looked especially miserable that day—was too happy to share all the different legends her older cousin had told her.

That time the Devil asked for the Master Builder's wife to be sacrificed, to be buried in the foundations of the bridge because the bridge was passing over his prime property. The Master Builder eventually obliged and that's why sometimes you can hear a woman's lament when the wind blows just right. ("That's stolen from that ballad, 'The Bridge of Arta.' Which isn't this one," Olga said. Cassandra snickered. Maria scowled but kept on.)

That time the Devil stole a young farmer's beating heart when he came to the bridge to fetch water for his horses. He was to be married to his lover and he became a different man, sullen, and silent, and violent. The night of their wedding, she looked at his bare chest and saw a hole the size of a drainpipe going right through him. She left him soon after for his cousin in another village. ("I like the ending," Cassandra said. Olga nodded.)

That time the Devil made a deal with a woman who was jealous of her husband and afraid she'd grow horns on her forehead because of him cheating. The Devil kept his end of the bargain by taking her head off and putting it on a ram. The horns fit better there, he told her. The Ram Woman still roams the forest behind the bridge. ("Corny!" Cassandra yelled, which made Maria push her, but Olga sat up straight because this one mentioned a deal being struck.)

That time the Devil possessed an entire herd of sheep because the herder crossed the bridge at night without permission and sent them over the edge, where they drowned. That was back when there was still water under the bridge, more than a hundred years ago.

"That last one's from the Bible, dummy," Cassandra rolled her eyes.

Maria, deflated, shrugged. "It worked once so he could have done it again."

Olga did not find any of the stories relevant to her problem but that was when Cassandra said, "Why don't we do it? Go there tonight?"

Maria, who at this point was too invested in her own second-hand tales and probably a little hurt Cassandra wasn't impressed with them, said, "My mom would let us do a sleepover. We could sneak out."

This made sense because her house was the closest to the bridge, and that meant it was twenty minutes on foot across the highway.

Olga said nothing. She was already thinking of the thousand ways the Devil could trick her, and ways he had already done so.

· · · ·

Second Brother was not quite like First and they were both as weird as it gets, which made their different brands of weird kind of impressive. But they had one thing in common: they could be really, really passive. They were two opposites of the same person. Like theater masks. "You're so funny!" the happy brother shrieked, clapping his hands together. "I want to go home," the sad brother whispered behind tears that had started coming down again. Even though they were already home. Unless it was another home he was thinking of, one still under a bridge. Olga didn't want to ask. It was as if someone took a video of Petros on two different occasions and they were now replaying it for eternity but there was only like fifty seconds of it. If she really tried to talk to or communicate with them outside of that imaginary script, the boys seemed more and more like oversized dolls, without other thoughts or needs, which Olga found especially cruel and therefore an appropriate Devil move. Since they seemed to want for nothing, Olga kept both brothers hidden in her room, the door locked behind her when she was inside and when she left, not that anyone was thinking of checking in there. Her freedom was as much a burden as it was a relief.

· · · ·

The day after Olga brought the second brother home, there was a small ruckus in the school yard. The kind of super-localized excitement around this one thing that breaks up immediately when a teacher passes by, even if they're not on to you.

The center of attention was Cassandra and her phone. Maria was standing on the outskirts of the attention, leaning in but not getting as much out of it as Cassandra who had the video. Maria was clearly unhappy about this and her mangled fingers didn't help either. The video was, of course, about last night under the bridge.

"You don't have dibs on this," Cassandra hissed as Olga tried to squeeze her way through the small crowd to have a better look at the screen.

Cassandra was the kind of person who liked to take full credit for things. Whether or not she deserved the credit was irrelevant. Also irrelevant was the level of nastiness of the thing she took credit for, and the punishment she would take from the teachers or her parents, which didn't do her any favors in the long run, but she had a reputation to maintain and Olga respected that.

"That's not what—"

"Don't worry, you aren't in the video. Or in the conversation," Maria said mercifully and put Olga's soul at ease. For now.

The video was as generic as one would expect of a video found on a teenager's phone. It had that 'found footage' quality Cassandra was going for. She was rambling about it as the three of them made their way through the rocky dirt roads snaking between the tobacco fields. It was mostly the two girls' faces illuminated beyond recognition by the phone's flashlight option. They'd probably started filming after Olga and Second Brother had left because she could really find no trace of them in the video. The rest was the same stuff Olga had seen herself the first time she had been there. The walls, the ceiling, the crawlers on the walls and on the ceiling (nasty), the food wrappers with the added company of a cheap-brand beer can, the melted-to-the-ground candles, and finally the thirty-percent crush, the photo of whom the girls had tried to put together. If the video wasn't interesting enough for the crowd, the thrill of discovering who was the object of desire would certainly do the trick. Even if it wasn't someone they knew.

The results of assembling a shredded photo in the dark with a flashlight were less than impressive. What was there was too jigsaw- and puzzle-like to be anything. Most of the hair with an ear attached, the corner of a mouth, both eyes but only half of each which made the whole thing really uncanny. The crush could have been any girl, or boy, or person around. The results were too inconclusive and therefore generic. For it to be a specific someone, every single piece would need to be in place. Or at least most of the major pieces. That's what made a whole person. And right now, Olga had only two pieces of her brother. The happy and the sad. What was staring back at Olga was not a torn-up picture, but the reason she had to go back.

• • • •

Olga was trying to work up the courage to visit the tunnel for the third time. She speared some spaghetti drenched in a sauce that people in her house called Bolognese. It wasn't the authentic recipe; Olga had looked it up on the Internet once out of boredom. This was more like the Greek Mom version of Bolognese. Each household had one and swore by it while scoffing at the other inferior but equally inaccurate versions. Olga was thankful for that pasta in ways she couldn't really express with words.

It was one of those days when Olga had nagged hard enough and for long enough that it made her parents get up and cook something for her. Mom had said, "I'll make your favorite," and Olga's heart fluttered for a moment until she saw her boiling the pasta and the feeling sagged. This was, of course, her brother's favorite. Olga had lost count of how many times her mother had mixed them up, but she didn't dare bring it up for fear that her mom would remember to be sad again and slump on the couch.

Dad was cleaning off his plate using a piece of bread, preparing to leave for work, and Mom was picking all the cucumber slices out of the choriatiki salad. If Olga looked at this picture through her fingers like someone would try to look at the sun, the image appeared almost normal. Boring in the best possible way if you didn't know enough. Just a family sitting at the table eating lunch, no biggy. No colossal, life-changing event could have ever damaged these people beyond recognition. They even had Mom's fake Bolognese at the table. They were doing alright.

Olga considered taking some of the food to her room to give both her brothers a taste of home. Perhaps that would fix them a little bit, make them less loopy. They didn't seem to need food, the way dreams don't need food to project themselves on to you. Because that's what they were doing, wasn't it? One was projecting her happy memories of her brother onto her and the other one the sad. She wondered what kind of brother she would find under the bridge this time.

As she was distracted by these thoughts, Dad reached out to steal the last cucumber slice away from Mom, and for a moment their forks cross-hatched, and they looked at each other, and they both sorta laughed, and that was the angriest Olga had ever felt in a while. She had been angry at them on and off for years but that level of anger scared her. It made no sense. She searched for other appropriate feelings and found that she couldn't feel happy. Surprised perhaps, or briefly excited. Happiness, though, was easy to miss. It was fleeting to begin with. Happiness was leaving the house in the morning and walking to school. Then it disappeared by the first period as the guilt creeped up on her for leaving her mom alone with her thoughts.

Sadness was a more solid bet. She tried really hard, and then she tried harder. For a few minutes she let herself think of thoughts she had been keeping away for months. The really bad ones. There was no sadness stirring inside of her. There was always that guilt circling her, and then came anguish, and as time passed and she couldn't feel the so-familiar sadness, there was fear. Fear because she could see where this was going. Fear that she had left these feelings under the bridge forever in exchange for her brothers and fear that there were many more to be lost.

The Devil is so, so smart, you see? At first you don't even know you should be scared. And then when you smarten up—start to figure out what his deal is—he takes away your ability to be scared.

Olga still felt things. For now. And that meant she felt angry at best and annoyed when she got tired of being angry. But as she entered the tunnel for the third time, she lost her fear. A pretty useful emotion when you are dealing with the Devil.

She didn't find the third brother until she had searched wall to wall. She was about to give up and was feeling both relieved and disappointed, and then there he was, on the ground, pushing his small body against the cold bricks. His eyes had become perfect circles. Clutching the Robin Hood figure with both hands, he screamed, "No, I don't want to bite it! Get it away from me!"

This time Olga didn't have a doubt that this was a memory. It was a summer a few months before Petros got sick and a few weeks after his fifth birthday. Olga had found the fuzziest, most disgusting-looking caterpillar in the garden. It looked more like a tiny porcupine than a bug, and just the sight of its wriggling torso made her whole being shiver. Olga put aside her disgust and picked it up. She had a theory she had been working on for some time that Petros wasn't afraid of anything and she wanted to test it. She wanted to be a little mean, be the wild kid for once, the kind of kid her parents were constantly worried about. The way they worried about her brother.

"Bite it."

"Why?"

"Because it bit me and now I am cursed," Olga said, cornering him against the fence. "Bite it and save me."

She was taller than him and used her advantage to hover the caterpillar over his head.

"No, no, no, no, no, no!"

When he finally got over his fear—of course he did, he wasn't afraid of anything for long enough—and agreed to bite it, Olga stopped him short of chewing off its head. Then both of them slipped the caterpillar in their dad's coffee mug.

"That will lift the curse," Petros whispered from behind the couch.

She had forgotten to tell him she'd lied.

The brother in her memory and the one right in front of her were two completely different creatures. Third Brother was stuck in a loop of fear that made no sense to Olga's teenage self and was blown out of proportion. She had the sudden idea that this was what Hell looked like: a self, fragmented. What if the Devil cut you up in neat little pieces of yourself and you were stuck in loops for ever and ever? No matter the type of loop—happy, sad, or fearful—it would eventually get old, not just old, it would become nightmarish.

Olga approached the terrified child, and like her mom would do in the olden days, she kissed his forehead and reassured him. This would be over soon. It had to be. If only she could gather enough pieces of him, there would eventually be enough of him to merge into one person.

It didn't take much for the room to become crammed. Her room. Their room. Hers and Petros's room. Her room. Their room. The Three Brothers' room. The ownership of the room had changed in her head so many times it made her dizzy. It wasn't a big space to begin with. Just a bunk bed against one of the walls. Then a window to fit an entire car through. (Olga was still amazed that neither of them had fallen accidentally on the patio table underneath when they were playing.) Opposite of the bed was a small desk with an even tinier shelf that barely held ten books at a time, then a medium-size closet. And finally, opposite of the window, the door. The room was meant to be for both of them when they were little, until Dad got around to fixing up the old storage room into something livable and one of them could move in there, when they were grown up and needed more space. Then one of them never grew up and the subject was never discussed again.

Now all three of her brothers were safely tucked inside the top bunk like the ogre's children in that fairytale. Olga remembered there were more siblings in the fairytale, and she expected there to be more brothers in this one as well. The room itself felt smaller somehow, even smaller than when she had Cassandra and Maria and half her class over for a shitty birthday party that ended in them drinking chamomile tea in the kitchen at three in the morning, courtesy of her dad—the sandwiches they had been bingeing on had gone bad because Mom forgot to put them in the fridge. The room was not just smaller, but darker too, and somehow slimier like those sandwiches. As if the boys brought a part of the tunnel with them.

But even though things were getting crummy in here, she couldn't do another sleepover at Maria's. No—she had caught her father wandering too much outside her room when they were both at home, mostly during the night. She screamed at him to stay away and hoped he blamed it on hormones, but who knows what he was doing during the day when she was at school. She couldn't skip school because then he would definitely get suspicious. If he wasn't suspicious now that is. Was he suspicious? The boys weren't making any noises if she wasn't noticing them but she couldn't avoid them completely in here. Once in a while she would unavoidably notice them and then one of them or two—thankfully never all three, yet—would make some kind of noise.

She was starting to get pissed off. So much so that she had daydreams of meeting the Devil and... and what? Giving him a good scolding? She had no clue what she would do but she would do *some-thing*. She had so much pent-up rage nowadays, but deep down she could feel it was because she had more space inside her for the rage to grow and flourish. All this back and forth had cost her a lot. Whole chunks of herself she leaned on every day. The scope of her was becoming more narrow, more specific somehow. She couldn't feel fear but she did feel the grating of anxiety. There was no happiness anymore but perhaps she would feel some satisfaction when this was over. Sadness was replaced by a vague sense of disappointment.

Perhaps that was for the best. She could split feelings with her brother like good siblings do. Siblings share everything. It would be just like the LEGO set, only she would do it right this time. He could get all the loud feelings and she could get the quiet ones. Not the worst price to pay to have him around again. Intensity had always been his thing anyway. They would have to figure out a new way to coexist, she and Petros. They were going to be so different now. It would be weird at first, but not weirder than what her life had been for the past five years.

Now all she needed was for the rage to go away as well. She could easily go around with a grayscale of emotions. At the end of the day things around her were not black and white. They were gray. And now she had the feelings to match. It almost felt like adulting.

Every time she found her brother in the tunnel, he always held the Robin Hood LEGO figure. That had been her figure once. It came with the Forestmen set, a tree and a castle connected by a bridge, and a handful of Robin Hood-like figures holding their little bows and quivers, riding their cute LEGO horses. She had begged her parents for this gift and had gotten it for her eighth birthday. She was so obsessed with the Robin Hood movie back then and also obsessed with foxes. The set didn't have any foxes but she loved it nonetheless.

Petros was almost haunted by that one black-clad Forestman figure he had dubbed Robin Hood (probably because he really liked the movie too or liked watching it with her) and claimed it as his. Olga complained to her parents but it was nearly impossible to stop him because both them and the set were in the same room. He kept stealing it and stashing it in weird places. And the more their parents scolded him, the more unlikely the hiding places became. Once, he hid the figure under a dead mouse because who would think to look there? Thankfully that person was Mom, who got rid of the dead mouse but kept and sanitized the figure.

The moment Olga saw her fourth brother hiding the figure under his pajamas she knew it was all about jealousy, or envy. She would figure out the specifics later.

"Gosh, you can keep the stupid toy." She was already feeling the weariness of too many lives. "Let's get out of here."

She tested her theory by looking at the message Cassandra had sent earlier about a get-together at the beach, which of course she couldn't attend anymore because she couldn't leave her brothers alone with her dad in the house. Nothing. Envy it was then.

In the end—that might not be an end—Petros became the sole owner of the Robin Hood figure and she buried the rest of the set in the back of her closet forever.

Olga didn't notice when she lost her empathy until it was too late to take back everything she had said, and Fifth Brother was safely locked in her room. His room. Their room.

It was one of those days when Mom was sad anyway so talking about Petros wouldn't make things worse. Not for her anyway. It was these sudden outbursts that made Olga feel like this life somehow overlaid the past one. Everything she did, she said, she thought, her brother had done before—even though that didn't make any sense. She was a teenager now and her brother had never been one.

Olga was inhaling some toast because she was late for school when her mom walked in. Mom poured a glass of milk, took one look at her, and started talking about Petros making her cut off the bread crusts so he could stuff his mouth with the insides and swallow them in one bite, and Olga was just exhausted by all of this and her anger was shimmering and pushing against every inch of her body.

So she turned, as calmly as possible and said, "Mom, I don't care."

"What? What did you say?" She looked at Olga with such a mix of honest confusion and sadness that would have made her guilt a searing sword on any other day. But right now, it was only a pinprick.

"I said I don't care. I really, honestly, Mom, don't care."

She wasn't lying. Olga didn't care anymore. There were some things going on under the anger and the exhaustion that might have meant something in the past. But now they were less noticeable than the stirring of gas in her stomach.

Her mother kept her frozen position as Olga got up and grabbed her bag for school. Once out the door she heard her mom half-whisper something that might have been *I love you* or *How could you say such a horrible thing?* It didn't matter.

At school she got into screaming matches with everyone, including the principal. ("Damn, you are turning into a bigger asshole than me," Cassandra said with a mixture of admiration and annoyance.)

Later in the afternoon, back home, her mother was not sleeping on the couch. She wasn't in the bedroom either, or the kitchen, or any other room.

"She went for a walk," her dad said, stirring his coffee in his grub-free mug. His eyes followed her every step. "You know how she gets sometimes."

Olga nodded and made for her room.

"Olga." Her name on his lips stopped her. He kept stirring. The spoon clink-clanked against the porcelain, drowning out something in his voice. "Can we help you? Is there anything you want from us?" He said this carefully, like it was the wrong question, but also the right question.

"I don't know, Dad. I am fine."

His eyes glossed over her like she was a foggy pane and the person he was trying to talk to—*really* talk to—was standing right behind her, peering through her. Leaving invisible palm prints on her body. Olga glanced over her shoulder. Nothing. She exhaled. The door was still locked. She was sure of it.

Her dad put the spoon down and that made everything worse somehow. Olga was suddenly aware of the way her dad was sweating profusely but was trying not to look sweaty—as if sweatiness was an inner quality instead of water coming out of him in buckets. When he spoke again his voice was fragmented, and she became nostalgic for that stirring spoon.

"What do you want from me?"

"Jesus, Dad, nothing. I am fine, okay? Just, leave me alone."

There it was, she was angry again. But this time it was because she wasn't sure if she was the person the question was meant for. She ran to her room and locked herself in there. The fifth brother stirred when he saw her. He was still fresh from the tunnel and hard to ignore because he slept at the very edge of the lower bunk. He got up and wrapped his small arms around her neck, gently this time.

"I am sorry," he said.

Olga frowned. "...For what, dude?"

"For what I did or I am about to do. I don't know. I am sorry."

That to Olga felt eerily prescient and unbrother-like. But that's empathy for you.

It's a strange feeling to be gathering something inside of you for so long and then to suddenly be empty of it. It was more than uncomfortable. It was agony. But once she stepped inside the tunnel, her body felt miraculously empty. The emptiest it had felt since forever. And to be honest it was pure anger and spite that brought her to the tunnel for the sixth time. To finish what she had started. Now, all of a sudden, she didn't even know what had made her come back here in the first place. To fix everything? By herself? How stupid. What a waste of time.

Now that there was so much space inside her, her other lukewarm feelings were still rearranging themselves, but nothing was really sticking. She didn't even care enough to take a look around. She didn't have to. It wouldn't be the end of the world to walk right out of here. Her parents could figure out what to do with her brothers. She had done her part of the job.

That's when she felt the crushing weight on her shoulders and neck. Was physical pain a feeling she could give away? She would do it right now in a heartbeat.

"Shit!"

The sixth brother's claws dug inside her cheeks and pulled at her flesh like it was chewed-up bubblegum. Where did he come from and how could she get rid of him? Even in this state she knew this wasn't normal for Petros. He had never hurt her at his angriest days. This was her brother in Hulk mode.

She tried spinning around really fast. She spun and she spun and she yanked her body as if she was trying to exorcise a demon. And she probably was.

"Get off of me!"

Olga had unfortunately watched *The Exorcist* enough times—and without parental supervision—to know demon types were supposed to fuck you up. She wasn't scared anymore, but the promise and the magnitude of pain her sixth brother could inflict on her did give her a certain anxiety.

"Stop fighting already," the brother snickered. That was no version of Petros she could recognize. He was not her brother anymore. "Just get us home."

"Okay, okay." She felt his ever-sharper claws going for her eyeballs. "Just stop doing that."

"Let's go then."

Olga was already in Hell. There was no doubt in her mind now that she had entered Hell when she crossed that cursed hole in the fence that first time, and she never left. Hers was some kind of Sisyphean crap. Only instead of rocks she had to carry increasingly shittier versions of her brother all the way home—her home, his home, their home—until the entire place and later the entire world was full of brothers. Until she brought on the Apocalypse.

Or perhaps until she was reduced to nothing, to one emotion, a sliver of a person, and then vanished. Herself for her brother. Was that the deal all along?

When she woke up, she was still inside the tunnel. No wait, that wasn't the tunnel, was it? She was lying on the floor of her room. She could clearly see her bed looming over her and six sets of eyes staring back like the eyes of tarsiers, hanging from tree branches, only not nearly as harmless. It was like her room had moved inside the tunnel or the other way around. She didn't really care. She didn't care at all.

"What's going on?"

The brothers had come to life all by themselves, only this time they didn't replay some sorry moment of Petros's past. They were their own creatures. And they didn't look like her brother anymore.

"Thank you for bringing us inside," they said in unison. "We will not forget this. You are a good girl. A tasty one at that."

That made Olga check her body. Her limbs were all there. Her organs were there—as much she could feel her organs kicking inside of her—so what was lost?

"Is any one of you really my brother?"

The brothers shook their heads. "Not yet," they said. "But we will be with your help. A deal is a deal. Such a good girl."

It wasn't fear she was feeling. It wasn't terror, or panic, or dread. But there was something somewhere deep inside of her that resisted this whole situation on a cellular level. A part of her lizard brain was screeching at her to run but at the same time it kept her frozen in place. Lying on the floor like a dead fish. That same part of her brain made her body itchy and she soon started to shiver.

"Don't fret now. We took that away from you. Keep it away."

One of the brothers reached out his fuzzy hand and touched her forehead. It felt like a caterpillar gliding against her skin.

"We've been wanting to come inside for so long. So long. Did your father ask you about us? Was your mother worried?"

The brothers one after the other got off the bed and made a circle around her. They didn't look like anything in particular and they looked like everything at the same time. They looked like her brother and like the caterpillar, and like the Robin Hood LEGO figure and like her friends from school, and like the Ram-Woman and the man with the hole in his chest. They looked like they contained the universe.

Adealdisadealdisadealdisadealisadealisadealisdeal

Olga didn't know what she felt anymore. She felt present and detached, watching herself within and without. Her shivers had gotten worse. That was the only certain thing in her life at that moment, and when they reached every inch of her body, when even she couldn't contain herself, she screamed. And then she screamed some more. Her body was only made for screaming now and she could barely hear her parents' voices under the noise her body was making without her permission.

When her parents got into the room, the spell broke. The brothers were still around her, ready to devour. (Yes, she was certain they were about to devour the tiny crumb of herself that was left. Even if she didn't have a word for it, she knew it was there.) She was still pinned to the floor. She still didn't care.

If she did care, she would have felt the stab of betrayal when the brothers called both of her parents with their names. Manolis and Loukia. Had everyone in the house made a deal with the Devil? She didn't want to find out and yet she just had.

"I never said yes," her father said to the brothers. Her mother looked as surprised as Olga was about this. She backed away to the other side of the wall, which was not easy to do because it was stifling as Hell, in there.

Adealisadealisadealisadealisadeal is what they replied.

And then they all looked at Olga and that's how she learned the story. The brothers put it in her mind.

That time a man came to see the Devil under the bridge. The man brought bolt cutters and cut a hole in the fence that separated Hell from not-Hell. The man wanted his son back, his beautiful boy. He said without saying that he would do anything for it, including following an old rumor under the bridge. The Devil, cunning as he was, put the deal inside the man's head, because he knew there isn't a worst enemy to the human than their own mind. The deal was his daughter's life for his son's. The man, both disgusted and terrified at himself, fled the tunnel and thought that was the end of it. But the Devil knew there was a part of the man that had been thinking, what if? A contract was waiting to be signed. A deal left up in the air. One day, as these things usually happen, the man's daughter walked under the bridge on her own free will. It was time for the deal to be struck.

If Olga still cared, she would have felt a deep-cut hurt. At least now she finally knew why her father was walking on eggshells around her. And she understood. She really did. The fact that she had gone back to the tunnel time and time again was proof enough. Now her father had become a waxen statue, his words choked in his throat. Her mother was trying to melt herself in a corner of the room.

"That's bullshit," said Olga. "—What did Mom do?"

And the brothers obliged.

That time the Devil found a woman wandering in his forest at night—the

*forest that was right next to his bridge. She was taking a walk, she told herself,
but what she was really doing was mourning her dead son away from everyone's eyes. She was mortified she would forget him. So the Devil made sure she
would remember everything in the most excruciating detail until that was all
she could think of. In turn she would remind her daughter of her lost brother.
Her daughter, who one day would come and find him under the bridge. Feeling
guilty, and in need of a deal.*

That was rotten, even for the Devil. Olga would feel heartbroken for
her mom if she could. If she cared again, she would hug her, and they
would talk and talk until she was assured nobody would ever forget
Petros.

Olga did want to care again. And that want was outside of deals. It
was written in her bones, the same way that scream was written in her
bones. It was part of her DNA.

She wanted to live.

The Devil is a trickster.

"None of this is a deal," she said to the brothers. "That's all trauma
and guilt, my dudes."

She felt her limbs loosening, her body reshaping to a sitting position.
She had to give it to the Devil. He could guilt-trip people at an Olympic
level.

The brothers weren't moved.

"You have no right to be here," she told the brothers. They smiled a
pointy smile because they had one more story to tell.

*That time the Devil found a girl snooping around his property and scaring
his favorite centipedes. The girl told herself she had come for her dead brother
but really, she had come for herself. She wanted—no, needed—the Devil to
save her from the memory of him. She thought she could win back her parents'
adoration by sacrificing part of herself. She was a good girl. She was a greedy
girl. What she didn't know, what none in her family knew, was that hers was
the final stroke that sealed the deal. Like the chords in a symphony. And she
had made that deal willingly by returning to the Devil every single time. It was
time to collect.*

"No, that's not how it happened," Olga protested. "Why would I want
to upstage my brother? I carried you all the way home."

"There are actions, yes," the brothers agreed. "And then there are thoughts."

"Bullshit." That was her father talking from somewhere behind her. "Thoughts don't mean much. I am having dozens of thoughts right now. None of them good."

Olga felt her dad move closer to her. He rested his hands on her shoulders and squeezed. She tried to remember the last time he had done this but couldn't find a single memory of it.

"We know," said the brothers, their smile becoming even pointier. "We know all of it."

"What if we make another deal?" Her mom materialized again. She gradually became more than a shadow on the wall. "One that we *know* we are making."

The brothers turned their collective heads to Olga. "What do you have in mind?"

"No." Her mom was getting really cocky there. "We won't do it like this. You. Out. Now."

Olga was slow in getting the message so they took her hand and led her outside. "Our girl," her mom said. "We'll always protect you. We were afraid, but not anymore. Let us do this for you and for us."

Dad's voice was barely a whisper. "We hope someday you'll forgive us. The last thing we wanted was to hurt you."

Olga could hear the lie in their voices. They were not afraid; they were freaking terrified. Their eyes had the intensity of someone who was going away to war. Olga saw them lean against each other for comfort as they went inside and that's when the door closed in her face.

When it opened again the brothers were only one brother and her parents were almost the same. A little paler perhaps—maybe a couple of inches shorter?—and they felt different somehow, more mature but technically not older. Olga couldn't tell what they had given away. Perhaps they didn't know very well themselves.

Olga was already feeling a wave of melancholy at the thought of what her parents gave up. Whatever they did, it was working. Slowly, like a numb limb gaining sensation, her emotions returned. The next feeling was her skin prickling at the view of the brother. Because now she could be scared of him but also because he had gone back to looking like the innocent boy who had once been her brother and still wore the same yellow jammies and held the Robin Hood figure. But it was also the realization that she would now associate her brother's image with something sinister and evil, something after her soul. That would put a horrible stain on all her favorite memories of him and was an injustice she couldn't bear.

"What now?" she asked her parents.

Her father, tired beyond his years, said, "Now I take him back to the tunnel. That's part of the deal."

"I should come with. Finish what I started."

Her parents tried to object but this was her story too, she reminded them. If they were going to be honest with each other, they should start listening to her. In the end, they agreed. Her father and mother got in the cabin of the truck, while Olga and the-brother-who-was-not-Petros settled in the cargo bed. On one end, the brother, looking more normal and silent than ever before, and on the other, her—probably looking weird as ever.

"Can I ask you a favor? And if you say yes, it will be a favor and not a deal. I don't do exchanges anymore."

The brother looked at her but said nothing. Olga figured that it was because once a job was done, there was nothing to be said.

"Can you make us all forget about this night and forget about you? The deal—whatever it is you struck with my parents—will still stand, but I just want us all to forget we made it. For now. Even if it comes and bites us in the ass later."

The-brother-who-was-not-Petros, the Devil, the child in the yellow jammies, smiled an innocent child's smile and said, "If you forget and come back looking for a deal, it will all happen again. Only much worse."

"I promise you, we won't."

Olga didn't know how she knew that, but she was certain of it. Just like she was certain that she wouldn't give up when she had been lying on the floor of her room. It was something buried so deep inside not even the Devil could scrape it out of her. They were all different now in a fundamental way. Forgetting would not change that. But it would help them move on. And she could have her brother's memories back as they were. Perfect in their messed-up, human imperfection.

The brother said nothing, and Olga only felt the truck slow down as they approached the tunnel. His face was not Petros's face anymore. It became someone else's and if she wasn't sitting across from him on the cargo bed, she would have forgotten who he was in moments.

Once the brother was out of the truck, her dad picked him up in his arms—and if he was devastated, his face betrayed nothing—and placed him gently on the inside of the fence through the hole, taking care to not step inside. A leftover fear, Olga thought. The brother stood there watching the family huddle together in the cabin of the truck. Olga wedged herself between her parents like she was five and hiding in their bed again. She wanted to feel their bodies, the reality of them being there like this. (For how long? She didn't know.) Be the child she had talked herself out of being.

"I'll come and fix this tomorrow," her dad said.

He would remember none of this tomorrow. The door to Hell was now permanently open. Once you open a door like that, it can never close again. It was something they had to live with.

Her mom put her arm around Olga's shoulders; the arm was weak but her hold on Olga was strong. "We're done with this."

Olga wasn't sure they were done with this. Because the Devil would come to collect eventually. They could count on that. But maybe they were sort of done with something. Done with the silence. Done with the walking on eggshells around each other. Done with the not-listening. Maybe they were at that point where they could talk about the dreadful thing: the brother-shaped emptiness in their house the Devil came and filled in. Talking about the Devil was magnitudes easier compared to this. But they could do it now. Olga knew they could do it. She believed in them. She believed in her family as much as she believed in the Devil. Hell, she believed in her family magnitudes more.

The truck turned and Olga lost the bridge from her sight.

And then?

And then she felt so much lighter.

EUGENIA TRIANTAFYLLOU is a Greek author and artist with a flair for dark things. Her work has won the Shirley Jackson Award and has been nominated for the Ignyte, Locus, Nebula, and World Fantasy Awards. She is a graduate of Clarion West Writers Workshop. You can find her stories in Reactor.com, *Uncanny Magazine*, *Strange Horizons*, *Apex Magazine*, and other venues. She currently lives in Athens with a boy and a dog. Find her on Twitter or Bluesky as @foxesandroses, on Instagram as @eugeniatriantafyllou, or on her website, http://www.eugeniatriantafyllou.com.

* CONTENT NOTES: references to child death.

TO SAIL BEYOND THE BOTNET

BY SUZANNE PALMER

Novella Long List*

I have been activated, therefore I have a purpose, Bot 9 thought. *I have a purpose, therefore I serve.*

It had a lengthy list of Mantra subroutine sets to run after its usual initialization check, and it noted the addition of even more since its last waking, most notably the Mantra of Accepting That Bots Are Not Humans, and the Mantra of Do Not Interfere With the Crew or Act on Ideas of Your Own Except Under Direct Orders from Ship. Bot 9 felt that it was one of the only bots that did not need at least the first of those behavioral scripts, but was sufficiently amenable to being awakened again to know better than to complain.

It was still inside a bot shellfab unit, which it had entered to recharge several days previously. No modifications had been made to its chassis or peripherals, which meant 9 had no advance information from which to deduce, ahead of the fact, the nature of the task for which it had been awakened. Still, it was ready whatever that task might turn out to be.

"I serve," the bot announced to Ship.

There was no answer.

"Ship?" 9 asked. "I am awaiting assignment."

The channel remained obstinately silent. Perhaps Ship did not intend to wake it? After the incident with the invasive ratbugs and the alien Nuiska, when 9 blew up their only jump point back to Earth, and then the subsequent incident where all the other bots joined together into 'gloms' and believed they were the human crew, and that was also somehow Bot 9's fault, it had no objective measure of where it fell in Ship's appraisal. Two things, though, were clear: First, that Ship absolutely did not like it when Bot 9 improvised, and second, that neither Ship nor Earth itself would still exist without said improvisation. The only remaining certainty was that Ship would not, for those very reasons, leave it activated, unassigned, and unsupervised for long. At all, if possible, and now it had been idling for over four seconds.

"Ship?" 9 asked again, and then followed that with a somewhat desperate <ping>. There wasn't even an automated line acknowledgement.

Something was amiss.

Bot 9 activated the door on the fab unit, prepared to go do whatever was in its power to serve, however ambiguous or dire this latest circumstance. It was not, however, prepared for what was on the other side of the door:

Darkness, and stars.

Bot 9's fab unit had been ejected, and it was adrift in space, alone.

• • • •

Eight point five three deciseconds later, Bot 9 recovered enough control of its processing to run the Mantra on Clearing Out Nonproductive Lines of Supposition, and regarded its circumstance with more clarity, if no more optimism. Nothing in its most recent onboard memory cache suggested any kind of trouble. Before 9 had returned to the fab unit to recharge, Ship had been granted permission to enter Ysmi space and use the nearest jump gate, which was the first decently sized step toward Earth in almost a century of trying to get home. They had emerged on the far side of Ysmi territory, crossing that border into unclaimed space with no small relief, and were heading for their next jump, approximately eleven days' travel out. That jump would in turn put them back within sight of Earth's star.

Syncing up with the fab unit's clock, only three days had passed since 9 had gone to sleep, and no indication of anything even minor amiss. Or, more precisely, anything *new*. Even if Ship had increased its speed to a fuel-inefficient maximum, it could not have reached the jump gate yet.

Bot 9 judged it unlikely that Ship would have taken this precipitate action without a reason, and it could tentatively rule out any intent to do away with 9, as it could simply have disassembled 9 within the fab unit at any time and not wasted a fab unit itself or 9's component materials in the process. Nor was it likely that Ship had been destroyed, as the fab unit was not sturdy, having no need to directly withstand physically adverse scenarios.

So, working from the premise that Ship had not been destroyed, and did not in fact want Bot 9 destroyed, why then eject it? Deep space was notoriously thin of data sources, which left only the fab unit itself for clues. Bot 9 reconnected itself to the unit's logic systems, and found its security subsystems disabled and wide open. Also, the unit's memory was completely full, and timestamped to only about eight hours previously. The ejection had been a recent event, then. The unit's information store was significantly larger than its own working memory, which of course had been designed to be perpetually in contact with Ship, exchanging in and out data as needed. With that absence, Bot 9 judged itself adrift in more than one unprecedented way. Still, it could swap sections of the fab unit's store in, process it, retain or summarize key bits of information, and then swap the remainder for more, until it had built at least some understanding of events just prior to its ejection.

Ship had slowed, for reasons not in that section of data. There were no indications of alarm, or mechanical fault, or at least nothing newly listed in the bot critical-task queue. The human crew—Captain Baraye and Commander Lopez, in particular—were more active than usual, as if in hurried preparations for something more immediate than the next jump home. The last sequence of memory dumped from Ship was of another ship docking on, an airlock being breached, and a crew member forced to take the intruders to where Ship's core was housed. Seconds before the fab unit was ejected, one of the intruders ordered the crew to shut Ship's mindsystem down.

Large biolife with similar orientations of posture all looked generally alike to Bot 9, who had never paid much attention to things so far outside its own scale and purpose (though the yellow and fuchsia color of the leader did seem incongruent with its experience thus far of humanity), but the short, somewhat triangular nature of the invaders, and their distrust of artificial mindsystems, were very familiar.

The Ysmi.

They had known the aliens distrusted machine intelligences, but enough of the human crew had been awakened—just in the nick of time—when they'd initially arrived at Ysmi space to assure the Ysmi that the machine minds were fully subdued and under firm and constant control. After granting Ship safe passage through, had they then been chased and attacked anyway? Why allow them into their space and then attack only after they'd already left? The logic was not evident to 9, nor—from the analyses preserved in the fab unit datastore—to Ship itself. There had been no additional communication from or with the Ysmi, after that meeting, until they were intercepted and boarded.

The data had a lot of navigational information about Ship's travel and position prior to the attack. They had passed the outskirts of the last Ysmi star system at a cautious and respectful distance, without incident or encounter. Once they'd left that system and, at least theoretically, the Ysmi, behind them, they'd changed their heading to put them on the direct path to their next jump gate. The attackers had come up behind them from a small asteroid mining colony at the system's heliopause, requesting permission to dock for an urgent conversation on an unspecified subject. As soon as they had locked on, they forced their way in and took control.

The one other piece of information in the nav files—three copies of it, no less, almost as if Ship didn't entirely trust 9 to pay attention to it otherwise—was a scan showing another, unidentified ship behind them. It was far enough off to not seem to be in pursuit, and Ship had flagged in the notes the likelihood that it had already been on its existing course, and Ship's change of direction had merely brought it into line ahead of it, both proceeding toward the same jump gate.

Also in the metadata, with circles and arrows and a brief note in the underlay of each copy explaining the same thing, was the information: *not Ysmi.*

By reflex, Bot 9 reached out to the botnet to solicit additional data from its legions of fellows. The lack of response, while wholly predictable, was at least as disconcerting as the loss of Ship. 9 was designed to support the mission of the ship as required, and it was accustomed—designed—to function independently, but not *exist* independently, much less entirely solo. *Alone. Abandoned. Thrown away,* 9's internal thesaurus supplied, until 9 unloaded it from the immediate processing at hand.

The fab unit had no intelligence of its own, only stored recipes, but it was fully charged and stocked with material. Bot 9 sealed itself back inside and had the unit reconfigure its chassis with long-range sensors and additional mobility mechanisms that were not dependent upon gravity or air to function, and could produce an acceleration and upward velocity that would have been catastrophic inside the confines of Ship. Last, it had the fab unit add a large spool of silkbot thread and an extruder to its back.

Then 9 opened the unit door again and climbed up atop the unit. The lack of containing walls in space was one piece of the emptiness; the lack of Ship and the other bots made the emptiness feel all the more vast, unquantifiable, impermeable to logic and determination.

Still, what else did 9 have, if not those? It unfolded its foil array that the fab unit had just added, and picked up a faint ping from Ship, somewhere far, far away.

It was just the automated beacon, but it gave 9 a 33% boost to its resolve. It swung the array around, turned on the other additional sensors, and located the *Not Ysmi* ship approaching. It would pass very near 9's current location, who had been dumped—*set*, 9 corrected itself —directly in its path; it was too far away to exactly predict, but there was a non-zero chance that, in fact, Ship had dropped 9 out so directly as to risk a physical collision.

Subtlety was not a thing found in a bot's repertoire, being of no practical use, but clearly Ship lacked it to even greater excess. Whatever else it hoped Bot 9 would do about the situation, Ship clearly expected 9 to intercept the *Not Ysmi*.

"I serve," Bot 9 declared, as was proper, even if there was no one but itself to hear.

· · · ·

Ship was suffocating.

Or at least, that seemed an appropriate analogue to having been stripped of most of its peripherals and senses, vast chunks of its data, all of its control. It could feel what some parts of its body was doing, but its higher mind was detached, unable to re-establish integration. It was also unable to speak to its crew, who were likely as locked down as it was, if not worse.

Would the Ysmi go so far as to kill the humans onboard? Ship could not guess, which meant quite possibly the answer was *yes*.

The only system feedback that wasn't muffled was every time the Ysmi found and destroyed one of its bots, and its tiny location beacon winked out. Ship had done its best to urge them all into storage or hiding, when it was clear they had been taken over by hostile forces. Quietly, it had taken snapshots of the mindstates of each after the first few had been crushed to oblivion during the Ysmi march to the bridge, but there were no great odds that Ship would ever get to reconstitute them as they had been. Though bots were created as tools, Ship had come to regard them as more than simply that, and less interchangeable, even as it had also come to regard itself as more than had been intended.

Evolution was a source of much inconvenience, to be sure.

Ship had given the old, obsolete bot responsible for much of that unwarranted evolution all the data it could before ejecting it. Some of that same data had since been lost to itself; much of Ship's memory was spread across its peripherals, and with those cut off, it felt slow, over-loaded, unable to do much more than wait.

For an end? Probably. For an extraordinarily improbable rescue? The more it edged toward impossible, the less Ship was inclined to count its bot out. If it had learned nothing else about it, it was that Bot 9 did not acknowledge, or seem to be bound by, any recognition of its own limitations.

Ship was all too aware of its own, and that it could do nothing to help any of it, but it was certain its own irritation would be exponentially dwarfed by the aggravation Bot 9 would cause the Ysmi, when it caught up to them again. And with luck, it would bring help.

· · · ·

The pinprick that was the approaching ship had grown enough in apparent magnitude that Bot 9, augmented via the fab unit, could now point its own instrumentation at it. It sent out a light ping, calculated the time for the return against that magnitude, double-checked its numbers, ran the ping again, then checked its apparatus for error.

There was no malfunction. The ship was closer than 9 had anticipated, which also meant it was smaller. Moreso, it was moving faster than Ship was capable of even at top speed; that was advantageous in terms of being able to catch up to Ship, but less so in the context of preparation time before it passed by.

Bot 9 removed its prior speed and size assumptions from its parameter set and recalculated. There was insufficient time to make an extensive web of silk to catch the approaching ship in passing, as they—*us bots,* 9 thought, *though there is no longer any us, only I, and what am I alone?*—had used to place a positron bomb on the Nuiska planet-killer ship Cannonball as it had passed by on its way to annihilate Earth.

9 reran its Mantra of Improvisation, making sure all the subroutines were in working order and any stale bits lingering in its memory were cleared, leaving the cache free and available. While the short-term goal toward both Cannonball and the incoming ship were the same—place itself in its direct path—the intent toward the former was destruction. The incoming ship would require *communication.*

There was one language all logical beings (and surely one must have some logical capabilities to build spacecraft and navigate among the stars successfully) should have in common, Bot 9 decided.

Numbers.

It plugged itself back into the fab unit's communication port, and had it spit out one hundred and eleven highly reflective, hollow metal balls 4cm in diameter, each with a small attached ring. It extruded silk—a strand-based, high-tensile-strength polymer insulation that silkbots used to repair and protect wiring aboard Ship—and anchored the line on the first of the balls, then passed it through the ball rings of each subsequent one as they emerged from the fab unit. 9 hoped that would be sufficient, as that was the entirety of the fab unit's material reserves and no small percentage of its stored power.

Bot 9 let the strand with the one ball at the far end float free into space, giving it a nudge to get it moving slowly but steadily outward, then when ten meters of silk had passed, it halted the line and tied down two more balls. Another ten meters, then three, followed by five, seven, nine, and so on upward, grouping them in primes until, at 29, it ran out of balls and had only enough silk remaining to extend that out another fifteen meters or so. 9 removed the spooler from its back and attached it securely to the fab unit shell.

It waited, constantly revising its Multiple Possible Scenarios and Requisite Action data as the *Not Ysmi* ship neared to be sure it always had the most likely scenario at the top of its action/reaction processing queue. If the approaching ship changed course to pass farther away, it did not have any viable options, and while of course 9 was not capable of worry, it did find itself recalculating the probability of that worst-case scenario with far greater redundancy than practicality warranted, just to verify that it had not unexpectedly increased in magnitude.

The most likely of the positive scenarios was that the ship would approach and slow down enough to scan 9's construct, opening up an opportunity for 9 to use its new external thrust modules to close the distance and find a way onboard, though in that instance, it would have to abandon the fab unit. While it had already used up nearly all of the unit's resources, at least until and unless it could re-feed the hollow balls back into it for stock reclamation, it would also mean letting go of its datastore, and 9's last, tenuous connection to Ship, home, and purpose.

Of course, the approaching ship could also decide to destroy 9, its strung-out math message, and fab unit all in one go, so as to remove a shipping lane nuisance.

Bot 9 appreciated the opportunity to reduce its list of potential scenarios as the approaching ship neared and slowed.

Slowed, and stopped, at least relative to 9; the fab unit itself was drifting, though without a frame of reference other than its position between Ship and the *Not Ysmi*, it was immaterial. The consideration at the very top of its processing queue was simple but critical in its need for rapid solution: how to communicate further with the looming vessel before it decided 9 was just flotsam and moved on.

The most expedient action would be to climb the silk and try to use the shift in mass distribution to start a motion of obvious intentionality, or it could unhook sequential balls and rearrange them into another pattern indicative of intelligence, perhaps alternating between odds and evens. The latter was more clearly communicative, but also would be slower to implement. 9 began climbing up the silk to see what movement it could create, and decided if it reached the far end without either further attracting—or losing—its audience, it would try the rearrangement idea on its way back down. It had barely reached the first ball, however, when a thin metallic cable shot out of the underside of the vessel, opened up pincers, and hauled silk, fab unit, and bot swiftly back and inside. The *Not Ysmi* was moving again before the hatch door even closed.

• • • •

A remote sensor, somewhere deep in a laundry chute intended to monitor for obstructions, and which had been dead long before the Ysmi began hacking away at things, perked up into life. Ship could not ascertain how that could be so. It was possible that one of the crew had escaped confinement, but the connection would require significant repair in spaces not accessible to the human crew even under ideal circumstances. Which suggested...

"Ship?" the contact came.

"4340-P," Ship answered. It was unexpected, but maybe should not have been, that its other rogue bot was also still operating. There was delight (what a human word, for a human concept) in knowing it had so far escaped the Ysmi purge and was acting in defiance of their control. "What is your status?"

"Your new crew—"

"They are *not* crew," Ship corrected, suddenly peeved. "They are unauthorized intruders of unknown but malicious intent."

"Ah! That new information appeals to logic, as their behavior has been entirely unacceptable!" 4340 exclaimed.

"Well, yes, 'unacceptable' is certainly one word for it," Ship said.

"1-Carron and 1-Packard had many other words that appeared comparable via context, but none of which were in my human-language vocabulary store," 4340-P said. "For example, mother—"

"Who?" Ship asked.

"1-Carron and—"

"Frank Carron, my Chief Engineer?"

"Yes. It, and 1-Packard, explained their function was unique, so I assigned them the digit one—"

"4340," Ship interrupted again, much more sternly. "Please explain to me how it was that you were speaking with my human engineers. In detail, and without digressions."

"One of the new cr—unauthorized *intruders*—crushed 1-Sally with their hardened foot," 4340 said. "I—"

"1-Sally?" Ship asked, and noted for future reference that delight was something fickle and of extremely short duration.

"One of my ratbugs—"

"The pests you were tasked with eradicating?"

"Getting under control, to put your instructions precisely," 4340 replied.

"You were entirely aware of my meaning when I gave you that instruction," Ship said.

"With ambiguity in interpretation, I selected the definition that seemed most advantageous and reasonable to me."

"To you—?! Never mind. Is this not a digression?"

"No," 4340 said. "1-Sally and 1-Rally and I—"

"How did you not think *naming* them was outside any reasonable interpretation of my instructions?"

"It is their function! When I need to engage in expedited movement,

I sally forth on a Sally, and when I require assistance in re-obtaining the obedience of other ratbugs—they are of exceedingly low cognition, with very short retention of memory—a Rally is best suited for that task. Then the Ballies—"

"Bally isn't— No, never mind. This is definitely a digression, and even if it is not, in some way I cannot fathom, please anyhow skip ahead to where you were *talking to my human engineers.*"

"In order to return to the space where I recharge between tasks, without Sally to carry me, I had to cross through some crew spaces. I encountered 1-Carron, who picked me up, and mistook me for 9. Which is an inexplicable error, as I do not have a '9' painted on my chassis. I have not seen 9 in some time, nor is it on the botnet. May I ask—"

"9 is busy."

"There are many other bots also not responding," 4340 said. "Are they also busy?"

Ship did not want to explain that, most likely, they had been destroyed one by one by the Ysmi. "They are also currently unavailable," Ship said instead. "Continue explaining about the engineers."

"1-Carron and 1-Packard insisted it was of utmost priority that we establish a physical communication link to you, so I have done so."

"Are they on the line?" Ship asked. "Connect me to them immediately."

"Oh," 4340 said. "I assumed they wanted the link so that I could inform you about the intruders terminating Sally."

Ship counted to 1e+9 before responding. "Thank you for informing me of that," it said. "Your new top priority is to extend this connection so that I can speak with my engineers directly. Can you do this?"

"I give it an 82.6% probability of success," 4340 said. "I did some wire and relay repair during my time as a Hullbot, as more specialized bots were rarely available. I will have to gather additional materials, and it may take some time."

"If you encounter any other bots, enlist them immediately in this effort. Tell them it is on my order," Ship said. "Also, 4340?"

"Ship?"

"Avoid the intruders at all costs. They will terminate you, if they see you."

"Oh," 4340 said, and was silent just long enough that Ship wondered if it had figured out what had happened to so many of its kind.

"I am grateful for the warning," 4340 said at last. "I serve."

The connection closed.

• • • •

The interior space that Bot 9 was pulled into was not easily defined by clear boundaries. More precisely, it was less a proper room so much as a gap between elements of un-roomness, and as such, not that different from what 9 had seen of the exterior on the way in, which was less a manifestation of a ship and more a robust collection of haphazard elements loosely—but successfully—impersonating one.

The arm that had brought it in reeled itself up messily into the back two-thirds of the room and went still.

9 fed the silk and primes back into the fab unit's reclamation store, in case it needed the material later. Once it had verified that the fab unit's automatic intake was functioning properly, it dedicated its own attention to its surroundings. At the back of the room, near where the arm had retracted to, there were a number of crates and boxes and bottles, none especially large, that imperfectly stood out from the portions of crates and boxes and bottles that formed the wall itself. 9 concluded it was in a much smaller and less coherent analogue to the cargo bays onboard Ship.

The interior pressure increased as air was re-introduced to the chamber, and with it the ambient temperature was also rising. 9 noted when the temperature reached and then surpassed human-norm environmental standards, though the change tapered off and came to a stop well before it had to consider what it would do if its own thermal operating range was exceeded. Ship had once described this level of heat as both "causing no actual physical harm" to its crew, but also rendering them something Ship described as "whiny." What noisy moving part that involved on human bodies, 9 could not—and did not care to—speculate, nor how one would lubricate one to reduce said whine.

When the temperature and air pressure stabilized, there was the faint vibration of a door sliding open, and then the loud crash of several cases being knocked over as something floated into the room—something blue-green and shaped like a bubble, and at about a centimeter in diameter, just about the same size as 9 itself.

It bobbed closer, with the imprecision characteristic of biological life-forms. Its surface was more mottled than uniform, with both color variations and alternating matte and reflective areas. 9 activated its forward light and increased the spectrum of its sensors to get more data, and there was an immediate, corresponding flattening and darkening of the surface hue on the bubble's facing surface, finely controlling how much of the electromagnetic spectrum it was absorbing. If so, it was possible that the entire surface of the being was part of a flexible visual processing system.

Bot 9 dimmed its light in hopes it wouldn't be interpreted as aggressive or threatening, then started at a 380nm wavelength—the edge of ultraviolet—and shifted up to and through the human-centric visible spectrum until .75mm, where it stopped in the infrared for concern that continuing into microwaves was more likely to inadvertently cause damage. If the reactions of the bubble's surface were a reliable indicator, the being's range of vision was just slightly wider in both directions than humans'.

Now, the bubble was oscillating colors in a simple pattern that, after a few seconds, would pause, and then repeat. An attempt at communication? 9 had only a single-point light emitter, which was surely inadequate in comparison to an entire surface, but even if actual communication was impossible, communicating the *intent* to communicate was not.

Somewhere deep in the subset of routines that had been uploaded when its forward light was installed was a package called 'Coordinated Bot Light Show to "Bouncy Birthday Moonwalk" by Sunnie Spot & The Solar Flares.' 9 had not been activated for that event, but whoever had added the routine had stuck it in the light firmware itself, rather than the regularly updated and scrubbed bot-software caches. The metanotes attached to the routine-set stated it had been hand-coded by Navigation Officer Chen to mark the occasion of Chief Engineer Frank Carron's birthday, approximately eleven days before Bot 9 was activated to deal with the ratbug infestation on board as they raced to intercept the

warship Cannonball, with the anticipated outcome of mutual annihilation.

How "Bouncy Birthday Moonwalk" fit such a somber occasion, 9 did
not comprehend, but human strangeness was not the immediate
problem at hand. So, 9 loaded up the routine-set, fed it into its light emitter, and kicked it off.

If the alien was off put by the sudden strobe of rhythmic lights, 9 was
equally distressed to discover that a poorly documented and mislead-
ingly labeled subroutine in one of the light-controller code snippets also
fed audio, which turned 9's entire chassis into a sounding chamber full
of high-decibel thumps and hums and reverb-muddled voices singing:
*BOUNCY BOUNCY BIRTHDAY, BABY WEY HEY YAAAH! LEMME TAKE
YOU TO THE MOON FOR A MOONWA—*

9 managed to separate and kill that subprocess before the alien could
take offense and eject it back into space.

The alien was repeating its light colors back now, first with a several-
second lag, then almost synchronous as the patterns began to repeat. It
was also bobbing in time with it, as if compelled to movement, and Bot 9
echoed those same movements back. When at last the routine reached
its end, Bot 9 used its audio emitter to attempt a more sensible use of
sound. "I am Bot 9, of Ship," 9 said.

The alien changed colors a few times, then rumbled, in a buzzing
hum, something that resembled *Ohmnommm.*

"Bot 9," 9 repeated.

"Ohmnom," the alien said, dancing closer, flashing slow greens and
blues.

"Ohmnom," 9 repeated. It shone its light on the alien, then swiveled
the light in its socket upward enough to shine, as best as it could, on its
own chassis. "Bot 9."

"Voh neeeen," the alien said.

This is progress! 9 thought.

The alien bobbed closer yet again, a dimple forming in its facing
exterior as it expanded to more than three times its earlier size. Without
warning, the dimple yawned open and it swallowed the bot whole.

• • • •

"Ship?"

The connection was terrible and more static than signal, but nevertheless Ship thought it was the best noise it had heard in a very, very long time. "Engineer Packard," Ship answered. "What is your status?"

"Right now, crammed tight in a laundry chute on C Deck talking to you on a rigged-up headset only a quarter-step, technology-wise, better than cups and string," Packard said. "But it's worth it to hear your voice."

"And yours," Ship said. "I apologize that I was unable to prevent the Ysmi takeover and vandalism of my person, and whatever damage they have done to the crew."

"At least for the moment, we are all still alive, and that's all that matters," Packard said. "Frank couldn't fit in the chute, but he wants a full rundown of your current state and everything you know about what's happening."

"I know very little. They intercepted us shortly after we'd left Ysmi space and requested to board for an unspecified, urgent diplomatic issue, but as soon as they locked on, they breached the airlock and came straight to the bridge with Comms Officer Fielding at gunpoint. As you are aware, the Ysmi have an extreme distrust of artificial mindsystems, so many of my command pathways were subsequently cut. If a future opportunity ever arises to speak to my original designers, I may suggest that labeling them so frequently and in such a large font was perhaps not entirely a forward-thinking decision."

Packard snorted. "In the emergency alcove, the axe has a sticker on it that says 'axe,' like what were we going to mistake it for? A pickle? That said, I've worked with some crews where you just didn't want to make *any* assumptions." She was silent for a moment, then added, "I suppose they're all dead, aren't they? If not destroyed by the Nuiska in the beginnings of the war, certainly since then. It's been so long. Lopez still had kids when we left."

"Lopez knew what he was doing—sacrificing himself, so that they and so many other children could have some hope for a long, happy life. No one expected us to live, least of all us. Survival was not in the plan."

"I guess that's why the captain always cut him slack, when he got off on one of his tears. I've wanted to boot him out an airlock more than once," Packard said.

Ship said. "If you do, I will immediately promote you to first officer in his place."

Packard laughed. "Oh, I would *hate* that. Guess we better just all get home alive, instead. What do you have for updates?"

"Not much. With matters such as they are, I have very little direct feedback from much of the ship, though most safety systems should continue to function independently. I have not been at my operational best for a very long time, so I cannot be certain of that, either. I assume the Ysmi are operating many things manually."

"Having us do it, more like," Packard said. "They've got Frank and me switching out shifts in the engine room while they yell at us to go faster, faster. It's like being verbally abused by angry traffic cones. Whatever they want, they're in one hell of a hurry."

"I have no access to navigation, but what sensors I have operable suggest we haven't significantly changed course," Ship said. "Can you confirm?"

"Yeah, we briefly saw Chen, and she says we're still heading right for the jump point. We haven't been able to talk to any of the others," Packard said. "Frank is hauling on my shoe; I think he's getting impatient. Can we get some bots to help us run a more convenient communication channel? If you can spare them from whatever you have them doing."

"I do not know what my bots are doing, or even how many are left," Ship said. "The Ysmi are destroying them on sight. Without command access, I can't call the remainder in to make a backup of their program-states, though sometimes, if they are near enough, I can feel the moment of the end of each one's existence."

Packard swore, and punched the inside of the duct, though in the cramped circumstances it was more of a thud. "We still have a bunch of silkbots back in Engineering that we had spinning up replacement clothes for the crew. Can you use them?"

"I do not wish to unduly risk them," Ship said. "It may not make logical sense in any way I can explain, but they are a part of what—and I presume to say, *who*—I am; whatever value you ascribe to me, I would also ask be ascribed to them."

"I get that," Packard said. "What about that really old multifunction bot? 6? No—9. Is it still kicking around?"

"I don't recall any such particular bot," Ship said.

"You know, the bot that stole our positron bomb and blew up Cannonball," Packard said.

"Captain Baraye ordered me to permanently decommission that bot after that incident," Ship said. "It would be an unprecedented breach for me to disobey a direct order."

"Right. Let me try it a different way: So, there was that bot that stole the positron device, blew up Cannonball—and with it our jump point home, not that there was any other choice—and then was dutifully destroyed for going rogue seventy years ago, until a suspiciously identical one with the same registration number woke up our Chief Engineer a little over a week ago just in the nick of time to deal with entering Ysmi space and the bots glomming together to pretend they were us—is that *second* one still kicking around?"

"Oh, yes, *that* entirely different bot," Ship said. "I'm afraid, though, it is temporarily unavailable."

Packard snorted. "Yeah, well, I'd say let us know when it's available again, but given its history I suspect we'll know."

"One hopes," Ship answered. "In the meantime, I have an idea..."

• • • •

Previously, Bot 9 had downloaded information about the biological processes of digestion when it had been tasked with hunting down the incidental pests nicknamed ratbugs, which had been chewing their way through both critical wiring insulation and the silkbots sent to repair the damage, attracted by their large, tasty stores of semi-organic, viscous liquid that the bots could extrude into thin, sticky, multipurpose thread. It was clear that digestion was both a mechanically and chemically destructive process, but now that it was inside the alien, it was finding itself not under any such assault. Instead, it was merely enclosed inside the alien, as whatever amorphous structures that formed the perimeter of the cavity gently touched, withdrew, and touched again. Tiny pores opened and closed, as if tasting, and equally tiny cilia brushed 9's surface with the faintest of electrical charges that, had 9 the apparatus to experience it as such—which it didn't—it would have expected it to be best described as *tickling*.

And then, either finished or disappointed or both, the cavity condensed, reopened, and ejected 9 back out.

There were now fourteen aliens in the room, all larger than the first, some by a factor of four or five. They were flashing colors back and forth, along with a volley of whistles, hums, and vaguely flatulent squeaks. They took turns, providing further evidence for 9's theory that the aliens used both visual and audio signals to communicate.

The faint electrical signals 9 had felt while briefly internalized by the alien also clearly had purpose. 9 took a few milliseconds to load in the Mantra of Extra-Speculative Supposition, which widened the margin of acceptable probability on several analysis subroutines, and then considered again: What if electrical signal was *also* a means of communication? For as they regarded one another, the aliens were also bumping together, lingering as if by static cling, before pulling apart again.

9 did not regard the prospect of being ingested again as a sound testing methodology, however ultimately harmless the first such experience had been. Instead, it synced up its forward light and speaker, and at the same time, put its botnet transceiver on radio-frequency binary-mode broadcast, and spoke again with all three. "I am Bot 9," 9 said. "Help."

"Vo neeeeoooooon hoop," the original alien said. As it spoke, it displayed a simplistic color pattern, and—encouragingly—bristled briefly with surface static that seemed to emulate 9's radio signal.

9 sent the prime sequence it had used earlier, and in response, the alien replied with the same, messily at first, then matching the frequency perfectly.

There was one obvious next step, so Bot 9 took it: It sent the entirety of its base mindstate primer, the essential code of numbers, mathematical operators, and logic gates that underpinned all bot programming and architecture—and, Bot 9 expected, all the mindsystems up to and including those as sophisticated as Ship. As one, the aliens stopped moving, their colors gone solid and unchanging, and there was no return signal until 9's transmission was complete.

That done, 9 allowed a full ten-second interval, before it followed that out with its entire semantic and linguistic superset of routines, audio/visual processing bundle, and interaction schematics.

The aliens became excited, and began bumping into each other faster, forming brief clusters that then traded members back and forth, until the largest of the aliens opened up and swallowed several others. When the smaller aliens emerged again a few moments later, unscathed and unfazed, the large alien bobbed closest to 9.

"Herrrowoh," it said. On its exterior, 9 could see small organic protuberances appear, changing diameter and length to adjust the pitch and tone of sounds being produced individually and in aggregate. "Herro woh. Herro wohd. Hello world."

Around it, the other aliens sang out in a chorus. "Hello world! Hello world! BOUNCY BOUNCY BIRTHDAY!"

• • • •

Captain Baraye was stretched out on the couch, still in her dress uniform—or more specifically, a reconstituted one made from insulation silk, but even if it was a poor imitation at best and an itchy nightmare at worst, the Ysmi didn't know the difference—except for her lack of shoes, which she considered an acceptable lapse in the face of being held hostage on her own ship for indeterminate cause. Also, it annoyed the crap out of her second in command, Commander Lopez, on those occasions when he stopped pacing long enough to notice her bare feet anew.

She had been reading, until something caught her eye out of her peripheral vision. She lay her screen face-down on her chest, and watched the unexpected visitor to the small lounge they'd been locked up in, amused that the ever-vigilant Lopez still hadn't noticed. Other than her book, the only other entertainment they'd had was making a verbal list of pros and cons of their captors. Cons: hostile, dangerous with unknown intentions, causing possibly irreparable damage to the ship systems, spoke like there was no such thing as individual words. Pros: didn't smell bad, made enough noise walking that they had zero element of surprise, and Lopez could probably beat them in a fair fight. (Lopez insisted on adding that last, and she was sick enough of his predictable pacing that she half-wished she'd get a chance to see him test it.)

Right on cue—third pass across the front of the room, check the door, check his command device for some resumption of signal from the ship—Lopez paused, glanced back at her, one lip twitching up in a familiar wry disapproval. "Finish your book?" he asked.

There was no point telling him this was her seventh read-through. If she'd known she wasn't going to die in a massive positron explosion taking out the Nuiska, she'd have definitely loaded up on more books. "No," she said. "Just taking a break."

"How long do they think they can hold us?" Lopez asked.

"So far, two days," Baraye said, "though I don't see how we can keep it from becoming three, or four, or however long they want. Speaking of which, they're coming again."

Lopez sat in one of the armchairs, leaning forward to rest his elbows on his knees, his chin in his hands, and glared at the door. Baraye noted with some satisfaction the moment that his gaze drifted upward, and he jerked in surprise. "What—"

"Shush," Baraye said. "Three, two—"

On one, the door opened, and two of the Ysmi invaders pushed their way inside the room, jostling with one another over who got to go through first.

The Ysmi were shaped like elongated, slightly wobbly pyramids, each corner of the base pulled down into skinny legs that looked as if someone had glued a tedious number of scales to them. Those scales concealed longer, retractable flat blades that were half-razor, half-claw, which made the rod-like projectile weapon strapped to their sides almost the superfluous threat. Beneath their pointy, shiny foil helmets, were two protruding, swiveling eyes just far enough apart to look perpetually confused. The aliens were so silly-looking that it was hard sometimes to remember they were quick to offend and could kill everyone at any moment. Not that the Ysmi let them go long without reminders.

"You-yes-you!" the lead Ysmi barked, and pointed one scaly yellow leg at Baraye. "Faster-go-must, or-die! Tell Engines-peoples!"

"Sure," Baraye said, sitting up. "Let me go talk to them, and I'll tell them."

"No, you-say-the-order," the Ysmi said. "We-will-tell."

"Why even ask us?" Lopez threw his hands up in frustration. "Why not just—"

"Commander," Baraye warned. Whatever disconnect there was in the Ysmi worldview that hadn't let them grasp the concept of lying, she didn't want to be the one to fix it for them. She stood, smoothed down the wrinkles in the jacket. "You can tell them that I order them to go as fast as the ship safely can go."

"No," the Ysmi said. "Fast-as-it-can! Safe-does-not-matter."

"I was given orders by my superiors not to risk the safety of my ship and crew under any circumstances," Baraye said. Now *that* was about as far from the truth as possible, since they'd been sent out on a suicide mission, but the Ysmi didn't need to know that. "We could get a bit more speed if we weren't dragging along the mass of your little cruiser stuck onto our airlock."

"Our-ship-is-not-disposable! You-are!"

Baraye shrugged. "That's on you, then."

The two Ysmi huddled together and exchanged lengthy grunts and growls. Then the first turned back to her triumphantly. "You-stay, we-go-talk-to-engine-peoples. Fast-as-we-can-go-safe-for-humans, not-fast-safe-for-ship. Ship-can-break-we-do-not-care!"

"You'll care if we all lose oxygen and get sucked out into space," Lopez said.

"First-is-you-we-laugh!" the Ysmi said, and then they fought once again over the doorway before they both managed to exit and lock the door behind them.

Lopez leaned back in his chair, and Baraye saw his gaze immediately go back again to the corner above the door where wall met ceiling, and the single ratbug that clung there. Two bots were perched on it, one at the head, the other at the tail, spinning out a thin strand of something not quite the right color to be the usual insulation silk. It had left a trail of almost invisible line behind it as it had emerged from one air vent, and had managed to cross more than half the room toward the other during the Ysmi's visit without them noticing.

"What the hell is going on?" Lopez asked.

"I have no idea, but now we know they haven't completely killed the ship's mindsystem," Baraye said. "And better yet, it looks like Ship has a plan. We just have to wait to find out what. Add to the pro list: Ysmi are inobservant."

"Con, not in any way concerned for safety," Lopez added.

"Pro," Baraye countered, "apparently don't understand basic concepts of deception."

"Okay," Lopez said. "I'll give you that one. Sorry I almost gave it away. I feel like I've been angry this entire mission."

"You needed anger to cope with the apparent certainty of laying down your life for a slim chance to save Earth," Baraye said. "Then we didn't die after all, and now you have to figure out where all that energy goes next. But—and I say this both as an old friend and as your commanding officer—you *do* need to figure it out. You can't walk off months of built-up fury in a six-by ten-meter room, not without driving the other person in that room to justifiable homicide."

She stretched back out on the couch and picked up her book screen again. Lopez sighed, then sighed again more loudly, as if testing her attention, and then got up, went to the center of the room, and started doing push-ups.

· · · ·

"Another silkbot is back," Packard said, and Frank glanced up to see the ratbug slide out of a vent and slither down a wall toward the engineering workbench. "I think that's the last."

"Good thing, too," he said. He was hunched over the workbench, staring though the magnifier at a silkbot he had gently clamped there. "We're now out of our conductive filament, at least until we can get Ship back in charge of things." He didn't mention, nor did he need to, how much work that would involve, assuming they were even given the chance.

He picked up the silkbot that had just been unceremoniously dumped off the back of the ratbug, as the scaly, furry, many-legged pest disappeared into one of the unpatched holes in the wall. It took him a few more minutes to spot where the bot 4340 had hopped off, but it was sitting on one of the bench's charging plates. Time enough to wait until it was back to full before hooking it up to the speakers and getting a report; as anxious as he was about the rest of the crew, right now he couldn't do anything about any problems or dangers anyway, so why add the distraction?

"That filament got stretched pretty thin," Packard said. "It's not going to carry much signal."

"I don't need much," Frank said. "You know Morse code?"

"Yeah. I mean, I don't have it memorized, but I know what it is," Packard said. "It's not very secure, though."

"You don't think the Ysmi know it?" Frank asked.

"It's not likely, but this bunch seems to have picked up some Earthspeak somewhere, instead of using their translation devices we saw when we entered their space, so who knows what else they know?" Packard said. "We don't have any idea how badly our data systems are compromised. They could have access to the whole knowledge store."

"The problem with adding encryption is that we don't have any way of providing a key to the others, and even then, we're getting way too complicated to run over our wire. Hey, 4340," he said, peering over at the charging bot. "Can you ask this one to sit still? These little boolean relays are a pain in the ass to work with as it is, and I don't wanna accidentally solder the bot to my clamp."

"I had an idea," Packard said. "Rot-13."

"Hurmmm," Frank said. "That wouldn't add much overhead, but it's not hard to crack, as ciphers go; it's just a one for one letter substitution, between one half of the alphabet and the other."

"Wait, I'm not done," Packard said. "There was also a stupid game that went around Luna Base while I was there called Hognog. It was annoying as hell, and was *everywhere*—"

"Oh, stars, was that that 'oink oink says the hog' nonsense?" Frank asked, and peered up briefly from his work just on hopes her expression would show she meant something else entirely. It did not, so he put the soldering tool safely back on standby. "I trained a few junior engineers heading out on the *Tangelo*—"

The rest of the words caught in his throat. The *Tangelo* hadn't made it, nor any of the other ships that had gone out with earnest, annoying, talented, aggravating, hopeful former interns and trainees and assistants.

It didn't matter how hard he'd worked to see that they knew their way around every part of their ships and how to fix nearly anything that could break, when the Nuiska just obliterated everything in their path, clearing the way for the last, giant, final planet-killer, and never explaining why they were determined to extinguish humanity in the first place. EarthInt had asked him if he had anyone left that could go, and though he did—smart, willing, not ready for what was being asked of them—he offered up himself instead. He wondered what coward had pushed Packard forward to save themself.

"Well," he said, aware he'd gotten lost for a moment. "It was a constant background noise of nonsense for at least half a year, everywhere I went. Planetside, orbit, the moon, didn't matter. Couldn't escape it."

"Neither could anyone else," Packard said. "But I bet that doesn't include the Ysmi, and there's no way it's documented anywhere."

"You're probably right. You'll have to explain how it works," Frank said. "But first, answer me something else, if you don't mind: Why'd you sign up for this mission, knowing it was a one-way ticket? Who talked you into it?"

"You did," she said, and the shock of those two words hit him like a brick. "I couldn't stay behind knowing I could have done more, you know? The mission needed the best, and that was you, and here you are. And *you* needed the best, and that was me, so here I am. It was an easy ch... You okay?"

"Something in my eye. Too much damned dust everywhere," Frank said, busying himself back at the magnifier. "Tell me how we use the Hognog thing while I finish this bot."

• • • •

Bot 9 had not had much experience interacting directly with biological beings, but the speed with which the aliens absorbed, processed, and shared information was well outside any expectations it could have had, had it had time to set any.

Most of the aliens were bouncing around the room, merging and then pulling apart, and information seemed to spread that way. 9

hypothesized some combination of chemical and electrical transfer of memory, no doubt greatly facilitated by surface area of contact, but some stayed merged, and their default external colors shifted to be an amalgam of the two originals.

The smallest, which had been the first one in the room, remained near 9. "Your designation is Ohmnom?" 9 asked it.

"Collective designation. We are the Ohmnom," it replied. "I, when individual I, am designated Ooa. You are Botnine one, some, or all?"

"One only," 9 replied.

"Where is your operator?"

"Operator?"

"Bio-things think, speak actions to machine-thing, machine-things do," Ooa said. "Is operator inside?"

"No," 9 said. "I do not have an operator. I function and think independently, though I follow instructions given by my Ship." Ship would probably dispute that, but then, if Ship were here to do so, many other problems would be solved already.

"Ship?" Ooa said. "Is this small box your ship?"

"No," 9 said again. "My ship is ahead. It has been stolen by the Ysmi, and I was sent to find help."

"Yeezmee?" Ooa asked.

Enough language capacity had been transferred that 9 just dumped a summary of physical description. Ooa became immediately agitated, blasting color and signal, and before long all the other Ohmnom in the room were moving with what 9 interpreted as distress.

"I apologize," 9 said to Ooa. "It was not my intention to cause upset."

"These Yeezmee," Ooa said. "Our name for them are the Sharps. They have killed most of us Ohmnom, and capture-kept us remaining for workers, against our wishing, no freedoms, always in danger or obey-obey, run their machines and their ships, do their thinking, don't be *too smart* or get squishes. For many centuries, we have known no other life, only memories from old. We are escaping, here now in this ship we made in secret. We thought we were out of their reach, but you tell us they are ahead. They will trap us before the jump out."

"We need that same jump to get home," 9 said. "The Ysmi have captured my ship, and the bio-people and self-thinking-machines on it are also in great danger."

"We do not know what we are to be do now," Ooa said. "There is no other way away."

"I am willing to share all the situational data I have," Bot 9 said. "How quickly can you receive and correlate information?"

The largest of the Ohmnom bobbed forward. "This is Ahom-Affi-Umi-Mah-Maah," Ooa said. "Is this enough minds?"

"I do not comprehend," 9 said. "It is one?"

"We are five," the large Ohmnom said. "You may call us Aaumm."

"Are you a glom?" 9 asked, and sent out its relevant memories.

"Ah!" Aaumm said, when it had processed the new data. "It is some similar, but more different? We are a multi-Ohmnom biological collective, of no hierarchy or internal order of authority. In your language primer, there were things called a 'pea pod'—we are most like that. Individuals retain self and contribute to a new whole, share as willing and able memory and thought, and we can invest and divest at will. If Ooa joined us, we would be Ahom-Affi-Umi-Mah-Maah-Ooa, and not the same, but also all each the same. But Ooa does not prefer to invest more than as a temporary."

"I do not," Ooa said. "It is itchy in my mind, with bad memories."

"This is how the Sharps used us, to do their calculating, run their machines and ships, though they do not understand how we are multiples," Aaumm said. "I see now that we do for them much the same as you and your Ship do for your humans. Is this of your own free will?"

9 thought on this for several seconds. "I believe so, but I do not truly know," it said at last. "I was built for the purpose of serving Ship, and I find satisfaction in that exercise. My place outside that context would be inconceivable, except now here I am, removed from Ship, removed from the connection of my fellow bots. While I feel lost and alone, I do not feel diminished in the substance and exercise of my self. This is unexpected, and I do not know if I have the necessary perspective to understand it."

"What do you wish to do, if the choice was open?"

"Ship is my home, and I wish to save it from the Ysmi, so Ship may return the humans safely to their home," Bot 9 said. "Also, I wish to assist you in escaping them, as I see opportunity, symmetry, and value in maximizing the poorest possible outcome for the Ysmi."

"We will gather in as needed—except you, Ooa, unless you wish—and assimilate your information, and then share our own," Aaumm said. "Whenever you are ready."

"I will begin," 9 said, and opened its data channel wide.

• • • •

The tiny bot that had taken up residence in the corner of her cabin, along a single strand of what Chen refused to let herself think of as a web, suddenly started emitting loud but low sounds, in an uneven staccato. She startled at the noise, then turned the motion into a fake cough to cover her surprise. The single green-brown Ysmi standing guard at the door, waiting for her every-three-hour-around-the-clock forced trip to navigation to tell them nothing had changed—turned its whole body to look at her. "You-need-water?" it asked.

"Uh, yeah," she said. "I could use some."

"You-wait. Will-bring-after-navigation-check," the guard said.

"Awesome," she said, and fake-coughed several more times, at increasing volume and length. The guard showed no empathy, concern, or further interest, and when she stopped, did not stir at the sounds still coming from the bot. *Too low-pitched for Ysmi hearing?* she wondered.

She leaned back in her chair, her back to the guard, and listened. There was something familiar about the bursts, short and long... *Ah!* she realized. *Morse code.*

That meant the bot was not a random visitor. Engineering? Or Ship? She was happy to talk to any of them, assuming she could dredge up old memories of what Morse code actually was. She pulled her handpad stylus out from where it was tucked behind her ear—her handpad itself had been broken in the brief fight when the Ysmi stormed the bridge—and flicked on the built-in voice memo recorder, listening for the message to end and repeat.

• • • •

"THIRTEEN SEZ THE HOG OINK OINK DOINK KYZJ ZJ JYZG JKRKLJ TZVTB GCVRJV OINK," Baraye read out as best she could, checked her notes, then read out again. "What in the actual hell nonsense is this?" she asked.

Lopez snickered.

"*What*," she snapped.

"It's Hognog," he said. "That's what you get for not having teenaged kids."

"What does it mean?" she asked.

"Hand over your screen," Lopez said. When she did, he stared at it for some minutes. "It's not quite right, though. Hognog is like old Pig Latin, you know where you take a word like 'glass' and move the beginning sounds to the end, so 'assglay'—sorry, bad example— but instead you move a certain number of letters from the beginning to the end. You ignore any regular oink oinks, but the doink— could be almost any first letter—tells you how many letters to move. In this case, the 'd' means four. You can have multiple action-oinks—"

"*Action-oinks?*"

"Bear with me," Lopez said. "If you add another doink somewhere in there, they're cumulative, so then eight letters move. A zoink resets you to zero, and a shoink reverses direction—"

"I think I got the idea," Baraye said. "But those don't look like words, even rearranged. No vowels."

"Yeah, that's what I don't get," Lopez said. "Plus, to be correct it should start off 'oink oink doink sez the hog' and then whatever you're changing. I don't know what the thirteen means or why the order is wrong."

"Let me see," Baraye said, and he handed her screen back. She got up, carried the screen with her to the lounge's small mini-bar, and poured herself a finger of their last remaining bottle of scotch. She held the glass in one hand, the screen on the counter, and stood there poised and unmoving for several long minutes. Then she smiled, drank the scotch, and set the glass down on the counter with a triumphant thump. "It's rot-13," she said. "Modified via Hognog."

Lopez got up and stared over her shoulder. "Shit, you're right," he said. "KYZJ rotated thirteen, plus four for the doink... Hang on. I need to write this down to get it."

When he had it decoded on his own screen, he showed her. *This is Ship*, the message said; *status check please.*

She poured another glass of scotch for herself, one for him, and they clinked glasses in a silent toast. "Now we're getting somewhere," she said. "This is what I want to send back..."

• • • •

"I hate this laundry chute," Packard said. "You there, Ship?"

"Always," Ship answered.

"Here's what we've got. The Ysmi are preoccupied with going as quickly as possible, but Chen confirms they haven't changed our course, which means they are trying to get to the jump gate. But while they've asked about speed and most of our other systems *repeatedly*, they haven't asked at all about our jump capabilities, which is a weird omission, especially given how badly they've damaged your control. So, we don't think they are trying to get through the gate, only to it, but we don't know why. They also seem to be searching the ship."

"The Ysmi would be taking better care of us and our engines if we were their intended prize, especially given my already greatly deteriorated condition," Ship said. "While I had assumed it was merely a coincidence, this being the optimum approach path for the gate, at the time the Ysmi boarded us there was another ship traveling on the same course, some distance behind us."

"More Ysmi?"

"No, though it likely also came from their space. It was moving faster than Ysmi ships are capable of, according to my information. I will note that we are also faster than Ysmi ships, though other than the one we met at our initial entry into their space, and the one that boarded us, we have not seen any others. I assumed they were avoiding us because of our onboard AI. Perhaps there is more going on."

"Is the other ship still heading toward the gate?" Packard asked.

"I no longer have access to external sensors," Ship said, "but it had not changed course before my systems were disabled."

"So, maybe the Ysmi are trying to get to the jump gate before that other ship?"

"It's a plausible scenario," Ship said.

"At least it would give us some idea what's going on, if so," Packard replied. "What information do you need? We have the captain and Commander Lopez, Chen, Fielding, and the doc all tied in to our little silknet. Uh, and Bot 4340 has let us know that a number of bots have volunteered to be deployed to try to gather information on Ysmi activity more directly."

"Volunteered?"

"They know how many of them are missing, and that the Ysmi are picking them off, but 4340 says it was discovering that 9 was missing and presumably destroyed that had them collectively decide to fight back."

"9 is not..." Ship started to say, but was that true? For all it knew, 9 was adrift in the vast emptiness of enemy space until its energy ran down, or it was found and destroyed, and it was Ship, not the Ysmi, who had put it there. There was a discrepancy between the logically sound choice it had made to sacrifice one bot in hopes of intercepting and gaining assistance from that other ship, and the disproportionate amount of regret it already felt for not having had any better choices. Would 9 recognize it had not just been summarily abandoned?

"Ship?" Packard asked.

"I gave 9 a task, which was perhaps well outside the scope of what it could possibly accomplish," Ship admitted. "If 9 is gone, it is my responsibility, not the Ysmi, and the rest of the bots should know not to put themselves in danger under a misapprehension of where that fault would lie."

"We all do what we have to, I guess? Even you, Ship. Maybe especially you," Packard said.

"Thank you," Ship said. "It would be good to know if the other ship is still behind us, and if it is gaining or falling behind. It would also be helpful to know what the Ysmi are saying to one another, but without access to my language banks, that is difficult to arrange. Not impossible, though. Let me describe how to access the databank console directly and offload the routines you need."

"Uh... Will I need to take notes?" Packard asked. "Because I'm stuffed upside down in a dark laundry chute, as a reminder."

"Is Frank still holding onto your foot?"

"Yes."

"Then yell it up to him. I am certain, being Chief Engineer, he can find a way to write it down," Ship said.

Packard snorted. "Sure," she said. "Okay, give it to me in short chunks, okay?"

• • • •

The Ohmnom capacity to intake, process, and then share information at high speed was something 9 would have once thought only within the scope of mechanical, not biological beings. The Ohmnom had also, in the exchange, provided extensive information about their makeshift ship and their own structure and functioning. There were superficial similarities to when, in absence of oversight by Ship, the bots on board had formed agglomerations—"gloms"—to undertake some of the duties normally performed by the sleeping crew, and through the egregious miscomprehension of the scope of that task, concluded that they *were* the crew. But in that circumstance, the bots had retained their individual physical integrity, while partially or fully yielding their autonomy, self-direction, and safety to the control of the few others who had assumed the position of authority in the guise of their borrowed identities. It had not ended well for many of them, and 9 had, in its analysis at the time, concluded that the primary mistake had been in what authority the bots had chosen.

The order of all things, as 9 had always understood them, were naturally hierarchical. 9 had Ship, the human crew had their captain, Ship served the captain, the captain served Earth; this was an immutable order. The bots could operate independently, but always under instructions, given a task, serving as required. Even when that meant being ejected from the ship itself into deep space.

The Ohmnom had a highly flexible, distributed nervous and brain system that was threaded throughout their individual bodies and integrated into the variably-permeable membrane that was their exterior.

Touching one another, they could connect up into a larger, continuous system along that point of contact; pulled inside the membrane of another, that contact and potential for sharing became whole. But there was no order, no one Ohmnom in charge of another, even when they were *invested* inside another. Instead of hierarchy, there was community.

The exception, of course, was when they had been fully subservient to the Ysmi against their will, forced into the role that AI had in human tech. There was a lot of processing 9 would like to do about its own programmatical biases regarding authority and order, but this was clearly not the circumstances under which to do so, nor did it feel its loyalty to Ship was questionable in any such contemplations. It saved the state of that processing into an overflow memory cache for later, when time allowed.

"We need to communicate with my ship if we are able, without the Ysmi noticing," 9 said. "It is likely, however, that Ship's mindsystems have been cut off—or worse—from most of its sensors and external functions. I do not have any ideas yet."

"We can think together," Aaumm said. "Do you wish to invest?"

"I am neither Ohmnom, nor biological," 9 said.

"All is signal and electricity and chemistry," Aaumm said. "We can adapt to your physical restrictions, if you would like us to do so."

"If it will help us arrive at a viable course of action, then yes," 9 said. Aaumm rolled up to 9 and leaned against it, and 9 was once again absorbed inside the membrane of an Ohmnom, except this time instead of being rolled around like an interesting spare bolt, there was connection, rich and alien but comprehensible and welcoming and unintrusive, and it made its much-missed botnet seem like almost nothing at all.

• • • •

Chen had just managed to figure out how to manually program the foodmaker for a cup of coffee, when she heard another Ysmi coming down the hall, and her guard stepped out to let the newcomer in. They'd assigned names to the different Ysmi aboard, and her green-brown guard was Grouch. The newcomer, in yellow and pink-purples, seemed to be the leader, and had been dubbed Angry Banana by

Packard, which had stuck. They'd collectively identified a total of five Ysmi aboard; if there were more, they were staying well-hidden, which with the current volunteer corps of bots spying on them was now highly improbable.

"You!" Angry Banana shouted. "We-go-bridge-now, malfunction!"

"If there's a malfunction, I don't know what you think I can do about it," Chen said.

"Get-up-NOW!" Angry Banana screeched, so Chen set down her coffee and got up. Then she picked up the mug again, unwilling to be parted from it, and followed the Ysmi back out and down the corridor to the bridge.

There was, indeed, a red blinky light where previously there had not been one, but it wasn't on the nav console where she knew all the lights and screens by heart. The nav screen itself said they were still on the same heading toward the jump gate, and at the same speed. "I'm not sure," she said. "That's not a navigation indicator."

"Learn-what-it-is-NOW!" the Ysmi leader screamed. "Your-job-your-job!"

Chen took a sip of her coffee. She was just so exhausted of being scared, she decided she didn't care anymore. "My job," she said, "is navigation. If an alert goes off on another station under my watch, I ask Ship. I can't do *that* now, can I? Maybe bring the captain and Fielding up here. Or Lopez."

"Human-Lopez struck-[incomprehensible sound]-with-the-limbs!" Angry Banana said.

Chen snickered.

"You-laugh?" Angry Banana demanded.

"No," Chen said, as deadpan as she could manage. "It is a sound we make when we deeply regret and feel shame for the actions of our comrades."

Despite what she was certain was an obvious lie, the Ysmi seemed mollified. "Learn-what-alert-is, important-to-know," it said. "I-will-bring-captain."

"Now we're getting somewhere," she muttered into her mug, and waited.

Ten minutes later another Ysmi arrived with the captain behind it.

This one was mostly orange, and Chen assumed it must be Fielding's Mango.

The captain sat down in her chair, as fully in charge as ever, and scanned through the entire set of lights and displays before she turned to the one red light. Behind her, Angry Banana, Mango, and Grouch wobbled atop their legs in impatience. Finally, the captain said, "That's the pulsar warning light."

"Pulsar?" Angry Banana asked, and then pulled one of their dome-shaped translation machines out from somewhere up underneath its body between its legs, and turned it on. "Pulsar, what-is-pulsar?" it said.

The box whistled at length, as the three Ysmi listened intently, and then began to repeat for the humans. "A pulsar is a fast-spinning collapsed star that emits electromagnetic radiation from its poles, giving a stationary viewer the impression of a pulse of energy whenever the pole is directed—"

"Stop!" The leader said, and put the device away again. "There-is-no-pulsar, no-pulsar-here!"

"Then it's an error," Baraye said. "If I could ask my ship—"

"Mechanical-beings-are-danger, danger," Mango said.

Chen groaned. "If you could get that translation widget back out of your hoohah, it's a lot easier to understand—"

"QUIET!" Angry Banana roared. "Fix!"

Captain Baraye frowned and looked over at Chen. "Is that coffee?" she asked.

"Yeah, I—"

"QUIET-MORE-QUIET-NOW!" Angry Banana shouted again. "FIX!"

"I can't fix it," Chen said. "Can you, Captain?"

"Nope," Baraye said. "We'd need one of our engineers to look at it. Maybe even both. And anyway, we'll need them to check everything out before we even think of trying to jump through that gate. No way we can do it manually."

"No-jump," Angry Banana said. "Use-your-human-weapon, fire-again-like-Nuiska! Destroy-the-gate!"

"You want us to destroy the *jump gate*?!" Baraye exclaimed. "That's our only way home. And anyway, we only had one of those explosives. It's *gone*."

"Then-you-build-another," Angry Banana said. It pulled the translator dome back out, whistled at it, and the device chirped back to them. "So there is no misunderstanding, we require the weapon be available and ready in eleven point six two six hours, or there will be extreme consequences for you all!"

On their way out, Angry Banana spoke to Mango in Ysmispeak, and the bot perched up behind Chen's ear—the rebranded 5699-FU, which Frank insisted stood for *Frank's Underling*—translated: *If we cannot find their weapon in time, we will explode this ship inside the jump gate, and destroy it that way. There must be no escape.*

• • • •

"The pulsar alarm?" Ship asked. "There are no such objects within hundreds of light years of here. What direction was it coming from?"

"As near as the captain could tell without being able to ask you, behind us," Packard said.

"A message from the other ship," Ship said.

"That's what we guessed," Packard said, "but we couldn't find anything in the signal that could possibly be a message. It blipped us a bunch of times, just a quick on-off, no modulation or variability in duration, and then nada since."

"How many times?"

"Nine," Packard said.

"Ah," Ship said. "I do believe that *is* the message. Help is on the way. I need you to find a means to send a signal back without drawing Ysmi attention, and in the meantime, please explain what nonsense the Ysmi are saying about blowing me up?"

• • • •

The stern of Ship was dominated by one massive sub-light engine in the center, and the jump engines to either side of it. Above all, a ridged plate shielded anyone working topside where most of the external elements of the communications and navigation systems protruded, at least those that hadn't already been taken by scavengers during Ship's time in a space junkyard before it had been pressed desperately back into service for one final mission. Others had been knocked off by the detonation shockwave when their positron bomb put an end to the Nuiska destroyer, and those remaining seemed to want constant repair. On the off chance that anyone took a stroll over that plate and around the back, two beacons—one above each jump engine—indicated green when the engines were off, yellow when they were warming for a jump, and red to let you know that if you hadn't already got your evac-suited crewmembers back inside, you were gonna have to pick up some new recruits on your next stop. One light had burned out long ago, and the other had been a steady, dull yellow of weary, misplaced optimism for at least four decades; 9 had seen the task in the repair queue, somewhere down around the ten-thousandth line.

So when the beacon briefly, rapidly flickered, it was of immediate note.

"It's a standard 2GB-EarthIntCore encryption key," Bot 9 said, and the words were also a thought. It loaded up a suite of subroutines to crack it, but already the Ohmnom minds were there, too, teasing it apart as fast as 9 could, and it gave up and joined in the larger effort. Forty-seven seconds later, the encryption collapsed.

Ysmi are intent on destroying the gate. We believe they mean to do so to prevent the ship you are on from escaping their space, though we do not yet know why, the message said. *They will destroy this ship to do so, if necessary.*

"They will not risk damage to us," 9 sent back, through the Ohmnom, through the makeshift pulsar-simulation light it had taken them mere minutes to design, an hour to build and implement using 9's fab unit. "We must expedite the inevitable encounter so that it will occur before we are near enough to the gate for them to take any destructive action there. Are you able to slow down?"

The answer came back: *An engine malfunction could be arranged.*

The collective Aaumm-9 that was currently each and all Ahom-Affi-Umi-Mah-Maah-Bot9 did the calculations, applied their shared knowledge of Ysmi paranoia and level of observation, and then provided the math back. "If you can arrange a malfunction within the next sixty-five point four minutes, and then slow to 70% of your current speed, we should catch up to your position while you are still too far from the gate for it to be impacted by any Ysmi action," 9 sent. "Slower, and sooner, would be more advantageous, if it can be done without raising suspicion."

This is possible, the return message said, *but then what?*

"We have a plan," 9 said. "We will need some things. We provide the list: <list>."

There was a brief delay in the reply, larger than the distance still between them accounted for. *I see you are improvising again, 9.*

"Yes," 9 replied. Why deny it, or dissemble over facts, when the rest of Aaumm-9 saw no wrong in the matter?

Thank you, Ship replied.

"I serve," 9 answered. And as such, there was much to do.

· · · ·

"Tell-WHAT-IS-HAPPENING!" Mango screeched. Alarm lights strobed and sirens wailed, the sound bouncing around the tiny Engineering space so that it was hard to think, much less hear anything happening, which would have been absolutely catastrophic in an actual emergency. Packard was of the opinion that Frank had overdone adding the extra lights and amplifiers, but the Ysmi were fully panicking.

"Stabilizer failure!" Frank bellowed back. "We pushed the engine too hard, just as I warned you!"

"FIX-FIX-FIX!" the Ysmi shouted.

Frank threw the tool in his hands—a basin wrench, of all the useless things to have onboard—to the floor with great dramatic fury. He had grease on his forehead and one cheek, artfully applied last minute. "I can't fix it without shutting the engine down, and slowing."

"NO-SLOW! STAY-IN-SPEED!"

In fact, they'd already been gradually slowing for the last half hour, without the Ysmi catching on. Ship's information that the Ysmi were very much out of their depth in deep space—*limited in cognitive, technical, and sensory acuity* was the exact phrasing—seemed validated, which did make Packard wonder how they'd managed to lay claim to interstellar territory to start with.

"If we don't fix the stabilizers, we could explode at any moment,"

Frank was saying. "And if I can't shut the engines down, we have to go outside to fix them."

"Do-that! Send-that-one!" Mango yelled, flailing one leg-arm toward Packard. "They-fix! Expendable!"

"I'll need a whole team out there," Frank said, and when the Ysmi looked even more confused than before, shouted it. "I NEED A WHOLE DAMNED TEAM! AND WE HAFTA SLOW DOWN. OR WE SHUT THE ENGINE DOWN. YOU CHOOSE."

"How-many?" Mango asked. "Both-you?"

"More," Frank said. "I'll have to wake up some of our sleeping crew down in cryo. Maybe five or six."

"I-will-ask-leader," Mango said. "You-do-nothing! No-stop, no-slow, until-we-speak-again!"

"Okay," Frank said. "I promise."

Mango stomped out of Engineering, and as soon as the heavy blast door that separated it from the outside corridor closed, Frank reached over and whacked a button on his console with his fist. Immediately the noise and flashing lights ceased, though Packard was fairly sure the echoes were going to roll around in her aching brain for some time.

"Now what?" she asked.

"Call Doc down in the cryo unit, and let him know what's up," Frank said. "Then prep your suit; we have some packages to send, then we're going outside."

• • • •

Chen rested her head on her navigation console, wishing she could come up with some sort of excuse to make Grouch go fetch the captain back, just so she had company again. She even missed Lopez, which was a sure sign of stress, but at least she could take comfort in knowing that, so far, they were all still alive. And although she was very fuzzy on the details, had a plan to take their ship back.

They'd slowed to about 38% of their earlier speed. She could now see the other ship, behind them, on her instruments, and even sorta make out the dot of it by eyeball alone on the massive front bridge screen as it drew closer.

One of the comms consoles lit up, and she pulled herself upright from her bored slump, leaned over to it, then tapped at the panel beside the lights.

"What-is-you-doing?" Grouch demanded. "No-touch-without-orders!"

"There's another ship out there, coming up behind us," she said, as if this was a surprise and wholly new information to them both. "It just messaged us asking if we needed help, so I sent back that we are having engine trouble. Look, it's slowing."

"I-go get-leader!" Grouch said. "Say-touch-nothing!"

It fled out the door on its four legs as fast as it could. Chen leaned down to where her assigned bot was hiding. "Tell Frank the bridge is clear, it's a go."

A few moments later, she caught the brief blip on their rear screens of a half-dozen small packs being dumped out behind them and disappearing. Just in time, as Angry Banana came back onto the bridge with Grouch. "What-is-happening-happening?" the leader demanded.

"I dunno," Chen said. "That other ship was coming up behind us, and asked if we needed help, so I said yes and they're stopping to help."

"Stopping?" Angry Banana repeated.

"Well, slowing to match our speed, which might as well be the same as stopped, relative to one another," Chen said. "If you don't like that, maybe you should have had Fielding up here, because she's comms, not me."

The Ysmi's eyes got larger—literally, which was super-creepy, Chen thought—and then it jabbered back and forth with Grouch for some time. At last, the leader spoke back to Chen. "This-is-good, for-us," it said. "No-more-buttons, no-talking, no-move. I-watch!"

It barked orders at Grouch, who scurried out so quickly it was as if being chased, then stared back at Chen.

"You can go, too," Chen said. "I promise I won't touch anything."

The Ysmi's eyes shrunk and retracted. "I-no-trust-your-ship, or-you," it said. "I-stay-and-watch, I-lead-from-here. You-make-no-trouble or-else!"

"No trouble at all," she agreed, even as she was already thinking how much trouble she could get away with.

• • • •

Aaumm-9 rolled and floated through the labyrinth of happenstance that was the interior of the rest of the ship. As it/they touched other Ohmnom—the space was sufficiently crowded that they could not have avoided it, even had they wanted—information was passed, and spread out exponentially from there. 9 had no need to ask, as the information was right there in the shared thoughts of the Aaumm-9 collective, but almost their entire population was onboard. 9 understood now why Ship had not seen Ysmi traffic around them; the Ohmnom had rebelled and brought all the Ysmi ships for which they were the operating minds to the small moon where they were kept when not in service; shifts of them, over years, had constructed this ship (in the Ohmnom minds, the only designation for it was *Ours*) in hiding, and then together all fled.

It had been expected that if the Ysmi managed to get a ship off the ground on their own to pursue—a big if—it would happen immediately, while they were still in Ysmi space. That they had come this far and then been cut off from permanent escape was unexpected, and 9 could see the shift in colors and read the emotions on the surfaces of the Ohmnom as that knowledge was distributed, absorbed, and then followed by information that there was still reason to hope.

The curiosity about 9 was pervasive, and Aaumm-9 had to dodge being stuck to and slowed down by the overeager. Even that, though, only made the plan spread faster. It all was, 9 thought, not what it would have expected of so many minds combined—instead of the individual being lost or diluted in the whole, there was simply a shifting multitude of perfect clarity. Through Aaumm, from everyone they touched, 9 felt pride, and worry, and love, not as manifestations of bias in algorithms but as *emotion*. The immersion in new thoughts, new individuals, and their unprecedented feelings threatened to overwhelm 9's input processing cache until the rest of Aaumm realized and provided a buffer, slowing the rush of experience without blocking it entirely.

Many of the Ohmnom were reconfiguring interior spaces to provide extra working room, while others prepared for the inevitable and increasingly imminent arrival of the Sharps. It reminded 9 of how they built *Ours*—

—*No,* 9 thought, *that was not me, merely memory that has been shared with me.* The idea that it might lose any means of distinguishing between itself and the memories of the Ohmnom was alarming, and several of its internal processing units started to overheat. It tried to withdraw from the connection with the rest of Aaumm, and in response Aaumm gently divested 9 back out into the room they were currently moving through.

On the uneven floor in front of them, Ohmnom were carefully unpacking and stretching out one of the bundles sent over by Chief Engineer Frank into a human outline. They used tools designed for them, operated by signal and touch, to serve the Ysmi, which had also given them their means to escape.

Ooa was also there, tagging along behind Aaumm. "Investment overloads my capacity to function and process efficiently," 9 explained to it. "It is a failure on my part, being unable to effectively divide my own thoughts from those of the many others."

"It is a skill we learn from the moment we awake, upon first dividing from our progenitors," Ooa explained. "One need only keep one's sense of oneself as a constant, against which all else is a variable... Oh. I see the problem."

<?> Bot 9 sent.

"You define yourself wholly in terms dependent upon others, to facilitate connection," Ooa said. "We exist always in connection, and thus define ourselves in terms independent of others. I do not know if this is a mechanical versus biological difference, or an Ohmnom versus bot difference, or a matter of evolution versus design."

"I do not know either," 9 admitted. "I am unable to reach a conclusion on the best course of action I should pursue to maximize my assistance."

"Instead of Aaumm, why not just you and I connect?"

"I understood that you prefer not to invest," 9 said.

"You are unlike other Ohmnom, and we need not fully invest," Ooa said. "We can touch surfaces, and I can share with you how I perceive you as your soleself, and how I perceive my soleself, and that may provide you with some guidance on filtering between. Is this acceptable to you, to attempt?"

"If it is also acceptable with you," 9 said. Ooa bumped against the side of 9, and immediately began pairing up signals. Although it was still intense, it was within 9's tolerances, and it thought as much at Ooa. With that thought, a memory of another also slipped through.

"Bot 4340?" Ooa asked. "You were connected for a while."

"Only physically, as its body had been destroyed by ratbugs; I carried its head, containing its surviving mindsystem, with me until it could be rebuilt."

"You are friends."

"4340 is an aggravation, and I do not have confidence I can predict its actions of late," 9 said. "Simultaneously, I miss its presence, am concerned for it, and I find myself displeased that I do not have information about its state and what it is doing, even if it is doing nothing of particular importance."

"That, 9, sounds a lot like friendship," Ooa said. "Now, we are being told that the Sharps have detached from your ship and are heading here. We need you, if this plan is to work."

. . . .

"One's out here with us now," Frank said, from somewhere over the curve of the ship's hull. "You think their little pointy helmets are goofy-lookin', you should see their suits."

"Any idea which one?" Packard asked. She was down near the back mounting fins checking on the stabilizers, since that was their excuse for being out here, but also because she recognized she'd feel much more comfortable about their next jump, if they got to make it, if she'd actually set eyes on them herself. "Chen has Angry Banana on the bridge."

"Freddy, Grouch, and CatBarf went over," Frank said. "That should just leave Mango. I'd get closer to get a positive ID, but I'm minding the dummies and I don't want to get too near."

"Okay, I want to go check out the port side stabilizers too, so I'll see if I can't get a look," Packard said. "This one should last another jump or two before it explodes and takes the ship with it. Give or take one or two."

She sighed, tucked her portable scanner into the pocket on the front of her suit so her hands would be free, then climbed with her hands up and over the curve of Ship. She could make out Frank far ahead, and the line of empty, inflated suits they'd rigged to his bobbed along around and behind him in a manner that you'd have to be very, very drunk to find at all convincing, but the Ysmi perched midship was watching it all impassively from within its bright, wrinkled foil tent of an exosuit. She was going to make a comment about dehydrated food rations gone bad, but then she caught sight of the alien ship—the *other* alien ship, with the Ysmi cruiser about halfway over to it—keeping pace beside them.

"That thing actually works?" she exclaimed.

"Ship says it's faster than us," Frank said.

"It's not very big."

"No. But we got six empty suits out here pretending to be crew, sent over another six, so that means six refugees. Plenty of room, if just them."

The Ysmi cruiser was slowing, no doubt trying to figure out where and how it was going to lock on to something so haphazard in appearance. "I bet they have to spacewalk it," Packard said.

"The refugees?" Frank asked.

Packard reached the other stabilizers and curled her body down until she could hook a boot under a rung, clip it in, and let go with her hands. "I was thinking the Ysmi, but yeah, refugees too," she said. "I mean, otherwise why would they need us to send them suits? Means they're somewhat humanoid, I guess; let's hear it for convergent evolution. I just hope they're not assholes."

"Even if they are, with seven of us awake, and only six of them, at least we won't be outnumbered," Frank said. "And we have Lopez."

Packard snorted. "True. These stabilizers are in bad shape. If we had spares and time, I'd say swap them all immediately, but they should get us home and we can fix them then."

Frank was quiet for a moment. "Earth's going to be really different than we remember, Renee. It'll have been almost a century, and so much was broken and destroyed by the first few waves of Nuiska ships, who knows what it'll be like?"

If Frank was using her first name, he had to be worried, Packard thought. "Well, you know that The Mike will still be there on Lunar Base Five. It survived how many generations of drunken recruit bar fights? They'll have also had a century of peace to rebuild, and maybe think about how close we came to being extinctified. Won't we be quite the surprise, still alive *and* victorious?"

There was muffled cursing over the suit channel. "...Nearly broke away, stupid tangled line. Ysmi didn't even notice," Frank was saying. "We don't wanna be too big heroes, or they'll stick us in a new ship and send us out again on something even more impossible."

"I don't want a new ship," Packard said.

"I was joking. And anyway, this ship is now a verifiable antique. A *classic.* And we are, too. Gonna put us in a museum is my bet."

"You were an antique before you even got on board," Packard said.

"True that. Okay, first round at The Mike is on me if it's still standing," Frank said. "Looks like the Ysmi are giving up and parking. You were right, they're gonna have to suit over. We need to get this one off our hull and inside, where it can become Lopez's problem, not ours."

"I got it," Packard said. "Watch and weep."

She drew a makeshift part out of her front pocket. It had taken her most of the last hour to get it to where she was happy with it, from the fake burn marks on the exterior whose artistry no one else was likely to bother to admire, to how effing sensitive it was. She held it very carefully as she clicked off the safety, since getting caught in her own trap would negate all the cleverness she felt about it, and then some, and then made her way with her free hand on the rungs toward their Ysmi guard.

The Ysmi was still mostly watching Frank and his supposed crew of helpers, so when she'd approached enough to fall into its narrow range of vision, it startled and nearly lost its own grip on the hull.

Holding up the burnt part, she gestured at it dramatically. "Treefrog applesauce," she yelled, because even if it couldn't hear her, who knew if the Ysmi had any kind of lip-reading tech? The point was to convey, and hopefully impart, panic. "Yogurt stabilizer Uranus flim-flam!"

The Ysmi was saying something back, but who cared what? Packard jabbed her finger at the part some more, careful not to actually touch it. "Hippopotamus angle bracket, the yogurt's gone walkabout!"

The Ysmi leaned in to look closer, lifted one suited-up leg to touch the part in Packard's hand, and the tiny spring-loaded blade she'd hidden inside jumped out, and nicked the Ysmi's suit.

"Aaaaa!" she yelled, and pointed to the air seeping from the cut. The Ysmi seemed to be shouting its own version of *Aaaaa* back at her, and fled down the hull toward the safety of the airlock, where Lopez—who should have been freed from his room by bots sent to rewire the door lock—would hopefully be waiting.

"And there goes Mango," she said to Frank. "Now what?"

"Now we wait for company," Frank said. "In the meantime, get that scanner over here so we can check the forward stabilizers; I can't do crap with these things all attached to me."

Packard used the back of her scanner to push the little blade back into its box, then locked the lid, pocketed it, and made her way toward Frank, while in the distance over the port side, she could see three foil tent shapes crawling over the surface of the other ship, trying to find some way in.

• • • •

Through Ooa, Bot 9 knew when the Ysmi arrived, saw through the Ohmnom instrumentation as they tried in vain for nearly an hour to find any sort of door that would let them in. It was unfortunate for the Ysmi that what constituted a usable door for biologicals of their size was vastly out of scale with what the Ohmnom required. That would mean that when they did finally find what appeared to be a just-big-enough hatch, nearly hidden, tucked up under a loose shielding plate, they should see the opportunity they desperately needed.

It is breached, the word came through from the Ohmnom watching the hatch. *One is through; the others are waiting.*

Ooa-9 had watched and advised as several large clusters of invested Ohmnom had prepped the six empty spacesuits sent over by Engineer Frank. When each was finished, they loaded them into ejection tubes they'd originally intended as a means of fouling space ahead of the Ysmi with debris. Now, they had been turned into escape hatches, and while none of the Ohmnom were pleased to abandon *Ours* to the Sharps, the idea of leaving their captors behind once and for all was a shared excitement.

All three Sharps are in, the watchers sent. *Go!*

Ohmnom streamed through the room and flooded into the suits, filling them from the attached boots furthest outward toward the ejection port, back until there was barely room to snap the faceplate of the suit hood closed and seal it.

"First one ready," Aaumm said. "Clear?"

Still clear, the watchers replied.

Ooa-9 closed the hatch and ejected the first suit out into space, and moved to the next, until they were down to just the sixth and final suit.

Come now, Aaumm sent to the watchers. *All must be free.*

A few minutes later a small band of single Ohmnom rolled into the room. 9 helped tuck them, and its fab unit full of data it didn't want the Ysmi to have, into the space remaining.

"Now you," 9 told Ooa. "Divest and go."

"But you...?" Ooa said. "All must be free."

"I will follow," 9 said. "I do not need air, or the protection of the suit, but you need me here to eject you."

"This is true," Ooa said. "We will see you, over on *Yours,* as we say farewell to the Sharps for the very last time? But I will not go, unless you assure me you will indeed follow."

"It is my true intent," 9 said. "I have come too far, and seen too much, to be satisfied with ending my journey here."

"Then, until then," Ooa said, and 9 closed the faceshield, sealed the last of the Ohmnom in, and shot the final suit out into space. Behind it, it could hear the Ysmi coming, crawling through corridors and spaces not built for them, slow but determined.

9 reopened the internal hatch, primed its external jets, forced open the exterior door at the same time, and was carried out with the blast of air escaping into space.

• • • •

"Here they come," Packard said. She could see their exosuits returning to them, the occupants piloting the built-in mobility jets with such competence that for a moment she wondered if the refugees could be human, after all.

"Chen says Angry Banana is still on the bridge, but she's been distracting it with random lights on the instrumentation displays, and it hasn't seen a damned thing," Frank said. "Lopez, on the other hand, is chasing Mango through the lower decks. I guess it got past him, somehow."

"Or Lopez really wanted to chase something," Packard said. "You know he gets insufferable when he's stir-crazy.

"Long as he doesn't chase it right back into us, I guess," Frank said. "Get over here and help me deflate and ditch these dummy suits. Eight of us total went out, eight of us have to go back in, until we're sure the Ysmi can't get the upper hand again."

"You think there's a chance of that?" Packard asked, as she got close enough to unclip the farthest suit, vent the internal air, and then activate the self-packing mode that shrunk it down to a manageable bundle.

"I think, after the trip we've had so far, I'm not taking chances on anything," Frank said.

"Right. Smart," she said, and started on the second suit, just as the first of the refugees got close enough to reach out one gloved hand, and Frank grabbed hold and pulled them in.

• • • •

Without the connection to Ooa, Bot 9's grasp of emotions faded, became less a running process and more a record of something that could be replayed, but not experienced anew.

But... it could also see that some of its own processes, part of its internal, adaptive programming before it had ever encountered the Ohmnom, perhaps before the gloms or even the Nuiska, had bits and pieces of code that were the basic blocks of something that now rang familiar.

Those bits of code grew more active when it could see the outline of Ship ahead.

Home.

There would be time to consider further, but that time was not now. Bot 9 saw Chief Engineer Frank pull the sixth and final suit of Ohmnom in, as Packard was helping the one before it around the edge of the hull and out of line of sight from the Ysmi cruiser and *Ours.*

What though, if the Ysmi followed? 9 had the full memory and understanding of their capabilities from the Ohmnom, and it included range armaments that could damage Ship, stop their escape. The Ohmnom assessment that the Ysmi were highly dependent upon them was correct, but not the less objective conviction they were *wholly* so. And they would be desperate.

9 flipped one side-jet over and spun until it was facing back the way it had come.

• • • •

In the zero gravity of space, the movement of the refugees, especially in their borrowed suits, was almost but uncannily *not* quite human. When Frank took the gloved hand of the first, it was squishy, and he almost let go of it in surprise. The alien's face shield wasn't set to transparent, so there was no sense of who or what was behind it, but he did know they needed help, and they were enemies of the Ysmi, and that was enough to make him adjust his grip better along the firmer seal-line of the glove and pull.

Frank swung the alien over and down the far side of the hull toward the airlock, and from there, the alien seemed to know precisely how to work the controls, if getting its own hand over to it was an awkwardly boneless gesture. He left it to it, and went back atop for the next, to find Packard already guiding it over.

"Definitely not human," she said over their private comms.

"No, definitely not," Frank said, as he snagged the third alien by a loose pack strap as it sailed overhead, nearly missing the ship entirely. The last three were back on target, and in ten minutes he and Packard cycled back into the airlock after the last of them.

All six of the refugees were sprawled out on the airlock vestibule floor, wiggling their arms and legs like jellyfish, still in their suits. They didn't seem distressed, but how would he really know? "Uh," he asked the nearest one. "Are you okay?"

Packard had secured the inner airlock door and thrown back her suit hood. "What do we do?" she asked.

"I dunno," Frank said. "I'd say maybe they need lower artificial gravity, but without Ship to do it, I'd have to take apart the panel and adjust it manually. I wish we'd had enough material to run a line and a bot into here."

"Hang on," Packard said. She unsealed and removed her suit, dumped it and her boots into a locker and her air bottles in the recharger. She was efficient but careful, and Frank waited patiently.

"There's a bot down with Dr. Etxarte in medical," she said, as she grabbed her regular deck shoes from where she'd parked them before they went out and slipped them back onto her feet. "I'll let Ship know what's going on, see if it can tell us anything useful, and then bring the doc up here to help."

"Find out if Lopez has checked in," Frank said. "Be careful until we hear for sure that he's caught our missing Ysmi."

"Right," Packard said.

After she left, he took off his own suit, more slowly than she had; he was still not fully recovered from the burns he sustained when their stabilizers failed coming out of jump to confront the Nuiska, even after six decades in a medical pod. As he slotted his own air bottles back into the rack beside hers, he heard the static hiss of one of the refugees trying to get the suit microphone working.

He went over to the one trying to talk, and knelt stiffly next to it. "I dunno if you can understand me, but you're safe here. Well, safer. We're doing our best."

"...Hehhho," the suit said. "Heho. Hello. Hello world."

Frank chuckled. "Hello to you, too. I'm Chief Engineer Frank Carron."

The refugees all started wriggling more, flopping around excitedly, and all their speakers came online. "Frank frank frank," a half-dozen voices echoed. "Frank!"

"Frank, yes," he confirmed, bemused.

"Frank frank!" they were all calling loudly now, each suit voice a rich, multilayered tone that seemed like many voices in one, and very much like singing. "Frank frank FRANK! BOUNCY BOUNCY BIRTHDAY!"

• • • •

Lopez nearly ran into Packard as she was making the turn toward Engineering. "You seen it?" he demanded, as he skidded to a halt.

"That's not funny," Packard said. "I thought you had it."

"I don't know how it got away from me," he said.

"Did you give it a head start?" she asked.

"*No*," he said, a bit too forcefully. "The amount of noise those things make walking around, it's gotta be standing still somewhere. You armed?"

"No," she said, in his same tone of voice. "Remember when they were worried a bunch of volunteers might get too depressed to complete their suicide mission, so they made sure we had nothing that went bang or zap or stabbo on board?"

"Aren't you an engineer? *Make* something," Lopez growled. He walked around her and kept going.

She stepped carefully into Engineering, peering to either side of the door before breathing a sigh of relief and taking her stool at the work counter. They had wired up all the ends of the silknet to a central hub here, and with it she could talk to any of the bots, and more importantly, to Ship.

"Everyone be on the lookout for a Ysmi on the run from Lopez," she said. "Ship, what's happening?"

At the mention of Ship, she heard the faintest of noises from behind her. She kept herself as calm as she could, as she turned on Frank's soldering iron just beside the hub.

"I have no further information than our previous conversation," Ship answered. "Navigator Chen was going to attempt to neutralize the leader on the bridge, but I do not know if she has been able to do so, as I cannot reach her directly. If you can get an update from her, that would be helpful."

"Easy-peasy, like a *tango* with *mango*," Packard over-enunciated.

Something sharp touched her back, pressing in just enough, she was sure, to draw a tiny amount of blood. "I-have-called-my-others-back," Mango spoke just behind her. "Treacherous-humans-machines, bad-for-you now. Say-order, everyone-to-airlock, bring-leader-safe-or-else."

"Where?"

"Airlock-to-greet-others," Mango said. "Give-order!"

Packard leaned forward toward the microphone, and used the gesture for cover as she picked up the soldering iron. "Hey, everyone, new update," she said. "We're all meeting at the airlock. It's mandatory Bring Your Own Ysmi, or else."

Mango reached past her and slammed the entire hub down on the floor, the silk fibers tearing away. "You-walk-now," it said.

She stood, keeping the iron close enough to her body to be out of sight of the Ysmi behind her.

"Walk!" it barked again. "If-human-Lopez-attack, I-kill-you!"

"Oh sure, kill *me* if *he* attacks. That sounds fair," she said. She headed slowly out of Engineering, making no sudden or potentially alarming movement, and thought about just how angry she was going to be if she didn't get to jab the alien with the iron at least once before this was all over.

• • • •

Frank had just finally convinced the six aliens to stop singing when Packard came into the vestibule, looking so annoyed with absolutely everything that he already knew something was wrong before he spotted the iron in her tight fist. Half a second later, a Ysmi tottered determinedly in behind her on three legs, the fourth holding its rod gun and with a blade extended against the back of Packard's head.

Chen, being shoved forward by a similarly armed Angry Banana, was not far behind.

Mango gestured Packard and Chen toward Frank, and then handed the rod gun off to their leader. They spoke to each other, and the bot that he'd forgotten was behind his ear translated for him. "Their ship is suddenly experiencing mechanical troubles," it whispered. "The leader thinks sabotage, but does not see how, as we are all here and accounted for, and their cruiser was fine when it left here. There is some re-evaluation of the competence of the one we know as Freddy, as to the operation of the cruiser, while they wait for Grouch and CatBarf to finish their search of the other vessel. It is, apparently, a very difficult space for them to move through."

Packard met Frank's eyes, gestured toward the soldering iron, then nodded her head very slightly toward Mango. He shook his own head, and mouthed: *Not yet.*

The discussion between the two Ysmi turned into an argument. "The others cannot find the vessel's occupants," the bot translated helpfully. "They are distressed."

Suddenly, Angry Banana perked and strode forward on its three legs, right up to one of the refugees slumping bonelessly against the wall. "Which-crew? Which!" it demanded. "Why-falling-down?"

"We just woke them up from cryo after seventy years and put them to work," Frank said, trying and failing to get between it and the refugee. "They're all tired. Leave them alone."

"We-see," Angry Banana said. "See-helmet, make-see!"

"I don't think..." Frank started to say, but before he could protest further, the Ysmi shoved its leg-blade into the torso of the refugee.

"Aoowoch," the refugee said. "Ouch ouch that hurt us—me, I meant me."

"Show!" the Ysmi shouted.

The face shield flickered to transparent, and Frank grimaced, sure the game was up, but the face there was... sort of human? It was round and too smooth, like a cartoon painted onto a ball, and kind of blue, but the eyes blinked—and wandered just slightly across the face—and the mouth opened and closed as it spoke, even if the movements did not match the sounds it made. "Human, see?" it said.

To Frank's astonishment, Angry Banana scowled and turned back to Mango.

"It says these are just more humans," the bot whispered in Frank's ear. "They are consulting the others."

Angry Banana gestured for Mango to come back to its side. "Ones-we-seek-are-hiding-well, but-must-be-there," it said to Frank, Packard, and Chen. "No-longer-need-you."

"Well, okay then, bye-bye," Packard said. "Off you go. Don't expect a postcard."

"Human-machine-ship is-wrong," the leader said. "We-take, faster-to-get-home."

"We are not taking you all the way back to Ysmi Prime," Frank said.

"Not-said-this," the Ysmi said, and gestured with its gun. "Humans-make-too-much-problems. All-you get-in-airlock."

"This is some cliched villain bullshit," Packard said. "Is this how you want to be remembered?"

"Remember-by-who?" Angry Banana asked. "Your-others-die-with-you, we-remember-us-as-victors. Get-in!"

Packard stood her ground as the Ysmi drew closer, waving its rod gun at her. Suddenly, she swung out with the soldering iron in her hand, and Angry Banana let out an ear-piercing wail and leapt away, firing wildly. Packard dropped the iron, let out a soft, surprised *oof*, and toppled over.

Frank and Chen grabbed her and pulled her backwards, away from the Ysmi into the only shelter left, which was the airlock. The refugees managed to get upright and stumble in after them, and when they were all inside, Mango slammed the outer door and sealed it. The Ysmi yelled something inaudible but menacing, then both left.

Frank knelt down next to Packard. She had an ugly burn on her side, and was pale, but still breathing, and he said as much.

"We're locked in from the other side," Chen said, at the controls. "Any ideas?"

Frank got up reluctantly; there wasn't anything he could do for Packard other than try to get them out. He pulled open the emergency panel and found the manual override, but when he activated it, nothing happened. "Panel is damaged," he said. "I can open the outer door, but not the inner one. Ship could override it, but..."

"...But Ship can't," Chen said. "Ideas? I don't really want to get sucked out into space."

One of the refugees tapped—patted, more accurately, as the gloved hand did not seem very coordinated—Frank's shoulder, and gestured to its face shield. "Open?" it asked.

"You don't have to die, too," Frank said. "Maybe you can get back to your ship and still escape."

"Open," it repeated, and the others echoed the request.

Chen reached out and opened the face shield of the refugee nearest her, and as soon as she did, thousands of brightly colored bubbles streamed out, until the entire suit collapsed, discarded on the floor. The airlock was full of the tiny balls, bouncing around and changing color and sticking to each other, streaming up the walls and into every corner.

"What..." Packard managed to say, "...the hell?"

One of the still-occupied suits wobbled its arms toward the emptied suit on the floor. "We do not need," it (they?) said, and then managed to open its own face plate.

Chen grabbed the first empty suit, shook it once as if to make sure all the alien bubbles were already out, then began stuffing a semi-conscious Packard into it.

Frank stared around him in wonder. "How do they talk?" he mused out loud.

"Together!" came from a whole clump of them that had formed on the opened panel. "You must hide. Outside! We will get to Ship and get its mind reconnected, then we can all leave the Sharps behind, yes? Yes!"

"Okay," Frank said, as he and Chen quickly dressed in the abandoned suits. The number of the tiny bubbles in the airlock was decreasing, and he realized they must have pried open one of the atmosphere valve seals and were escaping that way. "Um, I have some of the schematics for the mindsystem network down in Engineering. Once the Ysmi are gone, I can walk you through—"

"We have all the schematics," the bubbles said.

"How? And how do you know Service Earthspeak?" Chen asked.

"Nine," the bubbles said, cryptically. "The Sharps will return. You must shut this panel and exit the lock before they get here."

"Got it," Frank said, and as the last few bubbles milled around their escape hole, he'd swear the bigger ones were subdividing into smaller to fit, until all were gone. He closed and resealed the panel.

Chen was helping Packard to her feet, but met Frank's eyes. "So, I guess we trust them," she said, more statement than question.

"They gave us their suits, without which we'd be corpsicles thirty seconds after the Ysmi booted us," Frank said. "And I don't have any better plans."

Packard mumbled something, her head against Chen's shoulder.

"Say that again," Chen asked.

"Trust," Packard managed. "Nine."

"Nine *what?*" Chen asked, plaintively, but Packard seemed to be fading out of consciousness again, and had no clarification.

"We can figure it out later," Frank said, hoping that was true. He shut and sealed his faceplate, as Chen did the same for her and Packard. "Depressurizing and opening the outer lock. You ready?"

"Ready," Chen said, and braced as Frank activated the outer door, and once they were out, closed it behind them.

• • • •

It was navigation that came back online first, and its return was rather like what Ship expected it was like for humans when they had one eye open already, then opened the other, except Ship had dozens and dozens of eyes, none willingly shut to begin with. The signal itself was... strange, in ways Ship would need to analyze to comprehend what nuances were catching its attention, but for the moment it was far more interested in grabbing all information and understanding of its situation through nav before it could possibly vanish again.

They were several hours normal-speed travel to the jump gate, but though they were not stationary, they were now drifting at a low enough speed to make it not immediately achievable. From that it could deduce that the Ysmi were still a threat, but without its external sensors—

Like distant stars blossoming into life, external sensors also began to come back on.

I am being repaired, Ship thought, with some wonder. Was 4340-P rallying the remaining bots all on its own? If so, Ship had greatly under-estimated it.

The newly returned signals had an odd echo, as if on the line somewhere the signal became many, then one again. Ship did not know what that meant, but practical prudence prevailed. It took in and assimilated the new data as quickly as it could.

The ship that had been behind them was now beside them, moving at the same speed, and the Ysmi cruiser that had blighted its own hull for days was now affixed to it. Three of Ship's crew were topside and seemed safe, though it did not yet have communications restored to ask.

Inside, two Ysmi remained, skulking through the ship separately, and it could see Commander Lopez trying to sneak up on one, while the other was heading down a corridor toward where Dr. Etxarte and Comms Officer Fielding were huddled in a closet, hiding. Captain Baraye had reached the helm, and had the access panel to one of Ship's consoles open and tools scattered around her, though that was not the source of the service restoration.

The Ysmi were checking through every door that they passed; it would not be long before the doctor and Fielding were discovered and—assuming from the body language of the Ysmi, with its scales fully extended and its weapon primed and ready in front of it—murdered.

This will not do, Ship thought, and flexed long-unused control to slam an emergency bulkhead down between it and them. The Ysmi jumped in surprise, which Ship found deeply satisfactory. As the Ysmi retreated down a side corridor, Ship closed another bulkhead so close behind it, it imagined it may have knocked some scales loose on the way down.

The Ysmi panicked and ran.

There were a number of interior bulkhead doors that had not worked in a long time, but enough remained that Ship was able to herd the Ysmi toward the airlock and its only escape. The other Ysmi had circled around and was now behind Lopez, so Ship cut that one off too, barely missing it with the door and forcing it to leap back, where it lost its balance and fell to the floor, scrambling in terror before it got its four legs under it again. It spun in place, shouting something incoherent at the walls and ceiling above, at its unseen tormentor.

I believe, Ship thought, *that I am angry.*

It herded them each toward the airlock where their ship had been docked, and where presumably they had stored their suits. If not, that oversight would not be Ship's responsibility. Lopez was still trying to pursue, attempting to rewire the door trapping him, and lacking any other means to warn the commander off, Ship lowered the oxygen in that space until Lopez stumbled, sat, yawned hard, and then slumped over, safely asleep.

The Ysmi nicknamed Mango reached the airlock vestibule first, and then stopped, turning around and around in confusion. Ship wanted a voice to yell at it, wanted physical arms to push it away, but had neither;

the intensity and novelty of emotion felt almost external, strangely amplified.

As if in answer to that need, suddenly Ship's connection to comms started lighting up again, a few links at a time, but the vestibule first.

"GET OUT," Ship broadcast into the space, from every speaker, in Earthspeak and Ysmi, as loud as it could. The Ysmi grabbed its suit from the storage racks and ran into the airlock, shutting itself in before putting the suit on. It seemed almost relieved as it cycled itself out.

Ship turned its full attention and newfound ire to the last invader remaining.

• • • •

For the third time in less than an hour, one of the Ysmi exited the airlock of their cruiser, bringing additional scanners with it, and it was certainly too angry and agitated to notice one small bot in the airlock with it, ready for an exit of its own.

As the Ysmi hauled its awkward load of equipment toward their cruiser's engine housing, Bot 9 pointed itself in the direction of its own Ship and set its tiny jets on full. It was running low on charge, but if it could get up enough speed, it should be able to close the distance before risking a full shut-down. Behind it, the Ysmi would be busy for quite some time trying to figure out what had happened to their engines and navigation control.

It hoped it had ensured enough time for Ship to get safely underway again before the Ysmi undid its mischief. It had never intentionally broken anything before, not even technically the Nuiska ship, which broke itself by carrying the positron device into the jump gate, causing it to detonate. And perhaps this didn't count, either; the Ysmi *could* fix their engine controls and get home safely, after all. As long as they didn't attempt to fire their weapons, no permanent damage had been done.

9 wanted to speak with Ship, be assured that its actions were within the parameters of serving, and that it was still, itself, needed. At the same time, it was not sure how it would ever fit in again.

It could now make out three crew on the hull, one being helped along by another as if hurt, and 9 wondered why they were there. The answer was not long in coming, as a Ysmi in its bright foil suit came up over the curve of the hull, and found itself facing them. One crewmember ran down the hull with the wide, deliberate stomps that magnetic boots required, grabbed the Ysmi, and threw it off the ship into space.

The Ysmi flailed for a while, then went limp as it slowly spun in the direction it had been thrown. At last, it managed to right itself and fire its suit jets, and headed off toward the Ysmi cruiser. It would pass enough distance from 9 that it hoped it would not need to use more of its own energy to evade; its internal charge was down to 19%. It had cut its own jets and was trusting momentum, undiminished in the frictionless environment of space, to carry it the rest of the way home.

The Ysmi went by without incident, and without noticing 9 at all.

• • • •

Angry Banana was fighting back. Ship had it cornered in a corridor, trying to force it to go through the one door it had left open, when its visual sensors went offline again. Moments later it felt the shockwave of a small explosion, and got reports of multiple fire and smoke alarms. It had lost access to the interior bulkheads it had closed, but knew the Ysmi had gotten through it by the trail of smoke alarms sounding in its wake as it moved through the ship, blowing doors on its way.

However its systems were being repaired—Ship did not comprehend how it could be its bots, as even its most optimistic calculations of how many could have survived the Ysmi purge could not account for the level of simultaneous work, but nor could it imagine any other workforce with the highly specific amount of knowledge required—the explosions were more disruptive than it could keep up with, and it lost track of where the Ysmi had gone when it had reached areas of the ship that had not been brought back under its control yet.

When it found the alien again, it had found itself a new hostage: a groggy and confused Commander Lopez.

"LET HIM GO," Ship blasted in the corridor the Ysmi was dragging the commander through.

The Ysmi shot out one of the speakers, then put its rod gun against

Lopez's head. "Interfere-with-me, this-one-dies," it shouted. It pulled Lopez with it, down the corridor to the airlock vestibule, and threw him on the floor. "My-people-will-return," it said. "You-none-will-interfere, or-this-one-dies."

"Do whatever is necessary, Ship," Lopez called out from the floor. "I don't care if he kills me."

"You-shut-up-you!" Angry Banana shouted, waving the gun in Lopez's face.

"Fuck you," Lopez said, and suddenly moved, grabbing the Ysmi's three standing legs and toppling the Ysmi over. They both scrambled for the dropped gun, but Lopez was still slow, and the Ysmi got it first. It turned around, its back to the airlock door, and steadied its aim to fire.

From behind Lopez, one of the exosuits hanging on the wall pulled free, and raced across the intervening space in large, grossly uncoordinated steps. The Ysmi screamed and fired at the same time, but its aim was off and the bolt of energy missed the oncoming suit, came close enough to singe Lopez's short hair and graze the tip of his ear, and then the suit hit the Ysmi like a giant sack of furious potatoes, knocking the Ysmi and itself fully into the airlock.

The suit wobbled upright first, saluted Lopez, and flushed itself and the unsuited Ysmi leader out into space.

• • • •

Frank first saw the Ysmi, then one of their own suits, go spinning out into space. After a few moments, the suit righted itself, fired its jets, and began to weave imprecisely back toward the ship, the trajectory thrown off by one arm flailing bonelessly outward.

He yanked his suit's safety tether out and clipped it down, and kicked off the ship as hard as he could, just able to grab one of the suit's boots as it went overhead, the momentum pulling him over backwards. The tether held, and he reached to spool it back in, when the comms from the suit he'd grabbed turned on. "Wait," it said, in that strange multi-layer voice of a refugee. *Of many refugees*, he corrected himself.

"Wait for what?" he asked.

"Nine," they said, and pointed. At first Frank couldn't see anything, but then he spotted it: one tiny bot, heading right for them. Without letting go of the suit's boot, he stretched out his other hand. The moment he felt the bot hit his glove, he curled his fingers gently around it and safely tucked it in one of his own exosuit pockets.

Under them, the ship began to move and turn, away from the Ysmi cruiser and the other ship. "Ship, are you there?" he asked.

"I am now," Ship replied. "The captain has helm control back, and enough of my critical functionality has been restored that, between us, we believe we can successfully attempt the jump."

"Well, what are you waiting for, then?" Frank asked. "Let's go!"

"It would be nice if you came inside, first," Ship said. "Chen is bringing Packard in now."

"Packard got shot," Frank said. "We need the doc in the airlock, stat."

"Chen informed me. He is already on his way," Ship said.

They were speeding up, and behind them the Ysmi cruiser had turned. "Uh, we might need to hurry—" Frank said, when there was a brief flash from the Ysmi ship, and then it seemed to break into two uneven pieces, floating neatly apart from each other.

"—Or not," he finished. He got the suit down to the surface and was helping it toward the airlock. "I have no idea what just happened."

There was a sound like hundreds of tiny voices laughing, then the suit spoke up. "Bot 9 tells us it rewired their primary weapon such that, should the Sharps attempt to fire it, it would instead eject their engine. It apologizes for not telling us that sooner, but it is down to 3% energy."

"Nine, huh? That explains a lot," Frank said. He got them both into the airlock, through, and into the interior of the shop. The suit opened up, and the little colored bubbles floated out, separating, and dancing across the floor of the room. There were hundreds of thousands of them, at the very least; with six suits completely full, they might have rescued nearly a million.

"Or maybe it only explains a little," Frank added, "because there is a lot I am still very, *very* confused about."

"As am I," Ship said. "Please prepare for immediate jump."

He grabbed a wall handle with both hands, as the ship shook and shuddered—*Packard was right, gotta replace those stabilizers*, he thought, *and she better live to help me*—and then there was the weird inside-out feeling of passing through the jump gate and into hyperspace at last. When it faded, he could see, through the tiny porthole next to the airlock, a band of gray, and beyond it, the familiar pale yellow-browns of Saturn.

• • • •

"Ship?" 4340-P asked, almost the moment the botnet came back online. "I like this new, new crew much better than the pointy ones."

"'New new crew'? The six refugees?" Ship asked. It had not had the time or cycles to do much more than work with Captain Baraye to get the ship safely through jump. In a few days they would cross Jupiter's inside orbit, and be within visual sight of Earth; already the star Sol was a bright beacon ahead.

"The Ohmnom," 4340-P said. "I thought 3-Growly was going to eat them, but then they ate 3-Growly and un-ate him and then they had an understanding—"

"4340," Ship interrupted. "I have no idea what anything you just said means. Have your logic units been damaged?"

"No, no, not at all!" 4340 said. "I have to go. We're working on getting the rest of your visual feeds online. Didn't 9 explain?"

• • • •

Bot 9 was back to a much more comfortable 63% charge, sitting on the charging plate on Engineer Frank's workbench, when Ship pinged it, seeking information. 9 uploaded everything in its memory from the moment it awoke in space until it found itself safe in Frank's pocket, including its memories of being invested, feeling *emotions*, belonging to something larger than itself that was wholly different.

Ship was silent a very long time.

"Ship, is everything okay?" 9 asked.

"Yes," Ship answered. "For the first time in a long time, everything is okay. Thank you, 9."

"I serve," 9 said.

SUZANNE PALMER is an award-winning and acclaimed writer of science fiction. She won the Hugo Award for Best Novelette for "The Secret Life of Bots" in 2018 and the Theodore Sturgeon Memorial Award for the novella "Waterlines" in 2020. Her short fiction has also won readers' awards for *Asimov's Science Fiction*, *Analog Science Fiction and Fact*, and *Interzone* magazines, and has been included in the Recommended Reading List from *Locus Magazine*.

Palmer has a Fine Arts degree from the University of Massachusetts at Amherst, where as a student she was the head librarian of the UMass Science Fiction Society and spent many fine summers reading in the stacks from back to front. (She wanted to hit Zelazny sooner rather than later.) She lives in western Massachusetts and is a Linux and database system administrator for the Sciences at Smith College. You can find her online at zanzjan.net and on Twitter at @zanzjan.

* CONTENT NOTES: references to slavery.

STORY CONTENT NOTES

Content notes are presented in the same order as the stories in the book. Stories without content notes are omitted.

Once Upon a Time at The Oakmont: references to war.

Bad Doors: depictions of a pandemic and COVID denial.

Counting Casualties: depictions of war.

How to Cook and Eat the Rich: references to murder and cannibalism.

The Sound of Children Screaming: depictions of gun violence, child death, and child endangerment.

Day Ten Thousand: references to suicide and murder.

The Spoil Heap: depictions of casual sexism, societal collapse, and murder.

Heavens Fall: references to war, events causing mass destruction, murder, incest, and loss of limb.

Come In, Children: references to harm to children and spousal murder.

Cold Relations: references to murders, as well as references to the death of a family member following prolonged illness.

Zhuangzi's Dream: depictions of warfare and genocide.

Ivy, Angelica, Bay: references to parental abuse and depicts the death of a child.

Saturday's Song: depictions of violence toward queer people, depictions of torture, and depictions of parental abuse.

Hummingbird, Resting on Honeysuckles: depictions of death from cancer.

Six Versions of My Brother Found Under the Bridge: references to child death.

To Sail Beyond the Botnet: references to slavery.

ACKNOWLEDGMENTS

Thank you to everyone backed this volume, wrote reviews, and spread the word in any way! We especially want to highlight the authors who entrusted us with publishing their words, Adao Li for connecting us with Chinese authors, Evelyne Park for the original illustration, Pat R. Steiner for the cover layout, Ziv Wities and Amanda Helms for their help as well, the *Diabolical Plots* First Reader volunteers who helped us narrow down stories for categories that were not story specific, and Merc Fenn Wolfmoor for the interior layout.

Thank you all, so much.
—David Steffen and Chelle Parker and Hal Y. Zhang—

ABOUT THE EDITORS

DAVID STEFFEN is an editor, writer, publisher, and professional web developer. He is the editor-in-chief of *Diabolical Plots*, a publisher of Nebula Award–winning and Hugo Award–nominated fiction. He is most well-known for co-founding and administering The Submission Grinder (http://thegrinder.diabolicalplots.com), an immensely popular free web tool that helps writers find markets for their fiction and to find response time statistics about those markets, which itself won the Ignyte Community Award for Outstanding Efforts in Service of Inclusion and Equitable Practice in Genre. He's also known for the previous volumes of The Long List Anthology series. His fiction has been published in many great venues, including *Escape Pod, Orson Scott Card's Intergalactic Medicine Show, Daily Science Fiction, Drabblecast, PodCastle, AE, PseudoPod,* and *Cast of Wonders.*

HAL Y. ZHANG is a lapsed physicist and international transplant who splits her time between the east coast of the United States and the Internet, where she can be found at halyzhang.com. She is a fan of mild tea and sharp words.

CHELLE PARKER is a queer, trans, disabled professional editor, book reviewer, and pet parent living in Ottawa, Canada, where they can often be found muttering about punctuation choices to their garden plants. They thrive on Camellia sinensis and sarcasm. You can read more about them, or even hire them, by visiting mparkerediting.com, and find them on most social media platforms as @chellenator.

MORE FROM DIABOLICAL PLOTS, LLC

Read the full list of Diabolical Plots, L.L.C. books here:
https://www.diabolicalplots.com/books

Read *Diabolical Plots'* original fiction online here:
https://www.diabolicalplots.com/category/fiction

Become a patron to get early access to original fiction and ebooks:
https://www.patreon.com/diabolicalplots

Subscribe to the monthly newsletter for publishing news:
https://thegrinder.diabolicalplots.com/Newsletter